Whispers on the Tide
Dawn of Alaska
Book 2

Naomi Rawlings

Praise for Naomi Rawlings Books

"Naomi Rawlings has crafted yet another series that delivers everything lovers of historical fiction will clamor for—a stunning setting, a big family that will make you want to be a part of it, women chasing their dreams, and men who know how to be both strong and loving. *Written on the Mist* will pull you in and make you glad it's just the first installment of the series, so that you can look forward to many more hours spent with these compelling characters!"—*Roseanna M. White, Bestselling and Christy-Award Winning Author*

"*Written on the Mist* by Naomi Rawlings will take you on a journey to Alaska from the comfort of your own home. You will experience history, adventure, mystery, romance and more as you peek into the lives of the Amos family of Juneau and Sitka. Get ready to experience the real scenery, the climate and more of Southeast Alaska without benefit of rain gear or cold weather gear."—*Susan Benton, Educator and Book Reviewer*

"Naomi Rawlings writes exciting novels that feature fresh, sharply drawn characters, fast-paced and fine-tuned adventure-romance plots, and gently pitched biblical themes. Her newest novel, *Written on the Mist,* is simply exceptional."—*Erin Healy, Multi-Published Author and Fiction Editor*

"An excellent storyteller with beautifully written characters and storylines. Her books shine."—*Jennifer Lonas, Editor and Book Reviewer*

"There were so many aspects to *Written on the Mist*: the love story, the historical perspective, the drama and adventure, the characters, the carefully woven messages against domestic violence and racial discrimination, it was an incredible read. I'm excited to see Naomi Rawlings has five more books planned in this series." —*Karen Hardick, Editor and Book Reviewer*

"Naomi Rawlings' writing style stirs emotions in an incredibly positive way. The characters come to life and in your mind and heart. You rejoice, cry, and laugh right along with them. *Written on the Mist* is one of my very top favorites." —*Keili Holmes, Book Reviewer*

Other Books by Naomi Rawlings

Dawn of Alaska Series

Written on the Mist

Texas Promise Series

Tomorrow's First Light

Tomorrow's Shining Dream

Tomorrow's Constant Hope

Tomorrow's Steadfast Prayer

Tomorrow's Lasting Joy

Eagle Harbor Series

Love's Unfading Light

Love's Every Whisper

Love's Sure Dawn

Love's Eternal Breath

Love's Christmas Hope

Love's Bright Tomorrow

Belanger Family Saga

The Lady's Refuge

The Widow's Secrets

The Reluctant Enemy

Whispers on the Tide

Published by **Naomi Rawlings LLC**

PO Box 134, South Range, MI 49963

All Scripture quotations are taken from The Holy Bible, King James Version.

The characters and events in this book are fictional, and any resemblance to actual persons or events is coincidental.

Copyright © 2024 by **Naomi Rawlings**

Cover art © 2024 by **Carpe Librum Book Design**

All rights reserved. No part of this book may be reproduced or transmitted in any form or by any means, electronic or mechanical, including photocopying and recording, or by any information storage and retrieval system, without permission in writing from the publisher.

Printed in the United States of America

To Jeremiah, for your strength, bravery, and amazing, creative mind. I love you.

Description

He gave up his badge and his gun after his last case went horribly wrong. But there's one thing that can make him pick them both up again...

Jonas Redding never wants to be a lawman again. He's spent a decade as a US Marshal, wearing a tin star on his chest and chasing dangerous criminals across the great state of Texas. But when a case goes wrong, Jonas finds himself standing over two tombstones—his mother's and his fiancée's.

Resolved to protect his sister from meeting the same fate, Jonas cuts off all communication with her, changes his name, and heads north to the vast, untamed Alaskan wilderness.

Jonas isn't even in Alaska for a day before meeting Ilya Amos, a boy with wide eyes, an endless smile, and a heart of pure gold. Before he realizes what's happening, Jonas finds himself sucked into the everyday life of the Amoses—a sprawling family of eight siblings who are more Alaskan than American and unapologetic about their heritage.

Yet Jonas is resolved not to get too close to the Amoses, especially Ilya's older sister Evelina. The last thing he wants to do is put another woman in jeopardy.

But when the unthinkable happens and dangerous men seek revenge against the Amos family, Jonas must decide between hiding from his past or putting his badge back on and risking everything to save the family he doesn't want to admit he loves.

Set against the sprawling backdrop of Alaska, this sweeping book brings to life the hope of second chances and new beginnings after tragedy, and the rich history of taming a land that was never meant to be tamed.

Want to be notified when my next book releases? Sign up for my author newsletter.
http://geni.us/DHKH7
(Subscribers also receive a free novel.)
Whispers on the Tide

1

Near Bellingham, Washington; May 1887

Sacha Amos was about to find out whether he'd made the best decision of his life, or his biggest mistake. If only he knew which.

From his position inside the wheelhouse of his ship, the *Aurora*, he stared out over the calm gray waters of the strait. A thick veil of mist clung to the land and shoreline, the air so dense it could be parted with one of the cook's knives from the galley.

It was a dangerous morning, with the mist shrouding not just the rocks that lay in the shallows of Rosario Strait but entire islands and mountains as well.

On mornings like this, vessels found themselves colliding with each other or veering into a dangerous rock that lay just outside the shipping lane.

But not the *Aurora*.

If he'd sailed these waters once, he'd sailed them a thousand times.

He gripped the wheel tighter, the wooden spindles familiar beneath his palms as he steered the clipper away from Sinclair Island and into the more open waters of Bellingham Bay.

"Are ya sure you don't want me ta steer her, sir?" Ronnie Dubbins, Sacha's helmsman, said from where he stood to the left of the wheel. "I've guided her into Bellingham plenty of times."

"But not on such a morning as this."

The helmsman shifted his weight from one foot to another. "Truth be told, yer makin' me a bit nervous, Cap'n. No ship should be sailin' on this kind of morning."

He knew it. The sane, rational part of his brain was well aware that he should have sought harbor at one of the numerous locations on the west side of Vancouver Island when the mist had started to roll in.

Thankfully the mist wasn't as thick over the water as it was on land. Because of that—and his familiarity with the waterways near Bellingham and Seattle—he could make out enough of their surroundings to keep the *Aurora* in the center of the shipping channel. Mostly.

"Cap'n Amos," a rusty voice called from the main deck below, followed by the clomp of boots on the stairs. A moment later, Gus Benson, his first mate, appeared on the quarterdeck and headed straight for him.

The scowl on the sailor's weatherworn face told Sacha all he needed to know before the man stepped fully inside the wheelhouse.

"The mist is only gettin' thicker the closer we get to the harbor, Cap'n. The foghorns'll be blarin' in another minute or two. You shoulda anchored off Sinclair Island back there."

"We're already a week late."

"The cargo'll wait a few more hours, Cap'n. I promise."

Ronnie's face seemed to grow paler each second they glided closer to Bellingham's harbor.

Or rather, what should have been Bellingham's harbor. Sacha couldn't yet make out the other ships docked there, let alone any of the town's buildings. It was almost as though the densest, thickest patch of fog they'd seen that morning had decided to descend squarely upon Bellingham.

"It ain't the cargo the cap'n is worried about." Gus eyed Ronnie. "It's the passenger we're pickin' up."

"We're pickin' up a passenger?" Ronnie asked.

Sacha gritted his teeth. This was not how he'd intended to bring up the subject with the crew.

"You may as well tell him," Gus muttered. "We'll be docking in a few minutes—iffin' we don't wreck first. Your brother'll have yer head if that happens. And it won't be anyone's fault but yer own."

"That's why I took the helm," Sacha growled.

The first mate clamped his jaw shut. He'd surely seen stupider things in his thirty years on the sea, but at the moment, Gus was likely drawing on every last bit of that experience to keep himself from arguing further with his captain.

Sacha couldn't blame the man for wanting to argue. He wasn't just captain of any ship; he was captain of the *Aurora*. A masterpiece of a ship that his older brother had designed after spending three years in school studying naval architecture. Built for the sole purpose of plowing through arctic ice, the *Aurora* had a double-lined hull with six-inch-thick oak boards and an iron frame like any other ship, as well as an outer hull of Australian ironwood. Tough and durable, the *Aurora* could travel places few other ships could.

But a rock could still put a hole in its double hull, and a collision with another vessel . . .

His stomach dropped. Maybe he was being a fool sailing

the ship through such dangerous conditions. But he had to reach Bellingham. Today.

He only hoped the man he was supposed to meet hadn't gotten tired of waiting so long for the *Aurora* to arrive. Only hoped that Dr. Torres had stayed in Bellingham and waited for him rather than heading back to Washington, DC. Never mind the *Aurora* was running a week behind schedule.

"If the mist don't let up by this time tomorrow, can we wait to leave port?" Ronnie asked. "Or do we gotta be in a rush to leave too?"

Sacha blew out a breath. "Getting to port is the part that can't wait, though if the mist lifts this afternoon, we'll set sail before sunset."

Both of his men looked at him as though he'd lost his mind.

He sighed. Could he spare a night in port, even if the mist lifted?

"Land ho!" a voice rang out from the crow's nest.

Sacha glanced at the top of the mast where Eric was perched.

"The wharf is just off starboard," Eric called down. "Can you see it?"

Sacha peered through the thick mist to where he could just make out the long, flat outline of the wharf, and the looming masts of a ship docked uncomfortably close to the *Aurora*'s bow. Fortunately the space on the opposite side of the ship was empty.

He gave the command to slacken the sails—not that there was much wind to fill them on such a morning—then he guided the ship toward an open space on the wharf, waiting as the vessel slowed to a crawl.

Usually shouts would ring out from the shore about now, the dockworkers realizing that a ship was approaching and preparing themselves to unload cargo.

But not today. The wharf looked completely deserted.

Sacha just hoped Dr. Torres was waiting for him somewhere in Bellingham, even if he wasn't standing on the wharf to greet the ship.

THE *AURORA* WOULD ARRIVE TODAY. It had to. Maggie McDougal stared into her nearly empty coin purse. When she left Wisconsin several weeks ago, it had been full. But now only two dollars and a handful of coins remained, and she didn't want to spend a cent of it to stay in their dirty hotel room for another night.

"Are you sure you want us to pack everything?" Ainsley, her seven-year-old half sister, asked from where she stood beside the sagging bed stuffing the few clothes they'd brought into their carpetbag.

Beside her, their younger brother, Finnan, lay curled on the bed, staring out the window.

"Yes. Check under the bed too, just in case something fell." She couldn't afford to spend money replacing stockings or a hairbrush, not when they'd need to spend every last penny they had on food.

Ainsley did as asked, though the room was too dim for her to see anything that might have fallen under the bed.

It wasn't that the thin curtains beside the windows blocked the light, though they were dingy and in need of a good scrubbing—just like the floor and the bedclothes. No. The sun had simply forgotten to shine this morning. The street outside was coated in a mist that seemed to grow thicker by the moment. And the small lamp in the corner gave off so little light that it didn't even reach the shadows on the opposite wall, let alone the space under the bed.

Maggie sighed. She wasn't going to complain about leaving this place behind.

It was not having anywhere to go that terrified her.

She looked into her coin purse once more, then pulled out the folded bills, just to make sure she hadn't actually missed a dollar—or mistaken a ten-dollar bill for a one.

But no. She hadn't miscounted. The money was exactly the same as it had been a few minutes ago. Two dollars and thirty-six cents.

She shoved the money back into her purse, a sickening sensation swirling in her stomach. Was this how the widow with no oil in the Bible had felt? Had she looked into her empty jug with a sickening sensation filling her belly? Had she uttered rushed, desperate prayers, asking God to spare her from what was sure to be a disastrous end?

Or maybe she prayed not for herself but for her son, that God would provide for him.

Maggie's breath shuddered in her lungs. Perhaps she should focus her future prayers on Ainsley and Finnan. Maybe God would look more kindly on the plight of children.

Because God sure hadn't looked kindly on her own plight.

"I'm hungry," Finnan whined from where he still lay curled on the bed beneath the grimy window. He'd spent most of the week they'd been in Bellingham in that very spot, watching the busy street that was so very different from the lonely road that ran past their shipyard in Wisconsin. But this morning, the fog was too dense to make out anything more than the occasional shadow of a horse or passerby.

"Can I have a biscuit?" He pulled his gaze away from the window and looked at her.

The sickening sensation in her belly gave a sudden lurch. It didn't matter that Finnan was ridiculously hungry all the time or that he seemed to eat more than she and Ainsley combined.

All that mattered was that she'd promised her mother she'd care for her siblings if anything ever happened, and that she didn't have any food.

And while they could purchase biscuits and sausage from the food cart down the street today, she wouldn't have the money to do so in another week.

She sunk her teeth into her bottom lip. The *Aurora* would arrive in Bellingham before that. It had to.

But if it didn't . . . if it was lost at sea . . . if she somehow couldn't manage to find her older brother . . .

"Sissy, did you hear me?" Finnan climbed off the bed and headed toward her. "I said I'm hungry."

"We'll get biscuits as soon as we leave. Enough to tide us over for the whole day." Could they survive on just biscuits and no meat, or would that only make the boy hungrier?

"I still don't understand why we're leaving the hotel." Ainsley threaded the leather strap through the buckle on the carpetbag, sealing it tight. "The *Aurora* might not come today, just like it didn't come yesterday, or any other days this week."

"Will the *'Rora* come today, Sissy?" Finnan tugged on Maggie's hand, his blue eyes round with all the hope a four-year-old boy could muster. "Will it?"

"Yes." She spoke with a ridiculous amount of confidence. Never mind that of the past week they'd been in Bellingham, today was the most unlikely day for the *Aurora* to arrive. Surely there would be no ships coming into or leaving port until the mist faded.

"I get to meet brother! I get to meet brother!" Finnan cheered, then started prancing around the cramped room.

Ainsley, on the other hand, let out a huff. "I still don't understand why we're packing. Even if the *Aurora* arrives today and Tavish says he'll come back to Wisconsin with us, won't we need somewhere to stay tonight?"

Maggie drew in a breath. She wasn't going to let her sister know how little money they had left. The past four months had already given Ainsley more burdens than any child her age should be asked to carry.

Besides, maybe Tavish would actually arrive on the *Aurora* today. Or maybe his ship had docked last night before fog shrouded the city. Maybe God had heard her prayers after all.

She moved to the bed, where she picked up the carpetbag that felt far too light to be holding three people's possessions. "Once Tavish arrives, I'm sure he'll treat us to a nicer room. Maybe we can even stay in the large hotel in the center of town."

Ainsley's eyes widened, filled with excitement rather than sadness for once.

During the time they'd spent in Bellingham, they'd walked from one end of the town to the other. It had been hard to miss the pristine two-story hotel with a wraparound porch and giant white columns flanking the entrance to grand wooden doors.

Maggie hadn't been able to afford such accommodations, but Tavish had been working as a sailor for years with no family to provide for. Surely he not only had the funds but would also be willing to splurge—once he finally reached Bellingham.

"Put on your coats. It's time to leave."

Ainsley and Finnan did as asked, not complaining about needing to wear coats in June, even though they'd never need to do such a thing back in Wisconsin.

Maggie opened the door and stepped into the dimly lit hallway, only to be greeted with the scents of sweat and grime. Her fingers tightened around the room key as she led her siblings into the open space that marked the entrance to the hotel, where the proprietor sat behind his desk.

She wordlessly set the key on the desk, then took a step back.

"You're leavin' then? You sure you don't wanna stay another night?" the man wheezed, his shirt and trousers just as stained and grimy as the quilt and curtains in their room. "I can give you a discount, seein' how you already been here a week."

"I'm sure."

"Ain't got news the *Aurora*'s arrived yet." He tapped the end of his pencil on his ledger. "And no ships'll be comin' in or leavin' on a morning like this."

Maggie slid the key farther across the desk, stopping just shy of the man's dirt-encrusted hand. "Thank you for the accommodations, but we're checking out."

"Are you out of money?" The man slowly drew his gaze down her, and something about the look made her suddenly wish for a bath. "I know a place that might hire ya. Might even provide someone to watch yer young'uns while ya—"

"No, thank you. I'm not looking for work." Or at least not that kind of work.

Thank heavens her siblings were too young to understand what the man meant—or what type of clientele the hotel so close to the docks catered to.

Maggie had realized it on their first night in Bellingham, but renting a more appropriate room would only have drained their coffers faster.

"Come along, Ainsley, Finnan. It's time to leave." She turned her back on the proprietor and opened the door for her siblings, the hinges squealing in protest.

"Can we please get food now?" Ainsley asked the moment the creaky door swung shut behind them. "I'm hungry too."

"Of course. That's first on the list."

The salty tang of the sea and the odor of fish hung thick in the air as they ventured across the deserted road. The harbormaster's office sat just a block down the street, and a vendor wheeled his food cart there every morning, making it the closest place to eat.

Usually the road by the harbor was alive with activity—gulls soaring overhead, ships bustling in and out of port, sailors and dockworkers calling to each other. But today it was as if the town had been abandoned under the cover of night and shrouded in a thick, eerie blanket.

"Sissy, where's the food?" Finnan gripped Maggie's hand. "I want a biscuit."

"It's just up . . ." Her words trailed off as they approached the wooden office building, which appeared just as deserted as the wharf. Even the little patch of road in front of the harbormaster's office, where the vendor always parked his cart, was vacant.

It made sense. Of course it did. Why would the vendor be here when there were no sailors or dockworkers to buy his food?

"The cart's not here." She gave Finnan's hand a gentle squeeze, willing her brother to understand. "We'll have to walk back into town to eat."

"But I'm hungry now!"

"Yes, but we'll have to go the opposite direction for food, and since we're already here, we should check the ships." She looked down the long row of ships docked at the wharf, their hulls shrouded in thick shadows. "Just to make sure the *Aurora* hasn't come."

She tried to tug Finnan forward, but the boy's feet rooted to the wooden planks of the wharf, his face twisting into a stubborn frown.

She crouched and met her younger brother's eyes. "We'll go uptown and get a nice warm lunch as soon as we're done here. I promise."

Their lunch would likely cost more than she could afford,

but without any street vendors around, she had little choice about where they ate.

Finnan's lower lip protruded, his chin quivering. "I want a biscuit."

"I know." She patted his hand. "I want one too, but this won't take long, and we'll get that biscuit as soon as we finish. Maybe even some flapjacks to go with it."

"With syrup?"

"With syrup."

Her promise seemed to appease him, at least for a few minutes, and he started walking again. They continued past the harbor-master's office, the echo of their footsteps against the wharf and the creaking of ships the only sounds.

They passed one ship, then a second and a third, taking time to read the names painted on each hull.

When Maggie approached the fourth ship, Finnan pulled back against her hand. "Are you sure the *'Rora* is coming today? No one's here."

Ainsley made a scoffing sound. "The *Aurora* isn't—"

"It could have arrived last night before the fog rolled in." Though she didn't want to think about just how small of a chance there was of that happening.

Ainsley sighed and crossed her arms over her chest. "Will we at least be able to go home once we find Tavish?"

"I want to go home now." Finnan stomped his foot against the wooden planks.

"Me too." Ainsley surveyed the shadowed ships towering around them. "I don't much care for Washington Territory. It always smells of salt and fish."

"Can we go home tomorrow?" A ridiculous amount of hope tinged Finnan's voice.

Maggie sighed. "I hope so." And she did. Because if they weren't on a train home before their money ran out . . .

Oh, how did one explain to a four-year-old that if they didn't find their brother, there would be no home for them to return to? That the uncle who'd worked side by side with them for the past twenty-five years was trying to steal their family's land—and the shipyard and home that went with it? That all he saw was the money he'd be able to earn if he controlled the shipyard and the forty acres of waterfront property it sat on. And he didn't care that she, Ainsley, and Finnan would be forced out of their home in the process.

That was why she had to find Tavish. Why she'd collected the small savings her mother and stepfather had kept in the bank, told her two half siblings to pack their clothes, and headed west to the coast.

And it was why she needed the *Aurora* to arrive today.

If it didn't—if she had to wire her uncle and ask him to send money so they could return home—then the three of them would lose everything.

2

"Sacha Amos, you dirty scallywag."

Sacha grinned at the sound of the familiar voice, then set the crate he'd been carrying down and headed across the deck to greet the harbor master.

The man tugged on his bushy beard, the corners of his mouth twitching, though Sacha couldn't tell whether he was fighting a smile or a frown. "I'm not sure whether you're a genius or a fool."

"A genius, I assure you." He stuck out his hand.

The harbor master shook it, then scanned the deck. "Your crew will have to unload the cargo on their own. I sent the workers home when the fog rolled in just after dawn."

"Then that's what we'll do. I can't afford to spend an extra day in port, not when I'm already eight days behind schedule."

"Was starting to worry you might not arrive at all," the harbor master muttered, the corners of his mouth twitching again. "You're not normally late this time of year."

Sacha heaved in a breath. "It's been a crazy spring up on the Bering. I swear half the men captaining ships up there have never seen an iceberg before, and the other half don't know how to read a navigational chart."

"Well, now, there's probably some truth to that." The harbor master slapped him on his shoulder. "Glad to see you arrived safely, even if you're a fool for sailing into port in this."

"Like I said, I couldn't afford to wait until the fog lifted."

"Don't suppose your rush has anything to do with the people who've been traipsing down to the port every day, asking if the *Aurora* has arrived."

"Dr. Torres?" Sacha asked, his voice rumbling out of his chest. "He's been asking about me?"

"He has, right along with the woman and children. Glad to see you're expecting them."

Woman and children? Sacha frowned. Dr. Torres hadn't said anything about bringing his wife or children with him, just his assistant.

The harbor master—Glendon, if he recalled correctly—patted his breast pocket, then pulled an envelope from his coat. "He left this for you."

Left it because he'd gone back to Washington, DC? Or left it so that Sacha would know where to find him after he'd arrived?

Please, God, let it be the latter.

He tore open the envelope, only to find a brief note accompanied by a hotel name, a room number, and a date next week when Dr. Torres planned to leave if the *Aurora* still hadn't arrived.

Sacha pressed his eyes shut. *Thank you, Father.*

"I'm afraid the woman didn't leave a note, but she's been staying in the hotel across the street."

What woman? Was she not Dr. Torres's wife? Now he was even more confused.

Though if she was staying in the hotel across from the

docks, he was probably better off not asking questions. It didn't matter what port or country he was in, hotels near docks were known for one thing only, and he didn't plan to make use of any of those services.

"Thomas?" a voice called.

A rather feminine-sounding voice.

Sacha scowled. Was his mind playing tricks on him?

He looked toward the gangway, only to find a woman was, in fact, standing on the deck of his ship. Right in the middle of the path of his crew members, who were busy unloading the hold.

With a child clinging to each of her hands.

"Thomas, are you here?" she called, stepping closer to one of the men with a handcart, as though trying to see his face.

"Name's Eric. Ain't no one by the name of Thomas on the *Aurora*," he answered, pulling his cart to a stop rather than attempting to wheel it around her.

"That's what I was trying to tell you," Glendon muttered to Sacha. "She and her children are staying at the hotel across the street. But they don't belong there. It was all I could do not to bring them home with me, just so they'd have a safe place to stay."

"I see." Sacha headed across the deck to where the woman had parked herself smack in front of the gangway, blocking anyone from coming up or heading down.

Not that his men were complaining about the distraction. They were all looking at her, but Eric was standing a little closer than was proper.

"I need to ask you to move, Mrs. . . . ?"

"It's Miss. Miss McDougal." She turned to face him. "And I'm looking for my brother, Thomas. He's a sailor on this ship."

She's beautiful. That was the only thing Sacha could think as he stared into bluish-green eyes the color of the sea. High cheekbones framed rosy cheeks and soft lips, which were a shade of pale pink that contrasted perfectly with her fair complexion. Indeed, everything about her was perfect, from the gentle curve of her jaw to the way a stray strand of blond, half-curly hair fell beside her face.

"Well, do you know Thomas?" Those pretty pink lips moved, but it took a moment for her words to sink in.

"I'm sorry. I'm afraid there's no Thomas who works aboard this ship. Perhaps you got it confused with a different—"

"Aren't you Captain Amos?" Her eyes flashed, shooting little sparks of seafoam-colored fire. "Isn't this the *Aurora*, registered to Sitka Trading Company? My brother, Thomas McDougal, has spent the past six years working for you, and I can prove it by the letters he writes me every Christmas."

"McDougal. Thomas McDougal." Sacha scratched his chin, covered in stubble because he wasn't fool enough to hold a razor to his jaw while his ship rose and fell on the waves of the sea. Wasn't that Tavish's legal name? Seemed he remembered seeing Tavish sign something once as Thomas McDougal, and the surname certainly matched. "Are you Tavish's sister?"

Why hadn't his friend mentioned he had a sister? A sister who was pretty enough to distract his men from their work.

Of course, it didn't help that she was still standing in front of the gangway.

He reached out and gripped her upper arm.

She stiffened, and he couldn't exactly blame her, seeing how he was a stranger and touching her without asking permission.

But he didn't let go, because his men needed to get back to work, and the last place this beautiful woman should be standing was in the middle of a bunch of sailors—half of which planned to head to the brothel as soon as they were given leave.

"Miss McDougal, I need you to step aside. My crew needs

to finish unloading the cargo, and I don't want you or one of your children to accidentally get hit by a cart."

Or any of his men to up and get the idea of proposing to her.

She blinked, then looked around, as though just now noticing that more than half a dozen strange men were watching her.

"Of course. I'm sorry. I didn't mean to hold up your workers." She let him guide her away from the gangway toward the stairs that led to the quarterdeck, where the wheelhouse and his cabin were located.

"Get back to work," Sacha called to his men. "The sooner she's unloaded, the sooner you can go ashore."

Glendon fell into step beside him as he tugged Miss McDougal away. "Come find me in my office when you're done. And let me know if you need any help with this, er, situation."

Sacha gave him a quick nod, and Glendon peeled away, heading toward the gangway. Hopefully whatever issue Miss McDougal had could be easily resolved, but it was nice to know someone in Bellingham was willing to help if needed.

"So do you know my brother? His name is Thomas, but we always called him Tavish at home. It's the Scottish version of Thomas." Miss McDougal took small, dainty steps compared to his own long strides.

"Yes, I know Tavish, but—"

"Is he here? With the workers somewhere?" She stopped walking, planting her feet directly in front of the stairs leading to the one place aboard the ship where they might have a semblance of privacy. "I must speak with him. Now."

Something about how she said it, about the desperation in her voice and the hope in her eyes made a hard ball form in his stomach. "No. He's captaining the *Halcyon*."

"The what . . . ? What do you mean, the *Halcyon*? He's the first mate on this ship, the *Aurora*." She patted the side of her skirt, then reached into her pocket and pulled out a worn, crinkled envelope. "I have his letter from last Christmas. It says so right here. He even mentions you in it."

He glanced down at the envelope but didn't take it, the lead ball from his stomach climbing into his chest. "He usually is my first mate, yes, but Captain Jones suffered a broken leg about a month and a half ago and needed to stay in Sitka to recover. So we made Tavish temporary captain of the *Halcyon*."

"Then he's not . . . You mean he isn't . . ." Her eyes grew large and round, then took on a watery sheen.

She wasn't going to cry, was she?

He shifted awkwardly from one foot to the other. What was he going to do with a crying woman? And on his ship, no less?

"Sissy, can I have a biscuit now?" The little boy tugged on Miss McDougal's hand. "I'm hungry."

Sissy? Was Miss McDougal these children's sister? He'd assumed she was their mother, though she'd been quite clear earlier that she was *Miss* McDougal, not *Mrs*.

And now that he looked more closely, she seemed too young to be mother to the red-haired girl, who looked to be maybe seven or eight.

"Sissy." The boy tugged Miss McDougal's hand again. "Can I have one? Please?"

"You'll have to wait," the red-headed girl snapped. "Finding Tavish is more important than a biscuit."

"But I didn't have breakfast!" the boy wailed.

"We have biscuits aplenty in the galley." Sacha turned and found a sailor nearby pushing a handcart stacked high with crates. "Vasily, go grab half a dozen biscuits and bring them to Miss McDougal."

"Yes, sir, Cap'n, sir." The man left his handcart sitting right where he'd stopped and raced belowdecks, a silly grin plastered across his face.

"Thank you. I'm sorry about my brother. I just . . ." Miss McDougal pressed a hand to her throat, her eyes still shimmering with unshed tears. "Where is this *Halcyon*? And how do we find it? I have to speak with Tavish."

He sighed. "If it's running on schedule, you'll find it in the middle of the Pacific Ocean, somewhere between Japan and Unalaska."

"Where's Unalaska?" A thread of hope twined through Miss McDougal's voice.

"It's part of the Aleutian Island chain, in the middle of the Bering Sea."

"Oh."

That was all she said. Just that one simple word. But with it, all the hope drained from her body and her shoulders deflated.

"Where's the Bering Sea?" the girl beside her asked, her own eyes filling with worry.

"North," Miss McDougal whispered. "Much farther north."

"It's the sea that separates Russia from Alaska." He looked down at the girl, intelligence lurking in her moss-colored eyes. "Think of it as the northernmost part of the Pacific Ocean. It stretches clear up into the Arctic."

"Do we have enough money to go there, Maggie?" The girl looked up at her sister.

Miss McDougal's jaw quivered, and he found himself patting his pockets in search of a handkerchief. Perhaps if he didn't have to see the tears trailing down her cheeks, he wouldn't be tempted to whisk her off to the middle of the ocean in an attempt to meet up with the *Halcyon*.

He finally found a handkerchief shoved into the bottom of his breast pocket and offered the crumpled wad of fabric to the lady.

Miss McDougal took it, but rather than dab at her eyes, she twisted it in her hands, almost as though wringing it hard enough would cause her brother to appear.

"Is there something I can do to help in your brother's stead? We've known each other for a long time, and he's the best sailor I have. While I might not be able to take you to him, if I know the situation—"

"No." Miss McDougal's shoulders rose on a sigh, only to cave back in on themselves once the air left her lungs. "Only Tavish can fix this."

"Our ma and pa died," the girl piped up. "And our uncle's trying to swindle our family shipyard out from under us. He says Tavish is dead and—"

"Hush, Ainsley." Miss McDougal squeezed her sister's arm, then sent her a harsh look. "We don't need to go airing our business to strangers."

"He asked if he could help." Ainsley shoved a hand in his direction. "We should let him. It's not like we don't need it."

Miss McDougal stiffened. "It's not a stranger's place to help us. It's our brother's."

"Easy for you to say." The girl crossed her arms over her chest. "I've never even met Tavish. What if Uncle Ewan is right, and he really is dead?"

"Tavish isn't dead." Sacha crossed his arms over his chest too, knowing full well that the stance made him look far more imposing than the slip of a girl in front of him. "He's alive and well; he's just not on the *Aurora*. Perhaps if I send a letter to your uncle, verifying that Tavish has spent the past six years working for me, that will clear things up."

But Miss McDougal was already shaking her head. "It

won't do any good. Uncle Ewan has already started court proceedings. I presented the letters I have from Tavish to prove he's still alive, but the judge says a letter from December doesn't mean he's alive now. So Tavish has until the end of October to present himself to the judge in Wisconsin, and then he'll be awarded the shipyard, house, and property on Lake Michigan, all inherited from our father. If he doesn't appear, it will go to my uncle."

"The boy here can't inherit it?" Sacha jutted his chin at the small, redheaded child who looked to be three or four.

"We have different fathers. My and Tavish's father died when we were younger, but then Ma remarried. Ownership of the shipyard wasn't an issue until Ma died. Now the uncle who's helped us with it all these years is trying to claim it for himself. He has some type of agreement Pa signed when he first bought the land and Tavish was a baby. Something about how if he were to die without an heir, everything would go to his brother, and . . ." She waved her hand. "I'm sorry. I'm afraid this is frightfully complicated. But as you can see, I must find Tavish. You said the *Halcyon* is headed to Unalaska next?"

"Here's the biscuits." Vasily appeared at Miss McDougal's side, holding a cheesecloth that had been tied into a sack.

"Thank you." She untied the cheesecloth, sending a small smile Vasily's way.

The man's entire face turned red. "Yer welcome, miss. Anything else I can do to help?"

"I can help too, iffin' the lady needs somethin'." Ronnie appeared on Miss McDougal's other side, a ridiculously wide grin plastered across his face.

A quick glance around the deck told Sacha that only half his men were working. The other half were all loitering around, trying to look busy but paying more attention to Miss McDougal than anything else.

"Get back to work," Sacha shouted. "All of you, or I'll confine you to the ship after the work's finished."

"But the hold's nearly unloaded, Cap'n," Ronnie answered. "That's why I came ta see if Miss McDougal here needed any help."

"She doesn't," he snapped. What she needed was her brother, and none of them could provide that.

"Are you going to Unalaska?" Miss McDougal asked. "Can we purchase passage from you?"

"Whoopie!" Vasily shouted. "Ya hear that, boys? We're takin' the pretty lady with us to Unalaska!"

"I said no such thing," Sacha barked, glaring at Vasily. "And you just volunteered to scrub the deck while everyone else disembarks."

"No, Cap'n." Vasily looked around the ship, panic creasing his forehead. "We just got to port. You can't mean fer me to stay behind and—"

"I said scrub the deck. Once it's clean, you can take your leave." He turned his back on Vasily and gestured toward the stairs. "Miss McDougal, I'd like to continue this conversation in the wheelhouse. You'll find it a bit more private."

"Oh." She looked around, as though once again surprised to find herself the center of so much attention. "I didn't realize . . . That is, thank you."

She turned and proceeded to climb the steps with her siblings and enter the wheelhouse. The small house atop the quarterdeck was open on three sides but had a roof overhead to shield both the helm and helmsman from the elements. The only wall stood at the back of the wheelhouse, and on the other side of it sat the only two cabins on the ship, his as captain and the first mate's.

"Captain Amos." Miss McDougal turned to face him the moment he entered the wheelhouse, her shoulders now firm with determination. "The sailor on the deck was right. We need to go to Unalaska. This is what I can pay for our passage."

She withdrew a coin purse from her dress, then unclasped it and held out the contents. "I know it's not much, but it's what I have. I'm willing to work on the ship too. I can cook or clean or whatever else you might need."

He held up his hands, refusing to take the small bit of money.

"I don't take passengers aboard the *Aurora*." Or at least not passengers he wasn't related to. "Just cargo."

"Is it the money?" Miss McDougal stared back down at the open purse. "Do I need to earn more of it first?"

"Don't worry, Maggie." Ainsley squeezed her older sister's hand. "We'll go back to the hotel and get jobs until we have more money. There's bound to be another ship headed to Unalaska."

The thought made Sacha's insides turn cold. First, because he could well imagine the type of work the proprietor had in mind for Miss McDougal. And second, because while there would be another ship going to Unalaska eventually, it wouldn't be fit for a woman and two children.

The *Aurora* was the only ship that serviced the small village on an island in the middle of the Bering Sea for trade purposes. Nearly all of the other vessels that stopped at the port were sealing ships. And while he couldn't claim that every man on his ship was upstanding and moral, he expected far more out of his men than the captain of a sealing vessel would.

In fact, he could already think of how most captains would demand Miss McDougal pay for passage to Unalaska. And it wouldn't be much different from what Miss McDougal would be expected to do if she returned to the hotel across from the wharf.

He pressed the heel of his palm to his breastbone, though it did little to relieve the pressure building inside him.

He couldn't take Miss McDougal and her siblings. Not on this journey. Not considering the study Dr. Torres would be conducting aboard the *Aurora*.

If the wrong person learned of the study, there was sure to be trouble.

He wasn't even planning to tell his crew the true purpose for Dr. Torres's study until after they'd left Unalaska and were heading toward the Pribilof Islands—when it was too late for any of his sailors to snitch.

But could he really leave this woman stranded in Bellingham with two—maybe three—dollars to her name? Especially when he was better suited than the captain of any other vessel to ensure she found her brother?

"I don't suppose you've got a fiancé back home," he muttered.

Her eyes widened. "I . . . no. What does that have to do with—?"

"Benny Fullsom proposed after our parents died, but Maggie said no."

"Ainsley!" Miss McDougal's cheeks turned a flaming shade of red. "What did I tell you about airing our family business?"

The girl shrugged. "He asked."

"And the proper response would have been not to answer."

"Can I have another biscuit?" The boy—Finnan, was it?—spoke around a mouthful of food, his chubby little hand held out to his sister.

Miss McDougal handed him another one, and Sacha waited until the boy was busy stuffing the flaky bread into his mouth before turning his gaze back to her. "I'm going to make an exception about not taking passengers, just this once.

Mainly because I feel a duty to your brother and, by extension, to you."

Miss McDougal stilled, her eyes latching to his.

"I'll take you to Unalaska to meet Tavish, and I'll also ensure you have a place to stay in the town while you wait for the *Halcyon*."

He was picking up cargo and foodstuffs to take to Unalaska and some of the other small settlements scattered throughout Alaska anyway. Then he was stopping by Sitka to pick up Captain Jones so he could join the *Halcyon* in Unalaska. Taking Miss McDougal and her siblings wouldn't cost anything in either logistics or time.

But having such a lovely unmarried woman on a ship full of female-deprived sailors? While there was also a scientist aboard whose work needed to be kept secret?

That was another matter entirely.

3

Dr. Torres was the exact opposite of what Sacha had been expecting. He had met his share of scientists over the years, each one sent to Alaska on some survey or study commissioned by a department within the US government. And every single one of those scientists had several traits in common. Like being over fifty with graying hair, a protruding stomach, and thick glasses.

But when Sacha finally made it to the hotel where Dr. Torres was staying and knocked on his door, he found himself eye level with a man who looked to be only a few years older than himself.

"Captain Amos, I presume." The man's intelligent, dark eyes blinked back at him. There was something lithe and strong in his steps as he moved deeper into the hotel room.

Dr. Torres might claim to be a scientist, but he carried himself like an explorer, strong enough to trek up mountains and across frozen tundra. In fact, the man reminded him of his brother Mikhail, who was always off leading one expedition or another into the interior, entrusted not just with finding safe passage to a new place but also with keeping the bumbling scientists and bureaucrats conducting their studies alive in a wilderness filled with bears and wolves and bitterly cold temperatures.

Dr. Torres seemed to be a combination of both a scientist and an explorer, because after spending a few hours moving crates of papers and ledgers and reports from the man's hotel room into the captain's cabin on the *Aurora*, there was no question the man was a scientist.

Or that his books, reports, and notes were sure to slide all over the place the second the ship left port.

"I must confess, I'm disappointed I'll have to wait so long to reach the Pribilof Islands. I was hoping to go there directly, especially after your ship arrived late." Dr. Torres sat down at the desk Sacha had emptied before turning his cabin over to his guest and made a notation on his calendar.

Sacha gave the man a tight smile and looked around the room. A few hours ago, it had felt like it belonged to him, the one place in the world where he could always lay his head, no matter what ocean he sailed or port he was docked at.

Now he barely recognized it.

"When are we scheduled to arrive?"

"I'm sorry, what?" Sacha blinked at Dr. Torres, the man's dark hair curling around the edges of the glasses he'd put on to study his notes.

"The Pribilof Islands." Torres raised an elegantly arched eyebrow. "When will we arrive?"

"Oh, uh . . . probably a week and a half or so. We have stops at several salmon canneries, then Sitka and Unalaska, before we continue to the islands."

The man pressed his lips together.

"You won't find yourself bored. There's plenty for you to study before we get to the islands, especially this time of year."

Again, that slender eyebrow arched upward, making the man look as though he belonged at an afternoon tea inside some fancy European castle, not a cramped cabin aboard a ship. "Yes, I'm planning to put together a preliminary report on humpback whales. The Bureau of Fisheries has commissioned a full study on that subject to be conducted over the winter in Australia and here again next summer, but I'm hoping to get a bit of early research done, since we'll be south of the northern fur seals' summer range for most of the voyage."

Sacha rubbed the back of his neck. "That's not what I was thinking you could study."

"What then?" The man made another note in his journal.

"The number of ships we pass with seal hides piled on their decks. I figure that should give you a good estimate of the true number of seals that are being harvested each year, not just the number that Alaska Commercial Company reports to the Bureau of Fisheries."

The scientist set his pencil down. "You expect we'll pass that many ships with hides?"

"Absolutely."

"Please assign a member of your crew to notify me whenever we're passing such a vessel."

"No."

Dr. Torres turned to face him fully. "I beg your pardon?"

Sacha drew in a breath. "I will not send a crew member down to notify you whenever we pass a ship with seal pelts, because no one on my ship knows that's what you're here to study."

The scientist crossed his arms over his chest, his rather thick, well-muscled chest.

Sacha's chest was thicker and the muscles of his arms more well defined, but he hadn't gone through the trouble of getting

Dr. Torres onto the *Aurora* to see which one of them could throw a better punch.

"And just how am I supposed to compile a report on the effects of hunting on the *Callorhinus alascanus* if I'm not actually allowed to study it?"

"You'll be allowed to study it—when we reach the Pribilof Islands. Which my crew doesn't know we'll be headed to, as the islands are uninhabited by anything other than seals and not near any trade routes. That part of our voyage needs to stay quiet until after we leave Unalaska."

"Is this some kind of joke to you?" The scientist pushed himself up from his chair. "Your letters said you were willing to facilitate a full study."

"This is the best I can manage, and seeing how no one in Washington, DC, wants any type of study to be conducted, you should be thanking me for allowing you to conduct your research aboard my ship."

"Thanking you?" Dr. Torres's voice turned deep. "You're the one who invited me."

Sacha blew out a breath. He had no intention of arguing with a man who'd volunteered his time for such an undertaking. Just like he had no intention of standing idly by and watching as a species of seal went extinct.

But he also didn't want this study to cause problems for him or his family, which meant the fewer people who knew about it for now, the better.

Sacha wasn't foolish enough to hope that any regulations would change as a result of this study. In fact, he suspected the quotas that the government set for the number of seals that could be harvested each year were reasonable. Poaching caused most of the problems, and he wanted that to stop. Hopefully after Dr. Torres concluded his study, the results would be significant enough for Washington to send more revenue cutters to the Bering Sea to patrol for poachers. That was all he wanted.

But the study needed to be completed first.

Sacha cleared his throat and met the man's gaze. "I still have trade routes to run and a crew that needs to be paid. But at the same time, I've rearranged part of my schedule and I've given up my cabin so you can have comfortable accommodations and a place to record your findings. This is the best I can do."

"I don't understand. Does your crew think northern fur seals should be hunted to the point of extinction, much like the sea otter?" Torres studied him from behind the thick rims of his glasses.

"My crew is made of sailors trying to feed their families, and half of them have worked on sealing or whaling vessels in the past. The pay's better than on cargo ships."

"Do your men even know I'll be aboard? Or is that supposed to be a secret too?" Exasperation laced the scientist's voice.

Sacha shifted his weight from one foot to the other. "They think you're studying sea otter habitat, perhaps so the government will open a season on them in the future."

"The sea otters are all but extinct." Torres threw up his hands. "It will be a hundred years or better before they can be hunted without damaging the population."

"Maybe so, but that's what I told my crew, and since everyone wants the sea otter to return, they believed it."

"They only want the otter to return so they can hunt them again."

"Does it matter?" Sacha leaned against the wall. "As long as the crew thinks your goals are aligned with theirs, they'll be happy to assist you."

"Until we reach the Pribilof Islands and the true purpose of my study becomes clear."

"Yes. But after that, we'll return directly to Bellingham and you'll disembark."

"And where will that leave you?"

Sacha rubbed the back of his neck. "Hopefully with more revenue cutters patrolling the sea for poachers next summer."

"What if your men mutiny?"

"Mutiny?" Now it was his turn to raise an eyebrow. "It's 1887, not 1643. My men have no need to mutiny when they can just disembark at the next port."

"So you don't expect your crew to leave you when we return to Bellingham?"

He didn't expect so, no. But he could be wrong. Feelings ran strong when it came to the sealing industry. "The faithful ones will stay, and regular seamen can be picked up at any port in California, Oregon, or Washington Territory."

The scientist's brow furrowed, but he turned back to his desk, picked up a letter, and handed it to Sacha. "I've spoken with Senators Randolph and Wells, and if the seal population is as devastated as you claim, we should be able to get the government to enact stronger penalties on the poachers by the end of the year."

"That would be amazing." He glanced at the letter, which bore the seal of US Senator Horace Randolf at the bottom. "I know this isn't a proper study, Dr. Torres. I know a man of your expertise certainly deserves a ship fully dedicated to executing a study at your direction. But I hope this will be enough to at least open discussion on the matter in Washington, even if it doesn't get things changed right away."

"On that we are agreed." Torres sighed, his large shoulders rising and falling. "Forgive me for being brutish. I like my studies to be as thorough as possible, but the political nature of this one . . ." The man tugged on his collar. "It's enough to drive a man insane."

"I understand."

"I was going to ask if you could spare a sailor to help with my notes, but I suppose that's out of the question now."

Sacha blinked, then looked around the desk, chairs, and bed all cluttered with papers. "You want someone to help you take *more* notes?"

"My assistant fell ill before we left and wasn't able to accompany me. A man usually doesn't conduct a study such as this without assistance."

Sacha shook his head. "No. At least not now. Like I said, I don't want word of the study getting out until I bring you back to Bellingham."

"Very well." The scientist nodded, then turned back to his papers. "I best get busy."

Sacha glanced around the paper-strewn cabin once more, pushing away the fact he barely recognized it. "If you need anything, you can find me on the other side of the . . ."

Quarterdeck. In the first mate's cabin. That was where he'd been planning to sleep for the voyage, but now that Miss McDougal and her siblings were accompanying them to Sitka, he'd be giving up that room. "I'll be in the first mate's cabin tonight, but once we set sail, I'll be sleeping in the cook's cabin off the galley. There'll be a woman with two younger siblings on board too. She's taking the first mate's cabin."

Torres looked up from his notes once more. "A woman? Aboard a cargo ship?"

"Only for the first leg of the voyage. Her brother works for my family. I'm taking her to Unalaska to meet him."

"I see. Thank you again for your help, Captain Amos. And thank you for caring about the welfare of northern fur seals. I wish others in your profession were half as concerned as you, but I fear many only care about how much money they can make off killing them."

Sacha's throat felt suddenly tight. "They're God's creatures, aren't they? I figure if the Bible talks about God caring for a sparrow, then he cares for a creature as magnificent as the fur seal. I figure God cared about the sea otter too—once."

The man made the sign of the cross. "Yes. I believe he cares very much."

"I'll leave you to your work." Sacha opened the door, then turned back and looked over his shoulder. "Just make sure everything is properly stored before we leave port tomorrow. I'd hate for all these notes to get mixed up with the rocking of the ship."

"Thank you, Captain Amos." Torres didn't even look up as he spoke. The man was already absorbed in a stack of notes on his desk.

Sacha closed the door behind him and stood there for a moment, his back pressed to the familiar wood.

God, is this right? Is what I'm doing really what you have for me? He tilted his head toward the sky, which had cleared somewhat of the mist, but he didn't receive any answer from above.

It was just as well. Like he'd told Dr. Torres, he had no doubt God cared about the seal population. But God wasn't the only one. Anyone involved in the sealing industry cared too—about how much money they could make off the hides, either legally or illegally.

He hoped he wouldn't have to answer to those men about his actions before he answered to God.

4

"You want us to sleep here?" Ainsley scowled up at Maggie, her pert little nose upturned as though she were the queen of a foreign country and not a child poised to lose her only home.

"It's just for one night." Maggie settled their carpetbag on the wooden planks in front of the door to the harbor-master's office. The door itself was recessed into the building by several feet, forming a small alcove with a roof overhead that would keep them dry and concealed. Besides, sleeping in the doorway of the harbor-master's office was still a lot more protected than sleeping in a park.

"Just think of it as an adventure." Maggie smiled, then gave one of Ainsley's braids a tug.

Ainsley's lips twisted into an even deeper scowl. "What about the hotel? Why can't we go back there?"

A shudder traveled up her spine. She wasn't going back, not after the offer the proprietor had made to help her find work earlier that day. Besides, she had no idea how expensive staying in Unalaska would be, or how long they'd have to wait for Tavish. And with under three dollars left to her name, she was better off saving every penny she could.

Even if it meant sleeping in a doorway for a night. "Just think, years from now I bet we'll laugh over the night we slept in a doorway in Washington Territory."

Ainsley crossed her arms over her narrow chest. "I won't laugh over this. Not ever."

"Finnan, do you want to sleep here?" Maggie sat cross-legged on the wooden platform, settling her skirts about her before she reached for her younger brother.

He nodded and went willingly into her arms, his eyes drooping heavily. "I like 'ventures."

"Of course you do." She smiled down at him and stroked a hand through his wispy hair. Finnan had skipped his nap that afternoon as they'd wandered around town, whiling away the time as they waited for morning, when they would board the *Aurora*.

"Are you making us sleep here because we're out of money?" Ainsley asked, still refusing to sit. "I saw you counting it earlier."

"We're not out of money." Though if they didn't find Tavish in Unalaska, they'd be all but stranded. She'd need to find a job in order to book passage back to Wisconsin, and she wasn't sure she'd be able to earn enough to make it back before their court deadline in October.

But if they didn't find Tavish, what was the point of returning to Wisconsin? It would be easiest to just forge a new life for themselves wherever they ended up. Maybe some upstanding man in the community would even take pity on their situation and marry her. She could keep house and cook in exchange for a roof over their heads and food on the table.

However, that was only if they couldn't find Tavish. First she planned to do everything in her power to stop her greedy uncle from stealing the legacy her parents had worked so hard for.

Yet it was hard not to feel like a failure. She still recalled the promise she'd made to her mother four years ago. Finnan had been curled on her mother's chest, sleeping soundly, a pink little newborn who wasn't yet a full day old.

But her mother's eyes hadn't been filled with the joys of motherhood as she called Maggie into her room. They'd held a deep sorrow instead. *Promise me, Margaret. I've got two little ones now, and should anything ever happen to me, you know how your stepfather is. He's gone more than he's home, and he won't care for Ainsley and Finnan as he should.*

And he wouldn't have. Her mother had been right about that. Hamish hadn't been lazy so much as greedy and selfish, always thinking about the easiest way to make a dollar, always putting what he wanted for himself above their family. He hadn't been anything like her true father.

So she'd promised to care for them if her mother passed.

Of course, when she'd made that promise, she hadn't imagined Hamish would die in the same accident as her mother. Or that Uncle Ewan would try taking their land and house and shipyard.

She hadn't imagined that she'd find herself huddled in a doorway as night fell, with less than three dollars to support all of them, and their meager belongings contained in a single carpetbag.

Would her mother say this was taking care of Ainsley and Finnan? Or had she failed in her promise only four months after her parents' deaths?

I'm trying my best, Ma. Truly I am.

"Is there a blanket?" Finnan curled into a ball beside her, using her lap as a pillow. "I'm sleepy."

Her heart gave a single heavy thud, as though even the organs inside her body recognized just how big of a failure she was.

"I'm afraid we'll have to use our coats as blankets." Maggie tucked Finnan's coat more firmly around him. "That and the heat from our own bodies, but if we snuggle up close, we'll be—"

"Hey there, pretty lady."

She stiffened, her hand turning to stone on Finnan's shoulder. She looked toward the front of the alcove, only to find two sailors standing there, their faces vaguely familiar. Were they dockworkers? Had she seen them here and there over the past week? Both had ridiculous grins plastered on their faces, and one leaned against the other as though he were already too drunk to stand upright.

"Whatcha' doin'?" the man who couldn't stand slurred.

"Nothing that concerns you." Maggie reached for the carpetbag, sliding it over so Finnan could use it as a pillow. Then she stood and faced the men.

Had the recessed doorway seemed like a safe, protected place just a few minutes ago? Because now it felt like a trap that she and her siblings had no way of escaping without somehow getting past the pair of drunkards blocking the exit.

"You need help with something?" The less drunk man squinted at them. Or at least, she assumed he was less drunk because he was standing on his own.

"We're fine, thank you." Could she ask them to leave? They were on a public street in front of a public building. It wasn't as though they were in the doorway of her house, and she could contact the police if they refused to move.

"If yer fine, then what are ya doin' 'ere?" The man's voice turned mushier with each word he spoke.

Maggie drew in a breath. Darkness was nearly upon them, and as soon as night came, no one would be able to see them camped inside the doorway. She just had to get these men to move on, and they didn't seem as though they had any ill intent. They were just curious.

And why wouldn't they be? It wasn't every day a woman and two children camped in the entrance to the harbor-master's office.

"We just paused for a moment to rest. My younger brother is tired, as you can see. Thank you for your offer of help, but we—"

"Where ya headed?" the more sober of the men asked.

"Eric, Vasily, what are you two doing?" a voice called from farther down the wharf.

A strong masculine voice that sounded somewhat familiar.

The sailors turned together, mainly because the upright one was forced to either move his friend or let him fall to the ground. "We're seein' if the woman needs help. She says she don't, but I don't believe it. Looks like she's plannin' ta camp here for the night, 'stead a on the ship."

Camp on the ship? Maggie frowned. Could these men be sailors from the *Aurora*?

"What woman?" The voice was closer now, giving her no doubt whom it belonged to—or who was about to appear.

Maggie slid past the opening that the sailors had left when they turned and stepped outside, leaving Ainsley to slink back into the corner and curl herself around Finnan, who had somehow managed to fall asleep on the carpetbag despite the commotion.

"Captain Amos, good evening." She mustered a smile and extended her hand to the burly man towering in front of her.

He didn't take it. Instead he cast a single glance at the doorway, where their things were piled, then turned his eyes back to her, his face hard.

She didn't know how long he stood there, staring at her with a small muscle pulsing at the side of his jaw. Perhaps it was seconds, or maybe it was minutes. All she knew was that she found it suddenly hard to breathe.

"Do you have a place to stay for the night, Miss McDougal?" When the captain finally spoke, his voice rumbled low in his chest, as though he'd not used it for the better part of a month and was just now testing it to see if it still worked.

"I . . . Yes, of course we have a place to stay." In the doorway of the harbor-master's office. But he didn't need to know that.

"She's lying." Ainsley poked her head around the side of the wall. "She won't go back to the motel and said we have to sleep here until the ship leaves in the morning."

"Ainsley!" Maggie snapped, her cheeks growing hot. "Go tend to your brother."

Captain Amos brushed past her and strode into the alcove.

"What are you doing?" She would have followed, but the doorway was already small, and the captain's broad shoulders seemed to take up every last inch of space.

Again, the man didn't speak, just bent and swept Finnan into his arms, then slid the handle of the carpetbag onto his forearm.

The image before her should have seemed ridiculous. A burly man with muscles as thick as tree trunks had no business cradling a child. But there was something tender and protective about how he held Finnan.

"You're coming back to the ship," he spoke in a commanding tone.

"But you said this morning that you're not leaving until dawn tomorrow."

"That's right, and it will be best if you're already aboard, not trying to corral your siblings up the gangway before first light."

She looked back at the alcove, then up at the captain. "Is this about us camping in the doorway? I truly think it will be safe once it grows darker."

He started walking, his legs carrying him down the wharf with long, fast strides.

"Wait. Stop!"

Part of her expected him to keep walking, but he stopped and turned, those tawny eyes with green swirls landing on hers once again. "Do you need something, Miss McDougal?"

"I'll let a room at the hotel. We'll sleep there for the night." She wasn't sure what possessed her to say it, not considering how she despised the place, but it somehow seemed better than throwing herself at the mercy of a man she'd met for the first time earlier that day.

Even if that man knew Tavish.

Even if he cradled Finnan against his chest in a way that calmed most of her fears.

But Captain Amos was still a stranger, and he was already being generous enough by taking them to Unalaska without charging for their passage. He didn't need to let them sleep aboard his ship for an extra night.

"Here, let me take my brother, and I'll let a room." She scurried toward him and held out her hands for Finnan.

Captain Amos flicked his eyes down the road, where a swinging sign marked the motel they'd called home for the past week. "You're not going back to that place."

Then he turned and started walking again, his arms tightening around Finnan.

"Truly, this isn't necessary." She and Ainsley followed behind him, nearly running to keep up with his long strides. Somewhere behind them, the other two sailors ambled along drunkenly, weaving their way toward the *Aurora*.

"We can find somewhere else to go," she tried again, panting. "It's only for a few hours and—"

He stopped walking again and turned to her. "I made a mistake earlier today, and I need you to forgive me."

"Forgive you?" She nearly tripped as she stopped herself from plowing into him and Finnan. "Whatever for?"

"For not inviting you to board the *Aurora* when you first arrived."

"No. You're already being far more generous than you should with a group of strangers, and—"

"You're not strangers. You're Tavish's family." He started walking again, moving closer to the sleek ship tied to the wharf that seemed a good two decades newer than anything else in the harbor. When he reached the gangway to the *Aurora*, his powerful legs hastened up the steep incline with ease.

She and Ainsley were both panting for breath again by the time they scrambled up it. But the captain didn't slow his steps once he reached the deck. If anything, his gait only quickened as he strode across the polished wood toward the stairs that led to the quarterdeck and the wheelhouse.

"Where are you taking Finnan?" She and Ainsley raced toward the stairs.

"To your cabin."

"We have a cabin?" That didn't make any sense, not considering this was a cargo ship. They usually had only two cabins, one for the captain and one for the first mate. Everyone else slept in the bunkroom, except for maybe the cook, who sometimes slept in a small closet off the side of the galley.

Maggie allowed Ainsley to precede her up the steps, then

followed Captain Amos to where he had stopped to unlock a door to a room that sat behind the wheelhouse.

"Where did you think you'd be sleeping?"

She stretched out her hands only to let them drop back to her sides. "Like you said earlier, this is a cargo ship, not a passenger ship, and we're grateful just to have passage. I assumed—"

"That I'd allow an unmarried woman such as yourself to take two small children and sleep in a bunkroom full of rowdy, half-drunk men?" That hard glint was back in his gaze again, the glint that made her throat suddenly too tight to talk. "I might not be able to provide the most luxurious accommodations for your voyage, but I can certainly do better than that."

He shoved open the door and stepped inside. "It's not very big, but it's better than sleeping with my crew. Or in a doorway. Or at the motel across from the docks."

Ainsley needed no invitation to step inside the room, but Maggie only peeked through the doorway. It was a standard first mate's cabin with everything they'd need for the next week. There was a double bed, a trunk, and a small desk with a chair. And it was all cleaner than their room at the Tattered Trawler.

The cabin did seem a bit tinier than usual, but once again, that might have had more to do with the large man standing in the middle of it than the size of the space itself.

"Are you sure about this?" Something hot pricked the backs of her eyes. Which was ridiculous. She shouldn't suddenly have the urge to cry just because Captain Amos was being kind.

But she was so far away from home, and so very alone, with two siblings to care for and a dwindling stash of money. And here Captain Amos was offering them a private room, even though he didn't know her and she wasn't paying for their passage.

She wasn't sure what she should say or do. But the captain didn't seem to notice her distress. In fact, he didn't even answer her question. He simply set the carpetbag on the floor, then turned and laid Finnan on the bed, tucking the covers around the boy in a gentle way that once again seemed at odds with his towering build.

It made her eyes prick all over again.

"Get settled for the night, Ainsley," the captain said, his gruff voice only contrasting further with his gentle mannerisms toward the children. "I want a word with your sister."

"Aye-aye, Captain." Ainsley saluted him, then sent him a toothy grin before kneeling on the floor and unlatching the carpetbag.

Maggie took a step back from the door, allowing Captain Amos to exit the room. Unfortunately the man could suck up just as much space on an open deck as he could inside an enclosed room.

Or at least that's how it felt as she stared up at him.

Again he was quiet, not spilling all his thoughts the second he had her alone, like her stepfather or Tavish would have done. He watched her instead. For one minute? Two? Ten? Once again, she couldn't tell. It seemed the man had a talent for suspending time right along with his ability to suck up space.

She also didn't know whether he could tell that she was fighting tears, or that she didn't feel deserving of his kindness.

When he finally did speak, his voice took on that deep, rumbly quality he'd used outside the harbor-master's office. "If you need help again, ask. Do you understand?"

"I didn't need your help. We would have been fine—"

"Sleeping on the docks after dark? With your pretty face and your pretty hair and your pretty eyes?"

"You think I'm pretty?" The words were out before she could think to stop them, followed almost instantly by a sudden burst of heat on her cheeks.

That small muscle ticked on the side of his jaw again. "I think you're one of my most loyal sailor's sisters, and you need to get to Unalaska, and I owe it to Tavish to make sure nothing happens to you en route. Do you understand?"

She gave a small nod.

"Good." Then he turned and stalked away, leaving her to stare at his broad back as he clomped down the stairs.

THE WOMAN WAS GOING to be the death of him. Sacha pressed his eyes shut for a brief second as he strode away from Maggie McDougal and trudged down the stairs to the deck. They hadn't even set sail yet, and already she was causing problems. Not that it was a problem to have her move into the first mate's cabin a night early. But being near her? Talking to her? Watching as those seafoam-colored eyes blinked up at him?

You think I'm pretty?

She'd been shocked by the notion, as though the thought had never once occurred to her, when the truth was every man with eyes would think she was pretty. There was no way for her to be anything other than pretty, not with all that blond hair and those seafoam eyes. Not with a face that looked delicate enough to have been formed by God himself.

What were the chances that he could lock her in her cabin for the next week and not let her out? That he could convince his men that Miss McDougal and her siblings had decided not to accompany them to Unalaska after all?

That would work for about two hours, until Miss McDougal needed to be served breakfast, and the sailor assigned to galley duty brought her a tray.

"Curse you, Tavish," he muttered into the night. Why couldn't his friend's sister have a big nose and a wide forehead and dull hair?

Why did she have to be both beautiful and stuck on his ship for the next seven days?

Because those two things were going to make for a very long week.

5

The ship left promptly at dawn without ceremony or fanfare. In fact, both Ainsley and Finnan slept right through it. Maggie might have stayed asleep herself had she not spent the night curled on the outside of the bed trying not to fall off.

But the lurch of the ship away from the wharf had nearly been enough to roll her to the floor, so she'd gotten out of bed and peered out their cabin's one and only window, which faced the stern of the ship. Yards of water had already separated the *Aurora* from the place they'd once been docked.

She'd dressed quickly in the dim light from the window, thinking to go outside and witness the departure for herself. But the moment she closed the cabin door behind her, Captain Amos stepped out of the wheelhouse and asked her to go back inside until they were a few hours into their voyage. He said the shipping channels in the Juan de Fuca Strait and surrounding waters were busy at this time of day, and he couldn't afford for his crew to be distracted. He also said he would come get her and her siblings and give them a tour later.

Maggie did as requested, resolving herself to staring out the tiny window above the bed as they passed a cluster of small islands, then came alongside a large body of land she assumed was Vancouver Island. Another ship glided into the channel behind them, following them through the maze of water and land. Then a ship passed them headed in the opposite direction, likely with a final destination of either Seattle or Bellingham.

Ainsley and Finnan eventually woke, and Finnan plastered his face to the glass, fascinated by the large ships with iron hulls and steam engines, the smaller ships with sails, and everything in between. Though Finnan's father—her stepfather—had been a captain, Hamish had felt very strongly about having women and children aboard a ship. In fact, in the seven years Hamish and her mother had been married, Maggie recalled only one occasion when he'd taken them on a voyage to Detroit to visit their aunt.

That single voyage had been so filled with Hamish's temper that her mother had never asked to travel with him again, at least not by ship. They'd also started taking the train for their yearly visit to Detroit.

But now that the three of them were all crammed into this tiny cabin, it seemed Hamish might have had a bit of wisdom in refusing to take them on more of the voyages where he served as captain.

What were they supposed to do for the remainder of their trip? Hopefully Captain Amos would give them a tour soon, and they'd be allowed to visit a few places aboard the ship, even if they needed to be conscious of staying out of the crew's way.

Or maybe they could find a way to help the sailors. It only seemed fair considering Captain Amos had refused to take money for their passage. She'd offered to work aboard the ship yesterday, but the captain hadn't given her a job.

Did the ship need to be cleaned? She and Ainsley could do that. Or maybe—

Knock. Knock. Knock.

Maggie opened the door to find the drunk sailor who'd not been able to stand up straight the previous night now standing on the deck with a tray of food.

He winked at her. "Hey luv, Cap'n told me ta bring this up."

"Thank you." She took the tray and tried to peer around him to see if Captain Amos might be nearby and ready to give them their tour, but the sailor in front of her seemed to be the only other person around. "Do you know when Captain Amos might be available?"

"Don't think he'll be doin' much other than helpin' with the navigation till after lunch. This part of the strait's always busy." The sailor ran his gaze down her, and a slow grin spread over his face. "But I'm happy to help with whatever ya need."

Her shoulders deflated. "I was hoping to speak with the captain. But is there something Ainsley and I can do to help while we wait? Perhaps we can clean the deck or . . ." She wasn't quite sure what else needed to be cleaned on a ship. Both her uncle and Hamish had always kept her away from the dry dock, insisting that she could only ever be of use in the shipyard's office. "Mop the kitchen?"

The sailor shrugged. "Don't think the cook would complain iffin' you did that."

A shout sounded, and the sailor looked over his shoulder, then turned back to her. "Gotta go. Bring the tray down to the galley after you finish."

"Thank you," she called after him.

But he was already gone, disappearing around the side of the wheelhouse.

She brought the tray inside and closed the door.

"Flapjacks!" Finnan's face lit up.

"They smell really good." Ainsley moved from the bed to the floor and crossed her legs. "Is this where we're supposed to eat?"

Maggie glanced around the room once more. While she was fairly certain there would be a table inside the captain's cabin, there was no table here. "Finnan should probably sit at the desk. And the two of us can sit on the floor."

Hopefully the boy would be less apt to spill if he could set his plate in front of him.

She divided the food onto three plates, all of which had high square edges to stop food from sliding off if the sea was choppy. Then she stood beside Finnan and held his plate still. The boy dug into his food, and the scent of flapjacks and bacon filled the cabin, causing her stomach to growl.

On the floor, Ainsley inhaled her own food at twice the pace of Finnan, then set her empty plate back on the tray and stood. "Sit and eat, Maggie. I'll hold his plate until he finishes."

"Can I have seconds?" Finnan spoke around a mouthful of food.

"Not for breakfast," Maggie replied. That would leave her only one flapjack, but perhaps she could ask for a slightly larger serving at lunch.

She sat on the floor and drizzled syrup over her flapjacks, then took her first bite. The texture of fluffy flapjack and sugary maple syrup filled her mouth, and she shoveled in another bite. She wasn't sure if the meal tasted so good because Captain Amos had hired an excellent cook, or because she'd grown used to eating nothing more than plain biscuits for one or two meals a day. But she understood why Finnan had wanted seconds. She was tempted to go down to the galley and ask for them herself.

"Can we explore now?" Finnan handed Ainsley his plate, then hopped down from his chair.

Maggie swallowed the food in her mouth. "Not until after lunch. That's when Captain Amos is giving us a tour."

"How long till lunch?"

Not soon enough. She speared another bite of food with her fork. "In a few hours. Why don't you go back to looking out the window? We're passing another ship."

"But I want to explore now!" The boy pranced around the small space.

"You need to practice patience, Finnan. Remember how we talked about that on the train?"

The boy huffed. "If I'm patient, can I go to the top of the mast after lunch?"

Maggie nearly choked. "You mean the crow's nest? No. Absolutely not."

"What about me?" Ainsley asked, her own eyes growing bright. "Will you let me climb up to the lookout? I'm older than Finnan. I won't fall."

"No one is climbing the rigging. Both of you put that idea from your heads this instant." Maggie slid her empty plate onto the tray, then picked it up and stood. "I'm going to return this to the kitchen, and I might offer to help wash the dishes or mop. I want both of you to stay in this cabin until I return. Do you understand?"

"If I help with the dishes, can I leave the cabin too?" Ainsley gave her a toothy smile. "Please?"

Maggie shook her head. "No. The captain was quite clear about us needing to stay put."

"Then why are you going to the kitchen?"

"Because the sailor who brought us breakfast told me to return the tray. And because finding some way to help on the

Aurora is the least we can do to repay Captain Amos for his generosity."

Ainsley slunk onto the bed. "Fine. I'll stay here and watch Finnan."

"Thank you." Maggie opened the door and headed onto the quarterdeck.

Captain Amos was in the wheelhouse with another sailor, but he said nothing as she passed and carefully took the stairs down to the main deck. The sun had turned warm and bright, painting in brilliant colors the landscape that had been smothered in fog the day before.

It made her want to pause for a moment, to tilt her head back and feel the sun on her face. Or maybe she should let down her hair and allow the breeze to toy with the long, curly strands. Instead, she settled for drawing in a deep breath that felt much more refreshing than the stale air inside the cabin.

The sailors all seemed busy, with one of the men tugging on the ropes to the rigging and another calling down from the top of the mast where he stood in the crow's nest. A ship was approaching on their left, but Captain Amos's calm demeanor in the wheelhouse told her there was little to worry about.

She didn't exactly know where she was going. She'd seen enough drawings of ships from back when her father was still alive only to know that galleys were usually at the back of a ship. That way if there were a fire, it was less likely to damage the entire ship.

But those lessons were from years ago, so far back it seemed like another lifetime, when the shipyard had built grand ships, not all that different from the *Aurora*. Now they mainly made fishing vessels and dinghies, small boats that were intended to be moored every night rather than cross giant seas.

Still, it wasn't hard to find the steep stairs that led from the main deck into the belly of the ship.

The dishes rattled on the tray as she made her way down the stairs, but she reached the bottom without dropping anything, then turned toward the stern.

Even if she hadn't known that bit of information about galleys being at the back of a ship, the sounds of clanging dishes and hissing water would have given away its location.

Maggie turned and headed down a narrow hallway, the air growing staler and the light dimmer with each step.

When she reached a set of swinging double doors, she backed through them so they wouldn't hit the tray and cause it to tumble to the ground.

The moment she turned herself around, she found two sets of eyes on her.

"Dishes go over there." A portly man stood at a table and used the knife in his hand to gesture toward where another sailor stood washing dishes in a basin of water.

"Thank you." She smiled at the man, who she assumed must be the cook. But he'd already gone back to chopping potatoes and tossing them into a big pot that was secured to the center of the table by a square, iron rack attached to the wood. She recognized the contraption, though once again, it was a memory from before her father had died, when he'd give her and Ma and Tavish a tour of each ship before they slid it out of the dry dock to embark on its maiden voyage.

Even all these years later, she still had to admit the iron rack was quite an ingenious way to keep the pot from sliding around with the gentle rocking of the ship.

Maggie turned and headed toward the basin on a different table where the sailor who had brought them food earlier had apparently been assigned dish duty. She set the tray beside him. "Is there something I can do to help? Would you like me to take over washing the dishes?"

The man looked at her, one eyebrow quirking, then worked

his gaze slowly down her, lingering a bit longer than was proper. "You wanna help?"

"It only seems fair, considering my siblings and I all ate this morning." She nodded toward the basin and the stack of dirty dishes beside it. "I can do that."

He smirked. "I bet you can, sweetheart."

Her cheeks heated. Was it just her, or was he acting as though she'd just suggested something improper? "You can call me Miss McDougal."

He handed her the rag, then stepped to the side. The moment she plunged her hands into the soapy water, the sailor stepped close. Too close. She could feel the heat from his chest radiating into the side of her shoulder. Then he bent down, his breath tickling her ear. "I can call you a lotta things, luv, but Miss McDougal ain't gonna be one of them."

She dropped the dish into the basin with a thud, then spun around to face him. He didn't step back, meaning she had to arch away from him so their bodies didn't brush. The scent of stale liquor lingered on his breath, reminding her that he was the sailor who had been too drunk to stand or walk by himself the previous night. "I said you can call me Miss McDougal. And I meant it. Are you even in charge here? Perhaps I should get instructions from the cook."

She slid away from the sailor, who still hadn't done anything to put a reasonable amount of space between them, then stalked over to the man she assumed to be the cook. Had he seen how the sailor had crowded her? Heard what the man said?

But he was still chopping potatoes, seemingly oblivious to everything that had just transpired. "Is there something I can help with down here? I'm good at cleaning, or making biscuits, or just about anything in the kitchen, and I'd like to assist in some way."

The cook still didn't look up from where he stood methodically chopping potatoes.

"Scully can't hear ya." The sailor came up behind her. Right behind her, once again standing so close that his trousers brushed against her skirt.

She lurched away from him, but the man didn't look the least bit abashed. He just nodded toward the cook.

"He's deaf as a post. Needs his ear trumpet ta hear." The sailor slapped his hands down on the table.

The noise was loud enough that Maggie jumped, but the cook just raised his eyes, as though the sailor had done nothing more than snap his fingers.

"Put yer ear trumpet in. The lady wants to talk to ya." He gestured to the ear trumpet that was indeed lying at the edge of the table.

The cook picked up the device and inserted it into his ear, then cocked his head in a manner that allowed the trumpet to be angled toward her while he could still see her face. "Ya need somethin', doll?"

Again, her face heated. She'd been out of her cabin five minutes, and she'd been called sweetheart, luv, and doll. Did no one aboard a ship use people's names?

She stepped closer to the table and raised her voice. "Can I help with lunch?"

The man huffed, his round belly brushing the front of the table. "No need ta shout. I can hear ya plenty fine with my trumpet in."

Right. Of course. "I can dice those potatoes or finish washing the dishes. I'm good at cleaning too. Is there something that needs to be done?"

The man looked her up and down. "First time I ever had a passenger volunteer ta help in the galley."

Yes, well, it was probably also the first time Captain Amos

had taken on a trio of passengers without accepting payment. She smiled as brightly as she could manage, seeing how the sailor had once again found a way to stand too close to her.

"Eric here's on dish duty fer breakfast and lunch, but you can take over choppin' potatoes fer the stew. As long as ya think you can handle a knife with the ship rocking and not slice open a finger."

The ship wasn't rocking terribly much. Of course, that might change once they reached the open waters of the Pacific, but the strait was as smooth as glass. "I think I can manage."

"Great. I got carrots and rutabaga that need choppin' too. I'll gather those." Scully stepped away from his place at the table and held out his knife to her, a kind smile on his face.

She smiled back, then set to work chopping vegetables.

She worked for over an hour, and every time she was nearly finished with a bowl of potatoes or carrots, Scully slid another bowl onto the table, and she went right back to chopping.

Once she'd started chopping vegetables, Eric had gone back to the dish washing station on the other side of the galley and left her alone. At some point, he finished the dishes and left, but she couldn't quite say when.

By the time they finally set the stew atop the stove to cook, the pot was nearly full.

The cook had a special metal lid that locked in place atop the pot. That wasn't something she remembered from when she was younger, but it seemed like a rather smart way to keep the stew from spilling if the ocean grew rough.

Once the stew was cooking, Scully set her to work making biscuits. She wasn't sure how many she made, but she'd counted well over two hundred before Scully told her they had enough to see them through the end of the week.

By then the stew was thick and bubbling, releasing a tangy aroma into the air.

"Smells good in here." Eric entered the galley and flashed her a smile.

"Hopefully it tastes good too." Maggie went back to wiping off the table where her biscuit making had left a floury mess.

He unlatched a cupboard and brought a stack of wooden bowls and spoons to the clean section of the table.

"What time is lunch?" she asked.

"Noon."

"And what time is it now?"

"Ten to."

Ten to noon? Goodness. She tucked a strand of hair behind her ear. She'd left Ainsley and Finnan for over three hours. Hopefully they'd stayed in the cabin and hadn't gotten themselves into trouble.

As good as the stew and biscuits smelled, she really should go check on them, even if lunch was only ten minutes away.

She turned to tell Scully, but he was standing at the pot, licking remnants of stew from a large wooden spoon.

"Tastes delicious. Glad we added the marjoram like you said."

She smiled at the praise. She had, in fact, suggested that Scully add marjoram after it became clear he wasn't planning to.

"Take the pot to the table, then dish yerself up a tray to bring back to yer cabin. The sailors will be down soon. And yer welcome to help in my galley anytime."

Maggie's smile grew even bigger. "I'll be back to help with dinner, but I need to check on my siblings, and Captain Amos said he'd give us a tour of the ship after lunch."

"What was that?" The cook reached for his ear trumpet.

"I said I'll be back to help again with dinner," she shouted before Scully managed to get his ear trumpet in.

"Oh, no need fer that." Scully waved her off. "Dinner's already done. We're havin' stew and biscuits fer both meals."

They were? So she'd just cooked enough food for two meals? That explained why she needed to chop so many vegetables.

"Don't listen to him," Eric said from behind her, his voice too soft for Scully to hear. "You can come back right after lunch. I might need help with the dishes."

She shook her head, her lips pressed together so she didn't grin. "Are you trying to get out of your responsibilities aboard ship, sailor?"

He held up his hands in a gesture of innocence. "Me? Never. The time just passes faster with a pretty woman around."

Again, she felt her cheeks warm, but there was nothing inappropriate about this comment, or about the way Eric was looking at her. Perhaps she'd read too much into his actions earlier. "Let's worry about serving lunch first."

She stepped to the stove and hefted the large pot into her hands.

Do ya need help with that?" Suddenly, Eric was right behind her, his chest pressed fully against her back, and his mouth close enough that the scent of stale spirits from the previous night twined around her.

She slanted a glance at Scully, looking for him to correct Eric, but the cook had his back to them as he gathered biscuits from the cooling rack and put them in a bowl.

"Please step away. I need to carry this to the table." She tried to move back, the pot heavy in her hands, but Eric stayed in place, their bodies now plastered to each other.

Then Eric's arms wrapped around her waist.

She squeaked. "What are you doing?"

But that became clear a second later, when one of his hands snaked up and touched her chest.

Not an accidental brush. An intentional, lingering placement.

She yelped and jumped back, her heart thundering against her ribs.

The pot of stew slipped from her grip and clattered to the floor.

Only then did she realize Scully must not have latched the lid after he'd tasted the stew, because it slid off the pot, allowing their lunch to spill all over the floor.

A string of loud curses unleashed from behind her, and Maggie turned to find herself staring at an irate Scully.

"She's the one who dropped it." Eric stepped back from her. "I asked iffin' she needed help, but she never answered."

She whirled on him. "Me? It was your fault. You're the one who—"

"What?" Eric smirked. "Just what did I do? Care to announce it fer the whole ship to know?"

"Out. Out of my galley, and don't ever come back." Scully pointed at the door, his face beet red and his shouting loud enough Captain Amos could surely hear it on the quarterdeck. "Eric, go tell the crew we don't got no lunch."

"I . . . I'm sorry. I wasn't . . . It didn't . . ."

"Don't worry, luv." Eric winked at her. "You can repay me fer the lost meal later."

Nausea churned in her stomach as she stared at the sailor; then she turned and raced out of the room.

6

"To the left, Dr. Torres. There's another ship." Sacha pointed at the clipper about to pass them in the shipping channel. Stacks of seal pelts were piled high on the deck, and who knew how many more were in the hold.

The scientist's knuckles tightened on the ship's railing. "It's the third one, and it's not even lunchtime."

"I'm aware."

"How many pelts do you think the ship is carrying?"

Sacha shook his head. "It's hard to know."

The scientist slanted him a cool glance. "Guess, Captain Amos."

He drew in a breath. There were maybe three hundred on the deck, but ships didn't go to the Pribilof Islands to trade. They went for seals or whales. So it wasn't as though the ship's hold would be full of lumber with just a few pelts on deck. No. Every spare inch of the ship was probably stuffed with salted pelts, which would then need to be drained and dried before being sold at market.

"Probably two thousand or so."

Dr. Torres was quiet as they pulled alongside the clipper, his dark eyes absorbing every detail about the ship. "Wait. Is that a Canadian flag? The US government hasn't authorized Canada to harvest seals."

"No." He scrubbed a hand over the stubble on his jaw. "The ship is hunting the seals at sea, in international waters."

"No, no. That can't be. The bachelor bulls isolate themselves on the islands this time of year. If these seals were taken at sea, then they have to be females who were searching for food for their young."

Dr. Torres turned to him, the muscles of his powerful body coiled tight. "Do you mean to tell me this Canadian ship is carrying two thousand *female* seal pelts? That will destroy the seal population in a matter of years!"

"Keep your voice down." Sacha looked around the quarter-deck. Most of the crew was on the main deck, but Ronnie was in the wheelhouse, and he didn't want their conversation to be overheard.

They hadn't seemed to draw any attention, so he moved his gaze back to the Canadian ship.

He tried to see it through Dr. Torres's eyes, tried to let his body fill with anger at the thought of so many seals being poached. But the truth was, these ships were everywhere this time of year, the price of a seal pelt too high for most captains to turn away from, even if they didn't have a license to hunt seals.

He drew in a breath, heavy from the moisture clinging to the sea air. "Now you see why I want the poaching stopped."

"None of this should be happening." Dr. Torres's voice held a small quiver, but Sacha didn't know the man well enough to tell whether it was from rage or sadness. "Most females have a pup on land this time of year. If the mother doesn't return to feed it, it will die."

"As will the pup in her belly," Sacha added. "Assuming she's pregnant."

"That means three seals are dying each time a mother is killed at sea." The scientist covered his face with his hand, his shoulders slumping. "I hadn't realized the situation was this dire. This study should have happened five years ago."

He felt his own shoulders deflate. "That's about how long I've been writing letters, trying to get a study done. The Bureau of Fisheries ignored every last one. Then I moved on to writing politicians directly. When one of them wrote me back last summer asking what evidence I had that a study needed to be conducted, I decided to switch tactics and see if I could finance a study myself."

The Canadian ship was nearly past them, likely headed to either Victoria on Vancouver Island or the city of Vancouver on the mainland, but Dr. Torres couldn't seem to tear his gaze away from it, as though staring hard enough at the vessel just might bring some of the seals back to life.

"Have you read the report that the Bureau of Fisheries commissioned in 1868?" the scientist finally asked.

"Parts of it." Enough to get the gist: only bachelor male seals should be harvested.

"Because of the highly polygamous nature of the northern fur seal, a bull can impregnate dozens of cows every summer," Dr. Torres muttered. "That means we can take up to a hundred thousand young male seals who aren't yet old enough to mate without damaging the population. But there's no room in any of this for females to be killed, especially not by the thousands."

Sacha might not be able to put it as eloquently as the scientist beside him, but he didn't need a fancy degree to know the northern fur seal was in trouble. "From what I've seen, Alaska Commercial Company is the only one abiding by the regulations, but that's because they have an exclusive license to hunt the Pribilof Islands. Otherwise, I'm sure they'd be poaching seals right along with everyone else. No one wants to walk away from that kind of money."

He stared out over the calm waters of the Pacific, the blue expanse stretching as far as the eye could see. "Which is why, this time of year, there's a constant stream of sealing ships coming into Vancouver or Seattle. Sometimes I think it's the only cargo unloaded on the docks. And as soon as the ships unload, they'll head straight back to the Bering Sea for more."

Dr. Torres pulled a small notepad and pencil nub out of his breast pocket. "I need to arrive at some sort of estimate for how many seals are being taken each year. And when we reach the Pribilof Islands, I'll need to estimate how many seals are still using the islands as breeding grounds."

Sacha nodded. A part of him wanted all seal hunting to be banned immediately, so an official study could assess the true state of the seals. But that would cause an uproar, so he'd started by focusing on the poachers.

"What about the whales?" The scientist stopped writing long enough to look over at him. "Are they being killed by the thousands too?"

"Not by the thousands, but probably by the hundreds. I'm not sure the whale population was ever as large as the seal population. If you go north to Barrow or Nome, the Inupiat will tell you the whales are disappearing. Just like the Aleuts will tell you the seals are disappearing."

"Inupiat?" Dr. Torres's brow furrowed. "I've not heard of them before. Who are they?"

He nearly rolled his eyes. "The Americans call them Eskimos, though that's not their name."

"Ah, and the Aleut you speak of? Are they Eskimos as well?"

He shrugged. "Maybe. They live on the Aleutians, not as far north as the Inupiat. They're a different tribe."

"I see." Dr. Torres made a few more notes on his pad, then closed it and slipped it back into his pocket. "Like I told you yesterday, this study has a highly political nature to it. Much more than what I've navigated for any of my previous studies. The truth is, considering the bounty that the US government receives from each of these pelts, they have no incentive to change anything."

"I know." He wished it weren't so. But the simple truth was, each time a seal pelt arrived in port, the government got a bounty of two dollars regardless of whether the seal had been poached.

"I reviewed the numbers before coming here," Dr. Torres said. "If Alaska Commercial Company harvests a hundred thousand bachelor bulls per year for a period of twenty years, paying a bounty of two dollars per pelt as agreed upon, it will be nearly enough money to pay for the purchase of Alaska."

He knew that as well. In fact, it had been the first thing his brother Alexei had said when Sacha had started writing those letters to the Bureau of Fisheries all those years ago. "Look, I'm not a scientist. I'm not smart enough to figure out whether men can kill a hundred thousand seals a year without hurting the population. But as a captain, I can tell you that with the market price of a pelt at ten dollars, it's too lucrative a proposition for most captains to pass by. That ship we just passed was carrying twenty thousand dollars' worth of cargo, a percentage of which will be split among the crew."

The scientist raked a hand through his hair, his face turned toward the ocean. "Don't suppose you have any ideas for driving down the price of a pelt."

"If I did, I'd have done it five years ago. But while our government is content to ignore when our own ships poach seals—because they still get a bounty—they don't take kindly to Canadian ships poaching."

"What do you mean there ain't no lunch?" a shout carried across the deck.

Sacha frowned and turned toward the voice, just in time to see Miss McDougal race up the stairs to the quarterdeck.

Why wasn't she in her cabin? He'd told her to stay put until after lunch.

She flew past him and Dr. Torres, her head down as she raced toward the door of her cabin. She flung it open, slid inside, then slammed it shut behind her.

More commotion rose from the main deck, raised voices all competing with each other.

"Excuse me, Dr. Torres. It appears there's a matter I must attend to." He strode across the quarterdeck, then took the stairs two at a time and crossed the main deck until he reached the crew gathered near the steps leading belowdecks.

"What's going on?" he shouted above the melee.

"That woman spilled the pot of stew, and now we got no lunch," Eric said, his face red.

"We got no dinner either." Scully poked his head out from the stairwell, his ear trumpet in place as he climbed the last few steps to the deck. "That pot of stew was fer both our meals."

"Why was Miss McDougal handling the pot of stew? She was supposed to remain in her cabin," Sacha growled, narrowing his gaze on Eric. "I told you to bring food to her cabin for breakfast and lunch."

"She's been in the kitchen all morning." Scully's loud voice rang over the deck despite having his ear trumpet in place. "Came down with her dirty dishes and offered ta help. She's a good cook, and I was happy ta have her, right up till I told her to take the stew to the table, and she dropped the whole pot."

Of course she did. He could just imagine the slender Miss

McDougal carrying the big pot of stew across the galley, the ship listing to the side on a sudden wave, and the stew spilling across the floor.

"So we got no lunch or dinner because of the woman?" Gus, his first mate, muttered.

"Why'd you invite a woman onto the ship, Cap'n?" Nikolai asked. "Don't ya know a woman aboard can turn into bad luck?"

"I agree with Nikolai." Eric crossed his arms over his chest. "It ain't worth havin' a wench aboard. I don't care how warm yer bed is at night."

Sacha turned to face Eric. The young sailor had been in a sour mood ever since Sacha had assigned him galley duty that morning, and he'd had enough of the whelp's attitude. "Miss McDougal is Tavish's sister and a respectable lady. I'll not tolerate any talk of her warming a man's bed, least of all mine."

"How do ya know she's respectable?" Scully tilted his ear trumpet toward Sacha, a stumped look on his face. "Sure ain't nothin' respectable about how Tavish treats ladies."

"Because I know," he growled, though there was truth to Scully's statement. Tavish McDougal might make a fine sailor, but he made a poor gentleman. He certainly knew how to charm ladies, but his intentions were never honorable.

Which was probably something his sister didn't know. That wasn't exactly the type of thing a man discussed when he went home to visit his family.

"My words stand." Sacha scanned his crew. "If I find any of you speaking so much as a word against Miss McDougal's character, you'll be in the galley with Scully for the rest of the voyage. Am I clear?"

The men clamped their mouths shut.

"Miss McDougal will only be with us until we reach Unalaska. I expect each and every one of you to treat her like a lady, which I know you're capable of doing, seeing how my sisters have been aboard the *Aurora* plenty of times, and there's never been any talk impugning their character."

A collective sigh seemed to rise from the group, but again, no one argued with him.

"Go scrounge up something for dinner." He turned his gaze to Scully. "We'll make do with biscuits for lunch."

Scully scowled at him. "I told ya, the stew was fer both meals, and now we don't got none."

"There's plenty of time for you to whip up something for tonight, and I don't want to hear any bellyaching about changing the menu. We'll be in Ketchikan tomorrow, and you can pick up more supplies for stew there."

Scully muttered something under his breath about rice and beans, then yanked out his ear trumpet and made his way back down the stairs, a frown plastered on his face.

The cook could grumble all he wanted. Sacha paid him to provide food for the crew, and there was no reason he couldn't make something for dinner. "As for the rest of you . . ." He surveyed the crew. "I don't want to hear a word of complaint about missing lunch. Anyone could have spilled that pot. It's not the first time we've lost a meal due to a mistake in the kitchen. Now get back to work."

Though most of his men glared, no one had the gall to argue.

Which was a good thing. Because he wasn't in the mood to deal with whiny sailors.

Sacha waited for his crew to go back to their stations, then headed across the deck. Why had Miss McDougal been in the galley? Never in all his years of captaining had he found a passenger voluntarily helping in the kitchen.

And here he thought the morning had gone well. They'd sailed through the strait and were now making their way north along Vancouver Island. He'd had time to speak with Dr. Torres and point out how he could spot ships carrying seal pelts. Plus, he'd been planning to take Miss McDougal and her siblings on a tour after lunch and show them some places on the ship where they could go without interfering with his crew.

But Miss McDougal hadn't listened to his instruction. And the idea of her being belowdecks without him knowing caused his chest to feel inexplicably tight.

Especially in an enclosed room with only one other sailor.

Granted, Scully had a wife in Wrangell, and the man wasn't one to visit brothels in every port of call.

But Sacha couldn't say the same about Eric and some of his other sailors.

He climbed the steps back to the upper deck, nodding at Ronnie as he passed the wheelhouse. Then he stopped in front of the door to Miss McDougal's cabin and knocked, the rap of his knuckles seeming overly loud against the wood.

The door opened a second later.

"I thought I told you to . . ."

But Miss McDougal wasn't the one standing in the doorway. It was Ainsley, with her bright-green eyes and freckled cheeks. She looked back at him expectantly.

"I need to speak to your sister."

Ainsley looked over her shoulder, then shrugged and opened the door wider. "Don't know that she's much for talking."

He peeked his head inside and scanned the room, only to find Miss McDougal curled on the bed, her face buried in a pillow while her shoulders shook with silent sobs.

"When's lunch?" Finnan pushed himself off the floor, where he'd been playing with a whittled figurine of a horse. "I'm hungry."

Sacha glanced at Miss McDougal again, the tightness in his chest traveling clear up to his throat.

Just how harsh had Scully been with her after she'd spilled the stew?

"Cap'n Amos," Finnan tugged on his trousers. "Can I eat now?"

Sacha pulled his gaze away from Miss McDougal and down to the bright-eyed boy who didn't seem the least bit concerned about his sister's distress. "Sure. Let me run down to the galley and grab a few biscuits."

But even as he closed the door and headed belowdecks, he couldn't seem to scrub the sight of Miss McDougal crying from his mind—or find a way to relieve the tight sensation from his chest.

7

Sitka, Alaska

Alexei Amos blew out a breath, letting the salty sea air fill his lungs as the door to the administrative building swung shut behind him. Free finally. After a morning of haggling over delivery prices with the representative for the Marine Hospital Service, he could use a bit of fresh air.

And some lunch.

And to not step back inside that dratted building for another month.

Though he'd likely find himself tromping back up to the building in a few more days. It might be his least favorite part of owning five ships, a trading company, and a shipyard, but it was also necessary.

Alexei drew in another breath, then headed down Castle Hill toward the shipyard and office where he spent most of his days. It was a beautiful day, the sky above a brilliant blue, and the sun creating glittering patterns on the clear water of the sound. Mountains rose around him, surrounding Sitka on all sides except for the small space where the sound opened into the wide expanse of the Pacific Ocean.

It was almost enough to calm a man's spirits. Almost enough to make a man smile.

"Alexei. Wait a moment."

At the sound of the voice behind him, he nearly kept walking. Nearly pretended he hadn't heard anyone calling his name.

But it wasn't just anyone calling for him. It was Milton Trent. The governor of Alaska.

So he stopped and blew out a breath, forcing his shoulders to relax as the other man wove his way through the trickle of people headed to and from the building located at the top of Castle Hill. It had once been the governor's mansion, back when Alaska had belonged to Russia. But the Americans had converted the lovely architectural masterpiece into an administrative building filled with serviceable offices, and it almost hurt to step inside it, knowing how grand the building had once been.

"The Tlingit at Hoonah are demanding four hundred blankets." The governor stopped beside him, his brow furrowed. "But Alaska Commercial Company doesn't want to pay it. I'm not sure what the best course of action is."

Alexei rubbed his brow. "Is this about the Tlingit man who died last month? The one who was working for the ACC?"

"Yes. I'd like to reach some type of settlement with the clan so that we can avoid what happened last time."

He grunted. At least the new governor that Washington, DC, had sent to Alaska was concerned about maintaining a semblance of peace with the Tlingit. "Someone needs to pay reparations for that man's death, so I suggest you get some blankets. Unless you want the clan to capture and kill the next white man who wanders their way."

"So you think the government should use its funds to purchase four hundred blankets?" The governor shifted. "It might be a bit hard to get approval for that from Washington. They watch the budget, you know."

"It shouldn't be that hard. Can't the Indian agent fill out one of your forms and have the money released?"

The governor scratched the side of his head. "Probably. In six months or so."

Alexei crossed his arms over his chest. "Chief Yèil isn't going to wait that long. He'll kill half a dozen men from Alaska Commercial Company by the end of this month if you don't start some type of repayment."

"Half a dozen men?" The governor squeezed his hat in his hands. "All because of one accidental death? If Chief Yèil takes such drastic actions, there's no way I can let something like that go unanswered."

"Now you know how Chief Yèil feels regarding the death of his clansman."

"But it was an accident!" The governor threw up his hands, then started stalking back and forth. "People die at sea all the time. Doesn't the chief understand that?"

Alexei tamped down the urge to roll his eyes. Barely. "They have their ways, much as we have ours. As I recall, this was rarely an issue when Russia owned Alaska. They simply paid whatever was required to atone for a death, then moved on. I'm not sure why the Americans have such a hard time understanding it—or why Alaska Commercial Company is refusing to compensate for the death of one of their workers. I probably have two hundred blankets sitting in the warehouse now, and I can have another two hundred here by the end of the month. I can even arrange for them to be delivered. I just need Alaska Commercial Company to pay me for them first."

The governor huffed. "Mr. Caldwell is claiming his crew

did nothing wrong, that the death was a natural risk that came with working on one of his ships."

Of course he was. Alexei pressed his lips into a firm line. He should have expected such a response from Preston Caldwell. "That man's stubbornness could well start a war."

"We'd win it." Governor Trent waved his hand toward the harbor, where three navy ships were anchored.

Alexei sighed. The Americans responded this way every time there was some kind of altercation with the native tribes, and he didn't understand it. "Seems you were brought here to prevent altercations between the Americans and the natives, not to condone them."

The governor picked at an imaginary fleck on his vest. "You're not wrong. No one wants to see the navy destroy another village. There will certainly be fallout from that, which is why I sought you out. I want to know how we can prevent it."

Had the man heard anything he'd said so far? "By giving Chief Yèil four hundred blankets."

The governor scratched the side of his head, a frazzled look on his face. "Can you just give the blankets to Chief Yèil? That would make things so much simpler. You already said you have them."

His jaw clenched. "I said I have half of them, and I can get the rest, yes. But a man wasn't killed on one of my ships, he was killed on Preston Caldwell's. When he pays me for the blankets, I'll happily deliver them. I'll even make up some type of believable excuse for why Caldwell doesn't deliver them in person."

Governor Trent huffed out another breath. "I told you, Caldwell is claiming he did nothing wrong, that the Tlingit man jumped into the ocean of his own volition in an unsuccessful attempt to save another sailor. He won't pay."

"And tell me, is Caldwell paying the white sailor's family some type of compensation?"

"Well, yes, but the man accidentally fell on a slick deck. He didn't jump into the water intentionally."

Alexei started walking. He didn't have time for this foolishness.

"Alexei." The governor scrambled to keep up with him. "Where are you going?"

"Back to work."

"But what about the blankets?"

He turned to face the governor. He wasn't an old man, maybe thirty-five, and lithe and smart, the kind of man who could probably manage the vast expanse of Alaska well—if he made half an effort to understand Alaska and its needs, as well as the people, who had been living here for decades—or even centuries—before it switched to American control.

And honestly, at least Governor Trent was trying to figure this out, unlike the previous governor, or the navy general before him, who thought nothing of sacrificing Tlingit lives to get their own way.

But giving up his own blankets? Without being paid? And all because Preston Caldwell was being stubborn?

Alexei unclenched his hand from its fist and forced his fingers to open and stretch. If it were anyone other than Caldwell being stubborn, would he give the blankets?

Could he afford to give the blankets?

"Like I said, I'm happy to get them here and deliver them to Hoonah, but I don't run a charity."

The governor's lips flattened into a line. "I suppose I understand your position. I know there's no love lost between you and Caldwell."

It was all he could do not to laugh. The man didn't know

the half of it, but Caldwell was powerful enough that Alexei couldn't afford to start a rivalry with him.

"Tell me, Governor. How would you feel if you were in my position, and Caldwell had stolen your shipping contracts last year?"

"He only did that because your brother got one of his ships detained for two months and an entire load of cargo confiscated."

"And rightfully so. The captain of the ship was poaching seals. What would you have had Sacha do? Turn a blind eye to such blatant disregard for the law?"

"Everyone hunts seals at sea. Why would Sacha turn in one of the ACC ships but not any of the others out there poaching seals?"

Alexei shrugged, though the movement was tight and jerky, his muscles suddenly tense. "Because he recognized that ship. Because it was flying an American flag rather than a Canadian one, and the ship's captain knew the Revenue Cutter Service had jurisdiction over it. Because Preston Caldwell can take a hundred thousand seals a year legally on the Pribilof Islands already, which means none of his ships should be poaching."

The judge, wanting to set an example, had ruled harshly against ACC and confiscated an entire shipload of seal pelts. Most of the pelts had been obtained legally on the Pribilof Islands. But because the judge couldn't determine how many pelts had been taken at sea, he'd confiscated everything.

By the time Alexei understood the consequences of what Sacha had done, Caldwell had already stolen three shipping contracts out from under him, taking away the little profit Sacha made on the *Aurora* running their Alaskan trade routes. He'd be lucky if the *Aurora* didn't lose him money this summer, and that was without giving away four hundred blankets.

"I really think that if you were to supply the blankets, it

would go a long way toward healing your relationship with Caldwell," the governor muttered.

Alexei raised an eyebrow. "I'm not sure Caldwell is interested in repairing anything with me."

But he was interested in stopping a Tlingit Village from being razed. The last time something like this had happened had been four years ago in Angoon, when a shaman had accidentally been killed aboard a whaling canoe. The Tlingit had demanded a payment of two hundred blankets for their loss, but when the company refused to pay, the clan took hostages.

In response, the US Navy—which had been in charge of Alaska at the time—sent a ship to Angoon to demand the release of the hostages. When the Tlingit refused to release them without receiving any blankets, the ship bombarded the village, completely destroying it and the food stores, leaving the Tlingit people in a dire situation as winter approached.

Alexei swallowed, his throat tight with the memory. He'd gone to the general before that ship had left harbor, pleading with the man to simply give the clan at Angoon the blankets.

The only good thing that had come of the situation was that Washington, DC, had taken the governance of Alaska away from the navy and started appointing actual governors to run the six hundred and fifty thousand square miles that made up Alaska.

Things had been more peaceful with the Tlingit since, but Alaska had also gone through three governors in two years. And there was a betting pool down at the bar over how long Governor Trent would survive here.

Alexei didn't want to have to clean up Caldwell's mess with the tribe in Hoonah. Didn't want to find himself in the middle of anything that had to do with Preston Caldwell.

But if he refused . . .

He couldn't risk another Angoon. Neither could Governor Trent.

"I'll get you a price for those blankets," Alexei said, his voice a bit hoarse. "I don't need to make money on them, but I don't want to lose money either. So if you find room in the budget to pay me for the blankets, then I'll give them to you at cost."

The governor beamed, then slapped him on the back. "Excellent, Alexei. That's just what I was hoping for."

Then the man turned and trotted back up the hill toward his office, leaving Alexei to wonder if anyone was ever going to force Preston Caldwell to clean up one of his own messes.

8

Ketchikan, Alaska, One Day Later

"You're supposed to be here every three weeks."

Sacha tried not to wince as he looked at Oliver Sandingham, the irate manager of the cannery, who was standing on the wharf with a clipboard in his hands.

"It's been nearly five!" The short man threw up his hands, causing the papers on his clipboard to ruffle in the wind off the sea.

"I know. I'm sorry." Sacha raised his hands in a gesture of innocence. "Like I said, a ship ran aground just south of here as I was leaving last time, and it took us some time to get it towed out at high tide."

"It took you two weeks?"

This time he couldn't hide his wince. "Three days, but then I followed it back to Sitka to make sure—"

"I don't have time for your excuses. We need to get the salmon loaded." The manager turned toward the warehouse, where a half-dozen men were stacking crates filled with canned salmon onto handcarts. "I can take extra cargo."

Oliver whirled on him, his face an unhealthy shade of red. "You'd better take extra cargo. You better take everything I have that's been piling up since you missed your pickup two weeks ago. If you don't, I'll be taking my shipping contract to Bering Shipping Company. They make runs every two weeks, not three. And they arrive when they're scheduled."

Sacha dragged in a breath, the morning air thick with the scents of salt and fish. Above him, gulls circled against the cloudy sky. "What would you have had me do, leave the ship south of here stranded?"

The cannery manager crossed his arms over his chest. "Did the ship belong to your family?"

"No."

"Then yes, that's exactly what I would have done. Unless you want to lose even more business to Bering." The man leaned forward, somehow managing to point his skinny little nose down at him, even though he was a good foot shorter than Sacha. "And if I take my business to your family's competitor, I'll let you explain why to your brother."

Sacha sighed. Was it just him, or was Oliver being overdramatic? Yes, he was late, but it wasn't as though the cannery warehouse was full. They had space to store probably six or seven weeks' worth of canned salmon.

But his family couldn't afford to lose any more shipping contracts, not considering that last year, alongside owning Alaska Commercial Company, Preston Caldwell had started a small branch of the company—Bering Shipping. Its only purpose was to compete with Sitka Trading Company—and see how quickly it could financially bleed dry the shipping part of the Amos family's business.

Caldwell's plan hadn't quite worked, though, and part of

that was due to men like Oliver Sandingham, who were honoring their shipping contracts until they were up for renewal.

But after that? Sacha fully expected Oliver and a few others to move their business to Bering Shipping Company, and without the lucrative cannery contracts to support the shipping runs the *Aurora* made to the rural towns of coastal Alaska, they might not be able to afford to run those routes.

By this time next year, they might not be able to have the *Aurora* even run these routes, and he might be on his way to Japan or China rather than north to the Bering Sea.

Sacha pressed a palm to his breastbone, which suddenly started to ache.

"Can we unload the food, Cap'n?"

He looked up to find his first mate standing at the top of the gangway with a handcart. "Yes, start unloading."

"I certainly hope you brought extra flour, vegetables, and salt," Oliver muttered. Then he spun on his heel and stalked back toward the warehouse.

Was that what Oliver was so upset about? Not the fact that canned salmon had sat in the warehouse for a couple extra weeks, but that their food was running low? The mountains of Southeast Alaska were filled with bear and deer. The sea was filled with halibut and salmon. But the damp, wet nature of this section of the coast made it impossible to grow wheat or corn or any other kind of grain. Just as it was impossible to grow potatoes or carrots or root vegetables without them rotting in the damp, loamy soil.

The last time Sacha had visited Ketchikan, he'd brought three, maybe four, weeks' worth of flour, potatoes, carrots, sugar, salt, and oats.

Just what had the cannery employees been eating for the past week—besides salmon?

Sacha waited for his men to stream down the gangway, their carts filled with the food Oliver needed, then he strode up the gangway, strode across the deck, and headed to the hold, located two floors down, deep in the belly of the ship.

The lanterns hanging on the walls provided dim light as he made his way to where the food was stored along the starboard wall. He pulled out three extra fifty-pound sacks of flour and two extra sacks of potatoes, as well as an extra bag of salt.

The first of the cannery men arrived in the hold, their crates heavy on their carts.

"Put as many crates as you can fit in the front of the ship for ballast. The rest you can put on the port wall there." Sacha gestured to where he wanted the cargo, then handed the first five men the sacks of flour and potatoes to carry back up the stairs.

He stayed in the hold for over an hour, directing the stacking of the crates and deciding just how much extra food he could leave in Ketchikan. The problem was, Wrangell and Petersburg would also need extra food, and he would be arriving two weeks late to each of those places as well.

And the *Aurora* would be quite laden down if he took five weeks' worth of salmon at each of his next two stops. He'd need to unload some of the salmon in Sitka and take some of the extra food they kept stored there before heading north to Unalaska. Hopefully Alexei could find room on one of their other ships heading south to get the salmon down to Seattle.

Sacha sighed. He didn't envy his older brother, always moving things around among their five ships, trying to find a way to meet their contracts and make sure their routes brought in enough money to pay their bills and give their family money to live on. He'd rather be a captain five times over than be stuck managing everything like Alexei.

When he finally left the hold and made his way back to the

deck, he had to blink several times before his eyes adjusted to the brightness, and it wasn't even sunny. Just gray and misty, typical weather for this part of Alaska.

Oliver met him on the wharf, a list of the cargo they were loading in his hand, and his face a little less red than before. "Thank you for the extra food."

Sacha shrugged. "It's the least I can do. I truly am sorry I ran late."

The manager nodded. "It happens, I suppose. The sea is nothing if not unpredictable."

"How much salmon is left to load?"

"Just what the last of your men are taking up now. You should be able to set sail by the top of the hour."

He nodded. "Good. I still have loads waiting for me in Wrangell and Petersburg."

"Hopefully those canneries had a bit of extra flour and lard put by," Oliver muttered.

"I hope so too. I also recommend keeping a bit extra on hand from now on."

Oliver nodded, then moved his eyes to the ship. "Who's the woman?"

"What woman?" He turned to find Miss McDougal standing on the upper deck, her body wedged into the corner of the railing on the port quarter—where the stern met the port side of the ship. Finnan and Ainsley stood on the deck too, pointing and shouting and bouncing around, with wide smiles plastered to their faces. But Miss McDougal didn't look nearly so happy.

Perhaps because the smell of fish hung too heavy in the air? Even he had to admit the scent near the canneries was rather cloying, and he was used to it. What must Miss McDougal think experiencing it for the first time?

At least she was out of her room. It was the first time since spilling the stew yesterday. Last evening, when he'd knocked on her door with dinner and offered to finally give her and her siblings that tour of the *Aurora*, she had repositioned the hat she'd been knitting on her lap and refused to leave.

Ainsley and Finnan had leaped at his offer, but Miss McDougal had said she had a commitment to make a certain number of hats for a charity back in Milwaukee and planned to spend most of her time in her room knitting until they reached Unalaska.

He'd pretended not to notice the watery state of her eyes, or the way she wouldn't look at him for more than a second. It didn't seem natural for her to still be crying five hours after she'd spilled something, and he didn't understand it.

But then he had three sisters, and he'd never been able to understand what brought on their bouts of tears either.

All he knew was he missed the curious woman with the inquisitive eyes he'd met two days ago.

"Well?" Oliver asked. "Who is she? One of your sisters? I thought they had dark hair."

"She's one of my sailors' sisters who came to meet the ship in Bellingham. But Tavish got transferred to another ship, so I'm taking her to meet him in Unalaska."

"She in the market for a husband?"

Sacha stiffened.

"What?" The skinny man shrugged. "It's not like I meet a lot of women running a cannery. At least not the kind of women I want to marry. And she looks pretty enough."

He should have expected it. For every ten men living in Alaska, there was one woman, maybe less. But for some reason the question rankled, almost the way it would if a man his sisters had never met tried to propose to one of them. "She's in the market to find her brother and go back to Wisconsin. That's all."

"Pity." Oliver pressed his lips together, his gaze still latched onto Miss McDougal. Never mind that the last of the cannery workers had come down the gangway and were wheeling their empty handcarts back to the warehouse.

"Time to set sail." He extended his hand and shook Oliver's, then took the cargo list so he could add it to the shipping manifest. "Thank you again. We'll see you in three weeks."

"Three weeks." Oliver tore his gaze away from Miss McDougal. "Yes. And you'd better be on time." Then the little man turned and left the wharf.

The crew was already busy raising the anchor and getting the ship underway. The moment Sacha stepped onto the deck, Eric, Nikolai, Gus, and Vasily started dismantling the gangway. They loosened the ropes that had been securing it, adjusted the winches, and hoisted the gangway back on board before stowing it in the well on deck with a practiced sort of precision.

A few minutes later, when he stood on the quarterdeck and gave the command to raise the sails, he couldn't help the sense of pride that filled him. Perhaps it was the swiftness and ease with which his crew performed their tasks, or perhaps it was the feeling of standing in the center of such a grand vessel, knowing that he could control and direct it with a few adjustments to the rigging and rudder.

But as the *Aurora* lurched away from her moorings on a gust of wind, there was no other feeling like it, not in all the world.

Mountains rose on either side of them as they left the harbor and headed north, into the narrow passageway of water known as Clarence Strait. He stood there for a moment, partly because they couldn't afford for the *Aurora* to go off course in such a narrow channel, but more because he needed a moment to take in the beauty of it all.

It didn't matter how many times he sailed this route or

stopped in Ketchikan, Southeast Alaska, with its mountain-filled islands and craggy inlets, was one of the prettiest places on earth.

The coast of northern Alaska was flatter. Sure, there were mountains in the distance, but in Southeast Alaska and the Kenai Peninsula, mountains shot straight up from the sea, and the water held so many inlets and islands and passageways that a man could get lost trying to explore them all.

"They're so big," a young voice—Finnan's—sounded from around the corner of the wheelhouse.

"I feel like they're surrounding us. Do you think they'll go on forever?" Ainsley said.

Sacha couldn't help but smile as he left the helm to Ronnie and stepped out of the wheelhouse, approaching where Miss McDougal still stood on the deck with her siblings. He couldn't blame her for not going back into her cabin.

"Miss McDougal." He tipped his chin toward her. "How are you feeling today?"

"Fine. Better. I . . . ah . . . thank you." She turned to him, a look of hesitation on her face, as though almost expecting to be reprimanded for some reason. "The children said it's all right for us to be on this part of the deck?"

"Yes, you can always use this part of the quarterdeck, unless it's stormy. Then I'll need you in your cabin. And if we're not entering or leaving a port, or in such a narrow channel as this, you can go down to the main deck or up to the bow. The view is quite beautiful from the bow. Especially on the open sea."

She wrapped her shawl tighter around her shoulders, as though the idea of venturing more than a few feet from her cabin door was somehow frightening.

"We'll be fine staying here, thank you. At least this allows Finnan and Ainsley to have a little fresh air and sunshine—if there ever is sunshine, that is." Her bluish-green eyes scanned the thick gray clouds above. "I expected the skies above the ocean to be sunny, but the sun rarely seems to show itself."

Sacha took a step closer, catching the faintest scent of citrus and vanilla. "It's not so rare on the open ocean, but when the moisture in the air from the water hits these mountains, it's trapped overhead. Places between two mountains, like where Ketchikan is located, with the mountains of the mainland on one side and the mountains of Gravina Island on the other, are particularly dense and misty."

Miss McDougal looked around them, seeming to absorb everything about the mountains they were passing. "It's so beautiful, I can't seem to look away from it, even with the mist."

Something inside his chest expanded at her words. Not everyone who came to this part of Alaska thought it was beautiful, even with the mountains. Many complained about the constant clouds and endless rain, about the lack of sunlight and stars. But Miss McDougal seemed to possess an innate love for the untamed land surrounding them.

"I agree," he whispered softly. "In fact, I'm quite enamored with the entirety of the Alexander Archipelago."

"The Alexander what?" She turned that seafoam gaze on his.

"Archipelago. It's what we call these islands. Or actually, it's what we call any chain of islands clustered closely together. It just so happens that this chain that covers the coast of Southeast Alaska is named for Tsar Alexander of Russia."

"The Alexander Archipelago," she said softly, as though testing how the words felt on her lips. "Will we see more of it before we reach Unalaska?"

"Yes, both tomorrow and the next day. We have ports of call in Petersburg, Wrangell, and Sitka. After we leave Sitka, we'll head across the Gulf of Alaska to Unalaska. That will mean sailing across open water."

"So we won't be able to see land?"

He shook his head. "Not until we reach the Aleutians. That's its own archipelago, but it looks and feels far different than this."

"How so?"

"There are mountains, but they're more rock than anything. It's not so rainy or misty, but it's windswept and bald."

"Is it pretty?"

Sacha stroked a hand over his close-cropped beard, trying to think of how to describe the differences between the two archipelagos. "It is, yes, but in a sparse, rugged way. You have cliffs that drop hundreds of feet straight into the sea, but no trees to cover them. I prefer the look and feel of the Alexander Archipelago to the Aleutians, but the Aleutians are sunnier."

Miss McDougal scanned their surroundings again, her eyes wide, and he could almost see her trying to imagine what the Aleutians looked like.

"Cap'n Amos?"

Sacha turned to find Eric had approached them. But at the sound of the sailor's voice, Miss McDougal gasped, then ducked her head and turned away, seeming to shrink into herself.

What was that about? And had her cheeks just turned red too?

Sacha frowned but forced his gaze onto Eric, his eyes narrowed. "Yes?"

"Do ya want me or Nikolai on lookout?"

"Who did Gus schedule?"

"Me, but Nikolai's up there. He says I can take the lookout shift after dinner."

"And where is Nikolai scheduled right now?" Sacha asked, even though he could guess the answer.

"The galley."

He sighed. What was it with young sailors wanting to avoid the galley? Men who'd worked on the sea for a decade or better never gave him any trouble. But the young ones? They always seemed to think another sailor should be the one to wash dishes and scrub floors.

"I'll take care of it." He started to leave, though Eric didn't follow him, acting as though he wanted to stay and speak with Miss McDougal. But Sacha had only taken two steps when Miss McDougal let out a small squeak, then reached out and grasped his wrist.

She hadn't uttered a single word during their exchange, but now she was looking down, as though the wooden planks beneath her feet were somehow fascinating. "Can you . . . ? That is, I think Ainsley and Finnan went down to the main deck. Or maybe they're on the starboard side of the quarterdeck? Can you send them back? Please."

He scanned the quarterdeck to find they were gone. Never mind he hadn't noticed them leaving. "Yes. Of course."

But Miss McDougal didn't look at him, or even offer a response. Instead she slid between him and the rail, then raced the few steps to her room, where she fumbled with her key in the lock.

Which didn't make any sense. Why would she lock her room if she was only a handful of steps away the entire time she'd been on deck?

He glanced at Eric, who was also watching Miss McDougal, but something about the look in the sailor's eyes caused Sacha's hand to flex at his side. Eric was one of the first men to visit the brothel when they arrived in port, and Sacha didn't think he'd ever heard the man say a decent, respectable thing about a woman. But he'd given the crew a strong warning about how Miss McDougal and her siblings were to be treated before leaving Bellingham. Had the sailor been ignoring it?

"Do you need help with your lock, Miss McDougal?" Sacha asked, his eyes still trained on Eric.

The second his words were out, the key turned, and she disappeared into her room without answering.

A second later, the lock clicked into place.

He crossed his arms over his chest as he stared at Eric. "What station were you working when we left port yesterday morning?"

Eric tore his gaze away from Miss McDougal's door, then blinked. "Ah, the galley, sir. It's like I said, Nikolai should be in the galley this afternoon. I ain't assigned again till after dinner."

"Right. Come along, then. Let's go solve this." He started toward the stairs, but something told him this business about who was lookout and who had scullery duty wasn't the real problem that needed to be solved.

There might be a bit more to the story of Miss McDougal spilling that stew yesterday morning than he'd been told.

9

Maggie stared at the yarn in her lap, forcing her fingers to move the knitting needles as she made yet another hat. She'd spent far too much time in her room knitting hats and gloves for the poor in Milwaukee. But every time she considered leaving her cabin, an image of Eric flashed into her mind. She could almost feel his chest pressing against her back, his breath hot on her ear as his hand crept up . . .

And then she remembered that there was a whole ship full of men just outside that door, and they might all be waiting for a chance to behave the way Eric had.

Not Captain Amos. He seemed both honorable and trustworthy. But the rest of the men? She didn't know them, and they didn't know her, and staying within the four walls of her cabin seemed far safer than stepping out onto the deck, even if they were surrounded by some of the most beautiful vistas she'd ever seen.

She thought Wisconsin was pretty, with its sandy beaches and rippling grass and towering trees that turned the most brilliant shades of red and orange and yellow every fall. But that was nothing compared to mountains that rose straight from the sea, the dark green forest that extended as far as the eye could see, and the narrow channels and small islands that the *Aurora* threaded its way around.

Maggie stared at her hands, her needles still now.

Oh, why had God allowed this to happen to her? First the *Aurora* had been late, then Tavish hadn't been in Bellingham. Now she was traveling even farther from Wisconsin to find her brother—as though Washington somehow wasn't far enough.

And she had a ship full of men waiting for a chance to get her alone.

"God, why?" she spoke into the silence. "I'm just trying to keep my family together. I just want Tavish to come home and inherit our land and the shipyard my father worked so hard to build. I just want a nice place for Finnan and Ainsley to grow up—and not with Uncle Ewan."

The man was harsh. He always had been, and he wasn't accepting of Finnan and Ainsley either, considering they were from her mother's second marriage and not blood relations.

"Am I really asking for so much, God?"

She stared up at the ceiling, waiting, but no answer came, nor did any sense of peace. It was almost as though God had forgotten her out on the sea, in this wild land filled with more mountains than people.

Knock. Knock. Knock.

Maggie looked at the door. "Who is it?"

"Captain Amos." Even through the wood separating them, his voice sounded strong and confident.

He must have brought Ainsley and Finnan back. Hopefully they hadn't caused any trouble. She set her knitting on the desk and headed to the door, unlocking it only to find the captain standing there by himself.

She frowned. "Where are Finnan and Ainsley?"

"They're on the starboard side of the quarterdeck helping Dr. Torres count whales."

Her brows rose. "Count whales? Who did you say they were with?"

"Dr. Torres. He's the scientist doing the study on sea otters, but he's taken an interest in whales as well."

"I didn't know there was a scientist aboard."

Captain Amos rubbed the side of his jaw. "I know I haven't introduced you yet, but did I forget to tell you about him completely?"

He must have. "I'm sorry. This is the first I've heard of any study." Of course, keeping to her room most of the morning and for a good part of yesterday hadn't exactly meant she'd been available for an introduction.

"He's a biologist from the Smithsonian Institution in Washington, DC, and he's doing a study on sea otters and their habitat—and now whales, apparently."

"Are you sure Finnan and Ainsley aren't in his way?" She tried to peek around the captain's shoulders, but his chest was so broad and his shoulders so wide, they took up the entire doorway.

"Dr. Torres is a pretty straightforward sort. If he didn't want the children there, he'd say so. Besides, it was his idea to have your siblings count whales. He's sitting there with his notebook recording the findings."

"Oh." She blinked, not quite sure what to do with that information, other than ask Captain Amos to make an introduction. This Dr. Torres fellow sounded a bit interesting. "Is he staying in your cabin, then? The one with the wall that adjoins this room?"

"He is. Why?" A crease appeared between the captain's eyebrows. "Is he disturbing you?"

She shook her head. "The opposite, I'm afraid. It's been so

quiet, I wondered if you spent any time in there." She'd also wondered if Finnan and Ainsley had been too loud for him, but it looked like that was a question she'd need to ask the scientist. "Can you take me to meet him? Do you have time?"

"I can, so long as you answer a question for me." Captain Amos leaned against the doorway in what was probably supposed to be a casual stance. But something about him looked tense. "Why did you drop the stew yesterday? I want the whole story."

Sacha watched as Miss McDougal shrank in on herself yet again. One simple question, that's all it was.

Yet she sucked in a breath of air and took a step back from him, her arms wrapping around her chest in a forlorn hug.

"Miss McDougal..."

"It's not important," she rasped.

He straightened, tempted to step inside the room and move closer to her, so close that he could see the exact shade of her irises, hear each intake and exhale of breath.

But he had three sisters, and he couldn't remember a single time he or one of his brothers had been able to force information out of them. Coaxing worked far better.

So he kept himself rooted in the doorway, where anyone could see him and no one would be able to question his propriety. Then he gentled his voice, trying to make himself sound patient and understanding, which wasn't exactly easy given his suspicions. "If one of my sailors treated you inappropriately, I need to know."

She said nothing, but that faraway, injured look from yesterday crept back onto her face.

Sacha shoved a hand through his hair. "Look, I'm going to

speak plainly with you. Having a woman aboard ship can be a bit of a distraction for my crew, but I have sisters about your age, and they've been aboard the *Aurora* plenty of times. We always get by just fine."

"You have sisters?" she asked softly.

"Three, two of whom are old enough to be married, and one who's fourteen. You're no different from them. You don't need to apologize for being a woman or needing passage to Unalaska. But if one of my sailors mistreats you while you're on board, I need to know so I can deal with it."

Her eyes met his, guarded and wary. "I . . . ah . . . Thank you for your . . . your concern."

That was it? She wasn't going to tell him what had transpired yesterday? "Please, Miss McDougal, I know something happened with Eric in the galley, and I need you to tell me what."

Her mouth fell open. "How . . . how did you know?"

"You should be able to walk freely around this ship, should feel comfortable leaving this cabin. Right now you don't."

She dropped her gaze to the floor, the way a deer might if it felt threatened.

"I want to fix it for you." He gentled his voice even further. "But I can't if you don't tell me what happened."

"He . . . he touched me. Without my permission. Somewhere he shouldn't."

A growl threatened to rip from his throat, but he somehow managed to tamp it down. "What did the stew have to do with things? Did you drop it because of Eric?"

And then Eric had told everyone else it was her fault? He was going to kill the man.

Miss McDougal was nodding, her head still bent. "He'd been in the kitchen for most of the morning, standing far too close, calling me things like sweetheart and luv, even though I asked him to call me Miss McDougal. I don't know if he was waiting for a chance to . . . to . . ."

Even though her head was down, he could see her cheeks and throat turn a flaming shade of red.

"When Scully told me to put the stew on the table, Eric was suddenly behind me the moment I picked it up. He pressed his chest against my back and wrapped his arms around me, and then his hand came up, and he . . . he . . ."

She crossed her arms over her chest protectively and turned away, showing him her back. "Please don't make me say it. Were you Tavish, it would be one thing, but you're not."

No. He certainly wasn't. But he had a sudden urge to toss Eric overboard and watch him swim to a nearby island.

"Thank you for letting me know. It turns out Eric will be helping in the galley and scrubbing the floors belowdecks for the duration of our voyage. Should you choose to walk around on deck at some point—any point—you won't run into him. The man's not going to see a lick of sunlight until we return to Bellingham. If he so much as tries, I'll drop him off on the nearest island. I don't care whether it's inhabited or not."

Miss McDougal turned back to face him, her eyes wide and luminous. "Are you certain?"

"Absolutely." That wouldn't be the extent of Eric's punishment either, though Miss McDougal didn't need further details. "I do not tolerate poor treatment of women aboard my ship. Not ever. And neither do any of the other captains who work for Sitka Trading Company."

"Thank you," she whispered, "for being so kind."

He wasn't nearly kind enough, not if one of his men had been inappropriate with Miss McDougal yesterday morning, and he was just now finding out about it.

He blew out a breath, trying to push some of his frustration out with the gust of air, then looked back at Miss McDougal. "Repeat after me. Captain Amos, I need help."

She took a step back. "What?"

"Back in Bellingham, when I found you trying to sleep in a doorway and brought you to the *Aurora*, what did I tell you to do the next time you needed help?"

She dropped her gaze again, staring intently at something on the floor, though for the life of him, he didn't know what was so interesting about wooden boards.

"Well? What did I tell you that night?"

"To ask for help the next time I needed it," she whispered.

"And did you need help in the galley with Eric?"

"Yes."

"And did you ask?"

She dug the heel of her shoe into the floor, a determined tilt to her chin as she met his gaze. "It's mortifying, all right? That's not the kind of thing a woman tells a man she barely knows. It's not even the kind of thing most women would tell their husbands."

He leaned forward, part of him tempted to stalk into the room, take her by the shoulders, and force her to meet his gaze—just so she'd know he was serious. "Good thing I'm not your husband, then, because I absolutely expect you to tell me if anything like this happens again."

She threw up her hands. "You're all but a stranger. I've known you for two days. That's it. Two!"

"I might be a stranger, but I'm also your protector, and the sooner you acknowledge that, the easier this voyage will be."

Her mouth fell open. "I don't . . . That is, I wouldn't . . ."

"Don't try telling me you don't need a protector. Seems to me that's the one thing you need more than anything else, out here all alone, with no one to help and no family to support you."

She clamped her jaw shut, and he could see the struggle inside her, the inner war flashing across her eyes, playing across the planes and curves of her face. He'd take that any day over the dull, flat look she'd worn since yesterday. "Very well. Next time I need help, I'll ask. Now if you'll kindly leave me be. I feel a headache coming on."

Then she turned and stomped back to her knitting.

And even though Sacha punished Eric, had another talk with the crew, and had gotten Miss McDougal to agree to come to him for help in the future, the fact she confined herself to that dratted cabin somehow made him feel like he'd lost more than he'd accomplished.

10

"Lower the sails. There's a ship in the channel."

Maggie heard the words from inside her cabin. Lunch had come and gone, and Captain Amos had brought her a tray. She'd told him she wasn't hungry, but he'd insisted on leaving all of it with her.

The whole exchange had happened without her looking him in the eye, because how could she look at him after what they'd discussed?

But he must have forgotten to return for the tray, because it was still sitting on the floor of her room, and lunch had been several hours ago.

Maggie heard more shouting from the wheelhouse, the captain asking in a deep, rumbly voice what had happened, then more words from the lookout, explaining that a ship was blocking the channel, and they needed to lower their sails if they didn't want to hit it.

A few moments later, she felt the *Aurora* slowing. It was enough to propel her off the bed and cause her to open the door of the cabin and peek her head out. Sure enough, there was a ship in the narrow channel ahead of them, and with islands on both sides, one large and the other small, there didn't seem to be room to go around it.

"Let down the anchor and lower the dinghy." Captain Amos's powerful voice carried through the ship. "I want to find out what happened."

The crew instantly got to work, each person on deck moving to do his bidding, and a few minutes later, the captain and one of his men were rowing a small boat toward the ship ahead of them in the channel.

Maggie was tempted to duck back into her room and shut the door. But the sun was almost shining, the clouds above soft white whisps rather than a dense gray that shrouded the land in gloom. And mountains rose from the water on every side, including on the small island to their left.

She hadn't seen Finnan or Ainsley in several hours. Were they still helping the scientist count whales? Perhaps it was time to find out.

She pulled the door to her cabin shut behind her, then locked it and took a few steps toward the wheelhouse, moving her gaze slowly over the deck. True to Captain Amos's word, Eric was nowhere to be found. But a childish shout rang out from the starboard side of the quarterdeck, followed by a fit of giggles.

She crossed in front of the wheelhouse, making her steps quick lest whoever was at the helm tried to talk to her. When she rounded the opposite side, she found both Finnan and Ainsley near the railing, and a man with dark hair seated on a chair beside them, writing furiously in a notebook.

"Sissy," Finnan cried, running to her with his arms spread wide. "There you are!"

"Here I am," she answered, wrapping her arms around her brother.

Chapter 10   111

"Did Cap'n Amos bring you food?"

"He brought us food to eat with Dr. Torres and said you needed to rest." Ainsley's brows furrowed in confusion. "Said we needed to leave you alone."

"Why were you resting before lunch, Sissy?" Finnan planted a hand on her cheek.

She offered the boy a faint smile. Had Captain Amos truly said that? Had he ensured she had some time to herself?

The man claimed he wasn't kind, but from what she could see, he was the very embodiment of kindness. From giving them biscuits the first time they'd met, to offering them free passage to Unalaska, to letting them board the ship and sleep in the first mate's cabin a night early, to ensuring her siblings were fed while she'd been preoccupied, he was the definition of kindness.

"You must be Miss McDougal." The scientist who'd been sitting in a chair making notations in some type of journal rose and came toward her. "Forgive me for not introducing myself sooner. I'm Xavier Torres, doctor of marine biology."

"Yes, I'm Margaret McDougal." She reached out to take his hand. It was strong and warm against her own, but no sense of comfort swept through her when she touched him—unlike when she touched Captain Amos. "Are my siblings really helping you count whales?"

"Yes, yes." The man turned and waved her toward the children. "Come see. They're quite good at spotting them."

"Look, there's another one." Ainsley had moved back to the railing and pointed toward the open water behind the ship.

"Keep watching." Dr. Torres instructed as he headed back to his chair.

He moved in such a way that told her muscles lay beneath his clothes, but he wasn't as tall or wide as the captain. In fact, looking at the man in front of her, he couldn't be more different from Captain Amos.

And what was she doing comparing a stranger she'd just met to the captain? Why should she care who was taller or had a broader chest? It wasn't as though Captain Amos was the standard among men, and every other man she met needed to be held up beside him and measured.

Dr. Torres sat back down and started scrawling. "Let me know how many you see."

"I see one too," Finnan cried, his small voice filled with excitement.

"A different one or the same?" the scientist asked.

"I think it's the same . . . Oh no, wait. There are two of them. Look." Ainsley pointed again, her face filled with a smile.

Maggie turned and craned her neck, looking toward the open water where her siblings were staring. They weren't terribly close to the whales, but sure enough she saw two smooth gray humps sticking out of the water.

"Oh, dear," she gasped. "It just sprayed water."

She turned back to the scientist, her smile almost as large as Finnan's. "Did you see that? It just sprayed water."

"They always spray water." Ainsley rolled her eyes. "That's why they come to the top, to breathe."

Maggie's brows furrowed. "How do you know that?"

"Dr. Torres told us. They dive down to get food, holding their breath the whole time—and they can hold their breath for a really long time—and then they come up again to breathe."

"We think." The scientist looked up from his notes to study the whales floating on the top of the water. "We think they're feeding. It's what makes the most sense. We know from autopsies that they consume a diet of plankton, krill, and small fish, but they are mammals, meaning they breathe air."

One of the whales disappeared beneath the surface.

"There she goes." Dr. Torres looked at her. "Miss McDougal, do you mind counting?"

"Counting what?"

Ainsley rolled her eyes. "Haven't you been listening? We're trying to see how long they can stay underwater."

"Oh. I thought you were just counting the number of whales you saw."

"That is helpful," the scientist said. "But not quite as helpful as knowing how long they stay underwater."

"Very well. I can count." And that's exactly what she did. She pressed her lips together and started counting. And counting. And counting.

At one point, she turned to the scientist. "It's been ten minutes, perhaps the whale swam somewhere else?"

"They can stay underwater for as long as thirty minutes, we believe."

"And you expect me to stand here and count each second for thirty minutes?" She raised an eyebrow. When she'd agreed to count, she hadn't expected it would be for so long. "Have you no pocket watch?"

He blinked at her. "It's more precise to count by the second —if you don't get distracted and stop counting, that is. In this case, we shall have to estimate. I'll make a note in my book that the count isn't precise." He looked back down and scrawled something with his pencil.

"There she is! There she is!" Finnan turned to her. "How long was she underwater, Sissy?"

"Ah... maybe twelve or thirteen minutes?"

Dr. Torres unclipped a pocket watch from his vest and handed it to her. "Here, use this next time, Miss McDougal. Perhaps it will aid you after all."

"Oh... I..." She ran her thumb over the smooth surface of the watch. Maybe she should offer to record the findings while he counted. She was quite good at taking notes and organizing files. Keeping the books and ensuring the office stayed organized had been her job at the shipyard.

But if he expected her to stand here and count how long the whales stayed beneath the surface, she was sure to fall asleep with all the waiting, even if she had a pocket watch to help. "I should really get back to my cabin and knit another hat for—"

"I'll pay you."

She looked up. "Pay me? To keep time?"

Maybe she could manage to stay awake after all.

"Keep time, take notes, organize my records." The man waved his hand in the air. "I need someone to help with all three. My understanding is that you'll be on the *Aurora* until we reach Unalaska?"

"Yes, but . . ." She glanced at the door to the man's cabin. Would this new job involve being alone with Dr. Torres? Inside his cabin? "Are you sure it's proper?"

The man blinked at her. "Why wouldn't it be proper? My assistant normally accompanies me on research trips, but he wasn't able to come. And I can't both record the activity of the whales and count how long they're underwater—at least not with enough accuracy to feel comfortable submitting the report. So I'm happy to pay for your assistance, assuming you have the time to help?"

"Yes," she blurted. She'd do whatever the scientist needed if it meant she'd arrive in Unalaska with more than two dollars and thirty-six cents in her coin purse.

Maybe God really had heard her prayers earlier. Maybe this was his way of finally allowing something to go right for her.

"What's going on here?"

At the sound of the voice behind her, she turned to find

Captain Amos striding toward them. Apparently she'd been counting whales long enough for him to return to the *Aurora*.

"Why is there a ship in our path?" she asked.

"Is everything all right?" he asked at the same time, briefly scanning Ainsley, Finnan, and Dr. Torres before bringing his gaze back to her.

"Yes, fine, actually. I'm going to assist Dr. Torres with his notes."

"He's going to pay Sissy," Finnan blurted. "Then we'll have more than two dollars!"

Maggie's face turned hot.

"Finnan!" Ainsley elbowed her brother. "You said you'd keep it secret."

"But now Sissy will have more money." The boy grinned, and Ainsley sunk her head into her hands.

"I . . . um . . ." Maggie shifted from one foot to the other, then glanced at Dr. Torres—who didn't seem to be paying the least bit of attention to how awkward she felt, or care that she had no money. He was still looking at the water.

"The whale just went under again. Please time it, Miss McDougal."

She glanced at the second hand on the watch, committing the time to memory, then slanted her body so she could both see the spot where the whales kept resurfacing and also see Captain Amos. "Why is there a ship in the channel ahead of us?"

The captain pressed his lips together, a look of consternation on his face. "It ran aground. We might be able to tow it out at high tide tomorrow, but I'm going to leave part of the crew here overnight to help repair what they can of the hull. Hopefully that will be enough that we can limp it back to Sitka, where the shipyard my family owns will be able to fully repair it. But first we have to get it seaworthy."

"I see." She moved her gaze back to the ship in the waterway in front of them. "Is it normal for ships to run aground?"

"No. Not unless it's too foggy to see."

"Is that why you're upset?"

"I'm upset because this is the third ship I've come across in the past month that's run aground or hit a rock. I don't know why helmsmen can't seem to keep their ships in the shipping channels all of a sudden. Ships have been moving around these islands for nearly two hundred years. All the channels are clearly marked. The sea level hasn't changed. None of this should be an issue."

Ah, now his frustration made sense.

"Now if you'll excuse me. I need to figure out which crew members I can spare and which need to accompany us to Wrangell." As he moved to turn, she reached out and laid a hand on his arm.

"But how will we get around the ship? It's blocking our path." Even she could see there wasn't room in the narrow strait for the *Aurora* to sail around it.

"We'll have to row ourselves backward out of the channel until we can turn the ship. And we'll change the order of our ports, which means we'll go to Wrangell tonight instead of Petersburg. We'll return at high tide tomorrow and hopefully get the *Thunderhead* unstuck. If we can't manage to do that, we'll have to go clear around Mitkof Island before we can get to Petersburg, which will take even more time."

She scanned the *Aurora*, trying to imagine moving it backward instead of forward. It wasn't something she'd ever seen done before, not even at the shipyard in Milwaukee. "Can you move a ship this big backward with oars? Especially if you only have half your crew?"

She could almost see the tenseness come over him, from the

way his jaw hardened, to the way he drew himself up to his full height, to the way his shoulders suddenly turned into two rock-like boulders.

"I've managed worse." Then he turned and stalked off, just as Finnan and Ainsley pointed toward the water.

"The whale's back, Sissy! How long was he under for?"

"Oh, I . . . um . . ." She looked down at the pocket watch. What time had the whale gone under?

"Perhaps," Dr. Torres muttered, "I'll hire you on a trial basis, and we'll assess your progress after a day or two."

11

Sacha stared out over the strait, the water smooth as glass until it met the mountain rising from the island on the opposite side of the passage. The caw of a raven filled the air, followed by another answering in response. But there were no human voices to add to the noise, no passersby on Wrangell's handful of dirt roads, no crew awake on the *Aurora* to provide any distraction.

Which made sense, seeing how it was nearly midnight. If he were smart, he'd be abed too, especially after having two ports of call today, the last of which they'd handled with only five crew members. And that was after they'd had to row the *Aurora* backward out of Dry Strait for nearly half a mile.

But instead, he sat in the wheelhouse, on the single wooden chair they kept in the corner, watching as the sun slid behind the mountains to the west, covering the world in a hazy hue of pink and orange.

The view would normally be enough to unclench his jaw and loosen the tightness in his chest.

But not tonight.

He wasn't even sure why he was out here, other than he was trying to let Scully sleep rather than keep the cook awake with his tossing and turning.

He just needed to focus on tomorrow, on how he planned to tie ropes that ran from the *Thunderhead* to the *Aurora*. Hopefully, with the high tide, they'd be able to get the smaller cutter to float. But first that meant staying in Wrangell overnight and leaving at dawn to get the *Aurora* into position for high tide.

And since they were docked rather than on the water, it also meant giving his remaining crew a chance to sleep the whole night through.

A door opened somewhere on the ship, then closed again.

He looked around. Who would be up at this time of night?

Soft footsteps sounded on the deck, too light to belong to a man, and too slow to belong to a child.

A moment later, Miss McDougal passed the wheelhouse. She took the stairs down to the main deck, not noticing him sitting in the shadows as she moved to the railing on the starboard side of the ship.

What was she doing? Her hair was down, tumbling around her shoulders and back in rich golden waves.

He watched her for a moment, standing completely alone on the large deck as she looked out across the water toward the mountains on the other side of the strait. And though he wanted to go to her, there was something about how she stood there, so at peace with her surroundings, that made him stay seated in his chair.

After watching her a few more moments, he pushed himself to a standing position and headed down the stairs. "Miss McDougal? Is something wrong?"

She jolted at the sound of his voice, so lost in wherever her mind had been that she must not have heard his footsteps. "No, everything's quite fine. Thank you."

"What are you doing?"

"Didn't you say I was free to roam this part of the ship? Or would you prefer me to stay on the deck by my cabin?"

The quarterdeck was far too small of a place to confine a woman and two young children for an entire week at sea. "You can be here, yes, but it's midnight. Are you unable to sleep?"

"I wanted to see the midnight sun." She glanced at him for a moment, then turned back toward the strait. "For the past two days I've watched it from the window, and it just doesn't seem real. That the sun would set so late, that it would be light hours past the time most people go to bed. But somehow..."

Her chest lifted, dragging in a breath of air tinged with salt from the sea and fish. Then she tilted her face up toward the dying rays of the sun, as though she could somehow feel it touch her face. "Somehow this seems more spectacular than a normal sunset, doesn't it? I can't quite say why. Is it the mountains that the sun is about to sink behind? Or the fact that it's so late? Or maybe both? Either way, the beauty steals my breath."

Sacha swallowed, half tempted to reach a hand up and rest it on her shoulder, like he would with his sisters. She was from a state thousands of miles away, known for its fields and cows more than its water. But somehow she understood the true beauty of a midnight sunset the way few others did, not even his brothers and sisters.

Alexei, Mikhail, and Yuri all thought he was crazy when he told them a midnight sunset was the prettiest thing they'd ever see in their lives.

Evelina shrugged and said it was pretty, but there were many pretty things about Southeast Alaska.

Kate was too busy to stop and notice the sunset.

But Maggie McDougal understood the beauty in front of her.

"You should stay up when we cross the Gulf of Alaska after stopping in Sitka." He swallowed again. "It's even prettier then, with nothing but water and dying sunlight surrounding you, as far as the eye can see."

She turned to face him, causing her shoulder to brush his arm.

When had she moved so close? Or had he somehow shifted nearer to her without realizing it?

"Let's do it," she whispered, her voice soft against the descending night. "Let's watch the sunset together then."

The edges of his lips curled up into a smile.

"Did you just smile, Captain Amos? You better be careful. Wouldn't want your crew to know you're capable of something like that."

He chuckled, then scrubbed a hand over his face. "Am I really so dour that you're surprised by such a simple thing?"

"I . . . um . . ." She looked down, a faint blush tingeing her cheeks.

"Good heavens, don't tell me I'm turning into my brother."

"Your brother?"

"Alexei. He's the oldest of the eight of us, and he never smiles. I'm usually not accused of being quite as severe as him, though." But between having both Dr. Torres and Miss McDougal on his ship, he'd probably been a little more serious than usual over the past few days.

"Eight of you?" she sputtered. "You have eight siblings?"

"Seven siblings, but eight children altogether in the family. You didn't know?"

She shook her head.

"I assumed Tavish would have written you about my family, like he wrote you about me."

"He only wrote at Christmas, and even then, I think he only mentioned you because he was on your ship. I remember him writing after he got promoted to first mate. He seemed quite excited."

Sacha smiled at the memory. "He was."

"What's it like, having so many siblings?"

"Besides being forced to endure life with a brother who never smiles?" He rubbed the back of his neck. "I also have to endure my third brother, Yuri, who smiles enough for all of us. Seems he's determined to single-handedly make up for Alexei's lack of smiling."

"A brother who always smiles?" Miss McDougal's own face lit up with a smile that made her lovely eyes come alive. "That doesn't sound like something to be endured."

"Except for when we need Yuri to be serious, and he can't stop smiling. Then it can be a little frustrating, but you'll have to form your own thoughts after we reach Sitka."

"I can meet your brothers?"

He chuckled again. "Absolutely. Yuri will be delighted to meet you. Alexei, on the other hand, will probably mumble some type of greeting and then ignore you while he inventories the cargo."

Miss McDougal shook her head, her eyes dancing at the thought of meeting his two very different brothers. "How many brothers do you have in all? You said Yuri was the third, and there are eight of you total, so that means . . . ?"

"I have four living brothers, and one who passed. But only Alexei and Yuri will be in Sitka when we stop. My second brother, Mikhail, is leading an expedition in the interior, and my twin sisters, Kate and Evelina, live in Juneau with my youngest brother and sister."

"That sounds very busy. And here I am lamenting that just

one of my siblings moved away. Your family is so large, I bet you rarely see each other all at once."

Was that true? He stared out over the water, thinking back to the last time they were all together. "Captaining a ship doesn't lend itself to being home on birthdays or going to church with the family on Sundays. We're usually together for Christmas and Thanksgiving and Easter, but that's about it."

"Well, I look forward to meeting Yuri, even if I'm not so sure how meeting Alexei will go. But until we arrive in Sitka . . ." She looked down, her hands picking at a fleck of paint on the ship's railing. "I'm sure it's difficult having a woman and children aboard ship, and I certainly hope we aren't responsible for driving your smile away. If there's anything we can do to make this voyage easier on you, Captain, please let me know."

"You can call me Sacha."

She sucked in a breath, her head snapping back until their gazes met. "I beg your pardon?"

He was about to beg pardon of himself too. Had he really just invited Miss McDougal to use his first name? On a ship where everyone called him Captain, even the acclaimed scientist?

"I was just . . . I was thinking I might smile more if you called me Sacha." Now what was wrong with him? Was his tongue no longer controlled by his brain? Had it sprouted a mind of its own and decided to mutiny?

He didn't need to become overly familiar with Miss McDougal, not when she'd be leaving his ship in a few more days.

Except, would she really leave his ship? Or would he end up taking her and Tavish back down to Bellingham after Dr. Torres completed his study? Alexei would need to look at the shipping schedule and see what arrangements could be made among the five ships their family owned. What if he didn't end up bidding farewell to Miss McDougal once they reached Unalaska?

But even if she did stay aboard the *Aurora*, even if Alexei couldn't work out a way for the *Halcyon* to take her down to Bellingham and he took her to the Pribilof Islands and then back to Washington Territory, she would no longer be his responsibility. She would be Tavish's.

"Sacha," she said, as though needing to test the name on her tongue. "Are you sure you want me to call you that?"

He looked down at her, at her fine features and eyes the color of the sea, at the tumble of golden hair cascading down her back. Did she realize how distracting her hair was? How he could think of nothing besides lifting his hand and drawing it through those waving, tumbling tresses? "It's my men who call me Captain Amos. And you are definitely not one of my men."

He couldn't remember the last time he'd made such an offer, not aboard his ship, where his authority and ability to lead as captain could mean the difference between life and death.

Yet he couldn't seem to stop himself from extending the offer to Maggie. Almost as though the moment he'd seen her hair down, his brain lost all ability to think rationally.

"I suppose you should call me Maggie, then." Her lips spread into a smile, and her eyes turned warm and soft. "It's only fair."

"Maggie." He'd heard Ainsley call her that once or twice. The name seemed to suit her. Not too proper or formal, but something that felt comfortable to say, as though they'd long been friends.

"So, Sacha, tell me about your family. You can start with the brother who doesn't like to smile."

"You want to know about Alexei?" Sacha let out belly laugh, full and free, one his father would be proud of, if he were still alive. "I'm not sure why. He's the oldest, and he's as severe a man as you've ever met. All business and seriousness."

"I know running a business can be difficult. I remember times when my father and stepfather rarely smiled, but that was only for a season. Their smiles always came back."

"There was a time when Alexei knew how to smile, back when my parents and my brother Ivan were alive."

"Your parents are dead?" she asked, a slight rasp to her voice. "I had no idea. I'm so sorry."

Fresh pain lined her face, and she wrapped her arms around herself.

"Hey." He rested a hand on her shoulder. It felt small and dainty beneath his wide palm. "It was a long time ago. A decade now. I can't say we don't miss them, or wonder what life would be like were they still alive, but we've adapted."

"Adapted," she repeated, staring at some vacant spot across the water. "I haven't adapted yet."

He took a few steps closer, pressing his side against hers as they stood on the railing, then he moved his hand from her shoulder and settled it over top of hers on the railing.

Just like he would if he were trying to comfort Kate or Evelina. Not because he had any romantic inclinations toward a woman who'd be heading back to Wisconsin soon.

Yet he couldn't exactly ignore the way the heat from her side radiated into his, or the way her skirts brushed against his trousers.

He cleared his throat. Heaven help him, he needed some sort of a distraction from this woman. "Ah . . . How did your parents die?"

"Oh, I don't suppose I've told you, have I?" She sniffled, then pulled a handkerchief from her pocket and used it to dab at her cheeks. "It was a train accident four months ago. My stepfather was headed to Chicago on a business trip, and my mother accompanied him. No one expected . . ." She sniffled again.

He tightened his hand over hers. "It's all right. I'm sure everything's a bit raw yet."

"Raw. That's a good way to put it. You would have thought, with all the time my stepfather spent aboard ship, that a storm would have done it, lost the ship and all the crew. But no. It was a quick business trip to Chicago to check on a possible order of twenty lifeboats. My mother decided to accompany him, and then the train derailed."

A train derailment? Sacha tried to think back to any newspaper articles he might have seen about a train derailment in Wisconsin. Surely an accident such as that would have been in the news. Her parents couldn't have been the only ones to die.

He had a vague recollection of spotting a headline or two that spring when he'd been in port, but he'd never taken the time to read the full article or been overly concerned about something that had happened so far away.

"I'm so sorry," he whispered into the growing darkness. "That must have been devastating."

Her face turned somber, almost as though she were looking at a storm approaching rather than a majestic world painted in golden-pink light and rich blue shadows. "And how did your parents die?"

"A sudden storm at sea."

She gasped, then turned to face him, which meant he had to take a step back if he didn't want to find himself standing in an embrace.

The trouble was, with her red-rimmed eyes and slumped shoulders and sad lips, she looked like she needed a hug.

But she wasn't his sister. She was going back to Wisconsin, and the last thing she needed was rumors springing up about her and the captain of the *Aurora*. Those types of rumors—true or not—had a way of ruining a woman's life and leaving the man unscathed.

"A storm? That's how my father died all those years ago." Her eyes filled with fresh tears. "It was so fast. One day he was hugging us and laughing and snitching the last piece of pie after Ma had put it away. And the next, he was gone. I can't imagine how hard it would be to lose both your parents at once. I'm so very sorry."

"It wasn't both my parents. It was my father and my stepmother. My actual mother succumbed to a fever seven years prior. And there's no need for you to apologize. Like I said, they died a decade ago now, and we've moved on."

"Do you think one day . . ." She pressed a hand to her chest. "One day I might move on too? That a decade from now, I'll be able to think of my mother without . . . ?" Tears misted her eyes.

"Do you still cry when you think of your father?" he asked.

She shook her head. "No. Though I wish he were still alive. He was much better at running the shipyard than Hamish. Hamish only cared about being a captain. But my father and I weren't close the way my mother and I were. I wonder if I'll ever stop missing her."

Again, he was tempted to reach out and wrap her in his arms, to fold her in a hug until the lines of pain left her face and the hurt left her eyes. "I feel the same way about my brother Ivan. There are times when I still miss him keenly, even after a decade."

"Was he aboard the same ship as your parents?"

Sacha's throat closed. "No. He died on land. On the same night. During the same storm, but he wasn't on the ship."

"Oh . . . I . . ."

She stood there for a moment, just staring at him, her eyes asking for more details, even though the words never left her mouth.

But he couldn't. What had happened to his parents was one thing, an accident in a storm. It was a risk every person took the moment they stepped onto a ship or boat.

What had happened to Ivan was another matter entirely.

Only made worse by the fact that justice had never been served.

Oh, there'd been a court case all right, where Ivan's killer had been put on trial. But in spite of America's noble ideas about justice, it seemed people in positions of power—or whose families were in positions of power—were still above the law.

"I'm sorry," she whispered, her hand moving back to his on the railing. "For a long time I struggled after my father died. I was young, and it hurt so much not to have him. But now when I look back on it, I have to think that if he were still alive and Ma hadn't remarried, Ainsley and Finnan would never have been born. And I can't imagine what my life would look like without them in it. So I keep telling myself that maybe, as much as this hurts, there's something good ahead, and I just can't see it yet."

"'And we know that all things work together for good to them that love God, to them that are the called according to his purpose.'" Father Andrew, the priest at St. Michael's Russian Orthodox Church in Sitka, had given Sacha that verse after his father, stepmother, and brother had died. He'd wanted nothing to do with it then, couldn't bring himself to see any good that might come of losing three family members on the same night.

"I forgot about that verse." Maggie looked up at him. "But I think you're right. I mean, God's not cruel to his children, to those who love him. And I go to church every Sunday and donate to the poorhouse. Surely God will bring good out of everything that's happening, won't he?"

He opened his mouth, then closed it, then opened it again. "I don't know what God has in store for you, but I know you're right about stepparents and half siblings. Because if my mother hadn't died of a fever, Pa wouldn't have remarried, and I can't quite imagine how my family would look without Inessa or Ilya."

"Wait. You have half siblings too?" she asked. "You didn't say so earlier."

"Yes. Though they're older than Ainsley and Finnan, and like I said earlier, they live with my twin sisters in Juneau, so you won't get to see them in Sitka."

"That's too bad. I'd love to meet them sometime."

"I'd love for you to meet them too." He didn't see them nearly often enough, considering he was at sea far more than he was home.

Was the air suddenly heavy, or were his memories causing him to feel as though a lead weight had been strapped to his lungs?

"How did it go working for Torres this afternoon?" he asked, more because he wanted to change the subject than because he wanted details about Maggie's afternoon.

Perhaps midnight wasn't the right time to be talking about family. All he could seem to think of was hurt from years gone by.

MAGGIE STARED UP AT SACHA, his broad shoulders taking up so much room that he completely blocked any other view she had of the ship. She didn't know what had possessed him to come down to the deck and talk to her at an hour when any sane person would be abed, but she wasn't going to complain.

In fact, she couldn't quite imagine watching the sun sink behind the mountains without him.

He'd asked her about working for Dr. Torres, but she didn't

want to talk about the scientist. She wanted to ask more questions about his family. Yet there was something about the way his shoulders had hunched in on themselves when he'd mentioned that his youngest siblings were older than Finnan. Something about the haunted look in his eyes when he'd confessed his family saw each other only a few times a year, that caused her to hold her tongue and answer his question about Dr. Torres instead.

"To be honest, working for him is a bit boring. He wanted me to stand there and stare at his pocket watch for fifteen minutes or better. Any time I tried talking to Ainsley or Finnan or asking him a question, he told me to pay attention to the watch." She gave her head a small shake. She might not know how to take a pile of lumber and turn it into a ship, but after that afternoon, she was eternally grateful she'd been born into a family of shipbuilders rather than scientists.

"Tomorrow he wants me to file papers." At least that was something she was good at. She'd been doing it at the shipyard office since she was fifteen. "But Dr. Torres still seemed to appreciate the help, even if he's particular about it. And as Finnan announced earlier, I'm rather in need of the money he's offering."

"You won't be as soon as we find Tavish."

She looked up at Sacha. Light from the ship's lamps threaded through the strands of his golden-brown hair, highlighting the messy waves until they nearly glowed.

"Your brother's never been one to spend every last penny of his earnings in port. He'll have enough put by to see you, Ainsley, and Finnan back to Milwaukee, and he'll still have money left over."

She drew in a breath. "That's good to know. It's been so long since I've seen him that I . . . Part of me isn't even sure he'll recognize me."

"How old were you when he left home?"

"Thirteen."

Sacha made a noise beside her, then looked her direction, his eyes roving her face. "You were little more than a child."

She sighed. "It feels like an entire lifetime has passed between then and now."

He ran his gaze the rest of the way down her, his eyes moving slowly over her hair, then the ruffled inlay of her bodice and the green fabric that comprised the rest of her dress.

It was somehow different from how the proprietor at the hotel had looked at her, different from the glint in Eric's eyes when he'd leered at her in the galley.

She suddenly felt warm all over, as though the temperature was increasing rather than decreasing with the setting sun.

As though Sacha had wrapped her in a thick blanket and pulled her against his chest.

And oh, heavens, why was she thinking about leaning against this man's chest? About feeling the warmth and strength of his arms wrapping around her?

I might be a stranger, but I'm also your protector.

His words from earlier today came back to her, and while they'd caused her to stiffen, she suddenly wanted nothing more than to step into his arms and ask him to be her protector.

Because she was far from home. Because her parents were gone, and her uncle was trying to steal her family's shipyard. Because it would still be several days until she arrived in Unalaska, and even then she might need to wait a fortnight until her brother arrived and she looked into his familiar green eyes, swiped the thatch of hair that always fell into his eyes off his forehead, and felt his arms around her.

And that made her want to feel a different pair of arms around her. Arms that belonged to the man who was standing with her at that very moment, tall and strong and broad enough to block an entire ship from her view.

But she couldn't let her thoughts wander down this path, not when she'd be saying good-bye to Sacha Amos as soon as they arrived in Unalaska. Not when she had family land to return to back in Wisconsin. Not when he was so married to the sea that even if he took a wife, he'd see her only a handful of times a year.

So she forced her gaze away from the man beside her and across the dark water toward where the night had finally swallowed the mountains.

Because it was easier than letting her heart get tangled up with a sea captain.

12

Sacha paused outside the captain's cabin, taking a moment to roll his neck and blow out a breath. It wasn't quite time for dinner, but it felt as though the events of an entire week had been packed into a single day.

They'd left Wrangell at dawn as planned to reach the *Thunderhead* at high tide. His crew had been able to repair more of the ship than he'd expected, and with the help of tow ropes and a strong wind, they'd been able to dislodge the *Thunderhead*. It was now on its way without aid to Sitka, where Sacha would likely find it in the dry dock when the *Aurora* reached the port tomorrow afternoon.

It had been about lunchtime when the *Aurora* passed through Dry Strait, and around two when they reached Petersburg. Now cargo had been both loaded and unloaded, and Sacha was ready for a nap.

Maybe he'd sneak one in after the ship got underway. But first, he needed to talk to Dr. Torres.

He drew in another breath, then knocked on the door in front of him.

It opened a second later, but the person inside wasn't Dr. Torres.

Sacha blinked, just to make sure he was standing at the door to the scientist's cabin rather than Maggie's. But sure enough, he was on the starboard side of the quarterdeck, and the bed, table, and chest of drawers behind Maggie all belonged to him, not the first mate.

What was she doing alone with Dr. Torres? Why was she inside his cabin, answering his door?

He shoved the door all the way open and swept his gaze over the cabin, but Dr. Torres wasn't there.

His chest filled with relief, and he let it out in a giant rush of air.

"Sacha?" She moved deeper into the cabin, giving him room to enter. "Is something wrong?"

It wasn't proper having Maggie in this room, even without the scientist. Had any of his sailors seen her enter?

Generally speaking, there was only one type of woman who would book passage on a ship full of men she wasn't related to. And even though everything about Maggie McDougal seemed proper and respectable, his sailors might not view things the same way.

Nor would the people in the various ports of call. The cannery manager in Ketchikan had given him the benefit of the doubt when he'd seen Maggie aboard and asked if she was his sister.

But the manager in Wrangell hadn't been so generous when he'd spotted Maggie. Nor had some of the cannery workers.

"What are you doing in here?" he managed to grind out, his eyes sweeping the room once more.

She blinked at him. "Filing papers, like I said when you asked last night."

All right, maybe she had told him that, but he hadn't realized that meant she'd be alone in Dr. Torres's cabin.

He shoved a hand through his hair. Was he making an issue out of nothing? Dr. Torres was well respected within the scientific community, and Maggie clearly needed money. Having her work for him seemed like the perfect solution.

Yet he still wanted to forbid it.

And look at him, being ridiculous. Had he drunk some tainted water? Or maybe some sour milk? He wasn't thirteen. It wasn't as though this was the first time he'd been around a beautiful woman.

But never before had he felt such an unexplained urge to protect her.

Perhaps because he felt a personal responsibility to see her safely to Unalaska. Maybe that was the difference.

"Do you want to see how I'm organizing things?" She turned on her heel and headed toward the bed, which was covered with orderly stacks of papers. "Dr. Torres is letting me change a few elements of his filing system, and I think it will make his notes easier to find. I must admit, I didn't realize quite how many records a scientist needs to keep. I think he has more papers stuffed inside this tiny cabin than we do in the entirety of the shipyard office back in Milwaukee."

Her face was glowing, her eyes dancing as she reached for a stack of papers, then slid them into a file and placed them in the trunk.

Who got that excited about filing papers? Organizing records for the trading company was the bane of his brothers' and sisters' existence, and here Maggie was, actually happy to do it?

She also looked rather beautiful as she took another haphazard stack of papers and began placing the various sheets into the appropriate pile on the bed.

She worked through the new stack of papers in a matter of seconds, then turned to him. "So is there something you need?"

He blinked. He should probably be thankful the woman had spent quite a bit of time inside her room the past two days. Because every rational thought seemed to flee his brain when she was around.

"I . . . ah . . ." He scratched the side of his head. Why had he come to the cabin? "We'll be leaving in about twenty minutes. I wanted to see if there was anything Dr. Torres needed in town."

"He's already in town. He said there was something he wanted to see. Last I saw him, he was right . . ." She took a few steps toward the door, then pointed at the beach. "Oh yes, he's still there on the beach with all those wooden frames. Do you know what's tied to them? Is it some kind of animal skin? Dr. Torres wouldn't say."

"They're seal pelts."

"Seal pelts?" Her brow furrowed. "That's the main thing Dr. Torres is studying, seals. I thought it was whales or otter or all sea life until I came to his cabin this morning. But after spending half a day cataloguing things, it seems that nearly all the papers in here are about seals. I don't understand why he even bothered to time the whales yesterday—or why he was so particular about how I kept time."

And that was yet another part of Maggie working for Dr. Torres that made him uncomfortable. Sacha moved to the door, then made sure no one was on the quarterdeck to notice he was about to shut himself inside the room with Maggie. Once he closed the door, he turned back to her. "How much has Dr. Torres told you?"

The words came out a little more forceful than necessary, and Maggie's eyes widened. "About what? The seals? Not much. He just told me where to file the different papers."

"Because no one can know that he's studying seals, at least not yet."

"Why not?"

"Because each of those pelts you saw drying out there on the beach is worth ten dollars, that's why."

"Ten dollars?" she squeaked.

He could almost see her doing calculations in her head, see her estimating just how many pelts were drying—over five hundred, to be sure—and figuring out how much money that led to.

Sacha tapped a finger on the desk, where a paper rested that looked to be some kind of tally of the number of seal pelts Dr. Torres had seen since boarding the *Aurora*. "If this kind of hunting is allowed to continue, it will mean the complete destruction of the seal population, much like what happened to the sea otter. The trouble is, all anyone sees when they look at seals is money. And someone doing a study that might result in their hunting being curtailed . . . Let's just say certain men might go through some rather great lengths to ensure the results of this study never reach Washington, DC."

"If they know about it," she whispered, her eyes filled with understanding. "That's why this needs to stay secret."

"Exactly."

"So all those dead seals out there—"

"Those aren't dead seals," he interrupted. "Those are pelts that have been fleshed and are in the process of being tanned. The tribe here is being paid to drain and dry the seal hides. It's about a six-week process. After that, they'll be taken to Seattle or Sacramento, China or Japan, and sold to the highest bidder."

"And killing so many seals is legal? There's no law against it?"

"No. That's incorrect." His jaw twitched. "Every one of those seals out there was poached for their pelts. There's only one company that has hunting rights to the seals, and they hunt them northwest of here, on a small cluster of islands—the Pribilofs. They have a quota, and they hunt with full permission of the US government, with oversight from the Bureau of Fisheries. They abide by the laws. Mostly."

The confusion in her eyes only deepened. "Why would the government let only one company hunt seals? That hardly seems fair."

"Because Alaska Commercial Company paid for sole hunting rights on the Pribilof Islands—the seals' breeding ground—for twenty years. To hunt seals anywhere else is illegal."

"But people are hunting them in other places. They have to be; otherwise there wouldn't be so many pelts outside, right?"

"They're being hunted at sea. It's called pelagic sealing. The seals are hunted far enough away from land that the Bureau of Fisheries and the Revenue Cutter Service have a hard time patrolling for poachers. That's how you end up with the five hundred pelts you see drying on the beach. And it's devastating the seal population."

Maggie's face turned ghostly white. "So if Dr. Torres completes this study and it's taken back to Washington, DC...?"

"Hopefully the government will take a stronger stance against the poaching."

"But the poachers won't be happy with Dr. Torres."

"No. But I'm sure once Dr. Torres is back in Washington, the politicians and bureaucrats there will be happy to have the information from the study." At least, the politicians and bureaucrats who aren't in cahoots with the sealing industry.

"What about you?" Maggie licked her lips. "After this study is published, won't it be known what ship Dr. Torres was on when he conducted his research? What will happen when word you assisted him gets out?"

"Once the government realizes how dire the situation truly is, I'm hoping they'll send more revenue cutters north to patrol for poachers." If the government could curtail the poaching, then maybe the seal quotas on the Pribilof Islands wouldn't need to be curbed. At least, that's what he was hoping, that Alaska Commercial Company would see the importance of hunting seals in a way that would allow the animals to survive for future generations.

Because if ACC didn't see things that way . . .

Sacha swallowed, then tried to put a reassuring smile on his face. "You don't need to worry about anything. You'll be back in Wisconsin by the time the study is released. As far as I see it, no one will even know you helped."

"I'm not asking about me. I'm asking about you." She kept her eyes pinned on him, her gaze somber in the light filtering through the cabin window.

The back of his neck burned under her scrutiny. What would happen if the government drastically lowered the seal quota? Alaska Commercial Company wouldn't be happy, but would the manager—Preston Caldwell—make him pay the way he had last fall?

He gave his head a small shake. No. He couldn't let himself think that way, couldn't let fear control him. Besides, he wasn't pushing to have the quota lowered. He was pushing for more aggressive action to be taken against poachers.

"It's nothing you need to worry about," he rasped. "Just keep quiet about what Dr. Torres is truly studying and give him whatever he asks for to accomplish his work."

Then he turned and strode out of the cabin.

13

Sitka, Alaska, That Evening

Alexei sighed as he studied the paper in front of him. The shipyard was bursting, both with new ships being commissioned and damaged ships needing to be repaired. They'd just had one arrive a few minutes ago. The captain had said they'd run aground in Dry Strait, and that Sacha had used the *Aurora* to tow them off the gravel bar.

"If we have any more ships come in for repair, you'll have to hire another worker. There's no way around it." Bjorn, the master shipbuilder who had worked for his family for more than thirty years, rapped his knuckles on the desk. "This paper here shows it."

"The paper shows I need to hire another two workers, and that's without any more ships coming in for repairs. Can you think of anyone in town we might be able to hire?"

Bjorn shook his head. "They're either already working on a ship or they've got gold fever. No one wants to learn how to build ships when they can go off prospecting."

Right. It was the same problem Alexei had hiring workers in Juneau, or sailors on his ships. Most of the men coming to Alaska were so filled with gold fever, they were useless when it came to any other line of work.

"There's a ship in harbor today, and several more scheduled to arrive before the end of the week. Head on down to the bar a few nights this week and see if we can find a couple sailors who might want to replace swabbing the deck with swinging one of your hammers—at least for the rest of the summer. If you can't find anyone, then I'll talk to Sacha and see if he can hire a couple men to bring back here the next time he's in Seattle. But that means we'll have to wait at least a month, if not six weeks, for more workers."

Bjorn crossed his arms over his burly chest, the muscles in both arms sculpted from over three decades of swinging a hammer. "Can't remember the last time we saw so many ships needing repairs in a summer."

His master shipbuilder was right. It seemed like twice a month, ships were limping into the harbor after running aground or hitting a rock somewhere in the shallow waters of the Alexander Archipelago, and he had yet to figure it out. It wasn't as though the sea level was abnormally low, so why were so many ships suddenly wrecking?

Alexei sighed, then jutted his chin toward Bjorn. "What did Kate say when she examined your shoulder?"

The Danish man lifted a big, bear-like hand to the area he'd been complaining about for a month or better. "That I should put my hammer down for a few weeks and give it a rest."

Alexei raised his eyebrows. "And . . . ? I'm sure that's not all my sister said."

The man pressed his lips together, his hand moving from his shoulder to the center of his chest. "She's concerned about my heart too. Says I might want to think about setting down my hammer for good, that maybe I should take a trip to Denmark."

Alexei sucked in a breath. He shouldn't be surprised. Bjorn had worked for his family for decades, and building ships was the type of job that wore on a man's body. But were they really talking about replacing Bjorn now? When the paper in front of him already listed too many jobs for their shipyard, and that was assuming their master shipbuilder could work from dawn until dusk? "Does she think you need to stop immediately? Or can you give me a few more months, maybe through the end of the summer?"

Bjorn rubbed his chest. "She didn't say to stop this second, just that she thinks my heart is growing weak. But she does want me resting my shoulder."

Alexei sighed again. Maybe he was the one who needed to take a trip down the coast to a few of the shipyards in California. Because he wouldn't be able to hire just anyone to replace Bjorn. He'd need to hire a skilled shipbuilder already working at another shipyard.

The sound of the door slamming echoed through the office, then sharp footsteps sounded on the stairs. He straightened behind his desk and moved his gaze toward where the stairs emptied onto the second floor of the warehouse, which functioned as the office for both the Amos Family Shipbuilders and Sitka Trading Company.

As soon as he saw the top of the man's hat, he knew exactly who it was—and every muscle in his body grew tense.

"Thank you, Bjorn. I'll look things over a little better and see what I can do."

"You're wel—"

"I heard you're trying to come up with four hundred blankets to give the Tlingit." The sharp sound of Preston Caldwell's voice filled the room.

Alexei narrowed his eyes at the man who appeared at the top of the stairs. "Who let you in?"

"Don't do it," Caldwell snapped.

Out of the corner of his eye, Alexei saw Bjorn edge toward the stairs, then disappear down them. But he kept his gaze riveted on Caldwell. "Excuse me?"

"I said, don't bother giving those savages beads or blankets or anything else they ask for." Caldwell stalked to the long, narrow table against the interior wall of the office and poured himself a glass of water from the pitcher.

How very like the man to assume he could help himself to anything he saw.

He drained the water in a matter of seconds, his clean-shaven jaw and throat moving each time he took a swallow. Then he set the glass back down on the table with a jarring thud. "The Indian who died on my ship jumped into the water on his own. I don't compensate people who die because they're idiots."

"My understanding is that he jumped into the water to save another worker who fell." Alexei pushed himself up from his desk. He wasn't going to let Caldwell tower over him, especially not when the man was wearing perfectly shined shoes and a sleek three-piece suit that looked as though it had been pressed five minutes ago.

"As I said . . ." Caldwell yawned, though Alexei doubted the yawn had anything to do with Caldwell being tired. "He jumped in of his own free will, knowingly taking the risk. It's not the job of Alaska Commercial Company to compensate people for idiocy, let alone to compensate the entire town where the person came from."

Alexei crossed his arms and leaned a hip against his desk, trying to at least look casual and aloof—even if the man who'd ruined one of his shipping routes was stalking around his office.

"You're not compensating the people of a town. You're compensating the man's clan. It's his family. Think of it as paying them for his bravery."

"Men die at sea." Caldwell crossed the room toward him, his movements as sleek as a cat's. A dark, dangerous cat.

Most of the men who'd come to Sitka since the transition of power from Russia to the United States had arrived in worn suits and balding heads. Alexei knew better than to run afoul of them if he wanted to keep his trading company and shipyard, simply because their boring, paperwork-filled jobs meant they wielded a certain amount of power.

Preston Caldwell wasn't one of those men. He came from two centuries of money and power on the East Coast, and he oozed it. He was only in Alaska because of the filthy amount of money his family was making in the sealing industry.

"I'd expect you, of all people, to understand my decision." Caldwell brushed an imaginary speck of lint off the sleeve of his pristine suit. "Tell me, did your father pay grandparents and great-uncles and third cousins whenever he lost a man on one of his ships? Do you?"

A muscle pulsed on the side of Alexei's jaw. "It's not the same. After the death of a clan member, the Tlingit require some sort of compensation. They say it restores balance. If there's no compensation, they will take the lives of white men. Their honor demands it." And the Tlingit wouldn't necessarily make sure that life belonged to Preston Caldwell or even someone else employed by the ACC. They would capture whichever white man they could when an opportunity presented itself. "Surely you don't want to repeat the bombardment of Angoon? And all over a few hundred blankets."

Caldwell shrugged, and the gesture reeked of arrogance. "Why would that bother me? We won the battle, and we ran off some savages. That leaves more whales and beaver and bear for us to hunt."

Alexei's hand clenched into a fist at his side. "If you think they're so savage, why do you employ them on your ships?"

"They know how to kill seals."

Right. That muscle on the side of his jaw wanted to pulse again, but he worked to control it. "I already told Governor Trent I'll come up with the blankets. Unlike you, I refuse to stand aside and allow bloodshed to happen when I have the means of preventing it."

Caldwell's eyes narrowed into two slits. "It's a wonder you have any money left at all, making business decisions with your heart rather than your brain. Tell me, just how profitable is your trading company proving to be this year?"

"That's none of your concern."

Caldwell tapped the map lying on the desk, the one Alexei had been studying before Bjorn arrived. "You won't be able to make the *Aurora*'s route profitable. Not unless you drop the trips to Barrow and Nome and use the time to make an extra run to Russia or Japan. People in California and Seattle want things like silk and tea and vodka, not a basket that takes a Tlingit woman two months to weave."

His blood felt suddenly hot, his skin too tight for his body. He leaned forward, meeting Caldwell's gaze evenly. "I'm not taking those stops off Sacha's summer route. The Inupiat in Barrow and Nome depend on us to bring them supplies and medicine every summer. We're the only company that includes those stops."

"No shipping company owner will look at the routes you're running now and hire you as their manager."

Alexei narrowed his eyes. "Why would I want to go work for another shipping company when I have one of my own to run? You might have hurt the *Aurora*'s route, but we're not in danger of losing our business."

"You will be. Eventually. Because one day those big iron ships will start darting across the Pacific to Japan and Russia as often as your little wooden clippers, and they'll run you out of business."

The moisture leached from his mouth. As much as he wanted to argue, he couldn't. His family owned five ships, yes. Wooden vessels that could flit about the Pacific Ocean and Bering Sea with ease. But eventually all shipping would be taken over by giant iron-hulled barges. Stopping that progression would be akin to stopping the tide from rising.

But that day hadn't come just yet, and he was working on broadening his family's holdings. He'd used the company's profits from last year to purchase shares in a railroad in January, and if gold were ever discovered in the interior, their trading company was in an excellent position to outfit miners and provide supplies. No other company had anywhere near the trade routes in the interior that they did or had bothered to develop relationships with native tribes like the Athabaskans. After all, Mikhail didn't just know an Athabaskan chief or two, he knew all the various tribes and spoke their language.

But gold had to be discovered first. In the meantime, he was saving every last penny he could to either invest in one of those giant iron barges being built down in San Francisco or invest more in railroads.

He wasn't oblivious. He'd just had a father who'd only been interested in opening the Alaskan interior up to trade, not expanding their holdings or looking for investment opportunities in other regions of America.

If his father had lived a few more years, he might even have closed the shipyard so he could focus entirely on trade.

Now the shipyard was the main thing keeping their family

afloat. He could afford to lose money on Sacha's route and send the *Aurora* up to Barrow and Nome because they were making money on the shipyard.

Everyone wanted a ship like the *Aurora*, and the letters of inquiry he had regarding building double-hulled ships made to withstand ice seemed endless.

"You're awful quiet, Alexei." Caldwell's lips tipped up in an arrogant smirk. "Don't tell me you're only now realizing how doomed your paltry little business endeavors are. I'll let you thank me for my advice later, after you've had time to think about it more. But in the meantime, you can stop wasting time trying to finagle more money out of Sacha's shipping route. After the stunt Sacha pulled last fall, I made sure you'd lose money on the *Aurora* this year. It's only fair."

"Fair? You stole half the cannery shipping contracts out from under us," he gritted. "And tell me, are *you* making a profit running that route? Surely you'd be making more money if you used the ship that's picking up the canned salmon for sealing instead."

"It's money I can afford to lose." Caldwell leaned forward over the desk, his lips still tilted in a condescending smirk. "Consider my little shipping stunt a warning. You should be thankful I didn't use more ruthless methods."

Alexei's stomach twisted. "Then tell your men to follow the law. Pelagic sealing is just as illegal for you as it is for the ships from Canada."

"As far as I'm concerned, you owe me money for the three thousand pelts the judge confiscated, pelts legally acquired. That's thirty thousand dollars. I'll consider our business settled after I'm compensated."

"Would you really?" He cocked his head to the side, his eyes narrowed. "Or would you still try to destroy the *Aurora*'s trade route?"

Something dark flashed in Caldwell's eyes. "My family paid for the exclusive right to hunt seals on the Pribilof Islands for twenty years. It was not cheap. And if you do anything, and I mean anything at all, to keep us from fully using the rights we paid for, I will personally ruin you and everyone you love."

Alexei planted his hands on his desk and leaned forward, bringing him nose to nose with Caldwell. "You made that clear last year when your men kidnapped my ten-year-old brother and his friend. If you try ruining us again, I'll see to it that you spend the rest of your life inside a prison cell."

Caldwell pushed himself off the desk, his face turning the slightest shade of white. "I never told Jacobs to kidnap Ilya. He did that on his own, and you'll never be able to prove my involvement, because I didn't have any."

Alexei knew that. His brother-in-law, Jonas Redding, was a Deputy Marshal, and he'd wanted to press charges against Caldwell for accessory to kidnapping after they finally found Ilya and Gushklin. But he and Sacha had talked Jonas out of it. Preston Caldwell might be ruthless in business, but he kept his cutthroat tactics limited to that realm. The outlaw Caldwell had hired last year, however, hadn't made the same distinction.

And he'd been sentenced to prison for the rest of his life.

While Alexei certainly didn't like how Caldwell had ruined the *Aurora*'s summer shipping route, he could at least understand why the man had done it.

"Well?" Caldwell asked. He was still looking at him, as though expecting some kind of answer.

Had the man asked him a question? "Rest assured, Caldwell, I have no intention of interfering in your sealing endeavors."

"Then why are you getting involved in the death of one of my workers?"

He threw up his hands. "That's not interfering. That's trying to prevent a massacre!" Couldn't the man understand?

"Alaska Commercial Company won't be paying a cent for those blankets." Caldwell jabbed a finger at him.

Alexei straightened. "If it will save lives, it's worth it."

Caldwell snorted. "I'll give it five years before you're out of business."

Then he turned on his heel and strode from the room.

14

Sitka, Alaska, One Day Later

"Sacha's here! Sacha's here!"

Sacha heard the excited voice coming from land before the *Aurora* was fully docked. Trotting down the stairs from the quarterdeck, he headed to the railing, only to find his youngest brother, Ilya, standing there, a smile as big as the ocean on his eleven-year-old face.

It took a few minutes for the crew to assemble the gangway and slide it down to the wharf. Ilya didn't stop grinning the entire time, and the second the gangway reached the wharf, he was the first person on it.

"What are you doing here?" Sacha held out his arms to catch the boy. It seemed he'd grown an inch since the last time they'd been together. "I thought you'd be in Juneau."

His two youngest siblings had been living there with Kate and Evelina for about a year, never mind they'd spent the first decade of their lives in Sitka, living in the large white house positioned on the rocky point that jutted out from the harbor, where the rest of their family had been raised.

"Everyone's in Sitka." Ilya wrapped his arms around Sacha's waist—arms that were suddenly long enough to touch Sacha's back. When had that happened? "Evelina has court, so the whole lot of us came over from Juneau."

"Evelina has court? Already?" He groaned. He'd wanted to be here for it, had even told Alexei to find extra time in the shipping schedule so he could watch his sister argue her case.

But that had been before he was delayed and then spent an extra day getting the *Thunderhead* off the gravel bar.

"Is she in court now?" Sacha turned his head toward the grand building on top of Castle Hill overlooking Sitka, which housed the courthouse and jail, as well as all the other offices the various bureaucrats running Alaska needed.

"No." Ilya released him and looked up, a thatch of dark hair falling over his forehead. "It's done for the day. But she goes back tomorrow. Are you going to be here?"

He wanted to. Oh, how he wanted to. But Alexei would already be in a snit over how late he was, and some of their salmon would need to be unloaded into the warehouse here, only so it could be loaded onto their next ship heading south. Plus, he and Alexei needed to figure out how to give three of his regular stops to another ship so he'd have time to go to the Pribilof Islands.

Could he somehow squeeze in enough time in Sitka to see his sister in court? "I'll have to talk to Alexei. Where is he?"

"At the house, trying to cheer Lina up."

Again, his heart felt heavy inside his chest, almost as if it had a weight strapped to it. "Did court go that poorly?"

Ilya shrugged. "She's mad about what the paper printed—again."

"And what did the paper print?"

"The usual. That a woman has no place in a courtroom. That Kaaguneteen would let her son stay at the Indian boarding school if she knew what was good for him. That pulling any child out of the boarding school would be sure to ruin his life forever." Ilya rolled his eyes. "You know. All the stuff they've been saying since Lina filed the lawsuit last fall."

"Right." His jaw hardened. As far as he was concerned, it didn't seem like there should be much of a debate—let alone a lawsuit—over how to answer these questions. Shouldn't parents decide where and how their children received an education? And if one year a mother wanted her son in an Indian boarding school, and then her husband died and she needed the son at home to work, then so be it. The mother was the best person to make that kind of decision—Indian or white.

Why the question needed to go before a judge was beyond him.

"Come on." Ilya grabbed his hand and tugged. "Everyone will be excited you're here. Let's go to the house."

Sacha planted his feet on the deck, then glanced over his shoulder at the white house where he'd been raised. "I need to see that the ship is unloaded first. And I need to speak with Alexei about some extra cargo. Can you let him know I'm here?"

Ilya beamed, something about his smile reminding Sacha of just how young his brother was, even though his body was quickly propelling him to that awkward stage between a boy and a man. "Time me. I want to see how long it takes to run to the house and back."

Then Ilya spun on his heel and raced down the gangway as though his shoes were on fire.

Sacha pulled out his pocket watch and glanced at the time, not quite able to help the smile on his face. Ilya might be getting older, but he was still a burst of sunshine and happiness, even at eleven.

Was it too much to hope Ilya didn't lose that as he grew older?

Sacha turned and headed up to the quarterdeck. The shipping manifest and a few of his other important papers were still in the desk in his cabin, and Alexei would need them.

"Dr. Torres?" He rapped lightly on the cabin door.

No answer.

Was the man in his cabin, or was he at the bow timing the whales they'd passed at the entrance to the sound?

He knocked again, then twisted the doorknob and stepped inside—only to find he wasn't alone.

"Sacha." Alexei turned to face him, his jaw hard. "You were talking to Ilya, so I decided to get the shipping manifest. I'm sure you can imagine my surprise when I stepped into your office and found a detailed map of the migration pattern of the northern fur seal in the drawer where you usually store the manifest."

Alexei set the map down on the desk, then reached for another paper. "And a tally sheet estimating the number of poached seal pelts on each ship you passed heading here."

His brother's voice was as cold as the Bering Sea on a December morning, but the look in his eyes had turned furious, and that fury radiated from the taut way he held his shoulders to the hardness in his jaw to the stiff way he set the paper he'd been holding back on the desk and picked up yet another. "You have ten seconds to tell me what's going on—and it better not be what I think."

Sacha swallowed. He'd been hoping he could keep some of the study hidden from Alexei. Hoping he'd be able to ask for an extra two weeks to spend at the Pribilof Islands without going into all the details. After all, the fewer people who knew about the study, the better. "You know how I've been writing letters for about five years, asking the Bureau of Fisheries to do a study on seals?"

Alexei crossed his arms over his chest, his lips pressed into a tight line.

"I . . . ah . . . I may have gotten tired of waiting, so I contacted a scientist from the Smithsonian Institution and invited him to conduct an informal study aboard the *Aurora*—and he may have accepted."

He'd seen his brother angry before. And he'd seen his brother devastated. But he'd never seen his brother go ominously still, never seen Alexei's eyes turn so black he couldn't pull a single emotion from them.

When Alexei finally spoke, his voice was deathly quiet. "Do you know how much money we're losing this shipping season because Preston Caldwell is trying to get revenge for you reporting one of his ships last year?"

That's what Alexei was so angry about? Money? Surely he knew they could earn money other ways. It wasn't as though the *Aurora* was their only source of income. "I didn't know last year would turn out the way it did."

"What, with Ilya being kidnapped?"

"That wasn't my fault. All I did was follow the law. Maybe if more people reported poachers, we wouldn't be in this situation." Sacha thrust a hand toward the open ocean, never mind they couldn't see it standing inside the cabin with a window facing land. "You know a study needs to be conducted. You know there are fewer and fewer seals. You know they'll go the way of the sea otter if no one does anything. When was the last time you saw a seal in Sitka Sound?"

"We can't afford to get involved." Alexei stayed where he was, his arms crossed stubbornly over his chest, the rest of his body still.

"If we don't, who will?"

They stared at each other, Sacha's light-brown eyes clashing with Alexei's dark ones. The accusations in his brother's eyes speared a place deep inside him.

"You and I both know that Preston Caldwell will see any action you or anyone else in our family takes to restrict the number of seals being harvested as a direct threat to his business," Alexei gritted.

"No, I don't know that," Sacha snapped. "I'd think the man would thank me. If Dr. Torres can present enough evidence to Washington, they might take a stronger stance against poaching. Might send more revenue cutters to the Bering and—"

"Or they'll lower the quota on the Pribilofs, and then the man will do everything in his power to destroy our family."

"He won't go that far. He can't. Besides, the quota won't get lowered based on one study alone. Caldwell should be happy that someone is trying to get the poaching curtailed. That benefits him even more than it benefits us."

"That's not how he'll see it." Alexei raked a hand through his hair, stalked across the cabin to the bed, then turned and paced back to the desk. "He was in my office yesterday threatening me, and all because I'm trying to come up with blankets to give the clan at Hoonah so we don't have another Angoon bombardment on our hands."

Sacha raised an eyebrow. No one wanted to repeat that massacre, but his brother would need to fill him in on how that pertained to Hoonah.

"Make no mistake, Caldwell will view this study as a threat. And as soon as he finds out about it, he'll turn around and use the money and political connections at his disposal to threaten our business. We can't afford to make a bigger enemy out of him."

"I'm not trying to make an enemy out of him or anyone else.

Now I need you to clear two weeks from my schedule so I can take Dr. Torres to the Pribilofs. You'll have to give the cannery route to the *Halcyon* or *Alliance* for a couple weeks."

Alexei sent him another unreadable look.

"You can't ask me to turn my back on what's right because of Preston Caldwell. The man would sell off his own daughter if she'd bring him enough money."

Alexei shook his head. "If you want us to have anything left to pass down to our children, if you want the Amos family name to mean something, if you want the reputation our father and grandfather and great-grandfather before that spent ninety years establishing, then you'll call off this study and let me make travel arrangements to get this scientist back to Washington, DC."

Sacha swallowed. It shouldn't seem like that hard of a thing to do. Family first. It was his oldest brother's motto, the reason Alexei had sacrificed his dreams and come home to run the family business after their parents died. The reason he had gotten up every morning for the past ten years and gone to work in the office above the warehouse, tallying ledgers and rerouting ships rather than doing the thing he'd always dreamed of—designing ships of his own.

He shifted his weight from one foot to the other. If Alexei could so easily sacrifice a decade of his life for their family, why did he find it so hard to call off a study?

He met his brother's eyes, then raised his hands halfway, only to let them fall back to his sides. "I can't. I'm sorry."

"Are you serious?" Alexei straightened to his full height, which was still an inch or two shorter than Sacha's. But there was no question which one of them looked more dangerous at the moment. "Do you want to continue drawing paychecks? Do you want to keep paying your men? You're well aware that Caldwell stole shipping contracts out from under us last summer. Not because he needs them but because he knows that without those contracts, the route you run, the ship you captain won't bring in enough money to pay your crew. He hasn't chased any of our other contracts, hasn't taken business from us in any other way. He's just gone after your route. Now you come around, secretly facilitating a study that no one on this island—or on this crew—even wants done?"

"The Aleut are struggling to find food. The Inupiat too. You don't run the routes, Alexei. You don't see their food sources getting slimmer and slimmer. You don't see the sealing vessels paying the Aleut less and less per pelt while their own profits grow. This is Inessa and Ilya's grandparents I'm talking about. Their uncles and aunts. In a few more years, they might not have any food left at all. How can you ask me to turn my back on that? Do you expect me to leave our siblings' relatives to starve?" He dragged in a breath, though the air only seemed to burn his lungs. "Our family can find a more lucrative shipping route to run if things go that far. We can send the *Aurora* to China and Japan and forget about Alaska if we need to. The Inupiat and Aleut don't have ships that can carry them clear across the ocean to find more food."

Alexei sighed, the tension once again leaving his shoulders. But he didn't agree to the study, didn't say he understood.

Because he didn't.

Alexei would always put family first, and Sacha wasn't sure he could fault him.

"Stop paying my salary." Sacha shoved a hand through his hair. "That will at least make up for some of the money we're losing on the *Aurora* this summer."

Though if Caldwell was already threatening Alexei, it wouldn't solve the problem of how the man might retaliate once Dr. Torres returned to Washington, DC, with his study.

"I can't just up and not pay you." Alexei scrubbed a hand over his face.

He shrugged. "I have a ship to live on and a place to stay when I'm in Sitka. Plenty of money in the bank, since I've no bills to pay other than for clothes and boots. I can get by for a few months without a salary, probably even to the end of . . ."

The door to the cabin opened without so much as a knock. Sacha turned to find Maggie standing there, her wide eyes moving between him and Alexei. "Oh. I'm sorry. I didn't realize anyone was in here. Dr. Torres sent me . . . That is, I just need his journal to, ah, see if there's a difference between how long the whales are—"

"Who are you?" Alexei snapped.

"Maggie." Sacha stepped to the door, holding out his arm for her. He waited until she rested her hand on it before closing the door and turning her to face Alexei. "I'd like to introduce you to my oldest brother, Alexei. You'll have to forgive him, as he appears to have woken up this morning without any manners."

Maggie dipped her head toward him, a nervous smile flashing across her lips. "I'm pleased to meet you, Mr. Amos."

Alexei didn't reach out to take her hand or make some kind of introduction. Instead, he pinched the skin between his eyebrows. "Please tell me this is the scientist's wife and not an extra passenger you've acquired who somehow knows about the study."

"Like I said, no manners," he whispered to Maggie, trying to make his voice light and carefree.

It did nothing to lessen the death grip she was giving his arm.

"This is Tavish McDougal's sister from Wisconsin. She was waiting for the *Aurora* in Bellingham. Seems Tavish is needed back in Wisconsin to clear up a legal matter. I'm taking her and her two half siblings to Unalaska where they can meet up with Tavish on the *Halcyon*."

"So she's not the scientist's wife," Alexei muttered, thrusting a hand toward the desk covered with papers. "And she knows about the study."

"I . . . uh . . ." Maggie licked her lips. "I've been assisting Dr. Torres, if that's what—"

"Sacha, you're back!" The door to the room burst open behind them, and Yuri rushed inside with as much excitement as Ilya displayed a few minutes ago, never mind that Yuri was twenty.

His younger brother's arms were around him a second later. Sacha could almost swear he felt the tension leave his body, and it seemed to drain from Alexei's too. "I heard the most dreadful rumor that you're not letting your crew disembark? Tell me it isn't so. There's a dance in two days, and Lina is back in court tomorrow in front of that dreadful judge, and you simply must find some time to stay in . . . Well, well, well." Yuri's gaze fell to Maggie, and he dropped his arms from around Sacha's chest, a half smile quirking the corner of his mouth. "Who do we have here?"

He extended his hand to Maggie, then bent low and kissed Maggie's knuckles, causing a faint flush to creep onto Maggie's cheeks. "What's your name, darling?"

"Maggie McDougal." She smiled ever so softly at Yuri. "I'm headed to Unalaska to find my brother Tavish."

"Tavish McDougal? A good sailor, that one." Yuri grinned down at Maggie, still not letting her hand go. "And why did Tavish never mention he had such a lovely sister?"

"Yuri, stop," Sacha groaned.

"Stop what?" Yuri asked, his eyes still riveted to Maggie.

"Is something wrong?" Maggie tugged her hand out of

Yuri's grip and turned to Sacha, a knot of confusion appearing on the smooth skin between her eyebrows.

Nothing was wrong, other than the fact that Yuri didn't need to turn Maggie into another woman who followed him around town, waiting for him to give her five minutes of attention.

What was it about his younger brother that caused women to melt into a puddle of syrup whenever Yuri was near them?

"I know you must be aching to find your brother, darling, but have you thought of returning to Sitka after leaving Unalaska?" Yuri jabbed a thumb over his shoulder. "See, Alexei here needs a wife. I'm aware that he seems a little dour at the moment, but he's got a heart like a puppy, I swear it. He just needs someone to sweeten him up and remind him how to smile every now and then."

"I . . . um . . ." Maggie slanted a glance at Alexei. "You want me to . . . He's angry I'm even here."

"I'm not angry," Alexei interjected. "I'm just trying to—"

"That's precisely why he needs a wife." Yuri patted Maggie's hand, then sent her a conspiratorial wink. "So he doesn't walk around with a giant thundercloud over his head."

Maggie slanted another glance at Alexei, then burst out laughing.

And why wouldn't she? Alexei was standing in the cramped cabin with a serious frown and dark eyes, looking like God himself about to call down fire and brimstone from heaven.

And Yuri was trying to convince her to marry him. The idea was so hilarious, Sacha found himself laughing too.

"Yuri," Alexei snapped, pinching his brows with his fingers again. "I do *not* need a wife."

"But you do, brother." A saccharine grin split Yuri's face. "You're just too serious to realize it."

Maggie shook her head, her eyes moist with happy tears. "Sorry. I don't think I'm the right woman to make your brother smile."

"What about Sacha?" Yuri sent him a wink. "He's not as serious as Alexei here, though he's gone more than he's home. Perhaps if he had a lovely woman waiting for him back in Sitka, he'd be more apt to stay. Are you keen on him?"

Yuri looped an arm around Maggie's shoulders, as though they'd been friends for years. "Don't worry, you can tell me how you feel about him. Then we'll go back to the big house and plot ways for you to get whichever of my brothers you choose. I've got another one that needs to be married off too, but he's in the interior right now."

Maggie laughed again, the sound loud and free, releasing the tightness in Sacha's chest that he hadn't even realized was there. "I hate to disappoint you, Yuri. Truly I do. But I'm not here to find a husband, no matter how desperate your brothers might be for a wife. I need to find Tavish, and then I must return to Wisconsin."

Yuri gave an exaggerated sigh. "Pity. Something tells me you'd make a lovely sister-in-law. Come now. Let's leave Sacha and Alexei to their argument and get you over to the house, where you can meet my sisters. Did you know one's a doctor and the other's a lawyer?"

"They what?" She looked at Sacha, then back at Yuri, as though almost expecting them to burst into laughter and claim it was all a joke.

Sacha rubbed a hand over the back of his neck. "Don't suppose I thought to mention that when we were talking about my family the other night."

"No. You certainly didn't."

"Don't worry." Yuri patted her hand. "Evelina—the lawyer —won't bite. She's a gentle soul. Now Kate, on the other hand . . . well, if she bites, at least she knows how to patch you up."

"Is this some kind of joke?"

"Absolutely not. I'd never joke about my family. Did Sacha tell you we've got ourselves a pair of mixed-race half siblings too?"

"Um . . ."

Again, she glanced at Sacha, but he only shrugged. He wasn't going to apologize for his family, even if they were a bit odd.

"I knew about the half siblings, but not that they were mixed race."

"After our mother died, our father remarried an Aleut woman from a tribe north of here," he said. It wasn't something he'd been trying to hide. It simply hadn't come up in conversation.

Yuri patted Maggie's hand and tugged her toward the door. "No worries, darling. I'll explain it all to you on the way to the house."

Sacha watched as she left, something inside his chest suddenly calm after seeing such a big smile on her face.

"Yuri's not wrong."

At the sound of Alexei's voice, he turned to find his brother staring at him. "She'd probably make you an excellent wife. And I could certainly use your help at the shipyard. We're trying to hire at least two new employees, but we've only been able to find one so far."

"Of the two of us, I'm not the one who needs to get married. Captaining a ship isn't a good job for a man with a family."

"Our father managed it well enough."

He had, yes, and Sacha often wondered how. Besides the fact that he took them with him everywhere, of course. But sailing was a dangerous job, and he couldn't imagine leaving his family subject to the mercies of a wild, untamable sea day after day.

Which meant he wouldn't be looking for a wife until he was good and ready to sign over the *Aurora* to another captain. And if that day ever came, it would be years from now. By then, he'd probably be too old and stubborn for any woman to want him.

"So, about that trip to the Pribilofs. Can you make changes to the shipping schedule to fit it in?"

Alexei sighed. "I don't like this, Sacha. Not one bit. The seals might need to be saved, but that doesn't mean we should get involved. Someone else can fight that battle. Someone who doesn't have roots in Sitka that go back ninety years. Someone who doesn't already have Preston Caldwell nipping at his ankles. Someone who doesn't have as much to lose as we do."

Sacha raised his hands in a gesture of innocence. "This isn't something I ever wanted to do. I'd gladly let someone else take this fight. But there is no one else. That's the problem. We're the only people who care. We're the only people with family who've been in Alaska long enough to hear stories about the sea otter growing up and how they disappeared."

"Let me think about it." And with that, Alexei strode off, leaving him standing in the center of the cabin by himself.

15

Maggie had known Evelina and Kate Amos less than an hour, yet she felt like she was sitting in her kitchen back in Milwaukee, sipping tea and eating her mother's cake while the scent of baking cookies filled the air.

She wouldn't call the kitchen fancy. She'd certainly seen fancier ones, but there was something familiar about the large wooden table where they sat, its surface worn and scarred from years of family meals. Something familiar about how the hutch in the corner was just messy enough to look as though it was regularly used, and wooden shelves holding the dishes had gaps where cups and plates hadn't yet been put away after lunch.

Yuri had dropped her and the children off about forty-five minutes ago. But about thirty seconds after they walked in the door, he convinced his two half siblings, Inessa and Ilya, to take Ainsley and Finnan on a tour of the town while the women visited. Ilya's eyes had lit up with delight, and he'd grabbed Finnan by the hand and pulled him out the door, leaving the girls to follow.

Then Yuri had walked into the kitchen, introduced Maggie

to Kate and Evelina, and stayed long enough to down a cup of tea and a piece of cake, all while telling his sisters that they needed to take good care of her because she was going to marry one of his brothers. After that, he'd stated he better get back to the *Aurora* so he could remind Alexei and Sacha they actually liked each other before one of them up and decided to kill the other over whatever they'd been arguing about.

Maggie had a feeling they'd been arguing about Dr. Torres's study. Though that seemed a bit odd. If Alexei ran the trading company, then surely he knew about the study and had built time into the shipping schedule for the *Aurora* to visit the islands where the seals mated every summer.

"Would you like more tea?" Evelina stood and reached for her cup, not really waiting for Maggie to answer as she moved to the hutch against the wall. Atop it sat a large, ornate-looking copper reservoir with a teapot on top and a spigot at the bottom. Evelina took the teapot off the top and poured a bit into the cups. The steamy scent of tea exploded into the room, but the liquid looked nearly black.

"What is that?" she asked. She'd had tea aplenty before, but she'd never seen such a unique kettle.

"The samovar?" Evelina used the spigot at the bottom of the kettle to release steaming water into the delicate cups, then turned and handed one to Maggie. "You don't have them in Wisconsin?"

Maggie shook her head. "I'm afraid not. We just use a teapot, like what you have resting on top of the"—What had Evelina called it?—"samserver."

"Samovar," Kate corrected from beside her. "It's a Russian tea kettle that boils water."

"You don't just boil water on the stove?"

"We could," Evelina said. "But that water cools quickly, especially in the midst of a Russian winter. With a samovar, we fill the reservoir with water, then build a small fire inside the pipe that runs through the center. It heats the water to boiling and keeps it warm, then we brew a concentrate of strong tea, which we keep in the teapot, and set the teapot atop the pipe, where it also stays warm. When we need to refill our tea, we use a bit of the concentrate, then mix it in with the hot water below."

"We can serve warm tea for hours without ever needing to reheat the kettle," Kate added.

Maggie smiled, studying the urn-shaped kettle as she took a sip of her tea. "That's the most wonderful thing I've ever seen. Warm tea without reheating the kettle on the stove."

Who would have thought such a thing was possible?

Evelina smiled. "We Russians are quite good at keeping warm during the winter."

"We haven't much choice if we don't want to freeze." Kate leaned over the table and cut herself a second piece of cake, her movements brisk and efficient. Then she looked at Maggie. "Would you like another slice?

"I really shouldn't."

"Go on, have a second one." Evelina nodded to the cake. "The filling turned out delicious today."

Maggie moved her gaze between the two sisters, both identical, with creamy skin and delicate faces and rich brown hair with hints of red. But they carried themselves so differently, one would never be mistaken for the other. Evelina left her hair long and free, cascading about her shoulders in glossy waves that made her look like a princess out of a fairytale. She had a gentle look on her face and moved about the kitchen so gracefully she seemed to float.

Then there was Kate, who wore her hair pulled back into a tight bun and sat with proper posture. She hadn't smiled once since Yuri brought Maggie over to the house and introduced her to his sisters.

"So what do you think of Alaska?" Kate slid a small piece of cake onto the plate in front of Maggie. "And I'm insisting you have a second slice. We've both had Scully's cooking before. He doesn't let you starve, but that's the only good thing I can say about it."

"Kate, be kind," Evelina admonished. "There's not much need for either tea or napoleon cake on a ship."

"Napoleon cake?" Maggie broke off the tip of the slice with her fork. The first piece had been delicious, filled with five or six flaky layers of pastry with a smooth, buttery cream between each one. The outside of the cake had been coated with that same creamy filling and coated with crumbs from the pastry too. The result was heavenly.

"It's a Russian dessert," Kate quipped. "And Evelina is an excellent baker. It's a shame she only bakes when she's upset."

Maggie raised her eyes to Evelina. She looked peaceful and content sitting across the table. Was the woman upset about something?

A child shouted from outside, and Maggie pushed herself up from the table, then went to the window. Had it been Finnan or someone else?

"Don't worry about the children." Evelina took a sip of tea. "I'm sure they want to run after being cooped up on the *Aurora* for the past few days. Ilya will entertain them, and Inessa will make sure they don't get into trouble."

"Are you sure they aren't being a bother?" Maggie scanned the rocks descending into the water but didn't see anyone.

"We're sure." Kate speared a bite of cake with her fork. "Ilya is always happy to meet new people. This is giving him something to do."

"Come back and sit." Evelina gestured to the table. "You've

barely touched your tea. Besides, I want to know what you think about Southeast Alaska too." She waved her hand toward the window, which overlooked the boats moored in the harbor. Beyond that, a series of mountains with rounded, tree-covered peaks jutted straight up from the water.

Lingering beside the window, Maggie sighed at the vista of mountains and water. "It's one of the most beautiful places I've ever seen. Even when it's foggy, it's still beautiful, though I much prefer it sunny."

"It's sunnier in Sitka than some of the other places you've stopped with Sacha. As much as I like living in Juneau, it's rather dreary. Always cloudy there." Kate lifted another bite of cake to her mouth. "The sun is the biggest thing I miss about Sitka."

"I've never been to Juneau." Maggie slid back into her chair and wrapped her hands around the ornate copper and porcelain teacup, letting the warmth soak into her palms. It wasn't that the air outside was terribly cold, but she wouldn't call it warm. Certainly nothing like the summer they'd be having back in Milwaukee.

"Not many people have been to Juneau, I'm afraid. It's little more than a mining base camp, filled with men and bars." Evelina raised her shoulders in a dainty shrug. "There's not much elegant about it."

"And yet you both like it?" Maggie looked between the two sisters.

"I teach school there part-time." Evelina's eyes lit up, turning the woman on the opposite side of the table even more beautiful. "Tlingit children who don't want to go to the day school or an Indian boarding school. I can't imagine leaving them."

"And there's need for a doctor in Juneau. Much need." Kate shifted in the seat beside her. "I'd rather go somewhere

I'm needed than be relegated to delivering babies here or telling women who keep fainting that they need to loosen their corsets."

Maggie raised her eyebrows. "A woman can faint because her corset is too tight?"

Kate rolled her eyes.

"Don't get Kate started on corsets," Evelina whispered. "We'll be here until dark."

"But how do you know if your corset is too tight?" Suddenly her own corset felt tight, even though she'd laced it that morning the same as she always did.

"If you need to ask, then it probably is." Kate ran her eyes down Maggie's form, narrowing in on her waist. "Anything that reduces the size of your natural waist is too tight."

"But isn't that the point of having a corset? To reduce the size of your waist?"

"Sure. As long as you don't mind not being able to breathe deeply, as a tight corset limits lung expansion. Hopefully you don't mind having a deformed rib cage either, because the persistent pressure exerted on your torso can misalign your bones and displace internal organs. That will affect your body's ability to digest food, by the way. Corsets can also weaken your back and abdominal muscles and impair circulation. Tell me, do your fingers and toes feel perpetually cold?"

"I . . . um . . ." Maggie's fingers suddenly did feel cold. Because her corset was too tight? She wrapped them back around her warm teacup.

"Tight-lacing can also impact your ability to conceive and carry a baby to term. I never recommend corsets during pregnancy."

"Ah . . . thank you," she squeaked, her face turning hot. It wasn't as though she was planning to find herself in the family way anytime soon.

"Kate, be kind." Evelina set her teacup back on its saucer. "It's obvious she's not lacing her corset tightly enough for all that. And now you've terrified her."

Kate sighed, a bit of the stiffness leaving her shoulders. "Just be careful not to lace too tightly. I'm aware they can help support your chest, but never lace your corset in such a way that it alters the shape of your body."

"I won't," she promised. She'd never be able to think of a corset in the same way after that lecture. "So, ah . . . is that most of what you do as a doctor? Tell women to loosen their corsets?"

Kate's shoulders turned rigid all over again, and the woman narrowed her eyes, as though she'd somehow said something wrong. "Yes. Right along with setting broken bones, retrieving bullets from gunshot wounds, and stopping people from bleeding to death."

"Oh . . . I . . . ah . . ." Could she say anything right around this woman? Evelina had made her feel welcome and comfortable, but the longer she sat beside Kate, the more she found herself wishing she was back on the *Aurora* with Sacha. "I just . . . I didn't know women could go to medical school, I suppose."

"I could and I did."

"And she's a good doctor," Evelina said, her voice as warm as Kate's was cold. "She saved my husband's life. Sometimes she just forgets most people have never met a woman doctor before."

"You're certainly the first woman doctor I've met." Maggie took a small sip of tea, trying to wash away the lump that had formed in her throat. "Not that I think there's anything wrong with a woman being a doctor. I just . . ."

And the lump was back again.

"It's a bit unusual, I admit," Evelina said, the kindness in her voice seeming to melt away a bit of Kate's stiffness. "Especially with my being a lawyer too. Kate and I both chose to work in fields that aren't necessarily kind to women."

"You're the first woman lawyer I've met as well." Maggie took another small sip of tea, trying to imagine the gentle woman in front of her arguing a case before an austere judge. "And I just don't know what to think, especially since the two of you are twins."

"I didn't necessarily set off to become a lawyer the way Kate did to become a doctor. I just wanted to be able to help people—particularly women who find themselves in difficult situations. I was already in Boston with Kate while she went to medical school, so I decided to study law." Evelina said it so flippantly, as though a woman lawyer was about as common as a female seamstress or teacher or secretary.

"Lina writes all the contracts for the trading company and shipyard." Kate took another bite of cake. "Having a lawyer in the family has proved to be quite helpful."

"I imagine so," Maggie muttered. "Probably much like having a doctor in the family."

The corner of Kate's mouth tipped up into a half smile. Maybe the woman could be soft—just not when someone was questioning her medical skills.

"What about you?" Kate asked. "Yuri said you're from Milwaukee? What do you do there?"

She looked down at the table and shrugged. "Not much, really. I keep the books for our family's shipyard."

"A bookkeeper?" Evelina set her teacup down with a small clatter. "We could use a bookkeeper for the trading company. Our books are always a mess, no matter how hard we try to keep them straight. Yuri's right. You really do need to marry one of our brothers."

Maggie's face turned hot. What was it with the Amos family always trying to marry their siblings off? Never had she met a group of people so concerned about matchmaking. "I'm afraid I need to go back to Milwaukee with Tavish, or we'll lose our family home and the shipyard my father started."

"You'll lose it? You mean legally?" Evelina frowned. "The lawyer in me is trying to understand just how that will happen."

"We have forty acres of land on Lake Michigan, and it's the prettiest land in all of the Midwest, with endless sand and waving beach grass. There's nowhere else quite like it. Our family home and the shipyard are on the land too. Pa died eight years ago, then Ma remarried, and Tavish left shortly afterward. He didn't get along all that well with our new step-father. But the land and shipyard never belonged to Hamish. It belonged to Ma, and after she passed, to Tavish. But after Ma and Hamish died four months ago, Pa's brother Uncle Ewan claimed he should inherit everything. That it shouldn't go to Tavish, since he's been gone for seven years, and we have no proof he's still alive."

"Don't fret yourself." Evelina reached across the table and patted her hand. "I was just trying to understand why you need to find Tavish so badly."

"Does it make sense to you, as a lawyer?" She swallowed the sudden tightness in her throat. "Uncle Ewan went to a judge and claimed that unless we can prove Tavish is still alive, he should inherit everything. And the judge agreed."

"It makes sense, yes." The skin between Evelina's eyebrows furrowed. "But I'm wondering, is there some kind of document that passes the shipyard to your uncle in the event of Tavish's death?"

Maggie nodded. "It was in the contract back when Pa first bought the land and started the shipyard. Uncle Ewan cosigned the loan, even though the land and company were in Pa's name. The contract said that should Pa die before the loan was paid off, the company would go to Uncle Ewan. It also said that should Pa, Ma, and any sons they might have die without heirs, the company would go to Uncle Ewan regardless of whether the loan had been repaid."

She stared into her tea. "That's what happened. Pa repaid the loan before he died, so the shipyard went to Ma, and after Ma, to Tavish as his heir. But now Ma is dead, and Finnan is Hamish's heir, not Pa's. And Tavish has been gone seven years . . ." This time she couldn't quite manage to swallow the lump that had reformed in her throat.

"I see." Evelina straightened her shoulders. "And I see now why a judge would want Tavish to present himself. I know this isn't the legal proof the judge is after, but I can assure you that your brother is alive and well. He's doing an excellent job captaining the *Halcyon* too. Kate and I both saw him when he was in Juneau a couple weeks ago."

"Thank you." Maggie blew out a breath. "Even if he didn't have to appear back in Milwaukee for the judge, he'd still need to come home. I don't see how the shipyard can run without him, and Uncle Ewan doesn't want to work for me or Tavish. He wants to own it."

"Maybe Tavish could keep most of the land but sell the shipyard to your uncle," Kate said, her voice brisk and practical.

Maggie snapped upright, her hands clenching into fists on her lap. "No. Tavish wouldn't do that. Pa worked too hard for it. He started the shipyard as soon as he came over from Scotland and scraped together a bit of money. That shipyard was always his dream."

"But is it Tavish's dream?" Kate looked at her. "He's an excellent sailor and a good captain. Maybe he wants to be on the water."

"No. He has to come back. He has to work in the shipyard. It's our family's legacy. Surely he won't let that crumble." Tears blurred her eyes. She simply couldn't imagine any other outcome than Tavish returning to Milwaukee to run the shipyard.

"You'll find out once you get to Unalaska," Kate said.

"There, there, don't cry." The chair across the table creaked, and suddenly Evelina was by her side, wrapping her in a warm hug. "I'm sure God will guide you through whatever happens next. And if nothing else, Tavish will be thrilled to see you. My goodness, I can't imagine Sacha or Mikhail being gone for seven years. What a reunion the two of you will have."

Maggie sniffled and nodded. "I'm sorry. I don't know why talking about this has made me so emotional."

"Because it's your family's legacy," Kate said matter-of-factly. "I'd be emotional, too, if our house and shipyard and trading company were at risk, and I was the only person who could keep them in the family."

She tried to smile, though it was hard to imagine the stiff, efficient woman beside her being emotional. "Thank you."

"Here, you've barely touched this piece of cake." Kate prodded the plate closer. "Eat some. Cake always makes things better."

She couldn't help but smile through her tears. Did cake have a way of making things better? There was only one way to find out. She picked up her fork and dug into the layers of custard and flaky pastry. "It truly is delicious. I think this is one of the best cakes I've ever had."

"Like I said, we all love it when Lina gets worked up." Kate sent her sister a smile, then dug her fork back into her own cake. "She's making teacakes too."

"Oh, the teacakes!" Evelina jumped up from the table. "I nearly forgot."

Maggie took another sip of tea, her eyes drifting to the fancy etched copper inlay on the porcelain cup.

"It's beautiful, isn't it?" Kate said from beside her. "The tea service and samovar were our great-great grandmother's, and I miss having them each time I go back to Juneau."

"I'd miss them too." They were so exquisite she almost wished she had a fancy tea service that had been passed down several generations.

"Our great-grandmother was the governor's daughter here on Sitka, but she married our great-grandfather, who was actually an American shipbuilder from Maine. That's why we have the last name Amos and not a Russian—"

"Lina, Lina!" Ilya raced into the room, his cheeks flushed and chest heaving as he waved a copy of a newspaper in his hand. "Look what the paper printed today! It's says you're a—"

"Ilya!" A masculine voice boomed from the front of the house. "Where'd you go? So help me, if you showed that paper to your sister . . ." A large man with red hair and a short beard rushed into the room, his eyes narrowing on Evelina, who was scanning the paper Ilya had just handed her.

The man hurried around the table in three giant steps and swiped it from her.

"I was reading that." Evelina scowled and tried to reach around him.

But the man's arms were too long, and he easily held the paper away while moving his body into hers, blocking her from stepping closer to the paper.

"No need to read it, love," he drawled in a tender voice that hinted of the South. "It doesn't say anything useful. I promise."

"But . . ."

The man ducked his head and planted a kiss on Evelina's cheek.

The gesture was so sweet, warmth bloomed in Maggie's chest.

"Stop it, Jonas," Kate muttered. "We have a visitor."

"You expect that to stop me from kissing my wife?" The man—Jonas, apparently—didn't even glance at Kate, just ducked his head again, this time finding Evelina's lips and giving her a slow kiss.

The man was obviously smitten. Maggie couldn't make herself look away from the tender way Jonas held his wife, from the soft way his lips moved over Evelina's. It was almost enough to make Maggie wish she'd accepted Benny Fullsom's proposal back in Wisconsin. Though he'd never looked at her as softly as Jonas did Evelina, and she didn't recall him ever tucking a strand of hair behind her ear quite so tenderly.

"Jonas," Kate snapped, then sent Maggie a look. "I'm sorry. I wish I could tell you they weren't always like this, but they are."

"I think it's sweet."

Kate humphed. "You only say that because you don't have to live with it. Drives the rest of us crazy."

Evelina broke the kiss and leaned back from her husband, her eyes trapped in his for a few moments, almost as though she'd forgotten where she was or that she had an audience. Then her cheeks turned pink, and she glanced over at the table. "Jonas. You can't just kiss me like that whenever you please. How many times do I have to tell you?"

"And how many times do I have to tell you that if you don't want me to kiss you so much, then you need to stop being so beautiful." He tucked another strand of hair behind Evelina's ear, letting his fingers linger there a few seconds longer than necessary.

Evelina shook her head, her gaze landing on the paper her husband now held at his side. "Will you at least tell me what the paper printed?"

"No, love. Just argue your case tomorrow. No worrying about what anyone else says." Jonas turned to Ilya, who had evidently helped himself to a large slice of cake while Jonas and Evelina had been kissing. "No papers for your sister while we're here. Do you understand?"

"But she asked me to fetch it," he said around a mouthful of cake.

"Did she?" Jonas turned back to his wife, his eyebrow quirked. "I thought we talked about this after what the paper printed yesterday."

Evelina huffed out a breath, then turned and grabbed a bowl and a brown sack from the hutch. "I just want to know what they're saying."

"Why? Is what the paper says going to change what's right? Is it going to change the fact that Kaaguneteen needs her son back in Juneau with her? That Gushklin needs his older brother at home? That the director of the boarding school has no business claiming his right to educate a child should trump the rights of the child's parent?"

"No, but . . ."

"But nothing." Jonas opened the firebox on the stove and stuffed the newspaper inside. "Reading the paper is only going to get you worked up, and you can't let someone else's opinion stop you from doing what's right."

"I was just telling Alexei the same thing," Sacha said as he entered the kitchen. "If you know what's right, then you do it. Other people's opinions be hanged." He sent a dark look over his shoulder toward Alexei, who had stopped in the doorway to the kitchen.

Alexei glared right back at this brother. "It's not that simple with the seals."

"Tell me about this court case, Lina." Sacha walked around the table and held his arms out for his sister. "I heard you were brilliant today."

Evelina sighed, her shoulders slumping. "I thought it went well too, but evidently the paper disagrees."

Sacha nearly swallowed Evelina when he wrapped his arms around her. Maggie wouldn't call Evelina or Kate small, but all of the Amos men were bigger than their sisters, and Sacha was the biggest. His chest was almost twice as broad as Alexei's, and when he hugged Evelina, all but her neck and head disappeared.

Maggie took a sip of tea. Maybe Kate had a point, and all this hugging was a bit much. Because now she was wondering how it would feel to have Sacha's arms wrapped around her too. To stand in the embrace of such a strong man.

Safe. She'd probably feel safe.

Like maybe the weight of the entire world wasn't on her shoulders.

Like maybe, just maybe, there was someone who could help her bear it.

She swallowed. Where had that thought come from? She couldn't think about hugging Sacha Amos.

But perhaps she could think about hugging Tavish. He was sure to hug her after she finally found him. And then he'd return to Wisconsin and take over the family shipyard and everything would be right in the world.

So as she sat there watching Sacha hug Evelina, followed by Kate, why could she only manage to think of how Sacha's arms would feel around her, rather than her brother's?

16

Alexei found his brother standing on the quarterdeck, his arms folded on the railing in front of him as he stared out at the sound. A few of the crew were on board, beginning the preparations needed for them to leave again in an hour or so, but most of the crew and passengers hadn't boarded yet.

He couldn't blame Sacha for choosing this spot to stand. It offered a beautiful view of the sound, with mountains rimming the turquoise water. As much as he'd traveled and seen the world, this view constantly pulled him back to Sitka, to the place where he'd been raised, and his father before that, and his grandfather before that. He couldn't imagine himself ever leaving, not permanently.

Sacha didn't turn to face him as he approached. If anything, his shoulders stiffened. Alexei couldn't exactly blame him. It had been a while since they'd gotten into such a big argument.

"I got you the two weeks you requested for the Pribilof study, plus the time you need to return to Sitka." He rested three papers on the ledge of the railing.

Sacha looked down at them. "You reworked the shipping schedule?"

"Yes. If we postpone the *Halcyon*'s trip from the Yukon to Petropavlovsk-Kamchatsky and have it pick up your canning routes, we can make this work. Then the *Halcyon* can bring the salmon down to Bellingham, where it can also drop off the McDougals. I'll have you stop by the Saint Michael trading post on the mouth of the Yukon on your way up to Barrow later this summer. And then on your way south, you can cross the Bering and do a supply run to Petropavlovsk-Kamchatsky."

Sacha stared at the paper for a long time, far too long for him to just be noting the changes. Then his Adam's apple bobbed. "Thank you."

"Next time, try to give me more notice. I understand there might be times when you want to make extra runs or unusual stops with the *Aurora*, but this is our busiest time of year, and with the cannery contracts and you already running late and . . ." He stopped talking. His brother already knew all of this, and there was no use repeating it.

"You're right. I should have told you sooner."

"I can't blame you for waiting as long as possible, not after how I responded earlier."

"And I can't fault you for being concerned about Caldwell." The air hung heavy between them, and Sacha pulled his gaze back to the sea, where a whale surfaced, then dove under the water. "The man has a dark streak in him that I don't trust. And he thinks he's above the law."

"He's from that class in Washington that *is* above the law—at least in the ways that count most."

Sacha didn't say anything, probably because he agreed. Or maybe he was thinking of the last time they'd had to deal with someone from a family that was above the law—Ivan's killer.

But Alexei wasn't going to stand here and think about things that couldn't be changed, so he tilted his head toward the deck, where the rest of Sacha's crew had just climbed aboard. "Tell me, what do your men think about the study, about going to the Pribilofs?"

Sacha winced. "They don't know."

"How can they not? It's impossible to miss the man on the bow of the ship watching whales and recording furiously in his journal." The scientist had spent a good part of the afternoon in that one spot, though he'd gone into town for a bit as well.

"They think he's studying all sea mammals. Whales, seals, even otters."

That was one way to hide the study, at least for the moment. "So what will they think once you set your course for the Pribilofs? It's not like that's a typical stop for a ship to make."

"I'm not planning to tell them until after we leave Unalaska."

"You're not?"

"The more people who know, the easier it will be for Caldwell to find out. And while I hope he'll support me going after the poachers, I don't exactly want him to know what I'm doing."

"So you do fear him, at least on some level. I was beginning to wonder."

"How could I not after what happened to Ilya last year? But sometimes a man just has to do the right thing." Sacha shoved a hand toward Dr. Torres. "And this is right, Alexei. You won't be able to convince me otherwise."

"I know. Why do you think I spent the past two hours redoing the shipping schedule?"

Sacha's gaze turned somber, his eyes losing a bit of their

usual warmth. "If this does come back to hurt us, or if anyone gives you trouble, put the full blame on me."

Alexei gave his head a firm shake. "Never. We're Amoses. We'll face this as a family."

Sacha's shoulders rose and fell on a large sigh. But he didn't attempt to argue, just stood there in silence, staring out at the sea as though if he watched the water long enough, it just might help him save the seals.

At the very least, Alexei hoped it would help him figure out how to tell his crew where they were headed and why.

THE BOY still was in the corner of the wheelhouse.

Before leaving port, Finnan had climbed onto the chair in the corner with his blanket and looked outside. Normally Sacha would have kicked him out, especially with them raising the sails and navigating away from the wharf and across the sound. But Finnan had been so quiet, just peacefully watching as the ship slid away from its moorings and headed toward the great expanse of sea known as the Gulf of Alaska.

At some point during the past hour, the boy had curled himself into a ball on the chair, and now he was soundly sleeping. Ilya and Inessa must have tuckered the child clear out earlier.

Sacha glanced around. Ronnie was at the helm, easily guiding the ship on a course that would have them reaching Unalaska in two days' time. But he saw no sign of Maggie or Ainsley. Were they assisting Dr. Torres? Did they assume Finnan was sleeping in their cabin?

He rubbed the side of his jaw. He couldn't bear to leave the little guy on the cramped chair. He'd wake up with a crick in his neck for certain.

. . .

So he walked to the back of the wheelhouse and scooped Finnan up in his arms. He half expected the boy to wake, but he curled himself naturally against Sacha's chest, as though somehow finding the fabric of his shirt comforting.

Ilya had been this small once, young enough not to stir when someone picked him up, young enough to curl into the warm chest of whoever held him.

But he didn't ever recall holding his youngest brother the way he now held Finnan. Because he'd had to captain the *Alliance* immediately after his father died. He'd never thought of himself as a homebody before that. He'd always enjoyed sailing, but he'd also enjoyed sitting around the table with a cup of tea and a plate filled with whatever Evelina had baked that afternoon.

But in the span of one night, his comfortable home life had been stripped away.

And now . . . Ilya might hug him, yes, but his youngest brother was closer to Evelina's husband, Jonas, than he was to Sacha.

Oh, hang it all. Ilya was closer to everyone than he was to him. Because he was never home.

"You all right there, Cap'n?" Ronnie asked from behind the wheel. "You can take 'em to his cabin. I got the helm."

Of course he did. Ronnie was more than capable, and Baranof Island, where Sitka was located, had faded into the distance.

"I was just lost in my thoughts for a moment." Sacha repositioned Finnan in his arms, the boy curling closer to his chest, then left the wheelhouse and headed toward Maggie's cabin.

He rapped on the cabin door, then moved to open it, assuming Maggie and Ainsley were with Dr. Torres.

But the door opened before he could turn the knob, revealing a worried-looking Maggie. "Sacha, have you seen...?"

Her gaze fell to Finnan. "Oh, dear, was he bothering you? I'm so sorry. Dr. Torres wanted help with his records as we were leaving Sitka, and I thought Finnan was in here with Ainsley. I only just discovered he was missing."

How to explain that he'd liked having the child in the wheelhouse? That he liked holding him? He didn't have the words, so he simply settled for "He wasn't a bother."

Maggie reached for Finnan, but Sacha found himself tightening his grip on the boy. "Easier to just let me lay him down. Less chance of him waking."

"Oh, of course." She pulled the door farther open, then stepped aside to let him enter.

"Captain Amos," a stern voice said from behind him.

He turned to find Dr. Torres standing behind him.

"I need to speak with you."

Sacha frowned. Had something gone awry with the study already? They hadn't even reached the Pribilofs yet. "Just let me lay Finnan down, then I'm all yours."

He ducked inside the room, setting Finnan gently on the bed and tucking the covers up around his chin. A part of him wanted to crawl into bed next to the child and cradle Finnan's warm body against his chest for a bit longer. But Torres clearly needed to discuss something, and any number of things could have gone wrong in Sitka, which was one reason why they hadn't stayed the night, as much as he would have loved to spend more time with his family.

He took one last look at Finnan, then dipped his head toward Maggie and Ainsley and headed for the door. "Let's discuss this in the captain's cabin."

Dr. Torres followed him without so much as a word, the sound of his boots sharp as they clacked against the deck.

No sooner had they reached the other cabin than Dr. Torres moved to his desk, opened a drawer, and then gave a small shake of his head as he pulled out a few sheets of paper. "Margaret does an excellent job recording and organizing notes. It would have taken me ten minutes to find these before."

Margaret? Since when had Dr. Torres started calling her Margaret?

And did that mean she was calling the scientist by his first name too?

"She doesn't like timing the whales, but she has excellent clerical skills. In fact, I've switched to having her record notes while I time the whales."

The scientist released a soft chuckle, and a small smile tilted the corners of his mouth. It was almost as though the other man was pulling up an image of Maggie in his mind. Would she be standing at the railing, with the wind ruffling her loose hair? Or holding a clipboard with her hair pinned up and her slender neck bent over the notes she took.

Sacha made a noise in the back of his throat. It was probably a groan, but hopefully the scientist thought it was a hum. Why had Dr. Torres called him here? Surely not to sing Maggie's praises.

As though sensing his thoughts, Dr. Torres stepped closer and handed him the papers he'd retrieved from the desk. "These are the results from the study that I've been able to compile so far. It's certainly not comprehensive, as the largest portion of the research can't be conducted until we reach the Pribilofs, but I've been able to extrapolate more information than I thought, just from seeing the effects of the poaching. While we were in port, I sent a letter with these results to the two senators I've been working with in Washington, DC, but I wanted you to be aware of how the study is progressing as well."

Sacha scanned the pages, then flipped to the third page and read the final paragraph:

If poaching alone continues at the current rate—with or without the quotas being adjusted on the Pribilofs—I estimate the great northern fur seal will become extinct in fifteen to twenty years. I will be able to confirm these estimates more conclusively in another month and will share the study in full with you both once I return to Washington.

A chill swept through him. He'd guessed as much, but seeing the words written so plainly—and at the hand of a professional who knew how to calculate such things—caused a heavy sensation to fill his chest. "Do you think the senators will take action? Do you think, at the very least, this study will be enough to make the government enforce its current policies on poaching?"

"I'm hopeful that it will do more than encourage the government to enforce current policies. I'm hopeful that it will also result in quotas being lowered on the Pribilofs, even though I know that's never been your main goal. If the poaching is curtailed but the quotas aren't lowered . . ." The scientist shook his head. "I need to go to the Pribilofs to know for certain, but I fear the seals might still go extinct."

Sacha pressed his eyes shut. Had they been conducting this study a year ago, he would have said great, that he'd do whatever it took to get both the poaching stopped and legal hunting further restricted. But not after the conversation he'd just had with Alexei.

Not after what happened to Ilya last fall.

How could he support something that would make a bigger enemy of Caldwell?

"Also, it would have been helpful to know that a Caldwell is living in Sitka before I arrived," the scientist added.

He jerked his gaze back to Dr. Torres. "Why? What happened? Did he approach you? Did he threaten you in some way?"

"No, he didn't threaten me, but he did recognize me and ask what brought me to Sitka."

A bead of sweat trickled between his shoulder blades, never mind that it was far too cool for him to be sweating. "I didn't realize you knew him."

"Vaguely. We've met at a handful of events in Washington. As I said before, his family is quite influential."

"What reason did you give him for being in Sitka?"

"I told him I was conducting preliminary research on the Pacific humpback whale in preparation for a larger study I'll be undertaking over the winter in Australia and here next summer."

"Did he believe it?" Now the bead of sweat started to itch, and it wasn't in a place he could reach.

"Caldwell didn't like that I was traveling on your ship." Torres tapped his chin. "He grew rather suspicious when he learned that. Much more suspicious than he would have had I been traveling on a different ship, I think."

"Last fall, I reported one of his ships for poaching a few seals. I expected pelts from a handful of the poached seals would be seized, but the judge ordered all the pelts seized, even though nearly all of them came from the Pribilofs. Things have been strained between us ever since."

Torres let out a low whistle. "His pocketbook is probably still hurting after losing a whole shipload of pelts."

"Caldwell responded by having my youngest brother kidnapped."

The scientist's face blanched. "What? Because you

reported one of his ships for breaking the law, and he didn't like how the judge ruled?"

"Caldwell told one of his henchmen to make my family pay, and that was the man's way of exacting revenge."

Dr. Torres sank onto the bed. "I . . . I had no idea. Is your brother all right?"

Sacha released a dark chuckle. "He's fine. Probably better than me, in fact. Because he doesn't go to bed every night knowing that his actions almost got someone he loves killed."

"Tell me the ruffian who kidnapped him is in prison for the rest of his life."

"One of them is. But do you think anyone in the Caldwell family paid for what happened?"

Torres pressed his lips into a flat line. "Is it terrible of me to hope the next ship Preston Caldwell boards sinks to the bottom of the sea?"

"I've found myself hoping for the same thing a time or two." Sacha shoved a hand through his hair and turned from the window, only to find Maggie standing in the doorway, her face white.

"Maggie," he rasped. How long had she been there? Had she knocked before opening the door?

"There's a man who would do that?" Maggie whispered, her throat working. "Someone who would kidnap Ilya to get back at you for doing the right thing? Is this the same person who's trying to steal your cannery contracts and bankrupt your family?"

He winced. "Did Evelina tell you about that?"

"Caldwell's trying to bankrupt you as well?" Torres asked.

He sighed, then quickly gave Dr. Torres the details on the arm of the shipping company Caldwell had started with the sole intention of taking their contracts.

"I just don't understand." Maggie raised her chin, her eyes

flashing seafoam fire. "It seems horrible that a man would go to such lengths, and all because you want to stop poaching, which is already illegal!"

"Kings have gone to war for less money than what those seals are worth." He jutted a hand toward where Dr. Torres's preliminary findings rested on the desk.

"That doesn't make it right," Maggie snapped, fierceness still lingering in her eyes.

Sacha scrubbed a hand over his face. "I don't have all the answers. I'm just doing the best I can. And right now, that means facilitating this study." He met Dr. Torres's gaze. "Once you return to Washington, DC, and publish your findings, I don't know what will happen. As I've told you before, I hope Washington focuses on curtailing the poaching, not on lowering the quota on the Pribilofs. Because if that happens..."

He shook his head. Would his family have a dime left to its name? "All I know is that I can't, in good conscience, ignore what I see happening to the seals, or how the native villages are struggling to find food and pelts to survive the winter because the seals are becoming scarcer and scarcer. That's all I can say."

Dr. Torres stepped forward, his brow creased with lines of worry. "If there's anything you need once I'm back in Washington, don't hesitate to send a telegram."

"Thank you," he whispered. "I appreciate it. Now if you'll excuse me, I need to check on my crew."

He turned and left the room, closing the heavy wooden door behind him. But he didn't race down the stairs to the deck or stand at the top of the quarterdeck surveying how his crew was handling the ship. Instead he paused outside the door and looked up at the sky. *Am I doing the right thing, God? Should I be the one trying to save the seals, or should I have left this fight for another man?*

He stared at the sky for another moment, endless against the wide expanse of the ocean, but no answer seemed to come from the heavens. No peace settled over his soul.

All he could do was pray that somehow, miraculously, the research that Dr. Torres and Maggie were doing wouldn't mean his family's ruin.

17

She couldn't sleep. Again. From her position on the bed, Maggie stared out the cabin's single window, watching as the setting sun turned the sky orange, then pink. She didn't know why she was so restless, not after such a long day. But every time she tried to close her eyes, she found herself replaying conversations from earlier in the day. Alexei being upset she was on the *Aurora*. Yuri asking her if she wanted to marry one of his brothers . . . Sacha explaining just how much publishing the study could end up costing his family.

She could still see the tight set to his shoulders as he'd recounted how Ilya had been kidnapped the previous year. Could still hear the tension in his voice as he'd explained why his family was building ships that might be used to kill seals—why they felt they had no choice.

She could hardly believe those conversations had all taken place the same day she'd sat at the table with Kate and Evelina, listening to Kate rattle on about the dangers of corsets and watching Evelina's husband swipe the newspaper from her hand and then tenderly kiss her.

Part of her wanted to be back there now, sitting at the table again, visiting with Sacha's sisters while Ilya and Inessa entertained Ainsley and Finnan.

Would they stop by Sitka again on the way home? If so, would Evelina and Kate still be there?

And what was she doing staring out the window at the sky and thinking of such things? She was headed to Unalaska to find Tavish, and then they'd be returning to Milwaukee. She had no business yearning to return to Sitka. God had clearly laid out his plan for her, and it didn't include staying in Alaska.

She flung the covers back and swung her legs over the edge of the bed. Perhaps she needed some air to clear her mind. Besides, Sacha had said midnight sunsets were the most beautiful from the middle of the ocean, and that's exactly where they were. She may as well get a full view of it.

She dropped her nightgown to the floor and slid into the dress she'd worn earlier that day, forgoing her corset—because she planned to be on deck for a short time, not because of the lecture she'd gotten earlier that day. Then she grabbed her shawl, wrapped it about herself, and headed out the door.

The ship was nearly as empty as it had been two nights ago, when she'd stood on deck with Sacha, watching the sun slip behind the mountains. This time she spotted a man behind the helm and another on the deck, but that was all.

Tonight there were no mountains for the sun to hide behind, and Sacha was right. It was the most beautiful sight she'd ever seen, with the water around them stretching like an endless carpet, reflecting the pink and orange of the sky. From her position on deck, it seemed like she could see to the very end of the world. She didn't wonder why sailors of old had thought the earth was flat, and that they could drop off the edge if they traveled too far. It suddenly seemed a distinct possibility.

"Couldn't sleep?" a deep voice asked from behind her.

She turned to find Sacha.

"My brain won't let me rest, and I remembered you saying that sunset on the ocean is even prettier than it is from land. I wanted to see if you were right."

"Am I?" He took a step nearer, close enough that she could feel the heat from his chest radiate into her back.

"You are. It's breathtaking. I feel so small, and like the world around me is so large. The sheer breadth of it is overwhelming."

"It gives that verse in the Bible about not being plucked out of God's hand a whole new meaning, doesn't it? Makes you realize just how much God's hand can hold."

"I suppose it does. Though I think the sunset would be beautiful from your house in Sitka. It had windows in every direction I looked, always showing off a view of the sound and mountains."

"It's beautiful from there too, yes," Sacha said, his voice seeming to grow richer and deeper as they spoke. Then he gave his head a small shake. "I hope my family wasn't too frightening earlier today. I know we can be a bit much at times, and there're a lot of us."

"Your sister and her husband, Evelina and Jonas, they love each other so very much." She wasn't sure why that was the first thing out of her mouth. Why, of all her impressions of his family, she couldn't seem to hold that bit in.

Sacha chuckled, the sound just as rich as his voice. "Of course. They've not even been married a year. Did you expect something different from newlyweds?"

"I . . ." Had she? "I don't recall my mother and Hamish being nearly that in love, not right after they were married, and certainly not at the end."

"They were a poor match, then?" He moved from behind

her and leaned his arms on the railing, his eyes riveted to her rather than the beauty surrounding them.

"They must have been, though I suppose I was too young to realize it at first."

"Was your mother still in love with your father when they married? Was that what caused the trouble?"

"No. Not that. It was more that my stepfather never loved her the way my father had. Hamish was a captain, and he cared about captaining his ship more than anything else. Maybe she never should have married him for that reason, especially since Hamish believed women didn't belong on a ship. It would have been one thing if he'd wanted her to travel with him, but he hadn't, and they never saw each other. And it was so very different from how it had been before, with my father."

She sighed as she stared out at the ocean. "Pa enjoyed building ships, not sailing, and he loved us all so very much. Looking back on it, I think Hamish just wanted to own the shipyard. His new wife and her children were more of an inconvenience to him than anything. Our kitchen certainly never felt as warm and welcoming as yours did this afternoon with Evelina and Kate there, at least not after Ma married Hamish."

She could have spent days sitting in that kitchen. It didn't matter that the room had grown loud when Yuri, Inessa, Finnan, and Ainsley had all returned. Or that the entire Amos family had crowded around the table and eaten the rest of the napoleon cake, plus half of Evelina's teacakes. Even with everyone fighting for a chance to have their say, the scene had never felt chaotic, only warm and welcoming.

"I wish you would have let us stay a few hours longer," she whispered, more to the wind than to Sacha.

But he must have heard her, because he took a step closer to her along the railing, causing his shoulder to brush against her coat.

"I wish we could have stayed longer too." His voice sounded a bit wistful.

"Though to be fair, Alexei's not the only one who could smile more. You and Kate could both take a few lessons in that as well."

Again, a chuckle rumbled from his chest. "Why is everyone so obsessed with smiling?"

"Because it means you're happy."

The words stretched between them, filling the space as the sun sank lower in the sky, its hue changing from light orange to deep pink. She nearly asked if he was happy. But of course he was. He had his own ship—a beautiful one. He loved sailing. What could he possibly be unhappy about?

"What about you?" His words were soft on the wind. "You don't smile all that often either. Are you happy?"

"I will be, once I find Tavish and we return to Milwaukee."

"So you're happy in Milwaukee? There's no other place you'd rather be? Nothing else you'd rather do?"

"I . . ." How did she answer such a question? She'd already given Sacha the obvious answer when she'd said she wanted to find Tavish. After all, it was the thing she'd spent the past four months thinking about. "Milwaukee is the only life I know."

"Yes, but is it a life that makes you happy? Because you seem pretty happy here, sailing on the *Aurora* and stopping at the various ports, and having tea with my family."

Maybe she was happy here in Alaska, but Alaska wasn't her family's legacy, her father's dream. Alaska didn't have the house overlooking the water that her father had built with his own two hands. Her mother had begged him for that house on the beach. It afforded the most beautiful views of the sunrise. She could see herself sitting on the porch even now, rocking in a chair while sipping her coffee and watching the sun rise over the calm waters of Lake Michigan.

Eventually Tavish would marry and want the house for himself, but she'd marry too, and there was room enough on the property to add a second house. Their father had purchased a large stretch of waterfront property, right on the edge of Milwaukee. The shipyard was close enough to do business in the city, but far enough out that their house and everything but the little slice of land with the shipyard felt private and secluded.

It was the only home she'd ever known—the only home Ainsley and Finnan had known too. And she still recalled the promise she'd made to her mother, that she'd care for Ainsley and Finnan if anything ever happened to her.

How could she care for them anywhere other than in Milwaukee?

But Alaska was mesmerizing. She couldn't deny that. This place had a beauty that sucked the breath from her lungs. And the Amos family was wonderful. Not just Sacha, but all of them.

And all of that suddenly made her wonder if she could be happy in Sitka too, staying the night in the giant white house by the harbor, watching Evelina go to court in the morning, and smiling as Ilya teased Finnan and Ainsley.

What was causing her to think such things? God wouldn't want her to turn her back on both her promise and her family's legacy so she could run off to Alaska.

So why did this place have such a strong tug on her? And why, the longer she was there, did it become harder and harder to imagine herself leaving?

Chapter 17

MAGGIE MCDOUGAL HAD no idea how lovely she was. Sacha ran his gaze down her, with her face turned toward the dying sun and her shoulders relaxed and her hair blowing in the wind.

"You should really leave this up." He reached out and touched a tendril of her hair.

It was a mistake, because her hair was even softer than it looked, its silky strands slipping easily through his fingers.

"I wanted to feel the wind in my hair. There's nothing quite like it."

He dropped her hair and swallowed. This woman was going to be the death of him. She was too perfect. If only she wasn't so determined to leave Alaska. "That's one of the things I love most about being at sea, the feel of the wind in my hair, the sway of the boat beneath my boots. The sight of nothing but water surrounding us."

"Do you ever get scared that something might happen?" She turned to him, those wide seafoam eyes seeking his. "I mean, we're so small, and the sea is so vast. Doesn't it ever frighten you?"

Sacha settled his hand over hers on the railing, letting the warmth of her hand seep into his palm. "'Fear thou not, for I am with thee: be not dismayed, for I am thy God; I will strengthen thee; yea, I will help thee; yea, I will uphold thee with the right hand of my righteousness.'"

She was quiet, her face still turned toward the sun for so long he began to wonder if she'd heard him. Then she finally said, "I shall miss this, when I return to Wisconsin."

"What? The midnight sun? Or the sea? A combination of both? I'm told the Great Lakes are just as vast as an ocean."

"They're not quite as big as this. Most of the time you can see land, or if you can't, it's only for half a day at a time. But out here, we're nearly swallowed by water. How many days will we have of this?"

"Of the open sea? Two. We'll arrive in Unalaska on the third day."

"And then after the *Halcyon* arrives, it will take another two days to go from Unalaska to Sitka on the way back to Bellingham?"

"Ah, actually you won't be stopping by Sitka on the way back. Alexei rearranged some things with the shipping schedule, and with Captain Jones's leg healed, we'll transfer cargo in Unalaska, and Captain Jones will stop by the canneries and then take you back to Bellingham. With fewer stops, the trip should take five days, and once you're in Bellingham, Tavish will be able to leave the ship."

"Does that mean we're parting ways in Unalaska?" She looked up at him, her eyes sincere in the dying light.

"It does. I need to take Dr. Torres to the Pribilof Islands, and Alexei is rerouting a different ship, the *Alliance*, to travel to Russia while the *Halcyon* takes over the *Alliance*'s route that runs from Los Angeles up through Juneau."

"That sounds like a lot of rearranging. Please tell me it's not all because of me."

"Not all of it, no. Things already needed to be rearranged to go to the Pribilofs. But even if all the changes were for you, it's the least we could do. Tavish has served our family well over the years, and the two of you need to get back to Wisconsin as quickly as possible."

"Did we pick up Captain Jones in Sitka?" A furrow formed between her brows. "Is he aboard now?"

"He is, yes."

"Is he sleeping with the crew?"

His hand reached out to squeeze her shoulder. "You worry too much. There's not a one of us who started out sleeping in a captain's cabin. We can all survive a week of cramped quarters."

"At least you'll only be stuck with me for two more days." She shivered with a sudden gust of wind, then tucked her arms around herself, the breeze toying with the free ends of her hair. "I suppose it must seem more tolerable for you now that the end is in sight."

No part of you leaving seems tolerable. He opened his mouth to speak the words, then stopped.

Since when was he thinking that? The truth was, having Maggie and her siblings aboard ship was a bit inconvenient. So why didn't he mind losing the first mate's cabin or having the cook make extra food? What had propelled him to come to her again, while she stood at the ship's rail?

"Tell me about your brother," he rasped, searching for something, anything to distract him from the direction his thoughts were headed.

"My brother?" Maggie's shoulders rose and fell in a dainty motion. "You can probably tell me more about him than I can. I already said I was only thirteen when he left, and while I have some memories of him, I'm sure you have more."

Thirteen. He still couldn't imagine it. Or rather, he couldn't imagine being Tavish and having been away from his family for that long. It felt like he barely got to see his family now.

In one way, he knew that Tavish had been gone that long, because the man had been sailing for him for six years. But to think that meant Maggie had been thirteen the last time she'd seen her brother . . .

Why, she'd have been three years younger than Inessa. And she would have looked nothing like the lovely woman who now stood by his side.

"Were you and your brother close?" he asked. For all the

times they'd discussed his family, they never seemed to talk much of hers.

Maggie shrugged. "Not particularly. He grew surly after our father died, always arguing with Ma and Uncle Ewan about how the shipyard should be run. He wasn't pleased when Ma got remarried—and neither was Uncle Ewan. Neither of them thought Hamish would know what to do with the business. But while Uncle Ewan stepped back and let Hamish make the changes he wanted, Tavish was determined to fight everything Hamish did. But Hamish was stubborn, and Tavish eventually left to find work in California."

"I'm sorry."

She gave her head a small shake. "It's not your fault."

"No, but I'm still sorry your family was torn apart, first after your father died and then after your brother left." He supposed that was something he could be thankful for, something that hadn't occurred to him before. He might have lost three family members on the same night, but that had only caused him and his siblings to cling tighter to each other.

At least until he'd needed to leave Sitka and captain the *Alliance*.

"Uncle Ewan and Tavish were right, though." Maggie leaned her elbows on the railing, her eyes distant with memories. "Hamish wasn't very good at managing the shipyard. Pa wanted to move into making larger iron-hulled vessels, and so did Tavish and Uncle Ewan. But Hamish saw no need for that. Said we should just focus on small fishing boats, that expanding would cost too much money."

Sacha grunted. Sounded like this Hamish fellow had no business running a shipyard. "And how did that work out?"

She shrugged. "Even those large iron ships need lifeboats. That's mainly what we make now, that and small fishing boats. Nothing meant to stay out overnight."

"Alexei would cut off one of his hands if it meant we could move into manufacturing iron-hulled ships. That's the way the industry is going."

"Really?" She turned to him. "So why don't you?"

"How would we get iron to Sitka?"

"I suppose you'd need to open up another shipyard, maybe in Bellingham or Seattle or even San Francisco."

"That was the plan before my parents died. Now there'd be no one to run a second shipyard. Every one of us is needed in Alaska."

"It seems death has a way of doing that," she whispered. "Of ripping your plans from you and forcing your life down a different path than you imagined."

He had a sudden desire to wrap his arms around her and tell her everything would be all right, that wherever she ended up in ten years, it would be better than anything she could imagine right now.

But he didn't know that for certain. He couldn't even say the same of his own life in the ten years since his parents had died.

And he'd be saying good-bye to Maggie in two more days. So he kept his arms by his side instead of wrapping them around her. Instead of turning her to face him. Or lowering his mouth to taste her lips with his own.

After all, he'd only known the woman a handful of days.

So why did the thought of her leaving the *Aurora* suddenly make him feel lonely?

18

Unalaska, Three Days Later

"What do you mean we missed the ship?" The words came out of Maggie in a rush. A moment ago, she'd been in the cabin, busy packing everything while the crew unloaded the cargo. It had been apparent the *Halcyon* wasn't there as they sailed into the harbor, but she hadn't been worried. According to the shipping schedule, the *Halcyon* was supposed to arrive in three days.

And seeing how Dr. Torres had just paid her, she had a bit of money to find someplace to stay until her brother arrived.

Everything had been going as planned—right up until Sacha had come knocking on her cabin door.

Now she stared at him, her throat turning dry and her eyes burning. "You must have misunderstood. The *Halcyon* isn't due to arrive until the beginning of next week, and it's only Friday. We can't have missed it."

"It arrived early," Sacha answered, his hands buried in his pockets and his broad shoulders slumped.

"Does that mean we can't meet Tavish?" Ainsley asked from beside her.

"But . . . How . . ." Maggie licked her lips, not even sure how to voice the thoughts suddenly flying through her head. "When will it return?"

"After it goes to Fort Yukon, and then Petropavlovsk-Kamchatsky." Sacha's voice sounded unnaturally deep as it rumbled out of his chest. Or maybe it was just her. Maybe her ears had stopped working entirely, and she'd heard Sacha wrong when he told her they'd missed the *Halcyon*.

"Where is Fort Yukon? Where is Petra Komsky?"

"Petropavlovsk-Kamchatsky. It's in Russia. But your brother's ship will go to Fort Yukon first and pick up a shipment of fox and beaver pelts for the Russians. That's the original route Alexei gave it. We were going to switch things around and have the *Alliance* travel to Russia while the *Halcyon* returned you to Bellingham, but it's too late for that now."

She pressed her eyes shut, almost afraid to voice the next question, though it had to be asked. "How long will it take the *Halcyon* to return from Russia?"

"Five or six weeks."

Heat seared the backs of her eyes, and she blinked to keep them from filling with tears.

Finnan tugged on her skirt. "No brother?"

"No brother." Sacha crouched down to Finnan's level and held his arms open. The boy went straight to him. "At least not right now."

"Where will we go? Do we need to stay here to wait for the *Halcyon*?" Ainsley twisted her hands in her skirt. "Maggie, do we have enough money to stay here for more than a month?"

"I . . ." She wasn't sure. They had enough money to stay for a week or so, but she hadn't thought much past that.

"Oh, I'm sorry." Sacha pushed to his feet, holding Finnan

in one of his arms. "I must not have been clear about the *Halcyon*'s route earlier. It won't be returning to Unalaska until August, which is far too long for you to wait here. But it will go to Sitka after leaving Russia, then down to Seattle, then to China."

Maggie pressed a hand to her mouth, the urge to let her tears fall nearly irresistible. Why, oh why had she left Bellingham? Why had she thought it a good idea to sail to an island in the middle of the Bering Sea? Why had she—?

"That means you'll be staying aboard the *Aurora*." Sacha gave Finnan's back a little rub. "We'll be returning to Sitka in about three weeks. That gives us a cushion of two, maybe three, weeks in which you'll be in Sitka before the *Halcyon* returns."

"Will you be there too?" Ainsley asked. "In Sitka?"

"No. Sitka will be just a quick stop for me before I head down to Bellingham to drop off Dr. Torres and then pick up Kate in Juneau and head north to Barrow to deliver medical supplies. But you can stay with my family. We'll send to Juneau for Evelina, Ilya, and Inessa, and they can come keep you company."

"Ilya!" Finnan clapped his hands. "I get to see Ilya!"

The smile that spread across her brother's face was so bright, Maggie had to look away from it, because all she wanted to do was cry.

How could God be allowing this to happen to her? What had she done to deserve being stranded on an Alaskan island—whether it be Unalaska or Sitka?

God, why? Did I do something wrong? I don't understand. Why aren't you blessing me?

First her mother and stepfather had died, then her uncle decided to try stealing the land her parents had loved so very much, and now she couldn't find Tavish.

Her entire body seemed to grow cold, and she suddenly couldn't stop herself from shaking.

"Come here, Maggie." Sacha set Finnan down, then opened his arms. A moment later she was engulfed in them.

But they didn't feel strong or warm or comforting like she'd imagined. They only made her want to cry harder.

"SACHA!"

At the sound of his name, Sacha scanned the shoreline. He, Ainsley, and Finnan were all sitting in a dinghy in the middle of Dutch Harbor, with the town of Unalaska on one side, the Aleut village on the other, and rugged, grass-covered mountains rising from the sea.

Sure enough, a group from the Aleut village had already gathered on the shore, never mind that he still had ten minutes of rowing before he'd reach the village. Though he couldn't pick out Kuluk from so far away, he knew the man would be there. The village had likely recognized the *Aurora* the second it sailed into the harbor.

"Are those Indians?" Finnan asked, his eyes wide as he looked from the group gathered on the shore to Sacha and back again.

The corners of Sacha's mouth twitched up. He couldn't help it. It had been apparent that Maggie needed time to herself after learning they'd missed the *Halcyon*. So he'd offered to take Ainsley and Finnan with him when they delivered cargo to the Aleut village.

"Just who did you think you'd be meeting when you said you wanted to come to the Aleut village?" he asked.

"Not real Indians."

"Oh, you're definitely about to meet real Indians. The man standing in the center of the crowd is Ilya's grandfather." He was close enough now that he could make out Kuluk's proud stance, the extra beading on his parka that indicated his position as an elder.

"Ilya's grandfather lives here?" The boy's eyes grew even larger.

"He does. After my mother died, my father took the daughter of a prominent elder from this village and married her."

"Your pa married an Indian?" This time Ainsley's voice filled with awe, as though the thought would never occur to her.

And it probably hadn't. Mixed-race marriages weren't nearly as common other places as they had been in Russian America. "Does that mean Inessa and Ilya are half Indian?"

"Yes." Sacha dipped the oars in the water. "Didn't you notice how much darker their hair was than yours? Or their skin?"

Ainsley shrugged. "I didn't think about it. None of my friends back home have red hair, so why would I pay attention to someone's hair being a different color than mine?"

Right. If only everyone could look at things that simply. Ainsley and Finnan had seen only similarities with Inessa and Ilya and considered them friends. So why did so many adult Americans look at Inessa and Ilya and see only their differences?

"Why are they dressed so funny?" Finnan stared at the tribe as Sacha heaved the boat closer to shore. "Ilya and Inessa weren't dressed funny."

"The Aleut wear parkas. Think of them as long coats that keep the people who wear them warm and dry. The hoods on the back are for when it rains, and it rains often here, just like it does in Sitka."

"Are they warmer than this coat?" Ainsley pressed the woolen fabric of her coat closed at her throat, but he still noticed a shiver travel up her spine.

"They're much warmer than wool. Why? Would you like one?"

"Can you really get me a warmer coat?" She turned to face him. "I've been freezing ever since we left Bellingham."

Had she? Of course she had. She wouldn't be used to the damp of the ocean or the constant wind. And the farther north they went, the colder it became. Seattle and Bellingham usually stayed around sixty degrees in the summer, Sitka usually stayed around fifty degrees, but Unalaska rarely got above the forties.

The Pribilofs would be even colder.

He should have thought to get warmer clothing for Ainsley and Finnan before now. And for Maggie too. She'd definitely need stouter clothes if she was going to traipse around the Pribilofs recording Dr. Torres's findings.

More and more villagers gathered on the beach as they approached. Sacha gave the oars a final heave, then let the bottom of the boat glide onto the sand covered in an inch or two of water.

"Sacha." Kuluk sloshed out into the water in boots made of skins that would keep his feet dry. "Who have you brought us? And where are my grandchildren?"

The older man spoke in English, but Sacha answered in the Aleut tongue. He'd done enough trading with the tribe over the years that he'd picked up the basics of the language. "This is Finnan and Ainsley. They're traveling with us, and I'm determined to show them every last part of Alaska, your village included."

"We are honored to have you." Kuluk helped Finnan and Ainsley out of the boat, while members from the tribe began unloading the cargo.

Then two of the other dinghies from the *Aurora* slid onto the beach, with more foodstuffs and medicine to be unloaded.

"Come." Kuluk motioned for Sacha to follow him to the shore. "We have much to discuss, starting with my grandchildren."

Sacha sloshed out of the water and gave the man a full report on Ilya and Inessa, then found himself promising he'd bring his two youngest siblings up to Unalaska for a visit before school started in the fall.

By that time, more of his crew had arrived in two other dinghies with supplies for the village. The Aleut men were taking their canoes over to the *Aurora* for the rest of the cargo, and the Aleut women had pulled Ainsley off to the side and were mumbling questions in broken English about the color of her glossy red hair.

He had known they'd be entranced by it. Native women across the whole of Alaska loved the color of Kate's and Evelina's chestnut-colored hair, but they were completely taken by the sight of a blond or redhead.

After a few minutes, Kuluk called to the women to help with the cargo, and the entire village got busy moving goods from the beach to the storehouses. This would be the village's biggest delivery of the year, and Sacha wasn't just delivering blankets and beads; he also had crates full of medical supplies from the Marine Hospital Service. This included everything from bandages to smallpox inoculations to laudanum. He'd bring Kate back with him when he took Ilya and Inessa for their annual visit, just like he'd take her with him up to Nome and Barrow. While all the native tribes had their own healers, it never hurt to have a doctor visit. And the tribes were more accepting of Kate's medical training than most American men.

"How much flour did you bring?" Kuluk asked.

Sacha rubbed the back of his neck, trying to remember just

how many fifty-pound sacks he'd told his men to unload. "Twenty, I believe."

"Good. That will make much bread."

"It will," he agreed.

The Aleut had lived on their own, completely isolated from the world for centuries, until the Russians arrived. And they could stay completely isolated if they wanted to. Sacha certainly didn't blame them for wearing fur parkas rather than wool and gathering dried seaweed and shellfish when the tide was out.

But after nearly two centuries of colonization, the Aleut had incorporated a good number of Russian dishes into their diet, meaning they needed corn and flour, both of which had to be delivered by ship.

And the village always seemed to go through the medicine and medical supplies the Marine Hospital Service sent every year. So much so that this year he'd even included some additional supplies in the delivery.

"We don't need those." Kuluk pointed at the blankets being unloaded from one of the canoes. "We have plenty."

"Plenty of blankets?" Sacha frowned. Since when did the Aleut—or any tribe—have plenty of blankets? They were the most sought-after item a white man could give a tribal member.

"Yes, Alaska Commercial Company paid us in them."

"Alaska Commercial Company..." His words trailed off as the full impact of Kuluk's statement sank in. "Traded you for what? Don't tell me blankets were the payment for the seal pelts you've been hunting all year."

Kuluk's face lit with pride, and his shoulders straightened. "We hunted so many seals that ACC didn't have enough money to pay us for all of them."

Sacha doubted that. Alaska Commercial Company and the Caldwell family had more money than they could possibly spend. It was more a matter of whether ACC felt they could cheat the Aleut out of full payment for their pelts by dangling blankets in front of them. "So they gave you blankets instead of cash money?"

"Yes, six hundred! Enough to supply our tribe for years!"

Sacha's jaw locked so tightly, he could barely force words through his clenched teeth. "And how many seal pelts did you give them?"

"Three thousand!"

He wanted to growl. Or shake his fist at the sky. Or do something, anything, to balance the unfairness of it all. Those blankets had cost ACC fifty cents apiece at most, maybe closer to a quarter. "Wasn't ACC supposed to pay you three dollars a pelt?"

"Two dollars, but the blankets are more valuable."

Two dollars a pelt to the Aleut, plus two dollars a pelt to the government, for a commodity that would sell for ten in Seattle. And all ACC needed to do was transport the pelts to make six dollars in profit. A business contract such as that should be illegal in the first place, but evidently that wasn't enough for the ACC, and they needed to find a way to trick the Aleut into being compensated less than two quarters for each pelt.

"The world trades in money, Kuluk, not blankets." If he'd told that to an elder or chief once, he'd said it a thousand times. "If you want food or supplies, money will be able to get them for you in a way that blankets and pelts can't."

Kuluk shook his head. "We aren't like white men. We don't need things always brought from afar. The sea and the island give us everything we need—except for blankets."

That might be true for a man of Kuluk's age. But for the younger men and women of the tribe? He'd bet a new bride would have trouble cooking for a month straight without cornmeal or flour. And the tribe certainly needed the medical supplies he brought. The sea wouldn't exactly give them smallpox vaccines.

Things would only continue to change as more and more Americans came to Alaska, but Sacha couldn't claim all the changes were bad.

It was the changes the tribes had no choice about that worried him. "If the sea and the island are giving you everything you need, then tell me, how many seals has the sea yielded this spring?"

Kuluk frowned. "Not as many as it used to, but they will return."

"Will they?"

"We will pray to the spirit of the sea, and they will come back. You will see."

The way praying brought back your otter? But Sacha kept his mouth shut. It would take far more than a single conversation to convince the man that an animal species going extinct had more to do with overhunting than whether one of their spirits was happy or displeased.

Just like it would take far more than a single conversation to convince Inessa and Ilya's grandfather that Alaska Commercial Company had cheated his village.

"Do you want us to give you blankets for the medicine and food you brought?" Kuluk asked. "The council met last week to determine a price for the cargo. We are prepared to trade you a hundred blankets."

The council had met before they'd even seen what he'd brought? He sighed. Sometimes he felt as if he was straddling two worlds when it came to the Americans and the native tribes. They both inhabited the land and lived off its bounty, but getting one side to understand the other?

It was as useless as trying to stop the tide from rising.

"Well, should I tell my men to load the blankets?" Kuluk looked around at the supplies being steadily unloaded from the canoes.

"No." Though Alexei would probably throttle him when he learned Sacha had refused payment for the cargo he was delivering. Especially considering Alexei was trying to come up with two hundred more blankets to give to the Tlingit.

But Sacha couldn't bear to take anything from the village, not after they'd been cheated so badly by the ACC.

While the natives had no trouble making clothes of animal hides like deer, bear, and seal, they didn't have access to wool or mills used to spin blankets. Wool blankets were lighter and easier to transport than animal hides, and switching to wool blankets meant that the hides from any animals that were hunted could be used for clothes.

Sacha couldn't claim the blankets held no value, at least not to the natives.

They just held very little value to white men.

Beads were equally precious among the natives. They took days to hand-make out of shells and rocks, and native women used them to decorate ceremonial robes and other articles of clothing.

The tribes didn't understand how easily glass beads were produced in factories, and much like blankets, they would trade things of significant monetary value for a few handfuls of beads. Unfortunately, their love of both beads and blankets had left them open to being cheated by white men too many times, without the tribe ever realizing it.

Sacha heaved in a breath, heavy with the scent of the sea. If only he knew of some way to make the tribes understand.

"I don't need blankets," he said again. "But I do need three parkas, and three pairs of boots—if you have any small enough for Ainsley and Finnan."

"The children need clothing?" Kuluk's face brightened. "Come, come, we will take care of you."

Right. If only he could promise to take care of Kuluk's village in return. Instead, he seemed to be failing at the most basic of things—stopping the entire village from getting swindled.

19

"What do ya mean we're headed to the Pribilof Islands next?" Gus raised his voice over the sound of the wind as the *Aurora* cut across the water, her sails filled.

Sacha scanned his crew. He'd called them to the deck as soon as Unalaska Island had faded from view, though that wasn't quite fast enough to stop the mumblings and whispers that had started the moment he told Ronnie to set a course due north, rather than south toward Sitka like his men had expected.

"I meant exactly what I said. Our next stop will be the Pribilof Islands."

"Why?" Eric leaned against the mast, his eyes fixed on Sacha. "Ya want us to go sealing?"

"No," he snapped, his voice carrying over the deck. "You all know that Dr. Torres has been with us since Bellingham, conducting a study on whales and otters and other marine mammals. He needs to study the seals next, and the Pribilofs are the best place for that."

Sacha caught Dr. Torres's gaze from where the man stood

at the back of the crew. He'd asked the scientist to be present for the meeting, even though he'd told the children they needed to go to their cabin with Maggie.

"But the Pribilofs are in the middle of nowhere," Vasily moaned. "Ain't we at least headed up to Nome and Barrow after that, or are we just goin' to the Pribilofs and then heading south?"

"Just the Pribilofs," Sacha replied. "It's too early in the season to head to Barrow. You know that. We need a few more weeks for the ice that far north to melt."

"So ya want us to go to the Pribilofs and then go down to Bellingham, then turn around and pass right by the Pribilofs on our way to Barrow?" Gus scratched the side of his beard. "All so the scientist can look at seals? Ain't the seals in Unalaska good enough to study? Or the ones in Sitka?"

There weren't any seals in Unalaska or Sitka—or at least not many of them. Hadn't any of the men noticed?

"Once we reach the Pribilofs, I'll be spending most of my days ashore." Dr. Torres weaved his way through the crew. "Miss McDougal is going to help me with my research, but I'm in need of two others to help carry supplies and record my findings. I'll pay a wage on top of your sailing commission. Is anyone interested?"

"I'll do it!" Nikolai volunteered, pushing himself away from the railing.

Sacha wasn't surprised. Nikolai was his youngest sailor and sent half or more of his earnings home to his family in Virginia each time they docked.

"Ya need to go ashore to study the seals?" Now it was his helmsman, Ronnie, who was frowning at Dr. Torres. "Why do ya need to go ashore? Ya been studyin' everything else from the water just fine."

"Wait just a minute. Does this have somethin' ta do with

the poaching last summer? With the ship you reported, Cap'n?" Gus shifted his gaze between Dr. Torres and Sacha. "Is that what this study is supposed ta do? Make it harder fer people to poach seals?"

"Ya want to stop the seal hunts?"

"Is he right?"

"Just why are we goin' to the Pribilofs?"

Questions exploded around him, and Sacha sucked in a breath of salty air. Why did Gus have to go bringing up the ship from last summer?

But then, he should have realized Gus would put things together. His first mate had been a sailor long enough to understand everything about the maritime trade—including the politics of it.

"Dr. Torres will be conducting an assessment of the seal population, not banning hunting," Sacha answered, needing to raise his voice above the wind.

"That's correct." Dr. Torres agreed. "All I'll be doing is taking count of the seals on their summer breeding grounds and comparing it to the study done in 1868."

"But what if the study says there ain't enough seals? Are ya gonna end up sayin' no one should hunt 'em?" Eric pushed himself off the mast, his body rigid. "Just like what happened with the sea otter. You'll say too many seals have been killed, and iffin' we don't stop huntin' them, they'll go extinct."

"I'm not going to say anything." Dr. Torres drew himself to his full height and turned to face Eric, looking every bit like an able-bodied explorer rather than a man who preferred to spend hours hunched over his desk studying numbers. "I'm merely going to conduct the research and see what the results conclude."

The men's eyes held, both the scientist and sailor locked in a silent battle while the air around them grew heavy.

"I don't wanna be on the *Aurora* no more." Eric finally pulled his gaze away from Dr. Torres and narrowed it on Sacha. "I woulda found another ship in Unalaska iffin' I'd known we was goin' to the Pribilofs."

Sacha crossed his arms over his chest. "My goal for the study is to have the government take a stronger stance against poachers. I have no trouble with the male seals being killed on land each summer. But when you add the females being taken at sea to that number, the results—"

"No one would be huntin' them seals at sea if people were allowed to hunt 'em on land," Ronnie answered from behind him, his voice measured. "But the government only lets one company do that. One. How is that fair?"

"Yeah, and they made the price of those huntin' rights so high, a regular man like me could never afford to pay 'em. Even yer family couldn't afford it." Gus shoved a hand in Sacha's direction. "Don't ya think it's unfair ta say only one company—owned by one family—can get the money from all the seal pelts?"

Sacha raked a hand through his hair. Around him, the midday sun glinted off the rolling waves, casting a dance of light across the crew that contrasted with their angry eyes and stormy faces.

"I never claimed any of it was fair or right. If I had any say . . ." He gave his head a shake, trying to imagine just what he would do, how he might change things. But that was if he was allowed to have a voice in the matter. Instead, things were decided by a handful of men in suits who had never stepped foot in Alaska. "We'd be hunting fewer seals, yes, but everyone would have a chance to hunt them. Or at least the bulls, and only on land, so they don't go the way of the otter.

"But I don't have any say," he pressed. "None of us do. And we don't have the power to change the laws either. But we do, through this study, have a chance to make sure the laws that are on the books are enforced. That's not what's been happening. Everyone here saw the pelts drying in Petersburg. There were over five hundred of them, and every single one had been poached. If Dr. Torres returns to Washington with a study that shows the seal population is in trouble, then maybe the Revenue Cutter Service will send more ships to patrol the Bering Sea, and the number of pregnant females being killed will go down. I know that won't fix everything, but it's a place to start. And it should be something we can all agree on."

"But what if them politicians look at the study, and they don't just send more ships fer the poachers?" Ronnie asked, the calm, thoughtful helmsman determined to probe the study from every angle. "What if they ban all the seal huntin'?"

"One unofficial study won't have the power to do that." Dr. Torres's answer was swift and sharp. "It might get more ships sent to the Bering, as your captain said. And it might mean a more thorough, official study gets commissioned in the future. But the United States government makes a lot of money off the seal bounties—too much money to be ignored. It would take years to get sealing stopped entirely. And honestly, I doubt a complete ban would ever be implemented. That's why we're pushing for better management of the regulations already in place."

The men all looked at each other, seeming to understand that the study wasn't meant to be a threat.

Or at least everyone but Eric seemed to understand that. The errant sailor was still glowering at both him and Dr. Torres. "I don't want nothin' ta do with a study that'll change seal hunting. I don't care iffin' it's legal or illegal. Men feed their families with money from them seal pelts."

Sacha stiffened. "They do. But men found ways to feed their families long before we were hunting seals."

"Yeah," Eric shot back. "By huntin' otter."

"And look what happened to 'em." Gus shoved a hand toward Eric. "There ain't none left. Can't fault the cap'n here for wantin' to stop that from happening to the seals."

"I don't want nothin' ta do with it." Eric's hands clenched into fists at his sides. "Other men'll find out I was on the ship responsible for this study, and then—"

"No one will find out, because no one except us knows about the study." Sacha took a step forward, trying to calm Eric, to get him to see reason. The last thing he needed was to drop off an angry sailor who would spread word about the study around the Pribilofs. "And most of you didn't even know until fifteen minutes ago."

"Yer gonna tell me Preston Caldwell won't get word of this?" Eric crossed his arms over his chest, his eyes blazing. "He'll know afore we return to Sitka. And I don't want that man fer an enemy."

Sacha didn't either. He held up his hands in a gesture of innocence. "The study isn't going to hurt his operations. I just want to stop the poaching."

Defiance dripped from Eric's eyes, etched itself into every line on his face and muscle of his tense body. "I don't like this one bit. It'll only bring trouble. Just like havin' that woman and those young'uns aboard caused trouble. Iffin' ya don't want me to get off the ship on Saint Paul Island, you better arrest me and throw me in the brig. Otherwise, I'm leavin' the second we reach harbor." With that, he turned on his heel, his footsteps heavy against the wooden deck.

Sacha watched Eric go. After the trouble with Maggie, he probably should have dropped off the sailor in Sitka or Unalaska. But Eric seemed to settle down after Sacha had spoken to him, and he'd been working dutifully belowdecks, keeping away from Maggie ever since.

"Does anyone else want to get off on Saint Paul Island?" Sacha asked.

"I'll support ya, Cap'n," Ronnie said quietly from behind him. "Seems like we need a new study of the seals, what with all the poachin'."

"I agree," Gus piped up. "The scientist said it's been almost twenty years since a study was done. Seems like time fer a new one."

"I'll do anything iffin' it means more people can hunt seals, not just the ACC," Nikolai said.

The rest of the crew all murmured their agreement, their faces open and accepting, not filled with spite like Eric's.

"Excellent. Then I expect each of you to do everything in your power to facilitate this study. If you have further questions, you can address them to me privately. Now get back to your stations." Sacha gestured to the helm, followed by the crow's nest.

No one moved for a moment, then Gus stepped forward. "I appreciate what yer doing, Cap'n. Tryin' to stop the poaching. I mighta been surprised ta learn of it, but now that you explained . . ." The middle-aged sailor scratched his beard. "Guess I'm tryin' ta say thank you."

"You're welcome," he whispered, his throat thick. Then he turned and headed up to the quarterdeck before he did something embarrassing, like hug the man.

He just hoped the politicians in Washington would be grateful for the study too.

20

Maggie tried not to sniffle as she shut the door of her cabin behind her and stepped onto the deck. Truly she did. She'd rather stay in her room, knitting hats and gloves, so that she didn't have to face anyone, after learning they'd missed Tavish's ship. Just when she'd started feeling a bit better earlier, she felt the ship slip from its moorings and set sail, and that had started another round of tears. It was one thing to have Sacha tell her they'd missed the *Halcyon*, but it was another thing entirely to leave the place she was supposed to meet her brother.

Now the ship was cutting across the open ocean, its sails filled with wind, and the sun casting jeweled patterns on the water behind them.

But there was nary a patch of land in sight. And it made everything feel so final. Would she ever find her brother? The longer she was in Alaska, the more distant her dream became of keeping the shipyard and land on Lake Michigan out of her uncle's hands.

She gave her head a small shake, the wind catching her hair

and tugging a slip of it free from its bun. Maybe she'd be able to save the land and maybe she wouldn't, but none of that changed the fact it was an hour past Finnan's bedtime, and she didn't have any clue where the boy and his sister had gotten off to.

She tucked her coat around her, her fingers already cold even though she'd balled her hands into fists inside her sleeves, then started toward the main deck.

"Is that you, Miss McDougal?" a sailor said from the wheelhouse.

Maggie looked beneath the shaded awning to find a familiar face standing at the helm. Russell, was it? Or Ronnie? "Yes, it's me."

"I'm awful sorry we missed the *Halcyon*, ma'am." The helmsman dragged a hand down his beard. "The whole crew was disappointed fer ya."

"Thank you," she managed, her voice still a bit rough from all her tears.

"Well, truth be told, the whole crew's anxious ta have Tavish back here. He's a good first mate. Not that I'm complainin' about Gus none, but some men just know how ta sail a vessel. It's instinct."

"I'm sure he's anxious to get back to the *Aurora* as well." She nearly choked on the words, and her tongue had the sudden urge to stick to the roof of her mouth. She shouldn't say such a thing, not when her most ardent desire was for Tavish to leave Alaska and return to Milwaukee for good.

Did Ronnie know that was what she intended? Did any of the crew?

"If yer lookin' fer the young'uns, I saw 'em head up to the bow with the cap'n about an hour ago." Ronnie jutted his chin toward the front of the ship.

"The bow? Thank you."

The man shrugged. "Yer welcome. Can't say as I blame the cap'n for takin' the young'uns up there. It's a great evening to be at sea."

It was certainly pretty, with the sun slanting low in the western sky, creating a pattern of glittering diamonds on the water. But that was about all she could say as she hunkered down into her coat—a coat that kept her plenty warm during a Wisconsin winter. But the only thing it seemed to do now that they'd reached the Bering Sea was let the wind through until she found herself constantly shivering.

She quickened her stride, keeping her head ducked against the wind and picking up her pace as she headed down the quarterdeck steps and across the main deck toward the front of the vessel.

"See this, Ainsley?" Sacha's voice carried on the wind as Maggie approached the foremast. Sure enough, he was sitting near the bow with Ainsley and Finnan on either side.

Maggie shivered again as another gust of wind buffeted the ship. Sacha might have taken the children to the prettiest part of the ship. But it was also the coldest, with nothing to block the wind that pummeled the nose of the vessel.

Except Ainsley and Finnan weren't shivering in their coats the way she was. In fact, they weren't wearing their coats at all. They were wearing different coats, long ones that looked to be made of animal hide and lined with fur. They even had hoods on the back.

Where had they gotten them from?

"Here. It's for you." Sacha held a wooden doll out to Ainsley.

Before she could take it, he pulled the top off to reveal another doll hiding underneath. Then he did it again, revealing yet another doll.

"How many are there?" Ainsley asked, her face dancing with delight.

"This one has seven, and they all nest inside each other. Like a story within a story. The Russians call them matryoshka dolls."

"I've never seen anything like it!" Ainsley threw her arms around Sacha.

He chuckled and wrapped her in a hug. "I was going to give them to you when we said good-bye today in Unalaska. But now that you're headed to the Pribilof Islands with us, I figured you could use something to play with around the ship."

Ainsley unwrapped her arms from Sacha's neck and picked up the nested dolls. "They're almost like magic." She took them all out, lined them up in a row, and then reached out to touch the smallest one.

"Not magic so much, but certainly a tradition."

Maggie shivered again, then brushed a strand of hair out of her face, watching as Sacha took the smallest doll from Ainsley, then set it inside the bottom of the next doll, his rough sailor's hands nimbly moving the small wooden pieces.

Ainsley pulled the dolls out of his hand and continued stacking them back up.

"Can I play with one?" Finnan asked. The boy was curled up beside Sacha, half sitting on the deck and half leaning on Sacha's lap with his thumb in his mouth.

Ainsley finished stacking the dolls and tucked them in the crook of her arm. "They're mine."

"You don't need to play with your sister's dolls. I got something for you too." Sacha settled one hand atop Finnan's red hair, then opened his coat and reached inside it with his other hand. A moment later, he pulled out a wooden boat. "A ship to sail the seas."

Finnan pushed himself up to a full sitting position and took the small replica. "It's a boat! Like the *'Rora!*"

Even from where she stood by the foremast, Maggie could see it had been intricately carved, with great attention paid to every detail of the sails and masts and bow. And the sight of it made her heart melt into a giant liquid puddle.

"It is, indeed." Sacha smiled, running a hand over the boy's hair again.

"Will you tell us a story about Russia?" Ainsley asked, still cradling her nesting dolls against her chest.

"A story about Russia?" There was something about the soft smile that flitted over Sacha's face, something about the tender way he looked at Ainsley and Finnan, that had Maggie's knees melting right along with her heart. "I know the perfect one."

Sacha wrapped his long arms around both children, hugging them to his broad chest, one on either side, before he started repeating what could only be a fairytale. It involved a firebird who stole golden apples from a king's garden, a prince named Ivan, and a gray wolf...

It was the most beautiful story she'd ever heard. She wasn't sure if it was because of the gentleness in Sacha's deep voice, or the way the sun cast golden rays over the sea, or how his rich, expressive words painted pictures of a distant land she could only imagine.

And somehow, amid the wildness of the sea and the burdens of commanding a ship, Sacha Amos found time to be gentle with Ainsley and Finnan.

There was a part of her that wanted to go to him, to tug Finnan onto her lap and lean her head against Sacha's shoulder, to feel the warmth of his body beside her and hear every lilt and pause in his voice.

"Maggie?"

She looked up to find that Sacha had finished the story and risen from his place on the deck, carrying a now-sleeping Finnan in his arms.

Ainsley stood yawning by his side, her eyelids heavy.

"I didn't realize you were there." Sacha headed toward her. "You should have joined us."

"I . . ." She shifted from one foot to the other. "I didn't want to interrupt."

Except that wasn't exactly true.

"Come, Ainsley, let's get you to bed." She held out her hand for her sister, but it took Sacha prodding the girl forward to get her to move.

Ainsley's steps were slow as they made their way across the ship toward the aft where their cabin was.

Maggie half expected Sacha to stride ahead of them on his long legs and have Finnan tucked into bed by the time she and Ainsley reached the cabin. But he stayed behind them, his steps slow and patient against the rocking of the ship.

When they reached the cabin, she reached for Finnan, but Sacha stepped inside and laid him on the bed, pausing only to strip a set of soft brown boots off Finnan's feet before tucking him beneath the covers.

"Where did those come from?" She gestured toward the boots.

"The Aleut village. The three of you will need warmer clothes on the Pribilofs. I got you a coat and boots as well. Give me a minute, and I'll be back with them." And then he was gone, disappearing out the door with a quick, confident stride before she could tell him the gift was too much.

"Here, let's get you changed." Maggie turned back to Ainsley, who looked about ready to fall asleep on her feet.

She helped her younger sister take off her dress and put on her nightgown, and by the time Sacha's footfalls sounded on the deck outside the door, Ainsley wasn't just in bed but was already asleep.

He rapped lightly on the door, and Maggie moved to it, tucking her coat tighter around her as she stepped out into the chilly evening. Sure enough, he was holding a fur coat that looked similar to the children's, just larger.

"The Aleut call this a parka, and shy of going up to Barrow and trading for an Inupiaq coat, it's the warmest thing you can find." He held it open, waiting for her to take her wool coat off.

The second she did, a fresh gust of wind buffeted the ship, causing her to tremble. But then she slid her arms into the soft material of the parka and found herself enveloped in a cocoon of warmth. She looked up at him. "It's one of the warmest things I've ever felt. But how did you know I was cold?"

"When I took Ainsley to the Aleut village earlier, she couldn't stop shivering." He reached out, his large hand gently touching a lock of her hair before tucking it behind her ear. "I realized you might be feeling the same. I'm only sorry I didn't notice how cold all three of you were sooner. I could have gotten you warmer clothes back in Sitka."

Maggie swallowed, the skin behind her ear still warm from Sacha's touch, never mind that he'd pulled his hand away several seconds ago. "How much do I owe you?"

"Nothing. It was a simple trade for some supplies I was already bringing to Kuluk's village. Getting you clothes stout enough to endure the weather on the Pribilofs was the least I could do."

She sighed, the warmth of the parka seeping into her skin. Or maybe it was warmth from standing so close to Sacha, because there was something about the man that radiated warmth and comfort and safety. And she didn't need to touch him to feel it.

"Speaking of the day . . ." Sacha peered down at her. "How are you feeling now? Better than this morning?"

Maggie looked away, taking in the vastness of the sea stretching around them. "I don't know."

"I feel like I owe you an apology. If I had even the vaguest idea the *Halcyon* would be running so far ahead of schedule, I would have left you in Sitka with my family. I never would have brought you—"

"No, don't apologize. You've been nothing but kind since we left Bellingham. And it's certainly not your fault the *Halcyon* arrived early. Sometimes I just . . . I struggle with . . ." She drew in a breath, then let the words pour out, one on top of the other. "Do you ever feel like God hates you?"

The moment the words were out, she regretted them. But that didn't stop the question from hanging in the air, heavy and unanswerable. So she pressed her eyes shut, unable to watch the look of disgust that was sure to flash across Sacha's face.

But when Sacha finally whispered, "No," disgust didn't lace his voice. If anything, his answer sounded soft, even sympathetic. "Or at least, I never would have phrased it like that. I assume you feel this way because you haven't been able to find your brother?"

She opened her eyes to find Sacha had moved nearer, his large frame so close they were nearly touching. "Why else would all this happen to me? Why else would God bring me so far from my home if he knew I would fail?"

"I doubt it was because God wanted you to fail. Or because he wanted to watch you suffer. You're his child, Maggie. He loves you."

"If he loves me so much, then why is everything going wrong?"

"I'm certain God has a purpose for it. Maybe God wanted

you to come to Alaska for a specific reason, even if you don't know what that reason is."

"I just don't understand." She shook her head. "I go to church every week. I give to the offering. I volunteer at the poorhouse and donate to a charity that distributes mittens and scarves and hats to poor families that can't afford them. I do all the things I'm supposed to do to live as a Christian and follow the Bible. God should be blessing me right now. And instead I feel . . . I feel . . . like he's cursing me."

"The Bible says Job was strong in his faith." Sacha reached for another strand of hair that the wind had knocked free and slipped it back behind her ear. But this time, he didn't pull his hand away. Instead, he widened his fingers, until his palm cupped her face. "Do you think God loved Job?"

She sniffled, trying to recall the Bible story. "I . . . I suppose he did, yes."

"And yet God allowed everything Job loved to be stripped from him, even when he didn't deserve it."

"But that doesn't mean . . ." She drew in a shuddering breath. "Surely you don't think God wants to do the same to me. What if I'm not as strong as Job? What if I'm not as good of a Christian? I feel like I made a mistake somewhere, that I offended God. But I don't know what I did or how to correct it so that God will look favorably on me again."

"Maggie, being a good Christian isn't a checklist or a tally sheet."

"Maybe not, but I still feel like . . ." Oh, she didn't know. She was just trying to find Tavish, to keep the land she and her father had loved so much, to watch her brother claim his place as rightful owner of her family's shipyard. What was so wrong with that? Why couldn't anything go according to plan?

"Come." Sacha held out his hand for her. "There's a beautiful sunset, and we're missing it standing next to the cabin. Let's move to the railing while I tell you my story."

She placed her hand in his, warm and soft, and let him tug her toward the railing, where the sun was painting a cloudless sky with various shades of orange and pink.

She hadn't realized it was so late, but she wasn't going to complain about watching yet another midnight sunset with Sacha Amos. At least that was one good thing that could be said for being stranded in Alaska.

"My father died the year I turned eighteen," Sacha spoke into the wind. "He was captain of the *Alliance* back then, and he spent his last five years on the ship working on opening the interior of Alaska to trade. Have you ever heard of the Yukon River?"

Maggie gave her head a small shake. "No."

"It's north of here, north of the Pribilofs, even. It's the only river in Alaska that reaches the interior and is big enough to take a ship down. The tribes that live in the interior are different from the tribes that live on the coast. They trade different goods, eat different foods, make different things. My father wanted to develop a trade route there, and I took over as captain of the *Alliance* after he died. But there's only four, maybe five months of the year where the river is navigable and not iced over. On a rough year, the river can freeze as early as September, without anyone expecting it or having a warning. And if you're caught in the interior . . ." Sacha's eyes seemed to go to a distant place as he stared out over the water.

"Is that what happened to you?" she asked softly. "Did you get caught in the interior?"

His shoulders slumped. "I did, yes. And I was so homesick. I just wanted to be with my family in Sitka, watching Ilya learn to walk and talk, and Inessa learn to read. Being away from them for months at a time while I took over my father's position was already hard. No seasoned sailor wants to listen to an eighteen-year-old captain, never mind that I'd spent half my childhood aboard the *Alliance* with my father. I'd been planning on returning home during the coldest part of the winter, getting to spend at least a few months with my family.

"Instead, I was trapped in a frozen land, hundreds of miles from home, with a crew that didn't respect me and resented having such a young captain."

She couldn't imagine being trapped away from her family so long, without any way to send word of what had happened. "That must have been terrible."

Sacha scrubbed a hand over his face. "It's funny, really. I never thought of myself as a homebody before that. I mean, I'd always enjoyed sailing, but I'd also enjoyed sitting around the table with a cup of tea and a plate filled with whatever Evelina had baked that afternoon. But once that had been stripped away, all I wanted was to be home. And that was the last place I could go."

"I can't imagine how that must have felt." The mere thought of it caused heat to prick the backs of her eyes. She felt too far from home too, but she could return at any time, at least if she chose to leave without Tavish.

"But in the midst of all that, God gave me a verse about how our trials bring us patience and hope." Sacha's voice carried out over the sea, growing stronger as he spoke. "It's from Romans five, and it says we should 'glory in tribulations . . . knowing that tribulation worketh patience; and patience, experience; and experience, hope.'

"Don't misunderstand. The last thing I wanted to learn that winter was patience. And I certainly didn't want to go through any trials to get it, especially not if those trials meant burying my father, stepmother, and brother. But in the end, well, it's just as God's Word said. I gained experience, and I learned how to hope in God. Learning that lesson wasn't fun, but I'm glad I learned it nonetheless." He reached out and gripped her hand. "And if it's the lesson you're learning right now, then please let me know what I can do to help."

Maggie looked up at him, her heart thundering against her chest. Was Sacha right? Could God be trying to teach her something through all of this, even though it felt like he was punishing her?

"You're so strong." And she wasn't talking about his muscles, though those were certainly strong too.

He squeezed her hand. "You're strong too. Much stronger than you realize."

"But I don't feel strong. I feel like I'm being crushed by the weight of everything."

He brushed his thumb over her knuckles. "Maybe that's the point. Maybe God needs to do that to get you to trust him."

Was Sacha right? Did God have some kind of master plan that she didn't understand? Would enduring all the things that were going wrong now somehow leave her stronger in the end?

"'I have learned, in whatsoever state I am, therewith to be content.'"

She looked up at Sacha.

"That was another verse God gave me that winter. I trained myself to be content. To be grateful only our small personal boat had been lost in the storm that killed my parents, not the *Alliance*. To be grateful for the time spent with the Athabaskans, where I was able to pick up their language. To find beauty in the snow and ice and frozen landscape surrounding me." He heaved in a breath. "I won't say it was easy, but the lessons I learned that winter still stick with me today."

Maggie stared out over the ocean. It wasn't frosty and frozen with winter, but vibrant with shades of sunset. Maybe she needed to find a way to be content with where she was too. To find joy in the fact that when she sucked in a breath, it smelled of man mixed with sea. And when she shifted the slightest bit closer, heat from his arm radiated into her shoulder.

She might not be standing on the porch her father had built with his own two hands, staring at the waving beach grass and calm waters of Lake Michigan. But this view was still lovely, and it was something she could be content with. Right now. Today.

As long as she didn't think about needing to say good-bye to the man beside her in a few weeks . . .

21

Assisting a scientist was miserable work. Maggie hadn't minded so much helping Dr. Torres—or Xavier, as he'd asked her to call him—aboard the ship. After all, she'd been able to put her bookkeeping skills to use by recording things in ledgers, tallying numbers, and keeping his notes organized. But now that they'd reached the Pribilof Islands, she was tempted to resign, never mind how badly she needed Xavier's money.

It wasn't the cold. The parka and boots Sacha had given her did an excellent job of keeping her warm in the constant wind. And it wasn't the sparse landscape. As Sacha had told her that day they'd passed through the narrow channel after leaving Ketchikan, the scenery surrounding her had gradually become sparse and barren.

There were mountains, but they were smaller and covered in stubby grass, with nary a tree to be found, almost as though the constant wind was too strong for trees to grow. She supposed this part of Alaska was still pretty in a way, with the ocean spreading around them on all sides, and cliffs jutting straight up from the ocean. But it wasn't nearly as pretty as Ketchikan or Wrangell or Sitka.

Almost as though knowing the lush, tree-covered mountains that had jutted straight up from the water in Southeast Alaska were too beautiful to witness the carnage taking place on Saint Paul Island.

The reason she wanted to quit was the seals, the dead, bloody seals. They were everywhere. She wasn't sure how many carcasses she'd seen so far that day. Probably at least three hundred, and it wasn't even lunchtime.

Each day their little group, comprised of her, Xavier, Captain Jones, and Nikolai, hiked across a different section of Saint Paul Island. And each day Xavier spoke with workers from both Alaska Commercial Company and the Bureau of Fisheries, trying to understand how many seals were being killed—or harvested, as Xavier called it—how old they were, and how the number of male bachelor seals on the island this year compared with the number of seals in previous years.

Maggie wanted to claim she'd retch if she saw another seal carcass, but the truth was, she was only three days into this two-week-long study, and she'd already seen so many dead seals that she was far past retching.

She'd seen the pelts being cleaned and their bloody hides hung up on frames to dry in the sun. She'd seen the meat that the workers couldn't eat piled into a heap and burned so it didn't attract other animals.

In short, she'd witnessed more slaughter, death, and carnage in the past three days than she'd ever imagined possible, and all because the pelts would sell for ten dollars apiece down in Seattle.

It was a horrid business, and she didn't need to ask why Sacha and Xavier felt so strongly about curtailing it.

"Miss McDougal, did you get that recorded?"

Maggie blinked, then looked toward Xavier, who was standing beside one of the workers for Alaska Commercial Company. "What was that?"

Xavier raised an eyebrow at her. "I asked if you wrote down the number of seals this man here says that he kills per day."

"Oh, um, yes." Maggie looked down at the journal she'd been holding, though the wind kept ruffling the pages, trying to make her lose her place. She'd done her best to record every last thing each person they interviewed said, no matter how gruesome the details. A successful study depended first and foremost on the accuracy of the notes. At least that's what Xavier kept telling her.

"He said ten." She looked up at the man with the long beard, whose frayed coat had been patched in several places. "Is that correct?"

"Yep. On a good day it might be more like twelve, but it takes time to skin them. It's not like I can just go around bashing their heads all day."

"Right," Maggie muttered. "How terrible that taking the time to skin them slows you down."

The man scratched his head, which was covered in scraggly, overly long hair that looked as if it hadn't seen a brush in two weeks or better. "Well, the killing part sure is easier than the skinning, I gotta say. But it's the pelts that bring in money, so you gotta do the skinning."

"And are you paid an hourly fee or by how many pelts you secure?" Xavier asked.

"By the pelt, of course. I get two dollars a pelt, and that's about how much I made in a day back home. The wife doesn't like me being gone over the summer, and my young'uns grow like weeds while I'm gone, but the money's so good, I don't feel like I got a choice."

"Does all the blood bother you?" Maggie blurted. "The killing?"

Xavier furrowed his brow at her, probably wondering why she asked such a thing when it had no bearing on the study, but the man was already answering the question.

"Not much different than hunting back home, except there's more of it."

"Are you concerned that too many seals are being killed each day?" Captain Jones looked out over the rolling field, where patches of grass were stained with evidence of seal blood.

"I'm sorry, forgive my colleague, sir." Xavier stepped forward, sending a dark look at the captain. "You don't need to answer that question."

"Oh, well..." The man looked between Captain Jones and Xavier, then slid his gaze to the side, where a group of five or six seals had climbed onto the rocks near the shore and started barking. "The Bureau of Fisheries monitors all that. I just kill as many seals as I can. The more seals I kill, the more money I take back home at the end of the summer. So, ah, if you don't mind. I'd like to get back to it."

"Of course. Thank you for your time." Xavier extended his palm to shake the man's hand.

"You're welcome." The man shook it, then unlooped his seal hammer from his belt and headed toward the seals.

A sour ball formed in Maggie's stomach. The animals were surprisingly docile, and they moved slowly on land, allowing the hunters to get so close they had no hope of escaping. Even as the hunter walked away, she couldn't stop her eyes from drifting to the blood stains on his trousers or the thick belt around his waist that held his skinning knife and other tools of the trade.

She turned her back to the man as he drew nearer the seals.

He would probably kill the entire group on the rocks while they congregated, then spend the rest of the afternoon skinning them and tying them to the wooden frames that allowed the hides to dry.

"Margaret, did you remember to get his name? I might have more questions for him in the future." Xavier peered over her shoulder at her notes.

"I did, yes." She took down the name of every person they interviewed—first and last—but as she blinked down at the page in front of her, she couldn't seem to make her eyes focus. Why would Xavier want to talk to the hunter again? He'd made it sound as though he were a decent man just trying to earn money for his family. But how decent could a man really be to work such a job?

"You wrote his name down right there." Captain Jones pointed to a line on the page. "Lynville Turring."

"Oh, yes. Mr. Turring." She blinked the blurriness away from her eyes.

A thud echoed on the wind, and Maggie pressed her eyes shut, her stomach roiling.

"Are you not feeling well?" Xavier was standing even closer now, his coat brushing her arm.

"I . . . um . . ." She forced her eyes open, but that only caused her to see the pile of seal carcasses in the distance, waiting to be burned. "I'm not quite used to this much killing, I suppose. Perhaps tomorrow . . ."

She swallowed, fighting down the bile churning in her stomach. "Maybe tomorrow you can find another sailor to accompany you. I'm not sure I'm the right person for—"

"Margaret, no." Xavier took her gloved hand in his own, then began massaging it with gentle, soothing movements. "I mean, if you're truly ill, you can stay back at the ship and rest, but if it's a matter of being disturbed by our findings, then I ask that you keep accompanying us. You are excellent at keeping records."

"I am?" Her eyes sought his, and warmth filtered through his intelligent gaze.

"Yes. One of the best record keepers I've ever seen. Should you ever find yourself in need of a job, I'd be happy to hire you at my office in Washington, DC. I could use your organizational skills and efficiency to maintain the records from other studies I've done."

He could? She blinked at him. He'd asked her to start calling him Xavier after leaving Sitka, and complimented her record keeping numerous times, but she'd thought he was just being kind. After all, she didn't do things any differently for Xavier than she'd done at the shipyard office back home.

"This winter I'll be headed to Australia to begin a study on the Pacific humpback whale," he continued, his thumb still rubbing little circles on the back of her hand. "I would love to have you accompany me on that trip as well."

"I . . . um . . ." Her throat felt suddenly dry. Xavier had just offered her a job. So even if she didn't find Tavish, even if she didn't have a home in Wisconsin to return to, she'd still have a way to provide for herself and her siblings. And she did enjoy taking notes and organizing records. It would probably be a fun job—just as long as he didn't ask her to start counting when a whale submerged itself.

"Pretty sure you need to marry the woman before you go carting her off to the other side of the world," Captain Jones muttered, his eyes moving between the two of them.

"Pretty sure Cap'n Amos won't take kindly to what ya just said neither." Nikolai crossed his arms over his chest. "Even if ya are some fancy scientist."

Xavier blinked, red climbing up the back of his neck as he dropped her hand. "I didn't mean it like that. I was inviting you to Australia in a professional capacity. I'll have another research assistant with me, and while he's a good scientist and better at timing whales than you, he's not nearly as adept at organizing research."

He shifted his weight awkwardly from one foot to the other, and she had to press her lips together to keep from smiling. Who would have guessed a few comments about marriage would embarrass the poor man? "I appreciate the offer. Right now I'm still planning to return to Milwaukee, but should that change, I'll contact you."

He gave an abrupt nod. "Very good. I'll leave you with my address before we part ways, then. Now we best get moving. There's a patch of rocks on the other side of that hill. Hopefully we'll find another ACC man and some seals there. I'd still like to conduct one more interview before we break for lunch."

And then he was off, striding across the island with his usual determination. But even as she ducked her head against the wind and pumped her legs to keep pace with him, she couldn't quite ignore the warmth still swirling through the hand he had held, or the way her chest felt lighter as she moved across the field.

"No. You need to growl louder. He needs to sound like a *scary* bear."

Sacha looked over at Finnan, seated beside him on the deck of the *Aurora*. The boy reached out and placed his small hand atop Sacha's on the wooden carving of a bear.

"Like this." Finnan yanked his hand forward, pulling the bear on top of the toy ship the boy had been playing with, and let out a fierce growl.

Or at least, Finnan tried to sound fierce, but Sacha wasn't

sure anything about the child with the runny nose and the sleepy eyes could truly seem that scary.

"That's not a very good growl," Ainsley said from where she sat on Sacha's other side with her matryoshka dolls. "And the ship needs to hurry up and fight off the bear so it can come to the island and rescue the princess." She tapped the bottom of the doll on the deck, as though the princess was getting impatient.

"Do you want to be the bear?" Sacha asked Finnan. "I can take a turn being the ship and rescuing the princess. Ainsley's right. You're taking an awfully long time to rescue her."

He suspected that had something to do with the fact he'd told Finnan it would be time for a nap after they played one more game of the princess and the pirate ship. The *good* pirate ship. Because the pirates on the ship rescued the princess instead of kidnapping her.

When he had tried asking if the ship that rescued the princess could just be a normal ship with a nice captain—like him—Finnan had insisted only pirates could rescue a princess.

"I don't want to be the bear. I want to be the ship," Finnan proclaimed, his bottom lip sticking out and starting to quiver. "But you need to be a mean bear, Mr. Amos. You attack the ship, but I fight you off, and then I save—"

"Cap'n?" Vasily strode toward the bow of the ship, followed by a man Sacha didn't recognize. "This man wants ta talk to ya."

Sacha pushed to his feet, leaving the wooden toys on the deck. The stranger was larger than Vasily, with a broad chest and shoulders covered in a fur coat. His lips were set into a firm line, and his dark eyes revealed no emotions. But the man's belt, holding a seal hammer and skinning knife, among other things, gave away that he was a hunter and not an official with the Bureau of Fisheries.

"Your children?" The man sneered, his eyes landing on the carved boat and chiseled bear at Sacha's feet.

"No. The siblings of a friend, but they were just headed back to their cabin to rest. Isn't that right?" Sacha sent the children a firm look, and they both started picking up their toys. "Vasily, take them to the stern while Mr. . . ." He raised an eyebrow at the man, silently asking his name.

"Thompson."

"While Mr. Thompson and I talk."

"Aye, aye, Cap'n." Vasily held out a hand for Finnan, who took it without complaint, then started toward the back of the *Aurora* while Ainsley trailed them.

Sacha waited until they were out of earshot before turning back to Mr. Thompson. "What can I do for you?"

"Why are people from your ship traipsing around Saint Paul Island?" The words flew from the man's mouth like sharp little daggers.

Sacha stiffened. He shouldn't be surprised someone from ACC was seeking him out. The more surprising part was that they'd been on the island three days without any confrontations. There was nothing passive or invisible about Dr. Torres's work now that they'd reached the Pribilofs. The man made it a mission to talk to each worker he found, whether they were employed by ACC or the Bureau of Fisheries.

"Dr. Torres, from the Smithsonian Institution, is conducting a scientific study on marine mammals in Alaska." Sacha told the hunter. "That happens to include seals, which happen to congregate on Saint Paul Island at this time of year."

"And you expect me to believe this study is harmless?" The man spat.

"Why wouldn't it be? It's nothing but numbers and reports. No one from my ship is out there killing seals or competing with your business."

The man crossed his arms over his chest. "Why wasn't I told of the study before you arrived?"

Sacha narrowed his eyes at the man. "Who are you that you think you should have been informed?"

"Harold Thompson. Head manager for Alaska Commercial Company on Saint Paul Island."

Head manager? That meant Mr. Thompson wasn't a man to be trifled with. "Tell me, just how many of the Smithsonian Institution's studies are you informed of each year? And how much of the *Aurora*'s shipping schedule are you given? Do you know when the *Aurora* will head to Barrow next? Or Japan?"

The man's dark eyes turned as sharp as the skinning knife hanging from his belt. "The company I work for owns the sole right to hunt seals on this island."

"No one contests that. But while you may own hunting rights, you don't own Saint Paul Island—or any of the other islands in the Pribilof chain. Which means I don't need your permission to come here. Neither does Dr. Torres."

"I don't want your scientist talking to any of my men."

Sacha took a step forward, drawing himself up to his full height, which was a couple inches taller than the imposing man before him. "He's not my scientist. All I did was transport him here."

"Your sailors are working for him."

"I'm not paying them to do so. They either volunteered or Dr. Torres is paying them with his own funds. If you don't want your men talking to the researchers, then I suggest you have a conversation with them. After all, you're the manager."

The man huffed. "So help me, Amos, if this study results in our quotas being restricted for next year—"

"That's not the goal."

Thompson just stared at him, his eyes an inky black.

"The goal is to get the government to stop the poaching."

There was little point in hiding his intentions now, not when everyone knew about the study. "I have no problem with men legally hunting a reasonable number of seals. It's the tens of thousands of seals being poached at sea each summer that I want to stop. For anyone in Washington to care, I need some kind of concrete evidence. That's why I brought Dr. Torres here."

The man opened his mouth, then snapped it shut, his jaw as tight as a sprung bear trap.

"The scientist has been studying marine life the entire trip," Sacha added. "That includes seals. He's estimating the number of pelts on poaching ships and comparing the number of seals he sees in various harbors to the number that the Tlingit and Aleut claim were in the harbors five years ago. He's not just singling out the Pribilofs."

"I still don't like this. I'm informing Mr. Caldwell of what's going on. If he wants this study stopped, he'll find a way to do it." The man whirled on his heel and strode off, leaving Sacha to stare at his retreating back.

Sacha had no doubt Caldwell could stop the study if he wanted to, but the man wasn't stupid. Surely he'd understand why stopping the poaching was important. Maybe he'd even throw his support behind the study.

At least that's what Sacha told himself as he ignored the splinters of doubt in his stomach and headed to the back of the ship to check on Ainsley and Finnan.

22

Saint Paul Island, Ten Days Later

Maggie could hardly keep her eyes open. Every muscle of her body was exhausted as she trudged across the deck toward the stairs that led to the quarterdeck. Ten long days traipsing across one island or another while trying to take notes quickly enough to keep up with Xavier's endless energy and quest for information.

Earlier in the week, Sacha reminded Xavier that his two weeks of research were nearly up, and the *Aurora* was leaving the Pribilofs in a few days' time. Xavier had hoped to extend the trip a few extra days, but Sacha had been adamant the *Aurora* stick to its schedule.

She'd wanted to cheer at the thought of finally being done with the seals, but Xavier had taken Sacha's news to mean he and his team needed to work from sunup until sundown, using every last hour of daylight to gather as much information as possible on the seals.

And that's exactly what she'd done. Each morning she left the ship just after dawn, after only about five hours of sleep, and she'd return to the *Aurora* at sunset.

As she dragged her feet up the stairs to the quarterdeck, she could barely keep her eyes open. The sun was just beginning to set, meaning it was nearly midnight.

All she wanted was her bed. Well, maybe she wanted a warm bath and a cup of tea, but her bed would have to suffice.

She hadn't even gotten to see Ainsley and Finnan today. The cook had served the research team an early breakfast; then they'd eaten both lunch and dinner on the island, and now it was long past the hour when the children usually went to bed.

Maggie slowed as she neared her cabin, frowning at the crack in the door. Had Sacha forgotten to close it when he'd put the children to bed? He'd done such a good job of caring for them in her absence, never acting like it was a problem, even though she knew he'd spent most of his days ensuring they ate and slept, and finding some way to entertain them, whether on the ship or on land.

Perhaps Ainsley had left the cabin earlier and forgotten to pull it closed after she returned.

Maggie nudged the door open a bit farther, only to stop when she spotted Sacha inside the room, his large form crammed into the small chair beside the desk.

"But I dreamed Maggie died in the storm." Ainsley was curled in Sacha's arms, her voice filtering through the crack in the door. "She's not going to die, is she?"

Something pulled low in Maggie's belly. Was that why the door had been left open? Had Ainsley suffered a nightmare?

"No. She won't die." Sacha's deep voice carried into the night. "Certainly not in a storm, and certainly not on my ship."

"But that's how her pa died." Ainsley sniffled, then threw her arms around Sacha's neck and hugged him.

Sacha wrapped his arms around Ainsley in return, his hand rubbing her back in soothing motions. "That doesn't mean Maggie will die the same way."

"But what will happen if she dies and we never find Tavish?" Ainsley's voice trembled with unshed tears. "Who will take care of us?"

"Maybe my family. How would you like to spend more than a day with Inessa and Ilya?"

She sniffled again. "You mean it? We would go to live with you?"

Maggie's heart turned warm and liquid, her knees so soft she had to lean against the doorway to keep herself upright. Sacha was offering to take in Ainsley and Finnan if something happened to her and they couldn't find Tavish?

It was too kind. Too much.

And yet she couldn't quite make herself enter the room and say such a thing. So she stood by the door and listened as they finished their conversation, Sacha's voice deep and smooth as he assured Ainsley that all of her fears were unfounded. That they would find Tavish soon and then all return home, happy and healthy. That no one would die, and one day she'd come to look at her time in Alaska as a grand adventure.

By the time Sacha was done, Ainsley had drifted off to sleep in his arms, and he carried her to the bed, where he took painstaking care to tuck the covers around her before heading toward the door.

"Maggie," he whispered the moment he was outside. "I didn't realize you'd returned. Your sister had a nightmare, but you weren't here to calm her, so I—"

"I heard." She swallowed, her throat tight as she looked up at him. "Why are you doing this, Sacha?"

He blinked at her. "Calming Ainsley? Like I said, you weren't here, so—"

"Not just that. All of it. Why are you being so kind? Why are you caring for the children while I'm with the team? Why are you giving them toys and putting them to bed at night? Why are you helping me so much when we barely know each other, and I—?"

He pressed a finger to her lips, stopping her from speaking, then leaned close, his eyes gentle in the gathering darkness. "Because I want to."

The words were simple, and yet, in that moment, with her skirt caked with mud and her eyelids so heavy she could barely keep them open, she couldn't imagine a kinder thing he might have said.

"But why?" she whispered again, this time from behind his finger. "Why do you want to help? Is it a sense of obligation? Something you resent?"

Sacha pulled his finger away, a groove forming between his eyebrows. "Why would you think I resent this?"

"Because we're a burden. An inconvenience and a . . ."

He pressed his finger right back to her mouth. "You are not a burden, Maggie McDougal. You are a delight. A bit of a charmer, even though you don't realize it. You have a heart for your family and are going to great lengths to protect them. And you're also beautiful."

"Me? Beautiful . . . ?" She looked down at her filthy coat and boots. She didn't need to take off her parka to know the hem of her dress would also be muddy. "I'm filthy. In need of both a bath and a laundry tub. The last thing I am is beautiful."

Sacha reached out and stroked a strand of hair that had been hanging beside her cheek, wrapping it around his finger. "A pretty dress isn't the only thing that makes a woman beautiful." He gave the strand of hair a slight tug, which caused her to lean in closer to him until their lips were only a hairsbreadth apart.

He paused there for a moment, with his mouth just above hers. Time seemed to suspend between them, until the sights and sounds and smells of the ship faded away. Until they were the only two people left in the world. Then Sacha lowered his head a fraction of an inch, and his lips were on hers.

They were soft and warm and patient, just like the man himself, and Maggie found herself sighing into the kiss, her body melting against his as he pulled her closer and wrapped his arms around her.

His arms were strong, yet somehow gentle. And the longer she stood inside them, the more he seemed to surround her, engulfing her body with his large chest, wrapping her in his strength and warmth. Just being in his arms was almost as comforting as the kiss itself—or at least, how the kiss started.

But the longer he moved his lips against hers, the more she could only think about the gentle pressure, about the way he tugged her bottom lip into his mouth. About how he broke away to kiss the underside of her jaw, then her neck, then the soft place where her jaw and ear met.

"Sacha," she gasped, the combination of his hot breath and warm lips drawing a giggle from her.

"I know," he rasped, his voice unbearably deep. Then he pressed his forehead to hers, his arms tightening around her back. "I know. I shouldn't have done that. Forgive me, Maggie."

"Forgive you? Why am I forgiving you? We should do that some more." She pressed up on her tiptoes, her lips seeking his, but he turned his head away.

"Maggie, no. Go to bed, and we'll talk in the morning."

"But . . ." She tried to protest, but he was already pulling away from her and dropping his arms from around her back, where a flood of cool air rushed in.

"All right," she whispered. "We'll talk in the morning."

He gave her a stout nod, as though it were an established

appointment, then turned and left. The memory of his arms around her filled her mind as he clambered down the stairs and toward the cabin he shared with the cook.

23

They didn't talk in the morning. Maggie might have spent her entire night dreaming of Sacha's kiss, remembering the feeling of his arms wrapped around her and hugging her tight. But that didn't stop Xavier from knocking on her door at six the next morning, saying he needed to get an early start, since it was their final day of data gathering. A few minutes later, someone set a tray with breakfast outside her door. She ate quickly and was off the ship in a matter of minutes, ready for another day of grueling work while she left the children in Sacha's care.

Yet as she went about her work, she couldn't stop thinking about how safe and warm she'd felt in Sacha's embrace. How, for the first time since she'd left Wisconsin months ago, every last worry had fled her mind, and she'd felt protected and loved —or if not loved, then at least cared for. Cherished.

But here she was being foolish, because Sacha would be dropping her off in Sitka soon, and they'd never see each other again.

Was that why he'd apologized after kissing her? Because he'd started something that the two of them couldn't finish?

Maybe, after she returned to Wisconsin, she'd be able to find another man like him. Not someone who sailed, of course. She'd never marry a man who spent more time away from her than at home.

But maybe she'd be able to marry a lawyer. Or a police officer. A builder, even. A man whose job allowed him to come home to her every night. He'd be gentle and patient, and he'd look at her the way Sacha did, all kindness and warmth. He'd have time for Ainsley and Finnan, and a rich laugh that rumbled from a place deep in his belly and . . .

No. She couldn't imagine it. Because each time she thought about returning to Milwaukee and living in a house overlooking Lake Michigan that she shared with her husband, her husband always had golden-brown hair and tawny eyes and a chest nearly as broad as a doorway.

Each morning before breakfast, she could see him planting his arms on either side of her and leaning against the porch railing, caging her in as they watched the sun rise over Lake Michigan—just like Sacha had caged her against the railing of the *Aurora*. He'd whisper in her ear about how dawn over Lake Michigan still wasn't as pretty as a midnight sunset on the Bering Sea. And then he'd lean down and brush his lips against her neck, then her jaw, then her—

"Margaret?"

She snapped her head up to find Xavier, Captain Jones, and Nikolai all staring at her. "Um, I'm sorry. Did you ask me something?"

Xavier's gaze softened, and a furrow appeared between his brows. "I asked how this official's estimate regarding the decrease in population of the bachelor bulls compares to the others."

"Oh. I'm sorry. Let me look that up." A quick glance around the field told her that the official they'd been talking to was now heading toward three hunters and a cluster of seals on the rocks near the coast. She must have been too trapped in her own thoughts to realize he was leaving.

Maggie flipped back to the final page of the notebook, where she'd been keeping track of the estimated numbers after noticing a disparity between what the ACC workers were reporting and what the Bureau of Fisheries officials were reporting.

"Are ya feelin' well?" Nikolai asked.

"Yes, fine," she muttered while she scanned the page. "The official from a moment ago . . ."—She flipped back to double-check his name—"Mr. Simms, says the population is declining at a rate of maybe twenty percent year after year, which isn't too far off from what the other Bureau of Fisheries officials have reported. Some say a decline of about fifteen percent, and others have indicated a decline as large as twenty-five percent. But the ACC workers all continue to notice a negligible decline."

All three men kept looking at her, as though she'd grown a third ear on her forehead or antlers on her shoulders. "What? Is something wrong?"

Captain Jones slowly shook his head. "You don't seem like yourself today, is all."

"Thank you, Margaret." Xavier moved to her side, his eyes scanning her face. "But Nikolai is right. You look flushed. Are you feeling ill? I can escort you back to the ship if needed."

She sunk her teeth into her lip. She'd struggled her first few days on the island, but once she'd grown used to the gore, she became quite proficient with her note-taking. Xavier had a standard list of questions he asked each and every worker, and by this stage she could outline the interview questions before he asked his first one.

The last thing Xavier needed was to lose precious research time, and all because her mind kept drifting to Sacha. "I'm fine, I promise. I just . . . ah . . . didn't sleep well last night, and I'm having a bit of trouble focusing today."

Xavier slid the notepad out of her hand, then flipped back to the page where she'd recorded their most recent interview. He scanned it for a moment, then handed the notepad back to her. "This certainly looks thorough. Do you think you can continue for a few more hours?"

She nodded. "Yes, of course. I'm sorry for getting distracted."

Something soft glinted in Xavier's eyes. "I daresay it happens to all of us at times, even me. But if you don't need to return to the ship, we best get moving. There's more I'd like to cover this afternoon before finishing our research."

"Of course." She closed the notepad and slid it into the satchel she'd carried with her during their time on the islands.

A half smile tilted the corner of Xavier's mouth as he watched her; then he turned and looked at Captain Jones and Nikolai. "Let's continue." And he started across the field at a pace that left the rest of them scrambling to keep up.

Unlike the previous two days, they didn't stay out until sunset, which surprised Maggie. Dr. Torres had hoped to return to Saint George Island for a few hours and then spend the rest of their final day sailing to the two smaller islands, Walrus and Otter, to observe the number of seals and their behavior. But he felt they'd collected enough data to complete his final report for the various government agencies in Washington.

Maggie truly didn't care why they were returning early.

She was just happy to climb the rope ladder from the dinghy to the ship without being so tired she nearly slipped.

She spotted her siblings the moment she stepped onto the deck. They were at the front of the ship with Sacha, which seemed to be their new favorite place.

Even though she could use a nap, she headed toward the bow.

"Where will you go after you take us to Sitka?" Ainsley's voice carried on the wind.

"Down to Bellingham." Sacha absently ran a hand down the back of Ainsley's glossy-red hair. "I need to drop off Dr. Torres."

"And then?" Ainsley looked up at Sacha.

"I'll pick up my sister, Kate, in Juneau, and we'll head to a town called Barrow. It's as far north as a ship can sail. I can only go in July and August. No other months are safe. There's too much ice."

Maggie stopped a few feet away and blinked, trying to imagine a place that was icy for so much of the year. Would it be beautiful? A frozen land locked eternally in the icy crystals and snow of winter? Or would it be windswept and barren, like the Pribilofs?

"What do you do up there?" Ainsley asked, as though she, too, had tried to imagine such a place and failed.

"I visit the Eskimos. Though they don't call themselves Eskimos. They say they're Inupiat, and they don't call the name of their town Barrow. They call it Utqiagvik."

"Utqiagvik," Ainsley repeated, the name awkward on her tongue.

"Do you bring them food?" Finnan asked from where he sat beside Sacha, pretending his toy boat was rolling with the sea.

"No." Sacha shook his head. "They don't need food. They get everything they need from the ocean."

"Will you bring them blankets?" This from Ainsley.

"A few, but they live so far north that even our wool won't keep them warm the way caribou pelts will. I'll take medicine and beads, some firearms and bullets for shooting caribou, and lumber. They live too far north for trees to grow. Any wood they use to build things needs to be brought in by ship."

"No trees?" Finnan looked up from his toy boat.

"How can people live without trees?" Ainsley asked.

Sacha reached out and tousled Finnan's hair. "It's hard to imagine, isn't it?"

"I want to go with you." Finnan puffed out his chest. "I want to visit the Eskimos."

Something tugged at Maggie's chest. She wanted to go too, wanted to see this barren land of eternal winter. Would there be time for them to go with Sacha? If Tavish met them in Sitka, she could send him back to Wisconsin without them for a month or so, just long enough for her and Finnan and Ainsley to explore this new part of the world.

"No," Sacha said. "You can't come. You'll be headed back to Wisconsin about the time I reach Barrow."

Maggie found herself stepping forward, opening her mouth to explain that there might be a way for them to go, but Ainsley spoke first.

"But what if we miss Tavish's ship again? Can we go then?"

"I'm sorry, but no. Not on a trip like that. It's dangerous, and I'm very careful about who I take with me. My sister Kate comes, but she's the only doctor willing to travel so far north to treat Eskimos. And I never know what the ice will be like. It should be melted by the beginning of July, but if they had a harsh winter, I might not be able to get through. Most ships can't make the trip at all, but the *Aurora* has a double hull for that exact reason, so it can plow through ice."

Maggie blew out a breath, her shoulders sagging. How

many times had she heard Hamish tell her mother the same thing? That she couldn't go on a trade route with him.

She remembered overhearing one argument where Hamish refused to take her mother on a quick trip to Chicago. She pressed a hand to her throat, willing the painful recollections of that fight to fade from her mind.

She needed to keep in mind that what she'd experienced on the *Aurora* with Sacha was the exception. Even if she somehow stayed in Alaska—which she had no plans to do—even if they married one day, she wouldn't be accompanying him on trips or get to stand next to the railing on the *Aurora* with him each night as they watched the sunset at midnight.

Because captains didn't travel with their wives.

She didn't mean to make a noise, but she must have, because suddenly everyone turned to look at her.

"Sissy!" Finnan hopped to his feet and came running toward her. "You're back before bedtime."

Sacha stood as well and came toward her, running his eyes down her parka. "And in need of a bath by the looks of it. Shall I tell Scully to boil some water and have it sent to your cabin?"

A bath sounded heavenly. "Is there a tub aboard the ship?"

"There is. I'll have it moved to your room."

"Thank you."

"Is there anything else you need?" Sacha ran his eyes down her again, then brought them back up to meet her gaze. "Are you hungry? I can rustle up a snack from the kitchen."

Did he have to look at her with such gentleness? Have to go so far out of his way to make her comfortable?

"Stop," she whispered, heat pricking the backs of her eyes. "Please just . . . stop being so kind to me."

His brow furrowed. "Why? What's wrong?"

She clamped her lips together, not trusting herself to explain.

Sacha jutted his chin toward Ainsley and Finnan. "Go play for a minute while I talk to your sister."

They both scrambled back to where they'd left their toys on the deck, and Sacha turned back to her, his eyes soft as he studied her face. "What's going on in that pretty little head of yours?"

"It's like I said. I need you to stop being so kind." Her voice emerged rough and scratchy, as though she'd just swallowed a fistful of gravel.

"Why would I do that?" Sacha searched her face, his expression somehow growing even gentler.

"Because . . ." She sniffled. "Because we never should have kissed. You were right about that. Because we'll be in Sitka soon, where you'll drop me off, and then we'll never see each other again."

Sacha's shoulders rose and fell on a sigh, but he didn't speak. How could he? It wasn't as though he could argue that they'd be able to keep up their acquaintance after he left her in Sitka.

"So while I appreciate how kind you've been to me, how helpful you've been with the children, there's a part of me that wishes . . ."

What? She squeezed her eyes shut. That they'd never met? That they hadn't become such close friends?

Because that's what they were. Friends.

They couldn't be more.

The trouble was, now when she thought of Benny Fullsom's proposal back in Milwaukee, when she thought of returning home and saving the shipyard and letting another man or two court her, she couldn't imagine herself falling in love with anyone other than Sacha Amos.

"Maggie . . ." Her name was little more than a whisper on his lips, and when she opened her eyes, she found he'd taken a few steps closer, bringing him near enough for her to see swirls of green in his light-brown eyes.

"You're a beautiful woman, Maggie McDougal, both inside and out." His breath brushed her chin as he spoke. "Reckon one day you'll make some poor sap the luckiest man alive when you decide to marry him."

"But it won't be you. At least, not unless you want to move to Wisconsin and run a shipyard."

A muscle clenched on the side of his jaw, even though his eyes stayed soft. "I could never move so far away from my family."

"I didn't think so."

He heaved out a sigh, then raked a hand through his golden-brown hair. "I best go talk to the cook about your bath."

Then he turned and left her there, standing in the middle of the deck, with Ainsley's and Finnan's giggles rising from a few feet away and the crew milling about, preparing to raise the sails.

Yet she didn't remember the last time she'd felt so lonely.

24

Gulf of Alaska, Four Days Later

He never should have kissed Maggie.
Sacha sighed as he gripped the helm of the ship, the wood familiar beneath his palm.

Even now, nearly a week past that kiss, with the sun shining and the wind blowing and the *Aurora* gliding through the water with the precision of one of Kate's scalpels, he still couldn't wipe it from his mind.

They'd only talked about it that one time, when Maggie had said they never should have kissed, and then he'd left to draw her a bath.

The problem was, the *Aurora* was a rather small ship to be stuck on with someone he was trying to avoid. And now that they were all stuck aboard, without any islands for Maggie to venture to with Dr. Torres and the other sailors, he seemed to run into her every time he turned around.

And every time he saw her, he couldn't stop thinking about

how it had felt to hold her in his arms and press his mouth to hers.

But just like he'd felt her lips respond to his and heard her soft gasp as he'd kissed her jaw and throat, he'd seen the look in her eyes after he told Ainsley and Finnan about his trip to Barrow and how it was too far north and too dangerous to take them.

And she was right. He didn't plan to move to Milwaukee, not now, not in six months, not ever. His family needed him here too badly.

And her family needed her in Milwaukee.

Even if Tavish decided to stay in Milwaukee and run the family shipyard—and he wasn't sure the sailor would want to stay in Wisconsin—he couldn't quite imagine Maggie agreeing to leave her home and move to Alaska, not when her family's land and that shipyard meant so much to her.

And if he could somehow convince her to move to Alaska?

He shook his head. They'd still be stuck. Maggie's mother had been married to a captain, and that hadn't gone well. Even now, he could still hear her words come back to him from the night they'd stood on the deck together after leaving Sitka.

She never should have married a captain, especially one who believed a woman didn't belong on a ship. It would have been one thing if he'd wanted her to travel with him, but he hadn't, and they never saw each other. And it was so very different from how it had been before, with my father.

Sacha couldn't blame Maggie for wanting more for herself. He had men on his crew who were married, and they barely saw their wives. That wasn't something he'd ask of Maggie. Being married to a captain had even been difficult on his own mother, and his father had taken his family with him on his trips far more than most captains.

"Captain Amos!" a panicked shout carried on the wind.

Sacha looked around, trying to figure out which of his men had called for him, especially considering most of the crew was belowdecks having lunch.

"Captain, come quick!" The voice was louder this time, coming from the back of the ship near Dr. Torres's cabin.

Sacha headed out of the wheelhouse, leaving the ship unmanned as he rounded the corner and found Captain Jones holding Nikolai against the rail, gripping the sailor by the collar.

"Did you order papers to be dumped overboard?" Captain Jones thundered.

"Papers?" Sacha looked over the railing to find a mass of papers littering the sea. "No. What papers are those?" Though he had a sinking feeling he knew, especially after he glanced at the open door to Dr. Torres's cabin.

"Tell me those weren't from the study." Hadn't Dr. Torres locked the cabin when he'd gone down to lunch? How had Nikolai managed to get in?

Nikolai's jaw turned hard, never mind that Captain Jones still held him by the collar. "It ain't no secret my family needs money. Not with my pa dead and five siblings still at home back in Virginia. Alaska Commercial Company offered me more than Dr. Torres did. A lot more."

"You're fired." The words boomed from Sacha's chest, but what difference did it make? Even he knew it was an idle threat.

Nikolai didn't laugh or sneer. "Ya think it matters? I got paid five years' worth of wages fer what I just did there."

A sickening sensation twined through his stomach. How many of the papers had he gotten to? All of them? The ones on the whales too? The original seal study from fifteen years ago?

"What is the meaning of this?" Dr. Torres strode toward Nikolai and Captain Jones followed by several of the crew members, who must have heard the commotion from belowdecks.

Then Maggie rounded the corner of the wheelhouse, with Ainsley and Finnan in tow. She took one glance at the water, and her face turned white. "Are those the records from the study?"

"He emptied the desk clean out before I found him." Captain Jones said, releasing his hold on Nikolai's collar but keeping the sailor pinned against the railing. "He never came down to lunch, so I went looking for him. Caught him lurking around the deck up here last night without any explanation too."

"Not the entire desk. Please tell me he didn't get everything." Maggie rushed into the office, and the strangled cry that echoed through the door a moment later told Sacha everything he needed to know.

He pressed his eyes shut. How much had been sacrificed for this study? Dr. Torres had given up part of his summer, he and Alexei had sacrificed over two weeks' worth of paying work for the *Aurora*, and Maggie, Dr. Torres, and Captain Jones had spent hours upon hours on the Pribilofs gathering information and recording it in a way that could be compiled into a study.

"How bad is it?" Dr. Torres brushed past him and stormed into the cabin.

"It's everything." Maggie's voice filtered onto the deck. "Every last thing, except for a few papers from the bottom drawer."

"Take him to the brig." Sacha raised his voice, his eyes trained on Nikolai.

"The brig? Wait." Nikolai fought against Captain Jones's hold. "There ain't nothin' illegal about throwin' papers over the side of a ship."

"No? Well, it turns out there's something very illegal about breaking into another person's cabin, stealing their items, and destroying them. And if you don't believe me, I have a brother-in-law who happens to be a US Marshal, and a sister who's a lawyer. I'm sure they'll both be happy to sort out just how 'legal' your actions were once we get to Sitka."

Nikolai's face twisted into a scowl. "I don't know what yer thinking, tryin' to get seal hunting banned. A man can work on the Pribilofs fer two months and earn enough money to feed his family fer a year. Nobody wants that to go away."

Was no one listening? He wasn't trying to get it banned. But he was done explaining that. So he took a step closer, letting his body loom over the smaller man. "It's going away one way or another. If not because of government policy, then because the seals will be overhunted to the point of extinction."

"That'll take ten years, maybe more," Nikolai shot back. "A man can still make a lot of money 'tween now and then. Least-ways, Washington can't do nothin' 'cause you got no papers ta prove what Dr. Torres claims."

Sacha jutted his chin at Captain Jones. "Get him out of my sight."

Vasily stepped forward to take Nikolai by his other shoulder, and the rest of the crew cleared a path as the men led him away.

Sacha turned to face the rest of his crew, all of them looking at him as though they expected some type of speech. Could he even trust them, or had ACC offered to pay others to destroy the study, and Nikolai was just the first sailor who'd found a way into Dr. Torres's office?

"Does this mean it was all useless?" His first mate stepped forward. "All that trackin' the scientist and the lady did? All those days the team went ashore?"

Sacha dragged in a breath, the salt from the air burning his lungs. "I'll let you know just how bad it is after Dr. Torres and Miss McDougal go through the office."

Gus loosed a string of cusswords, and Sacha didn't bother to correct him for swearing near a lady. Truth be told, he wanted to do the same thing.

"Back to work," he commanded, then waited as his crew disbanded, though no one was quick about returning to their stations.

Once the quarterdeck cleared, he headed into the cabin. Perhaps it was possible Nikolai hadn't gotten everything. Perhaps he'd missed a desk drawer or...

The tears streaking Maggie's face stopped him just inside the door. She looked at him with such hurt that he was tempted to hold out his arms and wrap her in them, never mind that Dr. Torres would see their embrace. "We worked so hard on this. All those notes, all those days on the islands. I just—"

"Close the door," the scientist snapped.

Sacha shut the door with a bit more force than necessary, but the second it latched, Torres spun on his heel and strode across the room to where a chest sat at the foot of the bed. "It's not lost."

"What do you mean?" Maggie pressed a handkerchief to her face. "You saw those papers the same as I did. The ocean has surely swallowed them by now."

"I never risk having only one copy of my research, not with a study as involved as this. Any number of disasters can happen to papers at sea. Or in the desert. Or even on a train. That's why I always bring a mimeograph with me and store the papers in two separate places."

"So the papers aren't lost?" Maggie rasped, dabbing her eyes.

"One set of them is, but the second set survived."

"Thank heavens." Sacha stepped closer, relief trickling

through him, even if he wasn't quite able to believe the study remained intact quite yet.

"It seems too good to be true, doesn't it?" Maggie looked at him, her watery eyes growing bright with hope.

"What's a mimeograph?" he asked, though he guessed it was the small rectangular box the scientist pulled from the trunk.

"It's a way to copy papers using a stencil and a roller," Dr. Torres answered. "Have you not heard of it? It's one of Thomas Edison's inventions."

"Thomas who?" Maggie stepped forward, surveying the box.

"Thomas Edison, the scientist who invented the phonograph."

"He invented a way to copy papers?" Maggie picked up the small box while Dr. Torres began emptying more things from the trunk. An extra pair of boots, a sheaf of papers, a tent, and several other supplies he would need if he stayed on land for a night or two. Then he finally knelt beside the trunk and raised a board that looked to be some type of false bottom.

"We'll need to make another copy of these, Margaret. I'll show you how the mimeograph works, but I'm afraid you'll need to spend the rest of the afternoon and most of the evening in this cabin."

"That's all right. I'm happy to do it if it means we haven't lost the study." The corners of Maggie's mouth tipped up into a small smile, and she dabbed the last few tears away with her handkerchief.

Dr. Torres smiled at her in return. "I knew I could count on you."

Sacha shifted. Was it just him, or had Dr. Torres's voice just turned soft? And was he looking at Maggie with a bit more fondness than was appropriate for a scientist and his employee?

"I want to keep these papers secret," Dr. Torres continued, already beginning to separate them into different piles on the bed. "I'd much rather have everyone think the research was lost. That way we don't need to worry about someone trying to destroy it again."

"I agree," Sacha said. "Keeping the papers secret is the best course of action."

"I'm just glad the study isn't ruined." Maggie sent Dr. Torres another smile, and Sacha found himself wanting to growl.

Instead, he turned and left to find Ainsley and Finnan—who never had trouble showering him with smiles—and told himself he needed to be grateful that the study wasn't lost, rather than complaining about Dr. Torres and Maggie being alone together.

25

Sitka, Alaska, Two Days Later

Almost home.

Sacha stood in the wheelhouse as Ronnie guided the *Aurora* around the rocks that marked the entrance to Sitka Sound, the waves of the open ocean transforming into a calm, serene blue while mountains rose around them. He could already see his family's house, sitting atop the rocky little promontory that jutted into the water. Beside it sat the wharf and shipyard that had belonged to his family for ninety years.

The town sat behind the house, a jumble of wooden buildings wedged between the sea and mountains. Some of the peaks were still dusted with the last remnants of winter snow.

He drew in a breath, the air tinged with the scent of salt and pine. It didn't matter how long he'd been gone—a day or a week or six months—the sight of home always calmed him.

On the deck, the crew moved with a sense of purpose and efficiency, lowering various sails and preparing to dock at the wharf, each sailor knowing his job and expertly executing it.

That morning, he'd told his crew they would be staying the night in Sitka. Originally, he'd planned to stop for only a few hours, worried that he needed to get Dr. Torres and his study to Bellingham as quickly as possible. But now that everyone thought the study had been destroyed, there was no reason to rush. He had to admit, as sick as he'd felt watching those papers float away on the waves, he was happy that the study was once again a secret.

And since they were no longer running behind schedule, he'd decided to give his sailors a night docked in a real town, not moored off the coast of an uninhabited island with only seals to talk to. They'd earned it.

But tomorrow morning, all the peace and contentment that had filled his soul at the sight of his home would drain away.

In the morning he'd say good-bye to Ainsley and Finnan.

To Maggie.

It shouldn't hurt so much. He'd only known them a month. So why did it seem like this would be harder than getting trapped on the Yukon River his first winter as a captain?

Sacha rubbed the heel of his palm against his breastbone. None of this should hurt. It's what he kept telling himself over and over again. Maggie would soon be meeting her brother, then heading back to Wisconsin to save her family's land and shipyard. It was exactly what she wanted, and it would all work out perfectly, even if her reunion with Tavish had been delayed.

So why—

"Captain Amos?" Sacha looked over to find Dr. Torres standing at the edge of the wheelhouse. "May I have a word?"

They were nearly to the wharf, but his crew knew how to dock the ship, so he left the helm in Ronnie's capable hands and ducked out of the wheelhouse, rounding the corner toward the captain's cabin.

The second he stepped inside, Dr. Torres pushed the door shut behind him, his face etched with serious lines. "I've stowed the study back inside the trunk, beneath the false bottom. But I want to make sure my cabin will stay locked while we are in port, that you'll be able to keep your brothers and anyone else out of it."

"Absolutely. I took the shipping manifest out yesterday. There'll be no need for anyone besides you to be inside this cabin."

"What about Miss McDougal?"

Sacha raised an eyebrow.

"We've made copies of everything." Dr. Torres lowered his voice. "But we haven't quite finished organizing and filing it all. Since we're not leaving until tomorrow, I asked her to give me a few more hours of her time this afternoon."

"I see." And he did. Maggie and the scientist had spent the past two days copying reams and reams of papers.

It shouldn't grate on him. The two of them had been nothing but proper inside the cabin. And he knew because he'd checked on them. Frequently.

"She's been quite helpful to me on this journey, you see." The serious lines of the scientist's face grew soft. "You should know that I offered her a permanent position working for me in Washington, DC. I don't think she'll take it. She seems quite resolved to return to Wisconsin, but I told her I would keep the position open until after all that business is settled with her family's land."

"I . . . ah . . ." He had? When? Sacha raked a hand through his hair. And what was he supposed to say about it? "She'd make an adept assistant."

The man smiled. An actual smile that encompassed his full mouth, softening his face even more. "She would, yes. She brings quite a sense of civility and peace to the excursions, and she's athletic enough to keep up with the men. Having her on my team would be an asset indeed. I'm already planning to travel to Wisconsin after Christmas to restate my offer."

Sacha stiffened. Dr. Torres was planning to visit Maggie in Wisconsin?

Because Maggie was truly that much of a help, or because the man had feelings for her?

He wanted to tell the scientist no, that it wasn't right. That if anyone went to Wisconsin to visit Maggie, it should be him.

But even after things got settled with Tavish running the shipyard, even if Sacha could convince her to move away from the home where she'd grown up and the land she loved so much, she wouldn't want to be married to a man who was gone more than he was home.

And he didn't want that for her either.

And here Dr. Torres was offering to take her with him on his expeditions. The man even appreciated having her along. He wasn't sure just how deep the scientist's feelings for her ran, but he knew one thing. If Maggie took Dr. Torres up on his offer, his feelings would only grow.

How could they not? She'd make a wonderful wife for some man one day.

Just not him.

"Sacha?" a voice boomed from the shore. "Sacha, are you there?"

Sacha recognized Yuri's voice even through the thick door.

"Excuse me," he said, turning his back to the scientist and opening the door to the cabin. "I need to greet my family."

He headed straight for the railing, where his family would be able to see him. He always made it a point to stand at the railing when the ship docked, so whoever was on shore would know he was safe. But the discussion about Maggie had distracted him—just like everything else that pertained to Maggie McDougal.

"I'm here." He waved, looking over the railing to find Yuri, but no Ilya, Inessa, Evelina, or Kate. They should be back in Juneau by now, but a small part of him had hoped he'd somehow get to see everyone again. "Did Evelina win her case?"

Yuri grinned from ear to ear. "She did. You should have seen the look on Sheldon Jackson's face when the judge sided with her. Everyone's back in Juneau, including the student they pulled out of the school."

Sacha smiled down at his brother, but that ache returned to his chest. If only he could have been in Sitka when the judge issued his ruling.

"But that's not all," Yuri called. "We have a surprise for you."

"Did you plan a dance for tonight?" His sailors would love that.

"Not a dance. Just wait." Yuri glanced over his shoulder at the building that housed both the Sitka Trading Company warehouse and the office above it. "He should be . . . there. Right there."

Yuri pointed at the door, where Alexei was walking toward the ship with . . .

Was that Mikhail? It had to be. No one else wore their hair overly long or walked with a litheness that made him look as though he'd rather be scaling a mountain than traipsing down a boardwalk.

What was Mikhail doing back in Sitka? He was supposed to be leading an expedition into the interior.

"Mikhail?" he called.

His brother turned his direction, a smile wreathing his face. "Sacha! You've returned!"

"What are you doing here?"

"The expedition is being reorganized. The team wants to travel by foot, not water, and not as deep into the interior as originally intended. Though if they wait too much longer, the entire thing might get canceled and rescheduled for next summer."

"Is Ilya here?" a small voice said from beside him.

Sacha looked down to find that Finnan was standing at his side, clinging to the railing.

"He promised we could search for gold."

"No, little man," Yuri called. "He had to go back to Juneau."

A thud sounded from farther down the ship, and Sacha looked over to discover that his men had just slid the gangway down to the wharf.

"Come on, buddy." Sacha hefted Finnan into his arms. "Let's go give everyone hugs."

As he started toward the gangway, he noticed a bit of commotion below. It looked like a couple townsfolk had arrived, and maybe even one of the officials from the Revenue Cutter Service. Sacha paid them little mind as he strode across the quarterdeck and tromped down the stairs to the main deck. Only when he reached the top of the gangway and found not his family but three men in uniforms did he pause.

"What's going on?" He set Finnan down and looked between the men. "Is there some kind of problem?"

One of the men stepped forward, a man Sacha had seen around town a time or two, though he'd never bothered to learn the official's name.

Then the man unlooped handcuffs from around his belt. "Sacha Amos, you're under arrest."

26

Under arrest. Sacha looked around the dank cell with a single mattress in the corner and a bucket against the far wall for doing his business. A dim lantern flickered on the wall across from the cell, causing the bars at the front of the cell to cast eerie shadows over him.

Of all things.

He replayed the scene in his mind again, trying to figure out what had happened, where things had gone wrong. How he could be under arrest when he hadn't done anything illegal.

The Revenue Cutter Service officials had been tight-lipped, saying only that they needed to search the ship before taking him to jail.

What did they think he'd done?

How long would they leave him sitting here before they bothered to tell him?

Sacha heaved in a breath, the air damp and thick and filled with the sour smell of vomit. Laughter and teasing rang out from one of the cells near the front of the jail, the sounds of drunken men who had gone a little too far in their inebriated state, never mind that it was only three or four in the afternoon. Nikolai was in one of those cells too. Sacha had seen the Marshal bring him in at one point.

The door that separated the jail cells from the rest of the administrative building swung open, and he pressed his head to the cool bars in an attempt to see who had entered.

Alexei. He strode down the aisle as though he owned the prison, his steps strong and confident. The handful of other prisoners quieted as he passed, just like they had when the Revenue Cutter Service officials had led Sacha to his cell an hour earlier.

Sacha gripped the bars separating him from his brother. "Did you get them to release me?"

His brother sighed, his shoulders slumping as though they held the weight of the world despite his polished shoes and three-piece suit. "Your bail hearing is set for tomorrow. You'll have to stay the night."

Bail? So they were charging him with some type of crime?

"Don't worry. I can survive a night in a jail cell." As long as he could get his charges dropped in the morning. They'd leave port a few hours late, but he'd still be on his way to Bellingham with Dr. Torres and the study before noon.

"That's not what has me worried."

Sacha paused. It took some doing to get Alexei worried, and a misunderstanding that resulted in an easily cleared up arrest wasn't one of those things. "What is it?"

"They've seized the *Aurora* and her cargo. Getting everything released is going to be more complicated than getting you out on bail."

"They're detaining the *Aurora*?" The nausea swirled in Sacha's belly. Having the Revenue Cutter Service search his ship hadn't surprised him. They could search any ship they pleased, simply to make sure US vessels were complying with maritime law. He'd had vessels searched before as part of routine inspections.

But the Revenue Cutter Service had to have a reason to actually *seize* something. That implied illegal activity, and he'd done nothing to warrant such drastic actions.

That was why he'd been more impatient than worried sitting in the jail cell. Once the search turned up nothing, he'd expected to be released from jail and back on the *Aurora*, leaving in the morning as planned.

"I don't understand." Sacha scratched the stubble on his face, which seemed increasingly itchy inside the dank cell. "What are they saying I've done?"

"They didn't tell you?" Alexei raised his eyebrows. "You're being charged with transporting contraband."

"Illicit contraband? But they searched the ship. I know they didn't find anything. I haven't done anything illegal."

"They found vodka and sake."

"And?" Sacha crossed his arms over his chest. "It's all for the crew. I haven't sold any."

"It's still illegal to consume in Alaska."

He glared at his brother. "Is this a joke? Alaska might be dry as far as Washington, DC, is concerned, but you and I both know that everyone here alcohol. Sitka alone has three bars, and Juneau probably has twelve."

Alexei held up his hands. "I'm not saying the law is enforced, only that it's the law."

"And they're choosing to enforce it now? With the *Aurora*? What about any of the other ships sailing the Inside Passage or across the gulf? Is their cargo going to be seized too?"

Alexei sent him a dry look. "Don't play stupid. You know there's more to it than that. We both know exactly who's behind this—and why."

Sacha shoved a hand into his hair but managed to resist the

urge to pull it out by the roots. "You really think Caldwell is behind this? That it's some sort of retribution for commissioning a study on the seals? Penalizing poachers will only help Caldwell."

"He's not going to see it that way. I tried to warn you."

"I still don't regret it. This business with me and the *Aurora* and the alcohol will go away soon enough. But Dr. Torres's study? That could change things for decades, Alexei. Decades."

"What study?" A muscle pulsed at the side of Alexei's jaw. "I'm told one of your sailors threw it overboard."

Sacha leaned forward, motioning for his brother to step nearer the bars, then glanced around. No one new had entered the jail, but he still wanted to make sure another person wouldn't overhear what he was about to say. "It's not destroyed. Dr. Torres has a copy hidden inside his trunk. Whatever happens, you need to make sure that trunk is returned to him, with the study still inside. And then you need to get him back to Bellingham as quickly as possible."

Alexei stepped back and tilted his head up, as though studying ceiling. Sacha recognized that look. His brother was calculating a way to get the trunk released, to get Dr. Torres away from Sitka so the study could get back to Washington and the two senators who'd asked for it.

And he'd be successful. Sacha knew that as surely as he knew the sun would rise tomorrow. Because when Alexei put his mind to something, nothing could stop him. It didn't matter that Alexei had thought something like this might happen and tried to warn him. It didn't matter that saving the seals wasn't nearly as important to Alexei as it was to him.

Alexei would find a way to get him out of this mess anyway. Because Alexei loved him, and this was how he showed it.

"I'll see if we can have Dr. Torres's things released and get him on a ship south by the end of the week. But the rest of this?" Alexei waved a hand toward the jail bars. "It's not going to disappear easily. Caldwell is going to throw the full extent of the law at us. I've already sent for Evelina to help us sort through it."

"Let him," he growled. "I haven't done anything illegal."

"Except for transporting liquor."

"Transporting liquor isn't illegal, not if I transport it to San Francisco or Seattle or Bellingham. Selling it in Alaska is the only thing that's illegal, and I didn't sell it to anyone here."

Alexei looked at him, his face set with grim lines. "I'm not saying it's fair, but if Caldwell can get the *Aurora* detained because of that, what other things will he come up with if he has more time to look? And he'll have plenty of time to look with our cargo seized."

"I don't care how much time he has." Sacha threw up his hands. "He won't find anything!"

"He'll find something anyway. He's too bent on revenge not to. And then—"

"Well, well, well. If this isn't a lovely place for a family reunion."

At the sound of the oily voice, Sacha jerked his head up, only to find Preston Caldwell striding down the aisle toward them, his suit impeccable in the dim light of the jail.

"What do you want?" he snarled.

"I just came down to say hello." Caldwell smiled sharply, his eyes turning into two razor-thin slits. "And to warn you that if you ever try lowering the seal quota on the Pribilof Islands again, I will personally see to it that your entire family is destroyed. You should thank me for only taking your ship."

"The ship will get released," he growled. "And I'm not trying to lower the quota. You know that."

"I know what you claim. But what if those politicians Dr. Torres has been talking to decide my quotas on the Pribilofs need to be lowered?" Caldwell crossed his arms over his chest. "Tell me, what's your plan then? Just how do you plan to protect the investment my family made when we purchased those hunting rights?"

Sacha clamped his jaw shut.

"Nothing? Is that your answer?" Caldwell's gaze grew even sharper in the dim light of the prison. "That's what I thought. Good thing the study was destroyed."

Sacha gripped the iron bars separating him from Caldwell, the truth threatening to spill from his mouth, just so he could see the look on the man's face when he realized the study had survived.

But it wasn't worth the risk.

Caldwell glanced at Sacha's hands, his knuckles white on the jail bars; then he chuckled. "What's the matter, Sacha? A little frustrated you can't swing that fist at my jaw. You should try it after you're out on bail."

He wasn't that stupid. If he so much as bumped into Caldwell's shoulder, the man would find a way to send him back to jail for assault.

"Is there a point to your visit?" Alexei snapped, his voice sounding like steel coated in granite.

Caldwell flashed them both a sickeningly charming smile. "Of course. I came to see if Sacha had heard about the murder in Unalaska."

"What murder?" Had something happened to Kuluk? To one of the members of his village? Whatever had happened, it must be recent. No one had mentioned a murder when he'd stopped in port.

"The murder of a white man, committed by two members of the Aleut tribe there. They were drinking, and a fight broke out. It ended with one of the Indians pulling out a gun and shooting a man, Joe Renfield. Now both the Marshal and the

Revenue Cutter Service are looking for who sold the tribe that liquor." Caldwell made a show of studying his hands, as though there might be an imaginary speck of dirt he needed to brush off. "I was sure to mention that the *Aurora* was recently there, making a rather large delivery."

That's what Caldwell was playing at? Sacha's grip tightened around the bars until the metal cut into his palms. "That liquor didn't come from my ship."

"Didn't it?" Caldwell's smile turned sharp. "That's not what the sailor you dropped off on Saint Paul Island said. He said you sold two hundred dollars' worth to the Aleut village in Unalaska."

"Eric?" Sacha's blood turned cold. Eric had told the Revenue Cutter Service he'd sold liquor to the Aleut? And a man had ended up murdered during a drunken brawl involving two Aleut men who weren't supposed to have liquor?

Sacha couldn't help the groan that emerged from his lips. That was why the Revenue Cutter Service had seized the *Aurora* and its cargo. They were looking for someone to blame the ordeal on, and Caldwell had pointed everyone toward him.

"I see you know the sailor. Good." Again Caldwell smiled in that cold, cruel way of his. "Honestly, this all seems a little fitting, don't you think? Especially after the cargo on one of my ships was seized last fall—all because of you."

Then the man turned on his heel and stalked off, leaving Sacha to stare at his retreating back while he stayed stuck in jail for a crime he hadn't committed, with nothing to think about except for how big of a fool he'd been to assume Caldwell wouldn't retaliate.

27

The *Aurora*. Of all the ships. All the things they owned, did it have to be the *Aurora*?

Alexei ignored the ache in his chest as he stalked from the top of Castle Hill down the path that led to town.

Not that ship, God. Anything but that ship.

But it was already too late. Preston Caldwell wanted revenge, and he knew the best way to get it.

But he couldn't let Caldwell win. Not with the ship he had designed during what had ended up being his last year studying naval architecture. It was the best ship of their fleet and had become so well known that he now had four commissions for similar vessels waiting to be built.

Alexei clenched his teeth, forcing his legs to move faster as he strode toward the warehouse that his workers should have been busy filling with cargo from the *Aurora*. Instead, the RCS had moved the ship away from the Sitka Trading Company wharf and into the harbor, where they'd set it under guard.

There had to be a way out of this. Did he have anything

nefarious on Caldwell? Anything he might be able to use to pressure the man into backing away from the *Aurora*?

He shoved through the door to the office and took the stairs two at a time. Caldwell might be ruthless and powerful, but he was also cunning.

That was what made him such a dangerous enemy.

And it was why Alexei had done everything in his power to avoid ever becoming the man's enemy.

But now it was too late for . . . "What in the blazes?"

He reached the top of the stairs, only to find his brother Mikhail standing in the middle of the floor, swinging Indian clubs up and down in a series of alternating arm motions. He lunged forward with one knee, then brought himself back to a standing position, then lunged on another knee, all while rhythmically moving the clubs.

"Don't act surprised," Mikhail rasped, breathing hard. "You know I need to keep my strength up."

He crossed his arms over his chest. "You're the only person I know who trains for a strongman competition even though he never plans to enter one."

"I keep bumbling scientists—who spend more time in an office than outdoors—alive for a living in one of the deadliest places on the planet. That takes a certain amount of strength and endurance."

Alexei glanced around the room. A series of kettlebells sat along the far wall, beside a second pair of Indian clubs that looked a bit larger and heavier than the ones currently in Mikhail's hands. He knew his brother exercised when he was home, going for runs in the mountains, often carrying a pack filled with heavy objects, but it had been a long time since he'd seen him use his Indian clubs and kettlebells. "I take it this isn't the first time you've come to the office after hours and done this?"

Mikhail lunged a final time, then pushed off his leg into a standing position and lowered the weights to his side. Even though he'd stopped moving, his chest still heaved with exertion, and sweat soaked the upper part of his shirt. "As I said, it's in my best interest to stay strong, even when I'm not leading an expedition. Now what did you find out at the jail? Is there a way to get the *Aurora* back?"

"Not easily."

"Because Sacha had a few bottles of spirits? Everyone knows it's not enough to sell, and the second that ship crosses into international waters, it's not illegal for any of his sailors to consume either."

"It's not that. Caldwell is trying to convince the Revenue Cutter Service that Sacha sold alcohol to the tribe in Unalaska alcohol and it resulted in a man dying."

"What?" Mikhail dropped one of the weights to the floor, then winced and picked it back up.

Alexei scrubbed a hand over his face, then explained what Caldwell had said at the jail. The longer he spoke, the stiller and quieter Mikhail became. But quiet didn't mean Mikhail wasn't thinking. On the contrary, he probably had a plethora of thoughts spinning through his mind, and the quieter he got, the more dangerous he became. Like a mountain lion stalking its prey.

"So Sacha thinks that Caldwell is offering to pay Eric to lie, and that Eric will do it," he finished.

Mikhail strode to the wall and set his Indian clubs down, his gait sleek despite the weights. "Knowing Caldwell, it was one of his ships that sold the liquor to the Aleut."

"You're probably right, and that's why Caldwell's so certain he can pin this on Sacha."

Mikhail picked up the hand towel on the floor and used it

to wipe his forehead and neck. "You'll find a way to get us out of it."

Why did everyone keep saying that? This might be too big for him to handle. And if it wasn't, if he somehow could navigate the family through this, that didn't mean he'd be successful the next time something happened. Or the time after that. A man couldn't keep winning indefinitely.

Alexei had a sudden urge to ask if he could use Mikhail's towel, because the back of his neck had broken into a cold sweat, even though he hadn't touched his brother's weights.

"You need to find out who sold the alcohol to the Aleut." Mikhail wiped his hands on the towel, then tossed it on top of his weights. "That means going to Unalaska and asking the tribe directly."

Alexei raised his hands. "You can't expect me to leave Sitka now."

"Do you want me to go?"

He didn't. Mikhail was gone far too much, and unlike Sacha, once Mikhail left on an expedition, he didn't return for months. Sometimes he was gone so long, Alexei wondered if he'd ever see his brother again, or if he'd just use those powerful legs and shoulders to disappear into the vastness of Alaska's wilderness.

"Even if I wanted you to go, there's no ship to take you, not with the *Aurora* being detained."

"Let me talk to the Revenue Cutter Service. They usually send ships that way this time of year because of the poaching, and I'm certain they'll want to send someone to talk to the tribe and find out who sold them that alcohol, just like we do. Bet I can get passage with them."

Mikhail traveled with the Revenue Cutter Service often. After all, their ships were tasked with transporting scientists and government officials all over Alaska. If anyone from their family could convince the RCS to take them to Unalaska, it was Mikhail.

"Fine, yes, see if you can find a way to Unalaska." That certainly seemed like an option worth pursuing. "I've already sent word for Evelina. She'll be here in two days."

"Good." Mikhail came up and slapped him on the shoulder, the touch probably more powerful than he realized. "Don't fret. We'll get this sorted out."

He sighed. He hoped his brother was right. Because he couldn't stand to think about what might happen if they couldn't get Sacha cleared of all charges.

28

Sitka, Alaska; The Next Evening

Why was this happening? Sacha drew in a breath of moist sea air, so very different from the dank air of the jail he'd been breathing at this time last night. But it did nothing to lighten the heaviness inside him as he leaned his elbows on the porch railing and stared out at the calm waters of the sound.

Behind him, voices filtered out of the house, the sounds of cleaning up dinner and happy conversations, but he hadn't been able to stay inside and smile and discuss the price of lumber or the new ship that one of Alexei's friends down in Seattle had just purchased.

Oh, how could everything in his life have become such a big mess?

I have learned, in whatsoever state I am, therewith to be content. The verse came back to him, words he'd shared with Maggie when she'd been so upset they'd missed Tavish's ship in Unalaska.

They were words that had comforted him for years. No matter what port he was in or how poorly a voyage was going, he'd always been able to come back to that verse.

But not now, with the *Aurora* being dragged to the other side of the harbor, sitting under the watchful eye of the Revenue Cutter Service.

Not when that blasted study was still hiding at the bottom of Dr. Torres's trunk.

Alexei had tried to get the judge to release the trunk earlier, claiming Dr. Torres was needed back at the Smithsonian Institution. But the judge had said that Dr. Torres's items would be released with the rest of the materials aboard the *Aurora*, and that Dr. Torres could travel ahead without his trunk if he was needed elsewhere.

Sacha shoved a hand into his hair. Had he made a mistake by reaching out to the scientist? By pursuing a study on seals when nearly every man in Alaska seemed content to ignore their rapid decline in population?

"God, why?" he whispered into the misty sky. "Why are you doing this to me? I was only trying to save the seals. Don't you care about them? Don't you want them to survive?"

I have learned, in whatsoever state I am, therewith to be content.

Not that wretched verse again. He gritted his teeth, his fingers digging even harder into the weathered wood of the railing. Just how was he supposed to be content when he'd lost the *Aurora*? Didn't God understand how much that ship meant to his family? To him as the captain? To Alexei?

Few people understood how much that ship meant to his brother, who had dreamed of being a master shipbuilder one day. When he turned eighteen, he'd gone to school in San Francisco and studied naval architecture, intending to expand their family's holdings by building bigger, more powerful ships. But that had all come crashing down the day their parents and Ivan died. Instead of finishing his schooling and opening a shipyard in Seattle that built giant ships of iron and steel, Alexei had returned home to run the family businesses.

He'd brought the blueprint for one ship home with him—the *Aurora*. Nothing they built in Sitka contained much iron or steel. It was too expensive to have large amounts of those materials shipped to Baranof Island. But Sitka had wood aplenty, and that was the design Alexei brought home—a vision for a double-hulled masterpiece that could push aside ice.

And that had been it. The one ship Alexei had created.

There had been no time for anything else in those first few years. And now each month, when a new ship was built out of iron or steel, it put their family further behind, marking the days when the business that had sustained them for nearly one hundred years would become obsolete.

Alexei, to his credit, didn't seem upset that the *Aurora* had been seized. He seemed to view getting the ship released as a problem to be solved and was approaching it with the same logic a person might use to solve a puzzle.

But Sacha couldn't separate things the way Alexei did, couldn't stay as calm and controlled and emotionless.

Not when he might never again be able to step foot on the ship he loved so much. Because what if the jury found him guilty? What if the judge ordered the ship seized, not just during the trial, but after he issued his verdict?

He gripped the railing of the porch, the tips of his fingers digging into the splintered wood as he stared out over the waters of the sound.

The Revenue Cutter Service had commissioned their family to build a double-hulled clipper similar to the *Aurora*. But Alexei hadn't yet started on the ship, and if the judge awarded the *Aurora* to the US government, then the RCS could have the original ship in just a few weeks rather than waiting until next year for a replica. And they wouldn't have to pay for it either.

An ache opened up in Sacha's chest. He wasn't sure he could stand to see the *Aurora* sail into the sound and know it belonged to the government rather than his family. Know he was the reason his family had lost such a beautiful ship.

"Sacha?"

He stiffened at the sound of the feminine voice behind him.

"I came to see if you're all right." Footsteps padded on the porch, and a moment later Maggie came to stand beside him, her long blond hair cascading in waves about her shoulders. "And to tell you that I'm sorry about the *Aurora* and your cargo."

He sighed. "It's not your fault."

"It's not your fault either."

He jerked his gaze to her. "How can you say that? If not for me, the *Aurora* wouldn't . . . it wouldn't be . . ." His throat closed.

"Did you sell that liquor to Kuluk's tribe?"

"No."

"Then it's not your fault. It's Preston Caldwell's. You ought not blame yourself."

"I can and I will." His voice emerged hoarse, as though he'd just swallowed a fistful of sand. "Everyone tried to warn me he would seek revenge. And I was too foolish to listen. The Bible even warns about that. 'The way of a fool is right in his own eyes: but he that hearkeneth unto counsel is wise.'"

"No." She reached out and gripped his hand where it rested on the railing, her palm warm and soft atop his. "You're not a fool. You saw something beyond everyone's warnings, something bigger than your family's holdings, and decided to do the right thing anyway."

He shook his head, tugging his hand away from Maggie. "You can't say I did the right thing, not with how this is ending."

"Don't lose hope, Sacha. There's still good that can come of this. Alexei said Evelina will be here shortly, and once she arrives, she'll be able to get Dr. Torres's trunk released. Then he'll be able to go to Washington, DC, and—"

"Part of me hopes they find the study and take it."

"No." She grew still beside him. "You don't mean that. We worked so hard. Have you seen Dr. Torres's final report? He says that if the sealing isn't curtailed in some way, the northern fur seal will go extinct in fifteen years or so—"

"I don't want to hear it." He whirled on her. "Don't you understand? This isn't my fight anymore. It can't be."

"But what if God is doing all of this to teach you something? Like with Job, and all the suffering he went through. Sometimes God has a bigger purpose, remember?"

He pressed his eyes shut. His words, again, coming back to haunt him. "It's not the same."

"How do you know? You were just trying to do the right thing. There's nothing shameful in that. Do you remember the verse you told me? 'I have learned, in whatsoever state—'"

"This is hurting my entire family, not just me."

"Job's entire family was hurt by what happened to him too."

Was she right? He didn't want to think about it. He wouldn't complain if God wanted to take the money in his bank account, wouldn't even complain if God wanted to lock him behind bars for a few years. Maybe some good would come of it, just like good had come of Paul being in prison.

But to lose the *Aurora*? The ship that had been born of all Alexei's suffering and grief the year their parents died?

It was too much. Surely God wouldn't ask such a sacrifice of him and his family.

"I did what I could," he whispered, staring out at the water. "But this isn't a battle I can afford to fight anymore."

He pushed away from the railing and strode inside.

29

Two Days Later

Maggie stared into her tea, the dark liquid reflecting the light from the kitchen back at her. Outside the mist and rain that had covered Baranof Island for the past three days had finally lifted, and the sky and water were both a brilliant shade of blue. But inside the house . . .

Maggie inhaled the scent of baking sugar and flour around her and tried to smile. After all, the cake baking in the oven smelled delicious.

But she just couldn't force a smile to her lips.

"What are you thinking?" Evelina asked from the other side of the table, her hands busy kneading bread dough. She had arrived last night, bringing Ilya and Inessa with her—like Sacha said she would.

The children were now out exploring Sitka and happy to be together, never mind the world around them seemed to be falling apart.

"Do you think you'll be able to get Sacha acquitted?" The words tumbled from Maggie's mouth.

Evelina sighed, her shoulders sagging. "It's too hard to say at this point. Everyone from the crew is willing to testify that Sacha didn't sell any liquor to the Aleut. In a normal situation, that should be enough to get the *Aurora* and its cargo released, but lawyers are cautioned in law school not to predict how things might unfold in a courtroom."

"Yuri says the Revenue Cutter Service and the governor are determined to make an example out of whoever sold that liquor to the tribe."

"They are. Hopefully we can prove Sacha didn't, and the person who did sell the liquor can be found and held accountable."

"Hopefully." Maggie took a sip of tea, the brew tepid after sitting so long. But she didn't really feel like drinking it, just as she didn't feel like eating the teacake Evelina had slid onto the plate in front of her—or like eating anything else.

Sacha hadn't talked to her since their argument, when he told her he wished he'd never contacted Dr. Torres. And she still couldn't bring herself to agree with him. Surely Sacha had to realize that the seals needed to be saved. That God wanted him to have some role in it. Who could better understand how important the seals were? Who could better understand that he was seeing fewer and fewer of them as he sailed around Alaska?

And to think, a few weeks ago she'd been worried that God hated her simply because she'd missed Tavish's ship in Unalaska. But missing a ship seemed small compared to the Revenue Cutter Service seizing the *Aurora*.

She didn't wonder why Sacha was devastated, but oh how she wished she could find a way to cheer him up, to bring that bit of light back into his eyes, the smile that curved the corner of his mouth.

But she didn't have any ideas for how to do that, and even if she did, Sacha had spent the past few days almost entirely at the shipyard. And the handful of times he'd been at the house, he'd avoided her. She may as well be back in Wisconsin for all they saw of each other.

Yet somehow he still found time to spend with Ainsley and Finnan after dinner.

"Are you gonna be able to get Sacha's ship back?" Ainsley bounded into the kitchen, her eyes growing wide when she saw the teacakes on the table. "Can I have one?"

"Can I have one too?" Finnan rushed into the kitchen behind Ainsley, followed by Ilya.

"I knew I smelled food." Ilya reached out to snag one of the round little cookies covered in powdered sugar, but Evelina smacked the back of his hand. "Not before you wash up. The three of you were just outside."

Ilya sighed, then tromped around the table to the sink.

"You too," Maggie told Finnan. "You need to wash before you have any food."

Ainsley was already heading to the sink, her question about getting the *Aurora* back seemingly forgotten.

But Maggie hadn't forgotten it. The question hadn't left her mind once since the ship had been seized. She piled six teacakes onto a plate, enough for each of the children to have two, then waited for Ilya to carry the plate onto the porch, where the children could enjoy the sun.

But the moment the children left, she turned back to Evelina, her heart heavy. "What will happen if you lose the case? Could the RCS . . . Could they take the *Aurora*? For good?"

Evelina blew out a breath. "They could, yes. But I don't think it will come to that. As I said, we have multiple sailors willing to testify on Sacha's behalf, and Mikhail and the RCS are in Unalaska meeting with the tribe. I'm hoping Mikhail will bring Kuluk down to testify on Sacha's behalf."

"What about Dr. Torres? Will he testify?"

Evelina went back to kneading the dough. "He'll submit a written statement on Sacha's behalf to the court, but he should be on his way back to Washington, DC, before the court date. I filed a petition to get his personal effects released so he'd be free to go."

Maggie straightened at the news. She could see why Dr. Torres would want to return home shortly—especially if he was able to take the study with him. "When will you get an answer?"

"There's a court appearance scheduled for tomorrow morning."

At least something was going their way, even if it was small. "But the *Aurora* will still be detained until Sacha goes to court? There's not some way to get the *Aurora* released too?"

"Actually, I'll find out about that tomorrow. The *Aurora* will be detained until Sacha goes to trial, but I'm hoping to get his case moved up. There's room on the docket in two weeks, and Sacha is under contract with the Marine Hospital Service to deliver medical supplies to villages and outposts north of here, including Barrow. He usually runs that route in July, after the ice in the Arctic has melted. The voyage could possibly be pushed back to early August, but not any later than that. I've asked to have a rush put on the case because of the contract."

Maggie smiled, the first genuine smile she'd had in days. "That might even mean the trial will be over before I go back to Wisconsin. I'll testify if you want me to. Anything to see Sacha's name cleared."

"I'll keep that in mind. We just might be able to use your testimony." Evelina slid the group of bread pans on the table closer and sprinkled them with flour. "I noticed the two of you at dinner last night. You couldn't stop looking at each other, though you never let your eyes meet. Did something happen between you when you went to the Pribilofs?"

Maggie looked into her tea, her throat suddenly tight. "I suppose you could say that."

"Do you have feelings for each other?"

She swirled the tea in her cup. Had it been that obvious? "I suppose you could say that too."

"Then what's the problem? Do you feel more strongly for Sacha than he does for you? Or is it the other way around?" Evelina plopped the lump of dough into a bread pan. "Does he have feelings that you don't return?"

Maggie shifted on her seat. They'd never really talked about how Sacha felt about her—or how she felt about him. They'd both been smart enough to close the feelings tumbling inside them behind hard, solid walls. "I . . . ah . . . I can't claim to speak for Sacha."

Something about how she answered the question must have given her thoughts away, because Evelina cocked her head to the side, her brows furrowing. "What is it, then? Is it the shipyard in Milwaukee? Do you really feel as though Tavish will need you there that badly after he returns to run things? Can't you see yourself returning to Alaska eventually, even if it takes until Christmas or so to get things situated?"

Maggie pressed her eyes shut. "It's not that."

A thick silence emanated from the other side of the table, so thick, in fact, that Maggie almost swore she could hear the questions swirling through Evelina's head.

"I'm not willing to return to Alaska for a husband I'll never see. My mother's second husband—Ainsley and Finnan's father—was a ship captain, and it caused nothing but heartache."

Evelina took another mound of dough and plopped it into

the bread pan, her movements a bit slower this time. "I suppose that settles things."

Yes, it did. So why did the mere thought of leaving Alaska—of leaving Sacha—always make her throat grow tight and her eyes burn?

"You're brilliant, Lina!" Yuri slung an arm around Evelina's shoulder and gave her a squeeze.

Everyone in the family had come to watch Evelina in court the next morning, even Ainsley and Finnan. And Kate had come from Juneau just in time to testify about the need for the *Aurora* to deliver medical supplies to Barrow. She could only spare two days in Sitka and would be heading back to Juneau shortly, but this was the first time they'd all been together since Christmas, and it felt nice.

At the moment, the whole lot of them tromped down Castle Hill away from the governor's mansion with smiles on their faces.

Or at least everyone was smiling except Sacha, even Alexei.

Sacha had to admit, his sister had done a mighty fine job in court. She'd managed to get both his court date about transporting illicit contraband moved up, and Dr. Torres's possessions released so he could go back to Washington, DC.

Alexei was scheduled to pick up Dr. Torres's things in about an hour, and the *Alliance,* due in Sitka for a brief stop tomorrow, could take Dr. Torres back to Bellingham.

Sacha rubbed the back of his neck as he walked. It looked like the seal study would make it back to Washington after all, never mind that he was half tempted to throw it into the ocean.

Maybe the senators wouldn't care about it. Maybe they'd

just been humoring Dr. Torres and planned to dump the study into the Potomac River as soon as they received it.

And now he was just being petty. He slowed his steps, letting the others walk ahead of him. Dr. Torres and Maggie had spent hours upon hours working on that study. It was cruel for him to wish it destroyed. He just hoped that whatever happened with the study, his family didn't have to sacrifice anything else.

His heart wouldn't be able to take it.

Maggie's clear, bright laughter sounded from the group ahead, and he couldn't help but watch her for a moment. She walked beside Dr. Torres, her hand resting on his forearm as he led her down the hill. The scientist had spent most of his time in Sitka exploring. He'd hired a Tlingit man to take him to the mouth of the sound so he could study the fish. Then he'd hired the man again the next day to take him to the bay at the opposite end of the sound so he could study something or other there too.

But Dr. Torres had also made certain to sit beside Maggie each night at dinner, and he'd even found them talking on the porch one night.

The scientist had feelings for her. The more Sacha watched the two of them together, the clearer that became. Dr. Torres was bumbling and awkward and poor at showing what he felt, but the feelings were there nonetheless. And Sacha expected that when he visited Maggie in Wisconsin, he'd be a lot more forthright about his intentions.

That the man wasn't forthright now only made Sacha respect him. He knew Maggie needed to find Tavish and return to Wisconsin, and he was giving her the space to do so without any pressure.

He'd make Maggie a fine husband, indeed.

But was Maggie interested in him?

Sacha swallowed. He didn't think so. In fact, if he had to guess, he'd say her heart probably belonged to him.

Just like his belonged to her.

But nothing could come of their feelings for each other. Not with him being a captain, and not with him looking at spending the next five years of his life in jail if he didn't win his court case.

Which made him wonder if he should encourage Maggie to go with Dr. Torres to Australia this winter. To take the man up on the job offer in Washington, DC, and start a family in a new city once things were settled in Wisconsin. Her feelings for Dr. Torres would likely grow with time, and she'd get to spend the rest of her days with a man who adored her.

And yet Sacha couldn't quite bring himself to pull Maggie aside and tell her such things. Not now, and not an hour later when he, Alexei, Yuri, and Maggie accompanied Dr. Torres to collect his belongings from the *Aurora*. Not even later that evening, when she slipped back inside the house after sharing yet another conversation on the porch with the scientist.

He couldn't bring himself to speak to her earlier that morning either, when she came into the kitchen before dawn in search of coffee because she couldn't sleep.

All he could do was hope that someday she'd don a fancy dress and walk down the aisle toward him—not Dr. Torres. That someday she'd promise to love and cherish him for the rest of her days.

For some reason, he couldn't wipe the ridiculous vision from his mind—even though there was no chance the two of them could ever get married.

30

Two Weeks Later

Maggie had never met a family quite as amazing as the Amoses. She'd known they were special after her first visit to Sitka, but she hadn't realized just how special until she watched them work together over the past two weeks. Evelina had gotten Dr. Torres's belongings released shortly after arriving in Sitka, and Alexei had put the scientist on a ship to Bellingham the very next day—along with his study, which no one beyond her, Dr. Torres, and the Amos family knew existed. Then Alexei had turned his attention to reorganizing Sitka Trading Company's shipping schedule to meet all its contracts with only four ships.

Alexei's siblings might tease him about not smiling, but the man was a business genius, pure and simple. And when Maggie looked at all the things he oversaw—all the moving parts of owning both a trading company and a shipyard—she couldn't blame him for not smiling. She wouldn't be smiling either.

But Evelina hadn't just gotten Dr. Torres's belongings

released; she'd also managed to get Sacha's court date moved up to next week. Maggie had gone to court and listened as Evelina argued that Sacha had contracts with the Marine Hospital Service to distribute medical supplies to many of the tiny villages along the coast up north, and the *Aurora* was the best ship to use for the voyage because of its ability to sail through ice. She'd said detaining the vessel longer than necessary would put the native population at an unnecessary risk for disease. Kate had come from Juneau to testify to Evelina's statements, as had one of the doctors from Sitka.

Evelina alone had been quite convincing, but Evelina, Kate, and the local doctor together had been unstoppable. The judge had granted Evelina's request to move up the trial to next week with barely a blink.

Evelina and Sacha had been working feverishly on his defense ever since—and hoping that Mikhail and the RCS agent would return from Unalaska quickly enough that their testimonies would also work in Sacha's favor.

Meanwhile Maggie had made herself useful over in the shipping office. Evelina and Kate hadn't been lying when they said their family needed a bookkeeper.

To be honest, their family probably needed three bookkeepers. Maggie had done her best to check ledgers and organize as many records as possible. Or at least that's what she normally did, but the closer Sacha's court date drew, the more trouble she had focusing on the papers in front of her.

Which was what she needed to be doing at that exact moment—if she could just manage to stop thinking about the burly, muscular man who'd spent the past two weeks and three days avoiding her by working in the shipyard every spare moment of his time.

Maggie shifted in her chair and forced her eyes onto the mess of papers in front of her. She needed to know how many ships the shipyard was planning to build over the next year. The paper was buried somewhere on her desk. If she could just find—

"You're amazing, Maggs."

Maggie looked up to find Yuri standing in front of the desk, holding the paper she'd spent a good part of the morning working on—before she started thinking about Sacha.

"Alexei, come look at this." Yuri waved him over from where he'd been standing in front of the map of Alaska tacked to the wall, then sent her a wink. "Sacha's woman is a wizard when it comes to making sense of our records."

"I'm not Sacha's—"

"Did she run the cost projection I asked about?" Alexei strode toward the desk. "The one about how much money the *Aurora* could make if we took out the trip to Barrow every summer?"

"You're not taking Barrow off my shipping route," Sacha bellowed from the top of the stairwell, where he appeared just in time to glower at Alexei. He and Evelina had been at the house all morning preparing for court, but maybe it was time for lunch. "Someone needs to take medical supplies up to Barrow."

"You're right. They do," Alexei answered. "But the Marine Hospital Service isn't renewing our contract. The Revenue Cutter Service is going to start delivering supplies for them."

"What?" Every muscle in Sacha's body grew tense. Maggie could sense it even though he was on the other side of the giant room.

"Why?" Sacha stalked toward them. "Isn't the Marine Hospital Service happy with my deliveries?"

"I believe they are. While you were in Unalaska, the RCS was in my office asking about hiring you. That makes the second time so far this year. Of course, that was before you got charged with transporting illicit contraband. I'm not sure how interested they'd be in hiring you if you get convicted."

"Why do they want to hire you?" Maggie asked.

"Does it matter?" Sacha sighed, his shoulders rising and falling in a way that made her think this was far from the first time he had found himself caught in such a conversation. "I'm not interested in working for anyone other than my family. Never have been."

"Sacha's the best captain in the Arctic," Alexei answered in his brother's stead. "That's why the RCS wants to hire him. They don't just enforce maritime and customs law, but when needed, they deliver food and other supplies to remote villages and outposts. Sacha grew up sailing to remote villages back before any government saw a need for it, Russian or American. He's more familiar with the waters of the Bering Sea and Arctic Ocean than anyone else."

The best captain in the Arctic? Maggie looked at Sacha. She'd known he was a good captain. But was he really the best? He didn't walk around as though he controlled the universe. Didn't act condescending or arrogant. He was just . . . Sacha. The calm, kind giant of a man who had comforted her after they missed her brother's ship and entertained Ainsley and Finnan while she assisted Xavier.

"I don't understand," Yuri said. "If the Marine Hospital Service is happy with our ability to deliver supplies, why would they ask the RCS to start doing it?"

"Because the RCS has commissioned a double-hulled cutter from us, and it will be ready next spring and able to make the trip to Barrow. Once the government has a ship that can safely make that trip, there's no need for the Marine Hospital Service to rely on a private trading company to deliver medical supplies. The RCS will deliver those supplies. I've also heard talk that they'll be taking a traveling doctor from the Marine

Hospital Service to Barrow and some of the other villages at least once a year."

Yuri rubbed his jaw, his brows still drawn down in a frown, "They're going to send a doctor from California clear up to Barrow? Just to treat the Inupiat? That's an awful long trip, especially considering Kate already goes with Sacha. No one's ever complained about the treatment she gives the Inupiat."

"No, but the Marine Hospital Service is also considering building a hospital in Alaska to better treat the residents."

Maggie raised her eyebrows. The Marine Hospital Service's primary task was the health of sailors, particularly those in the navy. But in recent years, it had taken a large role in public health, helping with vaccine distributions and quarantining not just ill sailors but ill citizens as well. It made sense to establish a hospital somewhere in Alaska. Most major seaports in the US already had one, including Chicago.

"A hospital?" Sacha let out a low whistle. "Never thought we'd see anything that fancy in Sitka."

"We won't." Alexei picked up his mug from a nearby desk and took a sip of coffee. "It's being proposed for Juneau."

"What?" Sacha asked.

Yuri grimaced. "Does Kate know?"

Sacha was already shaking his head. "That's sure to take patients away from her."

"If the Marine Hospital Service decides to build a hospital in Juneau, then yes, I'm sure it will. But I'm not counting on that happening." Alexei's shoulders rose and fell on a shrug. "Alaska is too remote, and there aren't enough people. Chances are, even if we're not transporting medical supplies next summer, you'll still need to take Kate on the route so the tribes in the north can get at least a bit of medical care."

Sacha frowned. "I hope they don't build a hospital for Kate's sake."

"Me too," Yuri muttered, a crease appearing between his brows. "She's happy in Juneau."

"You realize Juneau is growing bigger by the month," Alexei quipped. "Eventually a real doctor is going to move to the town and hang out his shingle."

Yuri crossed his arms over his chest and glared at Alexei. "Kate *is* a real doctor."

"You know what I mean." Alexei didn't appear the least bit bothered by Yuri's glare. "A male doctor. One that's not a drunkard or an imbecile. The Marine Hospital Service might not come to Juneau, but to assume Kate will never have any competition from competent male doctors? That's ridiculous."

"I don't think any new doctor—or doctors—would come to Juneau with the intention of taking your sister's patients," Maggie offered.

Sacha glanced at her, his scowl nearly as big as Yuri's. "No, but that will be the end result."

"You never know." She shrugged. "If the Marine Hospital Service builds a new hospital, maybe the doctor in charge will want to hire her. She certainly seems competent."

Yuri burst out laughing, but the sound was a little darker than his usual carefree laugh. "She tried that here in Sitka, darling. It didn't go well."

Now Maggie felt herself frowning. "Whyever not?"

Sacha rested a hip against the side of the desk. "Because she's such a good doctor that most men can't tolerate it."

"They insist she see only women and children," Yuri added. "But as soon as she tells women they need to loosen their corsets, they stomp out of the office, claiming she's advocating for a lack of propriety."

"Oh . . . I . . ." Maggie looked around at the three men surrounding the desk. "Has this happened before?"

"More than once," Alexei muttered.

Sacha dug the toe of his boot into a crack in the floorboards. "Which is why, if the Marine Hospital Service builds that hospital, we should bring her back here before she can pick a fight with whatever doctor they send."

Alexei pinched the bridge of his nose, as though he felt a headache coming on. "Maybe he'll be old and out of shape and unaware of just how physical and demanding of a job he's getting into, and Kate can still find a way to practice medicine."

Yuri shook his head. "If this happens—and we don't know that it will—we need to let her decide where she wants to live. It's not our choice, and either way, she's going to be heartbroken."

"She's not the only one." Sacha slanted a glance at Alexei. "Are you sure the Marine Hospital Service wants the RCS to start delivering supplies?"

"Starting next summer, yes. They were quite clear on that during our meeting yesterday afternoon."

"But that tribe, going up to Barrow . . ." Sacha's throat bobbed, and he snapped his mouth shut.

He didn't need to continue for Maggie to understand how important the voyage was to him. He sailed the *Aurora* all over the Pacific Ocean to California and Japan and Russia, and those were just the places she knew about. But the only voyage she'd heard him talk about the most was the one to the Arctic, to Barrow. He loved it, probably for the same reason he loved visiting the Aleut village in Unalaska.

"I'm not trying to be cruel, Sacha." Alexei settled a hand on his brother's wide shoulder. "I know you like that route, but with the Marine Hospital Service not planning to renew our contract, this summer might be your last voyage there, especially if they take a doctor with them on their route."

"Not running the Barrow route will leave us better off,"

Yuri said. "We'll be able to find a more lucrative run for the *Aurora* instead."

"Is that true?" Sacha dragged a hand through his hair, his large shoulders heaving. "Just how much money do we need the *Aurora* to bring in over the summer? With all the commissions coming into the shipyard, aren't we on a bit better financial footing?"

They were, actually. Maggie knew because she'd seen the numbers. The previous year's financial statements had been low, especially for the trading company. It looked as though they'd lost several lucrative contracts to larger shipping companies. But at the end of last year, and for the first half of this year, the shipyard side of the family business had started making up for most of the lost shipping income.

"We're doing better than we were," Alexei agreed. "But I'd still like the trading company to generate a respectable profit margin on its own, and last year it didn't. That's why I asked Maggie to draw up this report." He snatched the paper Yuri had been looking at earlier off the desk, then blinked at it. "This isn't a cost analysis of the *Aurora*'s shipping route."

"No." Maggie reached for that paper on the desk and handed it to him. "I finished with that report an hour or so ago. Here it is."

But Alexei didn't reach out and take it. He studied the other paper in his hand for another moment, then turned to her and raised an eyebrow. "You put together a comparative analysis on which of our holdings—the shipyard or the trading company—bring in the most profit?"

She shrugged. "It seemed as though that report might be helpful. But here's the cost analysis of the *Aurora*'s shipping route like you asked." She nudged the paper a little closer to Alexei.

Sacha wasn't going to like what it revealed. Cutting out the trip to Barrow and using those weeks to run a profitable route would certainly put the *Aurora* in better financial standing. In fact, it looked as though canceling the cannery contracts as a whole and running more trips between Russia, Seattle, and San Francisco would be the best use of the *Aurora*.

"These are brilliant." Alexei's eyes soaked in everything on the pages. "Both of them. Sacha, why didn't you tell us your woman was so brilliant?"

His woman. There they went, saying she belonged to Sacha again.

There was a time when she might have imagined belonging to him, might have dreamed about a way the two of them could be together. But the man was a captain first and foremost. One who regretted commissioning a seal study she wholeheartedly supported. And one who had barely spoken to her since they'd arrived in Sitka.

But now, when she looked at him, her chest felt so heavy she barely had the strength to stand. Yet that's exactly what she did, then swept from the room before anyone could notice the tears burning her eyes.

31

Ten Days Later

They were going to lose the case. A sickening feeling rose in Sacha's gut as he stared at Eric on the witness stand. He'd been listed all along as someone who was going to testify, but Sacha hadn't realized just how brazenly the man would lie.

In fact, it seemed that the entirety of the case might boil down to whom people believed more, him or Eric.

And Eric was a very convincing liar.

"I done told him it was illegal ta sell alcohol to the Aleut," Eric's voice echoed over the room, his eyes wide and somber, an innocent look on his face. "But he unloaded a bunch of cases in Unalaska."

Murmuring broke out in the courtroom, but Eric kept going. "Iffin' I'd realized a man was going to end up dead after the Indians got drunk, I woulda stood up harder to Cap'n Amos. I regret not protestin' more."

Sacha tried not to scoff. Eric might have been on his ship

for only a handful of months, but the man was one of the biggest drinkers on his crew.

"Did Captain Amos sell liquor to any of the other tribes while you were aboard?" The prosecutor approached the witness stand.

"Why, sure he did. He sold it to the Tlingit in Petersburg too. You can go there and ask them yerself."

Again, more murmuring rose up from the gallery, where it seemed the entire town of Sitka had packed into the small room.

While Alaska might technically be dry, no one enforced the laws, except when it came to the native tribes. They had a reputation for being violent and mean when drunk, though Sacha wasn't sure Indians got any angrier or drunker than white men.

The judge banged his gavel on the bench and called for order before telling the prosecutor to proceed.

The prosecutor took a moment to straighten the lapels of his suitcoat. "In your opinion, Mr. Whitting, how competent of a captain is Sacha Amos?"

"I've been a sailor fer five years." Eric looked directly at Sacha, his eyes narrowed into two thin slits. "And Sacha Amos is the worst captain I ever worked for."

"Now just a minute . . ." Gus stood from his seat in the row of chairs directly behind Sacha.

"Ya can't say that!" Ronnie shouted.

The judge banged his gavel again, this time threatening to remove the next person who interrupted the proceedings. Sacha's crew, all of whom were seated on the bench directly behind him, settled themselves as the prosecutor asked the next question.

"What makes you say Mr. Amos here is a bad captain?"

Captain Amos, Sacha wanted to growl. But he settled for clamping his teeth together and glaring at the prosecutor.

Again, Eric's eyes turned to him, and Sacha dreaded what was going to come out of the man's mouth next.

"He didn't run a fair ship. He had favorites he gave the good jobs to and made me work in the kitchen after we left Bellingham. I ain't never worked on a ship like that before. You can ask any sailor here, and they'll tell ya the same."

"That ain't what happened," Ronnie whispered behind him.

"Hush or you'll get yourself kicked out," Maggie whispered back.

Evelina, seated in the chair beside Sacha, shifted slightly so she could see his crew. "All of you, settle down, or I'll request that you be removed from the courtroom."

"Thank you, Mr. Whitting, for sharing your experience aboard the *Aurora*." The prosecutor looked at the judge. "No further questions, Your Honor."

The judge blinked, then turned to Evelina. "Your witness, Mrs. Redding."

Evelina stood and approached the stand. "Mr. Whitting, did you see any money change hands between Captain Amos and any of the tribal elders in Unalaska?"

Eric's face twisted into a scowl. "I weren't with Cap'n Amos the whole time. I was busy takin' supplies from the dingy to the storehouse. But the cap'n was talkin' to the chief alone fer a long time, and I saw the chief give him things."

"Chief, you say? There was a chief? At the Aleut village in Unalaska? Has there been some type of change in the structure of Aleut leadership? Because as of this spring when I visited Unalaska, they were still using the elder system of tribal rule that they've been using for over a thousand years. Can you give me more information about this new chief in Unalaska?"

Eric's face darkened. "So maybe he was an elder instead, but he was still the man in charge."

"I see. And just to clarify, did you actually observe anyone from the Aleut village paying Captain Amos with cash money?"

Eric clamped his lips shut, but rather than pressing for an answer—which Evelina could have done—she switched tactics and asked if he had carried any crates of alcohol to the storehouse himself.

When the man claimed he had, Sacha found himself tempted to bolt from his chair and shout that Eric was lying. But at that exact moment, a slender hand from behind him reached out and settled on his shoulder. So he stayed seated, letting Eric spin his web of lies—and wondering how he was supposed to convince anyone of his innocence after the man got off the stand.

MAGGIE STARED down at her plate, where she pushed the carrots and bear roast around, rather than taking a bite. Everyone except Kate—who'd returned to Juneau weeks ago—was gathered around the large table in the Amoses' dining room, but no one spoke, not even Yuri. It almost felt as if she was attending a funeral dinner rather than a family supper.

But given how their second day in court had gone, how could it feel like anything other than a funeral dinner?

"I hate this." She stabbed a carrot with her fork, the action so forceful that the carrot split in half. "It's all lies. Sacha shouldn't even need to go to court. Eric is the one who should be on trial. For perjury."

"It's all right, Maggie." Ainsley laid a hand over hers on the table and sent her a small smile.

"Evelina will get Sacha out of this," Ilya said, though his smile wasn't quite as bright as normal.

If only she could be so confident, but Ilya hadn't attended court today—none of the children had. Alexei hadn't even wanted Inessa to go, seeing how her older brother might end up in prison if things didn't go their way.

"Sissy need a hug?" Finnan pushed his chair back from where he sat across from her, then tromped around the table.

Maggie scooted her chair back and held her arms open for the boy, who crawled onto her lap and nestled his head against her shoulder.

Sacha watched them from the end of the table, his eyes warm at the sight of Finnan snuggled against her.

He'd said nothing so far about court, and his face hadn't given away any of his thoughts. In fact he'd barely said a word since returning to the house with the rest of them. Now he was silently putting small bites of food into his mouth, almost as though the only reason he ate was because there was food in front of him. Not because he was hungry.

Maggie ducked her head until her mouth was only a few inches from Finnan's ear. "Go give Sacha a hug. He needs one more than me."

He perked up his head, looked at Sacha, and then scampered off her lap and headed straight toward him with his arms raised. "Sissy says you need a hug."

Sacha sent her a look she couldn't quite read, then scooted his chair back and hefted Finnan atop his legs. His chest was so large that Finnan nearly disappeared against it, but he tucked the boy into the crook of his arm, then tousled his hair. "Reckon I do. Especially from someone as good at giving hugs as you."

Finnan beamed up at him. "You think I'm good at giving hugs?"

"The best."

Maggie looked away from the scene, her eyes burning. How could she go back to court tomorrow and sit there while this tender, loving man had the next five years of his future stripped from him? "This is all so unfair. The only reason Eric's lying is because he's bitter toward Sacha. Because of me. Because of how Sacha punished him when he . . ."

She shook her head, then raised her gaze to meet Evelina's. "Can't we do something to let the court know Eric's trying to get revenge, not justice?"

Evelina dabbed at her mouth with her napkin. "I have several crew members who will testify that Eric is lying, that the *Aurora* never delivered any alcohol to the village in Unalaska. Plus the letters Mikhail brought back from Unalaska claiming Sacha's innocence. Keep in mind that it's not our turn to call witnesses yet. It always seems like the defense is losing at this point in a trial, when the prosecution is making its case. Even though today might have been disheartening, I don't feel as though the case is anywhere close to being lost."

"But shouldn't we tell the court what happened?" Maggie pressed. "Why Eric hates Sacha so much?"

"No," Sacha's voice rang out. "Absolutely not."

"But . . ."

"Wait." Alexei looked between the two of them. Then his gaze settled on Sacha. "Why does Eric hate you so much?"

"Did something happen aboard the *Aurora*?" Yuri set down his fork with a clatter. "Something the rest of us should know about?"

"I'd like to know what you're talking about too." Mikhail sat back in his chair, his plate cleaned. Though he'd barely spoken during the meal, his keen golden eyes told her he hadn't missed a thing.

The man had just returned from Unalaska with letters from several Aleut men saying that Sacha hadn't sold them any liquor. The problem was, the RCS had evidently found several other Aleut men who swore up and down that they purchased the liquor from Sacha. Mikhail thought Preston Caldwell was paying them to lie, just like he was paying Eric. But they had no way of proving it.

"Yes, can you explain a bit more?" Evelina set her napkin back on her lap, her gaze darting between Maggie and Sacha. "If I can prove Eric has motive to see Sacha imprisoned, that will go a long way to discrediting his statements. I might even be able to get him removed as a witness. And without Eric to testify about selling liquor to the Aleut, part of the case falls apart."

"There's nothing to explain." Sacha glared at Maggie, and she had to tamp down the urge to squirm in her chair. "The statements of my crew will be enough to counter what Eric's saying. We'll proceed with the defense as planned."

She sighed. Sacha was probably right. Accusing Eric of having a motive to see Sacha imprisoned meant she'd need to tell an entire courtroom how the sailor had treated her in the kitchen that first day. And she felt her face heat up merely at the memory.

"I still want to know what happened." Mikhail crossed his arms over his chest, his golden eyes locked on her. "Even if it doesn't get shared in court."

"Me too," Alexei said.

"Sacha made him wash dishes the whole time," Finnan blurted from where he still sat tucked into Sacha's lap.

"Finnan," Maggie snapped. "That's not our story to share."

"The whole time?" Ilya's eyes grew huge. "Why did he have to wash so many dishes?"

"Yes, why?" Evelina was sitting straighter in her chair now, her eyes bright at the possibility of discovering a new angle to help Sacha's case. "Like I said earlier, it will help if the jury thinks Eric Whitting is untrustworthy. So why does he have a grudge against you?"

Sacha sent Maggie a look, and this time she had no trouble reading the thoughts in his eyes. *Stop. Now.*

But he told the table, "Eric never liked me, is all. And I doubt he liked the captain he had before me, or the captain before that. The pup has a problem with anyone in authority."

"That might be true. But it's not the only reason Eric hates Sacha. You see, Eric was . . . He was . . ." Maggie ducked her head and drew in a breath, forcing the next words out. "He was inappropriate with me. And Sacha made him regret it."

"Maggie," Sacha growled, his voice low. "This is *not* the kind of thing that needs to be aired in court. There's a clerk who writes down every word of what's said. If you share the story, not only will the entire town know, but it will also be recorded for anyone to come back and read about later."

She raised her eyes to meet his. "But won't saying what happened help you?"

"Will one of you just tell me what happened?" Evelina asked again, her voice tinged with frustration.

"Sissy." Finnan tugged on her sleeve. "Privy."

Maggie looked down at the boy. He'd crawled off Sacha's lap at some point and was now standing beside her. And of course he had to go then. She'd forgotten to have him attempt to use the toilet when he washed his hands before dinner. Although maybe that was for the best. This wasn't the type of conversation she wanted Finnan and Ainsley overhearing. "Ainsley, please take your brother to the privy."

"But . . ." The girl looked around. "What did the sailor do to you? I don't understand."

And she didn't need to understand. Thank goodness Finnan had interrupted her, or she might have let slip things that were best left unsaid in front of young ears.

Sacha must have sensed the thoughts running through her head, because he straightened and looked at his two youngest siblings.

"Ilya, Inessa, leave." His voice carried a distinct sharpness and sounded commanding enough that she could imagine him using it when calling orders to his crew while navigating through a severe storm.

"But I'm still eating," Ilya whined.

Sacha merely raised an eyebrow, and Ilya shoved his chair away from the table, shoulders slumped. "I guess I'll finish my food later."

Inessa was already pushing back from the table. "Come along, Ainsley. Didn't you want to play checkers after dinner?"

Ainsley scooted her chair back and stood more slowly, still hesitant to leave, but Finnan jumped up and darted toward the door. "I want to learn how to play! Will you teach me?"

Ilya followed behind Finnan, his footsteps dragging.

"Ilya," Maggie said, "will you please take him to the privy before he starts watching checkers? The last thing she needed was a mess on the parlor floor.

"Yes, ma'am," he muttered, his shoulders still slumped. Then he tromped from the room and pulled the door shut behind him.

"What happened with Eric?" Seriousness filled Evelina's gaze, and her mouth was set in a firm line. "Tell me everything."

Maggie swallowed, suddenly aware of four sets of male eyes on her. "Eric touched me. He tried to force . . . That is . . ." Before they excused the children, the conversation had naturally fallen in this direction, and talking about it had felt a little simpler. But now her words dried up, and her tongue turned thick and cottony.

"See? You can't even say it in front of my family." Sacha shoved a hand in his sister's direction. "How are you going to say it in front of a judge and a courtroom packed with people?"

"You knew Eric assaulted her and didn't tell me?" Evelina jumped in, her eyes shooting daggers at her brother. "That's rather significant information to conceal from your attorney."

Maggie just stared at her plate, her eyes hot. Maybe Sacha was right. Maybe she shouldn't have said anything—couldn't say anything in court, where her words would be permanently recorded for all to read.

"It took me a couple days to put things together," Sacha answered his sister. "But after I found out, I relegated him to kitchen duty until Maggie left the ship. At first he complied, but he got bored with washing dishes after a few days. When he found out we were headed to the Pribilofs, he was quite adamant about not wanting to be aboard a vessel involved in any type of scientific analysis of the seal population. I forced him off the ship as soon as we reached Saint Paul Island. Though that wasn't much of a hardship for him. It took ACC all of five minutes to hire him to hunt seals.

"I honestly don't know whether he's madder about the kitchen duty or the fact I didn't let him anywhere near Maggie for the rest of the voyage," Sacha continued.

Maggie took a sip of water, hoping it would make her tongue feel a little less swollen, then looked at Evelina. "Do you need me to testify?"

Evelina's gaze softened when it met hers. "Yes. Is that all right?"

Part of her wanted to say no, that she'd rather do as Sacha suggested and leave all this buried in the past. But if she could play some small part in getting the *Aurora* released and ensuring Sacha didn't spend the next five years of his life in prison . . . "Yes. I'll do it."

"No!" Sacha's voice rang out with the force of a thousand

commands behind it. "This kind of thing ought not be aired in court. Ever."

Evelina's eyes flashed. "And what do you think happens during a rape trial? That a rapist gets convicted without the victim ever going into detail about what happened? It might be unpleasant, but sometimes these things need to be brought out for justice to be served."

"I'll do it," Maggie said again, louder this time. "I'll testify. But I want to run through some questions with Evelina a few times, so I know what to expect."

"Absolutely." Evelina stood from the table. "Come. The others can clean up dinner while we prepare to put you on the stand."

Maggie took another look around the table, where she found the gazes of four unhappy men directed at her. Then she set her napkin on the table and stood. She wouldn't let what any of them thought change her mind. She knew the next step she needed to take. Now she just needed to find the strength to do it.

32

Maggie wrapped her arms around her knees and stared out the window, her legs curled beneath her on the chair as the sun slowly dipped behind the mountains surrounding the sound. Normally the sight of the midnight sun calmed her, but not tonight. Her head was too full, her mind spinning with all the questions Evelina had put her through.

Some had been downright humiliating, like when Evelina had asked whether she'd wanted Eric to touch her or if they'd ever kissed. Evelina had even asked if she could have accidentally done anything that might have encouraged Eric to think his advances were welcome—and she'd asked the insulting question in multiple different ways.

At one point, she'd plead with Evelina to stop asking such questions, but Evelina had said that the prosecutor would try to discredit her testimony, and the easiest way to do that was by making it seem as though she'd encouraged Eric in some way. That, at its heart, the effectiveness of her testimony would boil down to whether the jury believed her or Eric more.

So they'd continued, with Evelina asking her mortifying questions, then giving her tips on how to answer.

Now her head ached, her throat felt thick, and her eyes burned with tears she'd refused to let herself shed.

She'd put Ainsley and Finnan to bed, then brewed herself a cup of chamomile tea, hoping to calm both her nerves and her mind so she could sleep before court tomorrow.

Evelina wanted her to be the first witness, which meant they'd only had tonight to prepare. But Evelina thought attacking Eric's credibility as a witness right away was more important than spending additional time working on her testimony. Evelina was quite insistent that they not go into the weekend with Eric's words ringing true in the jury's mind.

Still, testifying for Sacha, even on such short notice, had to be better than sitting in that courtroom watching him get lied about.

"I don't want you to testify," a voice said from behind her.

Maggie raised her head and looked toward the door to the parlor to find Sacha standing there, his lips set in a severe line.

He crossed the parlor toward her with determined strides and sat in the chair opposite her own. "I'm serious, Maggie, you don't need to do this. I'll get acquitted without you stepping onto the witness stand. Evelina is a good lawyer, and we've been working on my defense for weeks. Once she starts calling witnesses, she'll trounce the prosecution. I promise."

"You speak as though you suddenly have no doubts over whether you'll win, but the last time we talked, you were so worried about losing that you told me you regretted ever contacting Xavier about the seal study."

He sighed. "Must you call him Xavier?"

Maggie straightened. "Really? Of everything I just said, that's the part you want to argue about?"

Sacha's lips turned firm again, and thoughts she couldn't

quite read churned in his eyes. "Don't do it, Maggie. Please don't testify."

She gave her head a small shake. "Why? This case isn't cut and dry. There's still a chance you could lose, and I know you understand that, or you wouldn't regret contacting Xavier."

"That was before Mikhail returned with Kuluk's letter. His testimony will be enough to prove Eric's lying."

"If his testimony is believed. But how many of those jurors do you think will naturally believe the word of a native over the word of a white man? Now, if a white woman could also discredit his testimony, then perhaps the jury would be more apt to think Eric a liar."

The breath Sacha heaved from his lungs was so strong it might have ruffled the curtains on the window. "Maggie, please, don't do this."

She leaned forward and took his hand, the feel of his skin against hers causing a jolt of warmth to travel up her arm. "Thank you for being so concerned about how this might affect me. It's kind and sweet, and I appreciate that you care so much about me. But ultimately, this is my choice to make, and nothing you say is going to stop me from walking up to that witness stand tomorrow."

"But—"

"But nothing. If I sit by without attempting to defend you and you lose, I won't be able to live with myself. I have to at least try. And from how I see it, you're the last man who can grumble about this, because you would do the same thing if the situation were reversed. In fact, you did the same thing already, when you offered to take me and my siblings to Unalaska without charging us any money for passage. You even insisted we sleep on the *Aurora* a night early when you learned we had nowhere to stay.

"Both of those things caused you hardship," she continued.

"But you did them anyway, because they were right, and there's something inside you that won't let you turn away from the path you know is right, even when it will make things hard. Now it's my turn to do what's right for you, and I won't let you talk me out of it."

Sacha flipped his hand around so his palm cradled her hand, then squeezed. "You're a hard person to argue with, Maggie McDougal."

"I've weighed the consequences, and I'll gladly face them if it gives you a better chance of staying out of prison." She watched him closely, the familiar planes of his face, the tiny lines around his eyes and mouth.

He was quiet as she studied him, almost as though he didn't quite know what to say.

"Have you thought that maybe there's a reason for all of this?" she whispered. "Like how there was a reason for Job's suffering. Maybe God's trying to work here too, and we just can't see it."

He tugged his hand away from her and scrubbed it down his face. "The main thing I see when I look at my situation is Preston Caldwell's greed. I struggle to see how that has anything to do with God."

She looked back out at the water, letting his words linger between them. It was hard to argue, especially considering how much the *Aurora* meant to Sacha and his family. Some of what Job had gone through seemed like a series of accidents, natural situations that went horribly wrong. But Sacha was under a malicious, targeted attack. And it made her sick.

"I'm sorry," she rasped.

"It's not your fault."

She pushed to her feet, unable to sit still any longer, but she didn't leave the window. There was something calming about the sun setting over the water and mountains. If only she could find a way to get that same calmness to seep into her soul.

"Do you miss not being on the sea?" She kept her gaze pinned to the entrance at the opposite side of the sound, on the spot where the mountains fell away and the dying rays of sunlight glistened on the calm waters of the Pacific. "It might be silly of me, but I find myself longing for it."

She hadn't expected to miss it so much, not when she'd spent her entire life on land. And yet, there was a part of her soul that ached for the water.

"Yes," he croaked. He stood to face her, then his eyes dipped to her lips. When he brought them back up to meet her gaze, the softness she remembered from their time aboard the *Aurora* was back.

"I miss the sea," he rasped. "But not quite as much as I miss spending moments like this with you."

Warmth rose in her cheeks. "You ought not say such things, not when there can't be anything between us."

He reached out and cupped her cheeks with large, rough hands, then rested his forehead against hers. "There's a logical part of my brain that understands that. But there's another part of my brain that's keenly aware you and I are both still in Sitka together. That remembers how it felt to hold you in my arms and—"

"Don't." She slid her finger between their mouths, then she pressed it tight against his mouth to silence him. "It will make what needs to happen next too hard."

"And here you both claim there's nothing going on between you," a voice boomed from behind them.

Maggie jumped away from Sacha. But it was too late to try looking innocent, because Yuri and Alexei were both standing in the doorway staring at her and Sacha.

She didn't know where they'd been. Sane men would be

abed at this hour of the night. That's where Evelina and the children all were. But obviously Alexei and Yuri had been busy with something—probably working in the shipping office.

"Does that look like nothing to you, Alexei?" Yuri elbowed his brother.

"Looks like they were about two seconds away from kissing," Alexei muttered, his voice dry.

"We were nothing of the sort." Maggie stepped farther away from Sacha.

"Sure you weren't, darling." Yuri came forward and slung an arm around her shoulders, then turned her toward the hall. "Off to bed with you, darling. You have court in the morning, and you don't want to be sleepy. But next time you try kissing my brother, I suggest you lure him outside first. It's harder for people to find you when you sneak off, especially after dark."

"And how, exactly, would you know this?" Alexei quirked an eyebrow at Yuri.

Yuri just chuckled and led her toward the door, not even giving her a chance to say goodnight to Sacha as he escorted her to the foot of the stairs.

SACHA WANTED to crawl under the table and pull his hair out. Either that or get between Evelina and Maggie and tell his sister she had to stop. Or maybe he'd just stride into the middle of the courtroom and howl until everyone around him was forced to stop talking.

Any of that had to be better than sitting in a chair behind the defendant's table, watching as Maggie cried behind the witness stand.

Unfortunately, her tears didn't make Evelina hesitate for even a second as she went through question after question about how Eric had treated her, how that had made her feel, what Sacha had done about it as captain, and what Eric's response to his kitchen duty had been.

Part of Sacha couldn't believe they were even discussing this. Not the assault part. That was a crime, punishable by law, even if the sensitive nature of the crime meant such cases rarely landed in courtrooms. But kitchen duty? A sailor's response to it? Could such petty things really make a difference in his trial?

He'd tried to warn Maggie this would happen, had tried to talk her out of testifying last night, but she hadn't listened. And now the sight of the tears streaming down her face made him want to jump to his feet and wrap his hands around Eric's throat.

Then he wanted to wrap his arms around Maggie, brush the tears from her cheeks, and hold her until her sobs turned into sniffles, and her sniffles turned into a smile.

Or better yet, maybe he'd leave off strangling Eric and snatch Maggie out of the witness chair, then whisk her clear back to Wisconsin. Far, far away from all of this.

"That's why Eric was so mad at Captain Amos." Maggie's voice resounded through the courtroom, a bit stronger than it had been when giving her previous statements, though it still held a slight tremor. "Because Captain Amos punished him for assaulting me. So to pay him back, Eric's been on the stand lying this entire time."

"Objection!" The lawyer for the prosecution shot to his feet. "She can't claim my witness was lying."

The judge banged his gavel on the stand. "Let Miss McDougal's last statement be struck from the records."

Maggie looked up at the judge, her eyes wide and innocent. "Oh, I'm sorry. Was I not allowed to say that?"

The judge looked down at her. "No, dear, you can't claim

another witness is lying on the witness stand, at least not outright."

Sacha raised an eyebrow. *Dear?* Had the judge just called Maggie *dear?*

And while Sacha couldn't claim the man was smiling, his expression certainly looked softer than the one he gave Evelina whenever she appeared in court.

"No further questions, Your Honor." Evelina headed back to the defense table, the corner of her mouth tipped up in the faintest of smiles. She was evidently happy with how things had unfolded on the stand, though Sacha fully intended to scold his sister later. Surely she could have asked questions without making Maggie cry.

"Your witness, prosecution," the judge said.

The lawyer stood, then looked at Eric, seated on the bench directly behind the prosecution's table. "Ah . . . can we call for a brief recess? I need to speak with one of my witnesses."

The judge glanced at the clock hanging on the wall. "It's too late in the day to bother with a recess. We'll adjourn for the weekend an hour early and resume with the prosecution's questioning of Miss McDougal on Monday morning. That should give all attorneys plenty of time to confer with their witnesses."

"Thank you, Your Honor," The prosecutor said, though he didn't look very grateful for the extra time, not considering his face had turned whiter than a jug of fresh milk.

The judge banged his gavel again, declared court was dismissed, and then rose from the stand. Everyone around him rose too, in a sudden hurry to be one of the first people out of the room.

Sacha stood and tried to move past Evelina to get to Maggie, but Evelina reached out and grabbed his arm. "No. Not here. Don't say so much as a word to her until you're back at the house."

"But . . ." He glanced over at Maggie, who was dabbing her red eyes with a handkerchief.

"I mean it, Sacha. If the prosecution thinks the two of you are romantically involved, we'll lose all the ground Maggie just gained us."

"But we're not romantically involved."

Evelina raised an eyebrow. "Oh, so that's what I witnessed last night at dinner, when Maggie agreed to testify, and you kept trying to talk her out of it because you knew her feelings would be a mess. Good to know that's what *not* being romantically involved looks like."

He sighed. "Fine. We weren't involved when Eric assaulted her and I assigned him to the galley for the rest of the voyage. No one can argue with that, since I'd known her less than two days. Now if I'm not allowed to talk to her, can you? Because she's standing there all alone, trying not to cry, and—"

"Oh, you have it just as bad as she does, don't you?" Evelina sent him a soft smile, then looked over at Maggie, who was still dabbing her eyes. "And here I thought she was more attached to you than you were to her, but you're just better at hiding it. My only question is, why are you both trying so hard to ignore your feelings for each other?"

"Because I'm a captain, and that doesn't lend itself to having a wife or family."

"But do you have to be a captain? Couldn't you be happy—?"

"Miss McDougal! Miss McDougal!" The sound of Ilya's voice echoed from the back of the courtroom. There were still a few people gathering their belongings and moseying toward the door, but most townsfolk had already left.

The boy flew down the aisle, slowing only long enough to spot Maggie at the front of the courthouse before plowing forward. "The *Halcyon*'s here! It just entered the sound. Do you know what that means? You'll be able to see your brother!" He skidded to a stop in front of her, a smile as bright as the sun plastered to his face.

"The *Halcyon*?" Maggie rasped.

"Come on." Ilya grabbed her hand and tugged. "Ainsley and Finnan are already at the wharf waiting."

A wide smile broke out onto her face, and she gripped Ilya's hand, then rushed down the aisle with him. Sacha couldn't quite say she was running, but she was moving about as fast as a woman could while wearing heavy skirts.

"That's another reason, right there." Sacha kept his eyes pinned to the doorway where Maggie had just disappeared. "Maggie came to Alaska to find Tavish. And now that she's found him, she'll want to go home. The two of us were never trying to hide anything, no. We've been pretending it's not there. Then maybe saying good-bye won't hurt so much."

But now that Tavish was here, he'd be saying good-bye all too soon.

"Sacha." Evelina rested her hand on his forearm, the touch tender and soft. "You can move to Wisconsin, you know. You don't have to stay in Alaska."

Sacha looked down into his sister's bright-green eyes. He already didn't see her enough, just like he didn't see Kate or Ilya or Inessa or Mikhail enough. Alexei and Yuri were the only two siblings he saw with any regularity. Could he really be in a place so far away from his family? Even if he had Maggie with him?

He took a step back from Evelina. "Come on. Let's go meet the *Halcyon*."

33

Maggie raced down the path that ran from the administrative building on the top of Castle Hill down to the town, pumping her legs as fast as she could beneath her layers of skirts and petticoats. She could see a ship nearing the wharf in front of the Amoses' warehouse, its sails being lowered as it glided toward the port. It didn't look as new and majestic as the *Aurora*, but it was still large and beautiful, and obviously well kept.

Ilya ran ahead of her, reaching the town first and darting down a street before he turned and headed toward the water.

Maggie followed behind him, her chest heaving as she sucked salty air into her lungs. She'd been waiting so long, had tried so many times to find her brother. In a few more moments, she'd be hugging him, then telling him everything that had happened with their mother and stepfather's unexpected deaths, and finally explaining that he'd inherited the land and shipyard in Wisconsin.

She could almost hear herself saying the words, almost taste them on her tongue.

She turned down the road that led to the shipyard, dodging a rock in her path and willing her legs to move faster. A moment later she raced between the warehouse and the shipyard, where it appeared the usual workers had left their posts to greet the *Halcyon*. A crowd had gathered on the wharf. It included most of the Amos family, seeing how they'd left the courthouse before Ilya had come to fetch her, and the shipyard workers were there too, wheeling handcarts and waiting to unload the ship.

Ilya was already weaving his way through the crowd, and she followed his path, shouldering past people until she stood at the front of the wharf beside Ainsley and Finnan. Yuri, Alexei, and Mikhail had taken the thick ropes that the crew had thrown down from the deck and were using them to tie the ship to the wharf.

"Tavish," she shouted, scanning the crew on the deck above her. "Tavish, are you there?"

Several men peered down from the railing.

"There he is." Yuri came up beside her. "See him?"

Maggie frowned at the man he was pointing to. "No. I'm looking for Tavish. That's not my brother."

The gangway hit the wharf with a giant thud, and she was the first one up it, Finnan and Ainsley scrambling after her. It might be a bit presumptuous to insist on being first, but she hadn't come all this way, hadn't waited all this time, to stand back and let her brother be the last man off the ship.

Except she didn't see her brother standing on the deck. There was a man with brownish-blond hair, but he was far too short to be her brother.

"Tavish!" she called again. "Tavish McDougal?"

"That there is Tavish." A crew member nodded toward a man with dark hair standing by the mast, the same man Yuri had pointed to from the wharf.

She shook her head. "No. That man's not Tavish."

But she'd succeeded in catching the man's attention, because now he was coming toward her.

Where was Tavish? Was he belowdecks, preparing the cargo to get unloaded?

Ainsley reached out and gripped her hand, as though sensing something wasn't quite right.

Then Sacha appeared at her side, his chest heaving as though he, too, had run the entire way from the top of Castle Hill. "What's going on?"

"They're saying that man's my brother. But that's not him."

"Maggie?" The dark-haired stranger stopped in front of her, scrubbing a hand over his stubbly jaw. "Are you . . . ? Ah . . . are you Maggie McDougal?"

"I am." She scanned his face, the dark eyes and hair, the wide jaw and forehead that looked nothing like her brother's oval-shaped face and brownish-blond hair. "I don't understand. Why is everyone saying you're Tavish McDougal? You're not my brother."

She scanned the crew again, all of which had stopped working to watch her, just as all of Sacha's family had come aboard and was now watching her. Her heart thudded dangerously hard against her chest, and her mouth turned dry. "Is Tavish somewhere else? Belowdecks, maybe?"

"I . . . um . . ." The stranger shifted. "About that . . ."

"About what? I want to know what's going on here. Are there two Tavish McDougals?" Sacha ran his eyes between them, then turned to her. "I hate to say it, Maggie, but the Tavish in front of us is the man who's been sailing with me for the past six years. So you're saying he's not your brother?"

"No. But someone from your ship has been writing me letters and signing them as Tavish McDougal. That's how I knew I needed to find the *Aurora*." Her voice was getting higher, her breaths coming shorter and shorter as she stared at the man in front of her. Something wasn't adding up. Where was her brother, if not here? Did the man pretending to be Tavish know where he was?

"That, um . . . That was me." The stranger stepped forward. "You were always writing from Wisconsin, and I felt bad letting all of your letters go unanswered, so I wrote you a letter every Christmas."

"Why? And . . . and where is Tavish?" Tears pricked the backs of her eyes, but she blinked them away and sucked in a breath. This wasn't the time to turn into a watering pot. She needed answers. And she needed them now. "Where's the real Tavish McDougal?"

The man rubbed the back of his neck and ducked his head. "He's dead, miss. Died back in San Francisco all those years ago, before I ever came north."

"No." She stumbled backward as tears flooded her eyes. "He's not dead. He can't be dead. He's . . . I'm looking for Tavish. He's been writing me letters. He . . . he needs to come back to Wisconsin with me to inherit our father's land and his shipyard. But this, you're . . . It's not . . ."

Sacha reached out and wrapped an arm around her shoulders, drawing her against his warm, solid chest. But his touch only made her cry harder. She was vaguely aware that Ainsley and Finnan had started crying too.

"You'd better start explaining." Sacha's voice was hard as it rang out over the deck. "Because I want to know why you lied to me and everyone here for the past six years. Why you pretended to be someone you're not and didn't see fit to ever correct it. I'll let you start by telling me your real name."

The man in front of her—she wasn't going to call him Tavish—looked around the ship, then sighed, his shoulders slumping. "My name's Ed. Edward Fischer, really, but everyone used to call me Ed. And I didn't mean nothin' bad by saying I was Tavish. I was just . . . I needed a different name is all. Tavish McDougal seemed like it would work as well as any."

"Why'd you need a different name?" Yuri asked.

"How'd you end up using Tavish's name?" Alexei narrowed his eyes at the man. "And don't ask me to believe you made it up and then happened to accidentally start receiving letters addressed to the made-up name."

"I'm more interested in figuring out how you know Tavish died." This from Mikhail, who was standing at the back of the crowd. "Sounds to me like you might have had a role in it."

"No." The man—Ed—held up his hands. "No. I didn't have nothin' to do with how Tavish died. I found his body in an alley in San Francisco is all. He'd been stabbed and I didn't find a billfold, so I'm guessing he was robbed, and he'd been there for a day or better when I found him."

Maggie gasped, burrowing deeper into Sacha's side. Her brother had been robbed and killed, then left in an alley for an entire day or more?

"There was an envelope lying beside him, so I picked it up and read it. Suppose I wondered if maybe something in it was important, if that's why he'd been killed. But it was just a letter from his sister. She . . . ah . . ." Ed rubbed his mouth, their eyes meeting for a moment before he pulled them away. "She was a bit younger in that first letter. Didn't seem quite so womanly. But the letter left me with the man's name, Tavish McDougal. And when I was staring down at that letter, at that name, I realized that if I took the name, if I went somewhere else and pretended I was Tavish McDougal instead of Ed Fischer, it would get me out of the mess I was in."

Ed heaved in a breath. "So that's what I did. I took the letter, then checked Tavish's pockets to make sure there weren't nothin' else that would say his name was Tavish. After that, I reported him to the police and took a job on the first ship I could find that wasn't based in San Francisco—the *Aurora*. I didn't want no one realizing Tavish was actually dead, so I wrote his sister after I got to Alaska, told her I had a job on the *Aurora* an' all. Then she wrote me back, so I . . . ah . . . I figured I'd write her a letter once a year so everyone would think Tavish was still alive."

"You still haven't explained why you needed a new name." Mikhail looked at Ed with dark eyes, his body coiled tight enough, Maggie half expected him to leap forward and pounce on the man. "Or the mess you left behind in San Francisco."

"Oh, well . . ." The tips of Ed's ears turned pink. "That was because of the ship owner's son and the embezzlement."

"Just what type of embezzlement were you accused of?" Mikhail stepped closer.

Again, Ed raised his hands in a gesture of innocence. "It wasn't me. It was the ship owner's son. He was the captain, but he wasn't all that good of a captain. He spent more than he made and took the extra money from the ship. Eventually his pa figured out that the books weren't matching, that we were hauling more cargo than the ship was keeping record of. But when they went lookin' for someone to blame it all on, they tried saying I was the one altering the shipping manifest and keeping the extra money, and they were all mad about it. They had a police officer come and arrest me all official-like, and I had to pay bail to get out of jail. Then they said I'd need to go to court, but I didn't have money for a lawyer, not on a sailor's salary. And I didn't know what to do until I found Tavish's body."

The man pulled his hat off his head and looked at her, his eyes sincere. "I didn't mean to cause no trouble by it, miss. I promise I didn't. I just needed a different name and a ticket out of San Francisco."

There was something vulnerable in his face, something sincere in his wide brown eyes. And heaven help her, she believed him. It would be easy for a captain to doctor a shipping manifest and skim money from the extra cargo. And it would also be easy for the captain to blame such a thing on one of his crew members.

But Mikhail wasn't so quick to believe Ed. He was looking at the man with narrowed golden eyes, like a predator watching its prey before pouncing. "And how do we know you didn't embezzle from your previous employer, that you haven't been embezzling from us for the past six years?"

Ed's eyes went even wider. "I didn't . . . I would never. I swear I was innocent. I didn't do it the first time in San Francisco, and I didn't do it to Captain Amos either. I'm not good enough with numbers to even try. They get all jumbled up on me, same as words. Seems like they move around on the page. Just ask Sacha if you don't believe me."

Sacha straightened beside her. "He's right. He can read a map or navigational chart just fine, can repair anything that goes wrong on the ship. But he's never been able to read words well or make sense of the shipping manifest. Reckon it took him a long time to read the letter he found in that alley. And not once have I ever suspected he was stealing."

"I can promise he's not embezzling." Alexei stepped forward. "We have two people review the ledgers, and Miss McDougal has looked at them as well. Our books are clean."

Mikhail was still sending Ed a dark look, but everyone else seemed satisfied with Ed's explanation. Even Maggie couldn't help but feel a little bad for him. If he truly had been framed for embezzlement and he couldn't read, he must have felt like he had no choice other than to leave town.

She just wished she'd known Tavish had died before she left Wisconsin. "But why did you write and pretend you were Tavish? Why didn't you let us know Tavish had died instead? All these years, we thought Tavish was alive. I just don't understand . . ." Heat pricked her eyes, and she pressed them shut, unwilling to shed more tears while others watched.

"Guess I probably should have written and told you. But you sounded so nice in your letter. And you were so worried about your brother." Ed rubbed the back of his neck. "I didn't really want anyone knowin' he was dead, seeing how I was using his name. So I wrote you back. I didn't think you'd write again, that you'd want to keep getting letters from me. But once I told you I was working for Sitka Trading Company, every time I arrived in Sitka, one of your letters was waiting, so I kept them and figured I'd write back once a year or so around Christmas."

She couldn't claim she liked what Ed had done, but at least he hadn't done it out of spite or been trying to create trouble for her family. He'd had his reasons.

But letters or no letters, her brother was dead, which meant her uncle would inherit the shipyard and all the land on Lake Michigan—including the house her father had built.

34

Maggie stared out over the water of the sound, the waves lapping gently against the sand as she sat nearby on a piece of driftwood. But just like last night, the scenery didn't calm her, and no peace flooded her soul at the sight of the majestic mountains. Tears were the only thing flooding her at the moment, and she was too tired to try stopping them.

She'd tried to do all the right things. Had left her home in Milwaukee so she could save the land both she and her father had loved so much, the house her father had built with his own two hands, and the shipyard that had provided them financial stability long after he died. She'd fully believed Tavish would be able to turn the shipyard around, to expand their operations so they were once again building magnificent giant ships like their father had dreamed of.

Instead, her brother was dead right along with her parents.

He'd been dead for years, and she hadn't even known.

Had his killers ever been caught? Had their motive been as simple as Ed made it sound, a robbery gone wrong?

She'd never have those answers, not after so many years,

not considering the police in San Francisco didn't even know the identity of the man who'd been killed.

Now everything her father had once owned would go to her uncle, and it felt like her dreams were crumbling around her.

Why, oh why had God allowed this to go on for so long? Why had he let her believe Tavish was alive when her brother wasn't? Why had God allowed her to go all the way to the Pribilof Islands in search of him?

She stared up at the sky, still a bright-blue color, even though it had to be long past dinner. "What did I do to you, God? Why are you treating me this way? Why are you taking my father's land and house and business from me? Why can't Tavish still be alive?"

The questions all tumbled together, one after another, until they formed a giant, angry ball in her stomach. It wasn't fair. It wasn't right. She was a good Christian. She did her best to serve God, and yet he was still taking everything she loved from her.

Like God had done with Job?

She pushed the thought away. She wasn't going to start comparing herself to Job.

"Maggie?" A familiar voice called from down the beach.

She should have known Sacha would come searching for her, but she wasn't in the mood to talk to him. Or Evelina. Or anyone else.

"Leave me alone."

Footsteps thudded against the damp sand behind her. "I've left you alone for three hours."

She wrapped her arms around herself. It wasn't long enough. She wasn't sure three days would be long enough—or three weeks.

He stepped over the log where she sat and settled himself

beside her, his form so large, he almost looked ridiculous forcing himself to sit so low to the ground.

He didn't say anything, just covered her hand with his own.

"Did you know?" she rasped. "Did you have any idea he wasn't really Tavish?"

He gave her hand a squeeze. "No. Other than the fact you don't look anything alike, how could I?"

She sniffled, then ducked her head and pressed her eyes shut tight against the heat building there.

"Maggie," Sacha groaned from beside her. "Come here."

He scooted closer, then tucked her against his side. His warmth enveloped her, but that only made the tears start to leak. He was such a gentle man. So kind and caring and dependable. Always there to support her. Why did that only make her want to cry harder?

She didn't know. All she knew was that he sat there and let her cry. Without complaining that she cried for too long or making a comment about shedding enough tears for five people. He simply let her hold on to him and cry until his shirt was damp and her head ached and her eyes were so swollen she could barely see.

She couldn't begin to guess how long he held her for. It could have been five minutes or fifty. All she knew was that when her tears finally slowed, Sacha shifted her so she could see his face; then he rumbled, "Feel better?"

Only because he was there holding her. Not because her heart hurt any less. "I'm sorry. I've turned into a complete watering pot."

He stroked a hand up her back, then down again, the gesture soothing. "It's to be expected, Maggie. You've had a devastating day."

"How are Ainsley and Finnan?" She'd hugged them and cried with them and taken them back to the house before leaving for the beach, but they weren't nearly as upset as she was. After all, they'd never even met Tavish.

"They're concerned about you."

"I should go talk to them."

"What will you tell them?"

"What do you mean?"

"Now that Tavish is gone, where will you go? What do you plan to do next?"

"I . . . I'll go . . ." Heat burned her eyes again. She hadn't even thought that part through. She could go back to Wisconsin. Her uncle would probably still want her to help in the shipyard office. But she'd have to rent an apartment, and walking into the shipyard office every day, looking out over the land that had once belonged to her father but her uncle had kicked her off . . . She wasn't sure she could do that.

"I don't know where I'll go," she whispered.

Maybe she'd move to Washington, DC, and take the job Xavier had offered her.

"You can stay here, in Alaska," he offered.

She drew her hand away from his. "What?"

"You're already helping in the shipping office. I'm sure Alexei could offer you a job. And you like it here. I know you do."

"Yes, I like it here, but . . . you're sure you want me to stay in Alaska?" The words felt raw on her tongue. Was that really a possibility?

"At the very least, you can stay in town until we get a verdict on the case. Evelina thinks we'll win, but there's always a chance . . ." Sacha shook his head, his eyes moving swiftly over the beach, almost as though he was too scared to let them linger on anything in particular, including her.

"But if we win . . . If I don't have to spend the next five years of my life in prison, and you're here in Alaska, then the two of us could . . ." His jaw moved back and forth, and he gave his head another shake. "That is, I guess I'm trying to say . . . you could marry me, Maggie."

The breath clogged in her chest, the air growing still around them. "What?"

"I said, you could marry me if I'm acquitted." His eyes were gentle now, almost as though speaking the words gave him the courage he needed to focus on her. And his voice emerged both soft and confident as he spoke his next words. "We both know I can provide for you. Let me."

"Sacha, I . . ." She snapped her mouth shut. He would take care of her, yes. He'd always taken care of her, even from the first day she'd met him when they were strangers.

"I might not be able to give you the property your father had or the shipyard in Milwaukee," he went on. "But as I said, you can keep the books and organize the files here. Heaven knows we need a good bookkeeper."

Yes. She'd have plenty to do if she stayed in Sitka, and she'd have a family again, a place she could always belong.

But something was missing in all of this. Something Sacha hadn't said.

She wasn't quite sure where the clarity in her mind came from, not when her heart felt hollow and her lungs felt like they were on fire. But she somehow knew what she needed to do. What she had to say—even if it was going to break her heart all over again.

She scrambled to her feet, putting distance between herself and the warm comfort of Sacha's arms. "You have a good heart, and you're a helper. A problem solver. You've done nothing but help and support me since the moment we met. But this is marriage. It's not a project that will last for a few weeks; it will bind us together for the rest of our lives. And we need love for that, love and unity and a vision of what our future will look like together. I watched my mother marry a man who didn't share any of those things with her, and it was devastating. I won't do that to myself or to you. We both deserve better."

Sacha stood, shoving a hand into his hair. "It's not that I don't love you, Maggie. I have feelings for you. Too many feelings. I might even be able to call them love if I think about it. But I've been telling myself they're not allowed to grow, that I can never have you, and—"

"It's still not going to work." She met his gaze, forcing her voice to remain strong and even. "Not unless you intend to stop captaining the *Aurora*."

SACHA STILLED, every muscle of his body growing tense as he stared down at the beautiful woman in front of him, with her tumbling blond hair and creamy skin and wide, sorrowful eyes.

He hadn't exactly been happy to learn that Tavish was dead, to watch the devastation creep over Maggie's face as her dreams crumbled around her. But through those crumbled dreams, he'd seen a new path forward—for the two of them.

Provided he was acquitted.

But now the words on his tongue turned to dust, his fledging dreams shattering into jagged shards of glass in his chest.

"I'll still see you even though I'm a captain," he rasped. "It won't be the same as it was with your mother and stepfather. I'm not gone that much."

But it wasn't true. He knew that even as he spoke the words. He was gone far more than he was home, and even now, he didn't see enough of his siblings.

How would he feel once he was married?

"I know you love it here," he tried. If he made her think

about it long enough, surely she'd decide to remain in Sitka. "I saw the look on your face as we sailed around the Alexander Archipelago, and across the open sea to Unalaska. Now you can stay forever."

"You're right. I do like it here." She tucked a wayward strand of hair behind her ear, her voice soft against the breeze off the ocean. "I like the scenery. I like your family. I like being at sea. And I like . . ."

She shook her head. "No, that's not fair to either of us. I don't just like you, Sacha. I love you. Somewhere along the way, my feelings for you grew into love. I know you care about me too, even if you can't call it love yet. If I were to stay, you'd be saying those words soon. And I know how you feel about Finnan and Ainsley. I can see your love for them in your eyes whenever they run up to you."

Sacha nodded. Maggie was saying all the right things, what a woman might say right before proclaiming she wanted to become a man's wife.

But there was still something sorrowful about her words, something that made him hold his heart in check as she turned away from him.

"The trouble is, you love the sea more than all of us." Her throat worked as she stared out over the water, the wind toying with a strand of her hair. "Xavier offered me an assistant position with him in Washington, DC. I think I'm going to take it."

"No." He took a step nearer and reached out to grip her shoulders, as though doing so might force her to stay in Sitka. The movements brought him so close, he could see fragments of old tears still beaded to her eyelashes, so close he could feel the brush of her breath against his neck. "No, you're not. You can't. You belong here, with me."

She shook her head. "There is no 'here with you,' because you won't be here. You'll be sailing across the ocean. I've seen your shipping schedule. As soon as this legal matter is cleared up, you'll leave for Barrow. Maybe, were we to marry, you'd tell me that Ainsley, Finnan, and I could travel with you sometimes. But how many times each year would you leave us behind rather than take us with you?"

"I don't know." He stepped back. And he didn't. A lot. Too many. He shook his head. "I'm sorry."

"Sorry that you proposed?"

Was he? Or maybe he was sorry that they couldn't marry, or at least, that they couldn't marry and have a life that looked like Jonas and Evelina's, all happy and content as they lived together the way a husband and wife should.

"Thank you for proposing. It was kind of you to offer marriage considering my situation. But you're not obligated to take care of me. Tavish would have been—were he still alive—but like I said, I have a job offer in Washington, DC, so that's where I'll go."

"Who will watch Ainsley and Finnan when you go to Australia?"

She blinked at him. "Xavier told you the details?"

"He did, yes." And he'd wager by the time Dr. Torres left for Australia in January, the two of them would be married.

That made Sacha want to slam his fist into the piece of driftwood where they'd just been sitting, or stalk to the edge of the water and howl like a crazed wolf.

But he didn't. Instead he took a step farther back. Because Maggie was right. He couldn't be the husband she needed, and it was unfair of him to ask her to settle for the small part of himself he could give.

Then he took another step away from her, a part of his heart shattering with each inch of distance he put between them. "I best get back to the house."

A single tear slipped down her cheek. "Good-bye, Sacha."

They weren't saying good-bye, not officially. He'd see her at the house later. She still needed to finish testifying for him in court, so she'd have to wait at least until Monday afternoon to leave.

But something about the sadness in her eyes made her words stay with him long after he turned and walked away.

35

Sacha ran his hand along the curve of the clipper, the contours and grain of the wood smooth beneath his callused fingers. The ship, nearly finished, stood majestic and proud, its hull gleaming under the soft light of the lanterns. With a bit more sanding, then a few coats of paint, it would be ready to sail.

He lifted his hand from the wood and stood back to scan the vessel. He'd only been working on the ship since arriving in Sitka. He hadn't been here from the beginning, watching as the raw, unyielding lumber was transformed under the hands of Bjorn and his men into the strong, tall vessel before him. But he still couldn't help the sense of pride that swelled in him as he looked at it.

He reached out and touched the hull again, his hand pausing over a rough spot; then he reached into the pouch strapped to his belt and pulled out the light-grain sandpaper.

"What are you doing?"

At the sound of the voice coming from behind him, Sacha

blinked, then turned to find Alexei standing beside one of the lanterns.

"What does it look like? I'm building a ship."

Alexei quirked an eyebrow. "At dawn?"

Was it dawn? He tamped down the sudden need to yawn, then glanced toward the mountains in the east, where the faintest shade of pink was beginning to peek over their tops. "Guess I lost myself in the work."

"Guess you did." Alexei came nearer the ship, his hand reaching out to run along the hull. "Did you sand the entire thing last night?"

He shrugged. "It needed doing."

"You did a good job."

"She'll make some man a grand ship in a couple more weeks."

"That she will. Thank you." Alexei dropped his hand from the ship and turned to him. "I came to see if you wanted to go with me to deliver those blankets to Hoonah to make reparations for the man who was killed, but I hadn't realized you'd been awake all night. Are you up for the trip? I don't figure it will violate your bail since you'll still be on Baranoff Island, just the other side of it."

"Sure." Anything to keep his mind off the devastated look in Maggie's eyes as he'd walked away from her on the beach yesterday evening. "Reckon I wouldn't be able to sleep much even if I went to bed."

"Come on, then. You can help me load the blankets on the *Halcyon*." Alexei put out the lantern closest to him, then moved to the one Sacha had propped on a chair. "I want to leave as early as possible."

"I didn't realize you had all four hundred blankets." Sacha headed around the other side of the ship, extinguishing more of the lanterns until he met Alexei at the stern.

"The *Alliance* brought the last of them shortly before you arrived in Sitka. My plan was to use the *Aurora* to deliver them. But—"

"The RCS seized the *Aurora*." He finished, heaviness settling inside his chest. He started toward the warehouse, where he assumed Alexei was storing the blankets. "Does the *Halcyon* have time in its schedule for us to take her for a day?"

"Yes, she's still five days ahead of schedule."

Of course she was. That ship was always ahead of schedule. Never mind that this year he couldn't seem to make a single delivery on time with the *Aurora*.

Sacha pulled open the door to the warehouse, already looking forward to the feel of the wind in his hair and the swaying of the ship beneath his legs—the clarity of mind that being on the sea always brought.

Hopefully today it would help him forget about a woman with tumbling blond hair and bluish-green eyes too.

A SHIVER TRAVELED up Maggie's spine as she watched the three towering masts move through the trees. She couldn't quite see the wharf, warehouse, or shipyard from her position on the porch facing the water. She suspected that was intentional, that a large cluster of pine trees had been left in the rocky ground to give the Amos family a bit of privacy at their house.

But the masts were still tall enough to be seen through the tops of the trees. And on a quiet morning such as this, with pink and orange filling the sky to the east, she could even hear the sailors calling to each other. Soon the ship broke through the other side of the trees, moving farther into the water as the voices of the sailors grew softer and softer on the wind.

Maggie raised the mug of coffee to her lips and sighed. Was Sacha on that ship? She didn't know. He hadn't said anything about leaving today, even though Yuri had told her Alexei would be using the *Halcyon* to deliver some blankets to a local tribe.

But even though she didn't know for certain, it seemed like Sacha was there, like there was a place in her heart that could sense when he left.

Just like there was a place in her heart that could sense he had never returned to the house last night. She assumed he'd spent the night working in the shipyard, though she didn't know for certain. Perhaps she should have risen from the bed and gone to join him, asked if there was something she could do to help. It probably would have been better than staring at the ceiling, her heart too heavy to find sleep.

The door opened, and Evelina stepped out onto the porch, a cup of steaming coffee in her hand.

"Here." Evelina slid a small plate with a trio of teacakes onto the railing beside her arm. "You looked like you could use a little something sweet to go with that coffee."

"Do I really appear that sour?" Maggie picked up a teacake and bit into the dense, sweet bread that had been dusted in powdered sugar.

"Not sour, just sad. But you have good reason. And I happen to agree with Kate that cake always has a way of cheering people up."

Maggie offered her a small smile, then turned her gaze back out to the water. The *Halcyon* was nearly to the entrance of the sound. A few more minutes, and it would glide into the open waters of the Pacific and disappear from view. "I think I just might be the biggest fool in all of Alaska."

"Are you sure that's not my brother? I was certain he was

going to propose last night, after it became clear there's nothing waiting for you in Milwaukee."

Maggie swallowed. "He did."

Evelina raised an eyebrow. "And you said no?"

"See? I told you I was the biggest fool in Alaska."

"I thought you returned his feelings."

She sighed. "I do. I love him so much, the thought of leaving him makes my lungs ache when I breathe."

"Then what's the problem?" Evelina asked softly.

"His job."

Evelina straightened. "You mean he didn't offer to stay in Sitka when he proposed?"

Maggie didn't answer, just moved her gaze back out to the sea.

"Then no," Evelina huffed. "You're not the biggest fool in the state. My brother is."

"Maybe I was wrong to tell him no. I love him."

Evelina reached out and settled a hand over hers on the railing. "I don't think you were wrong, but that's not something I can answer for you. Would you be content marrying a man you saw only for a few nights at a time?"

Maggie took a sip of coffee, the liquid tepid in the cool morning air. "No. At least, I don't think so. You've been away from Jonas for a couple weeks. Tell me, how badly do you miss him?"

Evelina chuckled. "Rather badly, I'm afraid, but if he leaves Juneau, then there's no lawman, and he was in Sitka for my court case earlier this summer. I couldn't ask him to leave again. Besides, I'm headed home next week after the jury issues its verdict."

"That's how I would be too. I'd miss Sacha too much to be apart from him for so long." She pressed her eyes shut, then gave her head a small shake. "But I don't have much choice about being apart from him, do I? I just don't understand why all this is happening to me."

"What do you mean, 'happening' to you?" Evelina nudged her with her elbow. "Our world is full of sin and suffering. People get sick. People die. People go through painful, difficult times. If we focus only on those hard times, I suppose it's enough to make most of us want to give up. But don't forget that people also fall in love and get married; they have babies and hold parties and go through happy times too. You almost make it sound as though you feel like you deserve an easier life than everyone else."

Maggie blinked. Was that how she'd sounded? "No. I don't mean it that way. It's just that I do my very best to serve God, and I . . . I . . ." She shook her head. "When we missed the *Halcyon* in Unalaska, I told Sacha I felt like God hated me, like if he actually loved me, so many things wouldn't be going wrong. But Sacha said God still loves me, and that he's trying to grow me. He gave me a verse, from Romans five. He said it helped him when he first lost his parents and spent a winter stuck on the Yukon River. It says that we should be grateful for hardships, because they teach us patience, and patience teaches us experience, and experience teaches us hope."

"And has the verse helped?" Evelina asked softly.

Maggie stared into the inky blackness of her coffee. "I don't know. I suppose I'm still having trouble finding hope when everything about my life seems so very wrong."

"Maybe the answer is simply to trust God more. To remind yourself, over and over, that he has your best end in mind, even if what you're going through is painful. Because there should always be hope, not at the end but in the middle too."

A gust of cool wind crossed the porch, and Maggie shivered beneath her shawl. "What if I'm not strong enough to do that? What if I'm not strong enough to have hope?"

"'I have learned, in whatsoever state I am, therewith to be content.'"

Maggie slanted Evelina a glance. "Did Sacha tell you to quote that verse?"

Evelina blinked. "No, why? Have the two of you talked about it?"

"Yes, during the same conversation where he told me my hardships would bring patience."

"Well, then, it sounds like you know exactly what you need to do. It's just a matter of doing it."

Just a matter of doing it. Evelina made it sound so simple, like being content wasn't any more difficult than pouring a second cup of coffee or deciding which dress to wear for the day.

Had she been making things harder than needed? "Part of me can see the good of Tavish being dead. Don't misunderstand. I wish he were alive more than anything, but my future looks so very different now than it did when I thought I needed to return to Milwaukee. I can see God working in that. It's the part with Sacha that hurts."

"It would hurt me too." Evelina took a long sip of her coffee, her shoulders relaxed as she leaned against the railing. "In fact, I remember hurting in a similar way not all that long ago, because there was a time when I didn't know whether Jonas would ever be able to love me, at least not the way I wanted him to."

"You didn't?" Maggie wrapped her arms around herself, warding off another gust of wind. "That seems impossible. I've never seen a couple more in love than the two of you. Jonas adores you."

A smile wreathed Evelina's face, full and beautiful. "I know. But it took him a bit of time to figure that out."

"So what did you do after you knew you loved him, but you didn't know if he loved you back?"

"I told him I'd wait until he was ready to love again, no matter how long it took."

Wait until he was ready to love again? "How long did that take?" She was almost afraid to ask.

But Evelina laughed, her eyes filling with even more happiness. "At the time I was worried it could take quite a while. Maybe a year, perhaps more. Jonas had some rather tragic things happen to him when he was in Texas, and it was hard for him to move past them. But once I told him I would wait anyway, it took him about a day to come to his senses."

"A day?" Maggie pushed herself off the railing. "That's it?"

"That's it."

She sighed, her shoulders rising and falling as the breath loosed from her lungs. Then she looked back out at the water, at the place where the *Halcyon* had disappeared half an hour or so earlier. "Yet you don't think I'm a fool for turning Sacha down?"

The smile dropped from Evelina's face, and her green eyes grew serious. "No. I don't think a woman should ever commit her life to a man who might not love her fully. But I also think Sacha already loves you in the way you need. Either he hasn't realized it yet or he's not sure what to do about it. And don't forget he's devastated about the *Aurora* and Caldwell trying to pin that death in Unalaska on him. Men have a hard time sorting out their feelings under normal circumstances, and here Sacha might spend the next five years in prison."

Maggie shuddered. "I can't imagine him losing the case."

"I don't think he will. But until the jury delivers its verdict, that's still hanging over his head."

"Maybe I can stay in Sitka for a while. I mean, there's plenty of work for me to do in the office. I could stay until the end of August and see if Sacha changes his mind about being a captain."

"Yes, that's a good way to give Sacha time. I think you should stay at least until he gets back from Barrow."

"Barrow." Maggie drew in a breath. She'd forgotten about that. If he got acquitted and the *Aurora* was released, watching him board that ship and sail away from her would be one of the hardest things she'd ever done. "What if, in the end, he loves the sea more than he loves me?"

"Then you've still learned something, Maggie. You've still grown. You've still come to realize that it's not a list of things you do that make you a good Christian but how you respond and grow and trust God in the face of hardships."

Yes. Regardless of what ended up happening at the end of August, she'd still have learned some valuable lessons—lessons that God could use to make her stronger. That's what she needed to focus on for the rest of her time in Sitka. Not the things she felt God owed her for being a good Christian but the lessons he had for her to learn.

But there was still a part of her that hoped one day, in the not-too-distant future, she and Sacha would be as content and happy in their marriage as Evelina and Jonas.

36

Sacha had hoped being on the sea would bring clarity of mind, and with that would come some idea of what to do about Maggie.

But as he stood on the deck of the *Halcyon*, watching while Alexei finished talking to a very happy Chief Yèil, the head of the Tlingit clan in Hoonah, his mind wasn't any clearer, and his heart didn't feel any lighter either.

If anything, it felt heavier with each mile he'd put between himself and Maggie.

It was ridiculous. He'd only been gone for a morning, helping Alexei and their skeleton crew navigate the waters between Sitka and Hoonah. How could he miss her so much after such a short time?

Maybe the problem was that he hadn't invited her along. She'd just told him two nights ago that she missed being on the water, and here he was, spending a day aboard ship without her. It wouldn't have been any trouble having her and the children along for the day. Besides, she hadn't seen Hoonah yet, and she'd surely appreciate the views of mountains and islands they'd had to pass as they navigated to the small village, along with the view from the village itself.

He gave his head a small shake. What was wrong with him? He needed to think of ways to put distance between him and Maggie, not keep her closer. She'd be leaving Sitka in only a few days.

But if that was really the right choice, if she was supposed to go to Washington, DC, and work with Dr. Torres, then why did he miss her on such a simple, quick trip?

Why did he want nothing more than to be standing with her right now, watching the expression on her face as she surveyed the mountains enveloping Hoonah?

Marry me. His mind replayed the words he'd said only yesterday. He didn't yet know whether he'd be acquitted, but even with the possibility of prison time looming over him, the words had still seemed right coming out of his mouth, a perfect way to solve all their troubles.

And then she'd shattered his heart.

"When I invited you along today, I expected you'd at least get off the ship and help unload the blankets."

Sacha looked over to find Alexei standing beside him. He must have concluded their business, and now the crew was stowing the gangway and raising the sails.

"Sorry." He rubbed a hand over his face. "I'm a bit distracted."

Alexei leaned an elbow on the rail, then kicked his feet out in front of him, the stance rather relaxed for a man who usually held himself as straight as a ship's mast. "Honestly, I expected you to have proposed to her by now."

He sent his brother a glare. "I did."

Alexei quirked an eyebrow. "She didn't accept?"

He hunched his shoulders. "She doesn't want to be married to a man who's gone more than he's home."

"Ah."

Ah? That was all his brother had to say?

The ship lurched away from where it had been anchored near the shore. Around them, the crew was calling to each other, each man busy doing his designated task. He should probably be supervising. But the crew of the *Halcyon* was well trained, and they knew the vessel better than he did.

He and Alexei stood in silence for a while, watching as they passed a series of smaller islands before navigating into the larger waterway that threaded its way between the mountain-filled islands.

He expected Alexei to leave at some point, to go stand behind the helm or talk to the first mate. But his brother stayed at the railing, intently staring up at the sails as they filled with wind and propelled the clipper forward. He was probably studying something about them, wondering how many more sails they might need to add if they built a bigger ship, perhaps one with a fourth mast.

"Do you ever miss it?" Sacha asked.

"Miss what?" Alexei still didn't take his eyes off the sails.

"The fact that you're not designing ships. That you intended to be living somewhere else right now, doing something else, married to Clarise, and your life turned out nothing like you expected." It was the first time he'd voiced the words.

He might have known what Alexei had sacrificed ten years ago, might have stood silently watching his brother take control of the family and steer his siblings and the family businesses toward the future.

But he'd never once asked his brother how he felt, if he still had regrets all these years later.

Alexei was quiet for so long, Sacha thought he wasn't going to answer. But then his shoulders rose and fell on a sigh. "Parts of it, yes. On a day like this, when I can spend my time watching how the sails respond to the wind, noting what shift in the sails propels the ship faster and what slows it down, thinking about how many sails it would take to . . ." Alexei shook his head, as though he was intentionally catching himself, pulling his true thoughts back inside. "I'm sorry. I could ramble on for hours about the ideas in my brain."

"What about not marrying Clarise?"

That got Alexei to pull his gaze away from the sails, but the dark look in his eyes didn't invite questions.

"I know she's the one who left. That even after everything that happened, you still would have married her had she stayed." Sacha swallowed, his own throat growing tight at the memories. "But do you have any regrets that you didn't follow her back to Washington, DC? That you didn't fight harder for her?"

Again, he didn't expect his brother to respond. He had been quite certain Alexei would suddenly find something aboard ship that needed doing and stalk off.

Instead, Alexei met his gaze, as though he didn't even need to think about the answer before opening his mouth. "Every day of my life. It's not running the trading company or being stuck building the same old boats over and over again that's so hard. I feel like I could have managed all that—had Clarise stayed. Maybe I didn't do a good enough job convincing her. Maybe I didn't try hard enough to show her that I still loved her, even after everything that happened."

Alexei turned to face the water, his knuckles turning white as his hand gripped the railing. "I still tell myself I should have found a way to convince her I still loved her in spite of it all. Should have showed her that we could have a future together. But she's married to another man now, so I've learned to let her go—at least as much as a man who loves a woman ever can."

Alexei drew in a breath, his eyes scanning the series of

mountains they passed to the south. "But there's still the idea of her. I won't lie about that, or pretend I don't still dream about waking up next to the woman I love every morning. Or wrapping my arms around her after a long day and running my fingers through her hair. Did you know she used to come to the office above the warehouse in the middle of the night with a cookie and tea when I was stuck working late?"

"She did?" He never had any idea.

"She would watch for a light in the window, and if she saw one, and it was late . . ." Alexei shrugged, letting his words trail off.

And leaving Sacha to wonder just what kind of moments Alexei and his fiancée had shared in the office above the warehouse if memories of her still rose in his mind when he was alone.

Alexei turned to him then, his chin raised and his shoulders straight. "If you love Maggie even half as much as I loved Clarise, then I don't advise you to make the same mistake I did."

Sacha heaved in a breath.

"That's why you're asking, isn't it? You want to know if you'll regret letting Maggie go, so you're asking if I have regrets about Clarise. The answer is yes, more than you'll ever know."

Sacha raked a hand through his hair. "How can I be married and captain the *Aurora*?"

"You can't, at least not if you want to be a good husband."

"Then how am I supposed to choose?"

"If you need to ask, if Maggie's not already the most important thing in your life, then you have your answer." Alexei nodded toward where the helmsman stood behind the wheel. "And it looks like I don't need to worry about finding another man to captain the *Aurora* after all."

"Wait. You were looking for one?"

Alexei pushed himself off the rail, as though finally ready to head off and find something else to do. "I started looking for one the second Maggie stepped off the ship in Sitka on your way to Unalaska."

"Did you find one?" Sacha followed his brother across the deck.

"I was thinking Tavish—or Ed—at least until yesterday. While I understand why he took another man's name, I'm not sure I trust him enough to be a captain anymore. And I don't like the idea of having a captain who struggles to read either."

Sacha glanced at where Tavish—he wasn't sure he could call the man Ed—stood on the quarterdeck, talking to Captain Jones and the helmsman. "Me either. The men seem to like him well enough as captain of the *Halcyon*, but I don't have it in me to hand our most valuable ship over to him after how he lied. He makes a good first mate, though."

"He does." Alexei rubbed his jaw. "What if we move Captain White from the *Alliance* over to the *Aurora* and promote the first mate over there?"

"Raymond would make a good captain for the *Alliance*. He's been first mate there for several years." So good of a captain, in fact, that Sacha been a bit worried Raymond would leave Sitka Trading Company and find a ship to captain elsewhere. But now that Alexei had mentioned it, he could easily envision Tavish showing Captain White the finer points of sailing the *Aurora* while Raymond took over the *Alliance*.

And he'd just planned his way out of a job.

Which he wasn't even sorry about. If anything, his heart suddenly felt lighter.

There was only one question left to answer. "If I give up the *Aurora*, what will I do in Sitka? Don't tell me you'll put me in an office all day and have me poring over books."

Alexei chuckled. "Heavens no, you'd go crazy. And why

would I want you anywhere near our books when Maggie is so brilliant at managing them? You'd just muck everything up."

That was a little too true. "So what will I do?"

Alexei crossed his arms over his chest. "What did you spend all night doing?"

"Sanding a ship?"

"Bjorn is getting too old to work. When we got our newest commission, he asked if he could start coming in just two days a week. Said it's getting too much for him. And Kate backed that up by saying his heart is weak."

"So you want me to run the shipyard?" It was like they'd always planned, all those years ago before their parents died. Alexei would design ships, he would build them, and Ivan would manage the business aspect of the shipyard until their father grew too old to run the trading company, and eventually Ivan would take that over.

Now it was just Alexei and Yuri, and they were running the shipyard without Alexei's fancy designs and steel hulls down in Seattle. But they were still building good ships. It was why so many companies were commissioning clippers built in the model of the *Aurora*.

If he came along and helped too, it would bring them even closer to what they'd originally dreamed of doing.

But could he stay off the sea and spend his days on land?

It wasn't as though he'd never sail again. Sitka was only accessible by water, and someone from their family was constantly running between Juneau and Sitka. Maybe he could still go on a voyage or two a year. Even if the RCS was delivering medical supplies to villages in the Arctic, someone would still need to deliver lumber and flour, corn and potatoes. What if he made that trip to Barrow once a year but spent the rest of his time in Sitka?

He could imagine himself being very happy with a life that

looked like that. "Thank you." He looked at his brother. "Not just for finding a way for me to stay in Sitka but for everything else. You warned me the seal study would cause trouble. I didn't believe you, but here we are, going on three weeks since the *Aurora* and its cargo were seized, and you haven't complained once. You've just put every last ounce of energy into getting this mess cleared up. I don't . . ." His throat grew dry, but he forced the words out anyway. "I don't deserve a brother like you."

"You mean one who never smiles?" Alexei gave him a dry smile, but Sacha couldn't bring his own lips to curve up in response.

"No. I mean one who's sacrificed so much for his family."

Alexei rubbed a hand over his jaw. "You weren't wrong about the seals. The poaching problem should have been addressed years ago, but I was too scared to do it, especially after what happened to Ilya last fall. But you were right to pursue it, and we'll find a way out of this, Sacha. We've faced worse."

"But what happens if we lose the *Aurora*?"

"Then we'll build another. We're getting quite good at building double-hulled ships."

"Maybe, but we'll never be able to replace her." The ship meant too much to his family.

"Then we'll build something new, something that looks toward the future. Never forget that, Sacha. Even if you lose in court this week and you spend the next five years of your life in prison, you still can't let your losses destroy you. You always need to look toward the future."

"'I have learned, in whatsoever state I am, therewith to be content,'" he whispered. "Maggie's been trying to remind me of that, but I haven't wanted to listen."

Alexei rubbed the back of his neck. "I'm not sure this is

about being content as much as about growing. What's that verse you used to tell me after Ma and Pa died? The one from Romans five about having peace in God and rejoicing in tribulations because tribulations work patience, and patience works experience, and experience works hope?"

"'Therefore being justified by faith, we have peace with God through our Lord Jesus Christ: By whom also we have access by faith into this grace wherein we stand, and rejoice in hope of the glory of God.'" The verses rolled easily off his tongue. After all, he'd become far too familiar with them in the years since their parents died. "'And not only so, but we glory in tribulations also: knowing that tribulation worketh patience; and patience, experience; and experience, hope: And hope maketh not ashamed; because the love of God is shed abroad in our hearts.'"

"Yes, that's the one." Alexei gave Sacha's shoulder a shove. "So look toward the future, even if that means time in prison and rebuilding the *Aurora*. Because what you're facing isn't about being content or having a perfect-looking life, it's about God growing you."

Sacha stared at his brother. Alexei was right. How could he have missed it? How could he have spent the past two weeks moping and telling Maggie he wished he'd never contacted Dr. Torres? How could—?

Crack!

A sickening sound filled the air. In an instant, the ship's forward momentum ceased, throwing him and Alexei and the rest of the crew forward on the deck.

Sacha didn't need to rush belowdecks or look over the rail to know what had happened. The sound of the impact told him enough. It was the harrowing thud of a wooden hull against a rock.

37

"What in the . . ." Sacha looked around, the landscape of water and mountains and trees familiar. He didn't need a map to know they were passing the Inian Islands, but why were they so far to the north?

"Did we just hit a rock?" Alexei asked.

"Appears so, but we're not even in the shipping channel. We're practically touching the mainland." If he hadn't been so busy talking with Alexei, surely he would have noticed they were too far north.

Sacha shoved away from the railing and strode toward the wheelhouse, taking the stairs that led to the quarterdeck two at a time, while Alexei kept pace behind him.

"What's going on?" Sacha bellowed the moment he entered the covered space. "Why aren't we in the shipping channel?"

"I . . . ah . . . I think we hit a rock," the helmsman answered, his face white. "Cap'n Jones and Tavish are belowdecks inspectin' the damage."

"Of course we hit a rock. It was bound to happen considering how close we're sailing to the mainland. Don't you know how to read a navigational chart? The shipping channel runs through the center of North Inian Pass, not on the north side of it."

The man blinked at him. Sacha didn't quite recall his name. Ralph, maybe, or Roger. Possibly Roy. He'd been helmsman on the *Halcyon* for several years, and he hadn't once run the ship aground or hit a rock. It seemed ridiculous that he could navigate foreign waters without issue but not the passageways close to Sitka.

"No. The shippin' channel runs right next to the mainland, where the water's deep. The pass is shallower than it looks and littered with boulders. See?" The helmsman turned to the navigational chart tacked to the wall behind him and pointed to North Inian Pass, a strip of water about two miles wide that separated the Inian Islands from the mainland. Most of the body of water was deep enough to pass a ship through.

But not according to the chart in front of him. It showed all but the very northernmost route through the water strewn with large boulders and unnavigable shallows.

Sacha blinked, then rubbed his fingers against his eyelids. Surely he was reading the chart wrong. He knew these waters, knew the parts of the passage that were safe and unsafe.

But sure enough, the navigational chart showed that the only part of the water deep enough for a ship to pass through was right next to the mainland.

"Where did you get this chart? It's wrong." Sacha yanked it off the wall. He'd sailed these waters hundreds, if not thousands, of times, as had Alexei and everyone else in their family. The route from Sitka to Juneau led right past the Inian Islands.

"Sacha's right." Alexei came up beside him to study the map. "The shipping channel has always been in the middle of the water, never on the north shore."

"But that appears to be the only thing incorrect about this

chart. The water depths are correct around Baranof, Admiralty, and Douglas Islands. Look." Sacha handed the map to his brother so Alexei could have a closer look.

Pounding sounded on the stairs to the quarterdeck, and a moment later, Tavish raced into the wheelhouse and slid to a halt in front of Alexei. "Captain Jones wants you to know the hull's cracked and leakin' water, but not fast. He wants to try sealing it with pitch and movin' the cargo that can't get wet to the bunkroom for the afternoon. He thinks we can make it back to Sitka tonight."

"We have to get the ship off the rock first." Sacha studied the water surrounding them. That might be possible, considering the tide was coming in, not going out. It would be better if they had another ship to help dislodge them, but most of the ships heading to and from Juneau approached from the south side of Douglas Island, meaning this wasn't a very busy passage.

"The captain wants to know what happened." Tavish looked at the helmsman.

"I . . . well . . ."

"Your navigational charts are wrong." Sacha raked a hand through his hair. "That's what happened."

Tavish frowned. "That can't be. I got the newest ones last time we were in Sitka, when I took over for Captain Jones. They were straight off the press. The Revenue Cutter Service has been tryin' to get them out to everyone."

"This chart is new?" Sacha nearly choked.

"Yes." Tavish headed over to where Alexei still held the chart. "I can't imagine such a new chart would be wrong."

"Look around you." Sacha shoved a hand toward the water. "Tell me where we are and where the shipping channel is."

It didn't take more than a few seconds for Tavish to survey the landscape, then point toward the center of the passage. "We should be over there, not this close to the mainland. It's too shallow here, and the water is strewn with boulders."

"Now tell me what your fancy new chart says." Sacha jutted his chin toward it.

Tavish studied the chart for a few seconds, then raised his gaze, eyes flashing. "It's wrong. In fact, it's so blatantly wrong that it's almost like whoever drew up this chart wanted ships to wreck right here."

"That's impossible." The helmsman stiffened. "No cartographer is gonna intentionally publish a false chart. He'd never work again in his field once word got out."

"I wonder if any other charts are incorrect." Alexei rubbed a hand over his jaw. "We've seen an uptick in ships running aground or hitting boulders, both in the Alexander Archipelago and in the Aleutians. Bad charts would certainly explain that."

Could there be other wrong charts? It seemed impossible, and yet . . . "I've helped four wrecks so far this year." The most recent one had been coming into Petersburg on its way north to the Pribilofs, when Maggie and Dr. Torres had been aboard. "And it seems like every time I stop by Sitka, you're repairing a ship that ran aground."

"There's been a constant stream of them," Alexei said. "We even had to repair a revenue cutter that ran aground in May."

Sacha turned to Tavish. "Do you have the old charts?"

"They're in the captain's cabin with most of the new ones. We just pulled the one we'd need today from the book."

"I want to see both books." Sacha stalked out of the wheelhouse and toward the cabin.

He spent most of the afternoon poring over the navigational charts while Captain Jones, Alexei, and the rest of the crew worked to seal the leak in the hull. First he looked at the new charts and marked any areas that seemed wrong, particularly where the shipping channels ran too close to the shore. Then he compared those charts with the old charts. Every time, he found the old chart matched what he remembered, with the shipping channel passing through the deeper, middle sections of water rather than near the shore. He missed two of the discrepancies, though, and he found those only as he went through the painstaking process of comparing the old charts to the new. As the tide came in, he could feel the ship start to rock in the rising waters, a good sign they'd be able to dislodge the *Halcyon* soon.

In the end, he found eight discrepancies, rather large ones, like with the North Inian Passage.

And there was one thing all the errors had in common: their proximity to Tlingit villages that were drying seal pelts for poachers.

38

Sacha didn't care that it was after midnight, didn't care that a light rain had started to fall or that the wind off the ocean was cold for the end of July. No. He'd swung into action the moment the *Halcyon* had reached Sitka. There was a mess that needed to be cleaned up, and he didn't care about the time. He intended to see it cleaned up. Tonight.

So did Alexei, Mikhail, and Yuri, which was why they were with him, rain dripping off the brims of their hats as they stormed toward the large white house with fancy white pillars on the edge of town.

When Sacha reached the steps leading toward the large porch, he took them two at a time. It was the first time he'd been on Preston Caldwell's property, and if he had anything to say about it, it would also be the last. He banged on the door, waited about a minute, then banged again. He'd pound all night if he had to.

On his fourth round of knocking, the door opened, revealing a butler dressed in a housecoat.

"Can I help you?" the man asked.

"I need to speak with Caldwell. Now."

The butler didn't even blink, as though getting requests for his employer in the middle of the night wasn't all that uncommon. "Mr. Caldwell has retired for the evening, but if you leave your name, I'll be sure to mention in the morning that you stopped by."

The man moved to shut the door, but Sacha planted a boot inside the doorjamb. "I'm not waiting until morning. I'm giving him this one chance to talk to me, and if he doesn't, the next person I rouse out of bed will be the prosecutor."

Again, the man made no indication that his words were alarming. In fact, he still didn't blink. But he did push the door farther open. "Very well. You can wait in the parlor. I'll let Mr. Caldwell know he has guests."

The parlor was decorated like Sacha expected, with glossy wood trim and fancy, highfalutin furniture with intricate carvings on the legs and rich burgundy fabric on the cushions. The drapes lining the windows were thick and rich, descending from ceiling to floor, and an ornate rug sat in the center of the room. Sacha had done enough trading to know the rug came from Turkey, and it probably cost more than Caldwell's sailors made in a year. Even the light fixtures were a display of wealth, the chandeliers dripping with crystals that could only have been imported and would have taken much time and money to ensure they reached Sitka without breaking.

Everything about the stupid house shouted money. In fact, Sacha bet Caldwell's house was more richly appointed than the Russian governor's mansion had been. It was certainly fancier than the modest house the Department of the Interior provided for the current governor.

If he were standing in this room under any other circumstance, he'd feel awkward and out of place, like he had no business being in such a lovely home.

But tonight he was too mad to care, and judging by the grim looks on his brothers' faces, they felt the same.

"Yuri?" a soft voice said from the foyer. Then Rosalind Caldwell stepped into the room, a wrapper cinched tightly over what was likely her nightgown, and her blond hair tumbling about her shoulders.

Her eyes moved to encompass the four of them, then settled back on Yuri, her brow furrowed. "Is something wrong? Why are you and your brothers here?"

Sacha couldn't help but notice the softness in Yuri's eyes as his gaze moved to Preston Caldwell's daughter. Or the way he went straight to her, his touch gentle as he rested a hand against her upper arm and turned her toward the door. "We need to discuss a bit of business with your father. It's nothing to concern yourself over."

"In the middle of the night?" Rosalind halted a few steps from the doorway. "It must be concerning if you're here at such an hour."

"It's nothing you need to fret over."

It was a lie. If word of what Sacha had discovered got out, her father's reputation would be ruined, and he'd never be able to hire another sailor.

Sacha didn't know Rosalind well. She was about a decade younger than him, and she seemed as sweet and kind as her father was cruel. Like the type of woman a man would shield from the discussion they were about to have, so he couldn't blame Yuri for not wanting her to worry.

But she must have sensed Yuri's falsehood, because she stepped away from him and turned to Alexei. "What's my father done now?"

Alexei shook his head. "Yuri's right. It's nothing that concerns you. Go back to bed. Your father will be down momentarily. We'll say what needs to be said, and then we'll be gone."

She crossed her arms over her chest. "He won't be down soon."

"Your butler said—"

"He'll make you wait. He always does when someone doesn't bother to schedule a meeting—especially one that's an inconvenience. He'll take probably an hour to get ready, and when he comes downstairs, he'll be dressed as though it's morning."

"We'll wait," Alexei said.

"I don't need to wait." Sacha leveled Rosalind with a look. "I'll just go wake up the prosecutor assigned to the case against me."

"The prosecutor?" Rosalind's face turned white, and she looked into the foyer, where she spoke something softly, likely to a servant who was waiting there. "Let me see if I can hurry him along. Would you like some tea?"

"No," Sacha snapped.

"That would be lovely, darling." Yuri reached out and patted Rosalind's hand. "Thank you so much for offering."

Rosalind smiled up at Yuri, the look so soft that Sacha found his knuckles whitening around the navigational books he held.

"I'll be right back," she said, then turned and left.

"You know nothing can come of whatever's between you." Sacha jutted his chin toward the door where Rosalind had just disappeared.

"There's nothing between us." Yuri held up his hands. "I'm just being kind."

Mikhail snorted. "Is that what being kind looks like these days? Because I'd wager half of my pay for this next expedition that she's in love with you."

"We had a kind father. Not necessarily a conventional one, but a father who loved us." Yuri leveled his gaze at Mikhail, something hard flashing in his eyes. "Can you imagine being raised by a man like Preston Caldwell? Rosalind might live in the fanciest house in town, but I'm quite certain her life is miserable, so excuse me if I go out of my way to show her a little extra kindness. She needs it."

Sacha wanted to ask just how Yuri knew what Rosalind needed—and if it had anything to do with sneaking kisses after dark, like Yuri had alluded to after stumbling upon him and Maggie about to kiss.

But the clicking of shoes against the polished wood floor drew Sacha's attention to the foyer, where Preston Caldwell descended the stairs in a three-piece suit with perfectly styled hair.

He moved into the parlor with a catlike grace, powerful yet deceptively smooth. But there was something a bit off about the movements, almost as if he'd forgotten to add the final layer of polish he usually showed the world.

"I don't take kindly to being roused in the middle of the night." His eyes were sharp as he took in the four of them. "Whatever you have to discuss, it better be worth my inconvenience."

"Oh, it's going to be worth it." Sacha offered the man a sharp smile. "We'll start with how you're going to have Eric issue a formal statement saying he's been lying on the witness stand and then make sure all charges against me and the *Aurora* are dropped."

Caldwell let out a cruel laugh. "You think coming here to intimidate me in the middle of the night is going to change anything? All you've done is give me something else to report to the prosecutor. I'm not sure if he'll call it witness tampering or interfering in an ongoing investigation, but either way, it will make a lovely addition to the list of charges already stacked against you."

"Sure. Go ahead and get the prosecutor. I'd be happy to meet with him." Sacha set the book with the new navigational charts on the table in front of the sofa and flipped it open to the chart that held the map of Hoonah and the North Inian Pass. "I've got a hankering to explain that someone changed the navigational charts the Revenue Cutter Service has been distributing, making it appear that the shipping channel runs through dangerous shallows where ships are sure to either hit rocks or run aground. I'm sure he'll also be interested to learn that at least eight ships have been damaged this year in the Alexander Archipelago alone, and that all of the major errors in those charts are near Tlingit villages that are drying and tanning poached seal hides."

Caldwell released another laugh, though this one sounded strained rather than cruel. "You must be mistaken. Those are brand new charts, made with the most up-to-date advancements in cartography. There's nothing inaccurate about them."

"Then perhaps you can explain why both of your ships in port are using the old charts rather than the new ones." Sacha had sent a crew member to check the moment the *Halcyon* had docked. He'd known he'd never be granted access to one of the ACC's ships as a captain, but sailors were different. They all knew each other in one way or another and were willing to share plenty of tales. Having a crew member from another ship ask to compare navigational charts wouldn't cause any alarm.

"I've spent the past two weeks wondering why you were so furious about Dr. Torres's seal study. It didn't make any sense, not when the study has the potential of curtailing the poaching that's cutting into your company's profits." He narrowed his gaze at Caldwell. "Then I discovered you had your own way of stopping the poaching. You wanted to make the waters around those villages seem too treacherous to navigate, hoping to scare off the poachers, or perhaps damage vessels filled with seal pelts. Because if the pelts get wet after an animal has been skinned, they won't tan properly and are ruined."

"That's quite a story you weave." Caldwell sneered. "But it has nothing to do with me."

"The tea is ready." Rosalind entered the room, a tray balanced in her hands. "I brought cookies too. I figured—"

"Leave," Caldwell snapped. "Now."

Rosalind's cheeks turned pink, and she shoved the tray at Yuri, her head bowing. "I'm sorry, Father. I didn't realize you'd be accepting visitors so quickly."

She turned as though ready to scurry from the room, but Caldwell spoke again. "Wait."

He strode forward, fury evident in each stride. When he reached Rosalind, he spoke in a low tone, too quiet for Sacha to hear on the other side of the room, but there was no mistaking the anger in his posture or the threatening tone of his voice.

Was this what Yuri had meant when he'd said Rosalind needed someone to show her kindness? Sacha suddenly felt sick, and a quick glance around the room at his brothers told him they felt the same.

A moment later, Rosalind rushed from the room, her head down and arms wrapped tightly around herself.

"I'm sorry for the interruption." Caldwell turned back to them. "Do forgive my daughter. She can forget herself at times."

Forgive her for what? Sacha wanted to ask. She'd done nothing but act as a gracious hostess, never mind the ridiculous hour.

"Of course," Alexei said, his voice deceptively smooth. "Before the interruption, we were discussing why you changed several of the navigational maps that the RCS is distributing."

Chapter 38   377

An angry flush crept up Caldwell's neck and onto his face. "We were discussing nothing of the sort, because I didn't have any maps changed."

"Is this really something you want us to prove?" Again, Alexei's voice emerged unnaturally calm. "Because I know you had a cartographer up here working for you last summer. I can look him up if needed, see just what manner of work you had him doing."

"I vote we just hand over what we have to the prosecutor and let him deal with it." Mikhail crossed his arms over his chest.

"I don't." Sacha narrowed his eyes at Caldwell. "What if he pays the prosecutor off the way he's paying Eric to lie about me selling liquor?"

"You can't prove I'm paying Eric anything," Caldwell sputtered.

"Can't I? I can already prove that your men paid one of my other sailors, Nikolai, to destroy the seal study. You don't think I can find a way to prove that you're paying Eric too?"

"I told you not to do the study." Caldwell took a step forward, anger flashing in his eyes. "I told Alexei that if your family tampered with my rights to hunt the seals, I would make you regret it."

"I'm not a lawyer," Yuri muttered, "but it sounds like Caldwell here issued a threat first, then paid a sailor to lie second. That seems awful premeditated to me. Bet there's someone somewhere in the justice system who would care about that. Someone who's not on his payroll."

Caldwell clenched his hands into fists. "You can't prove anything."

"Do we need to?" Sacha took a step closer. "Even a rumor that you messed with the charts will be enough for half your sailors to up and quit, and it will scare away any captain from working for ACC for the next decade. All I'd need to do is compare the charts the Revenue Cutter Service is handing out to the ones you keep aboard your ships for everyone to see the truth in it."

"Don't forget, we keep pretty clear records on which ships we repair." Alexei nodded. "Right along with why they need repairs and where they became damaged."

Caldwell scoffed. "If there are incorrect charts somewhere, you can't prove they had anything to do with me."

Sacha tucked the book of charts under his arm and started for the door. He was done giving the man a chance to save himself. If Caldwell wanted to insist he wasn't responsible for the false charts, then he could answer to a jury. Sacha still might have enough evidence to get Eric to confess to lying and have the charges against the *Aurora* and him dropped.

He was nearly to the door before the word *wait* echoed through the room.

He turned to find Caldwell tugging on his collar. "You say I need to call Eric off? To see that the charges against you are dropped? In exchange for what?"

"You really did it?" Mikhail cracked his knuckles, the sound echoing in the room. "You tampered with the charts? You're lucky no one has died in the wrecks you've caused, that all the ships were able to be repaired rather than lost to the sea."

"The charts weren't supposed to go to everyone," Caldwell rasped. "Just about four or five ships. The ones that spend all season poaching. As you've said, something needed to be done, and no one in Washington, DC, is in a hurry to correct it. I wanted those captains too afraid to continue poaching."

"Either that or you wanted to damage their ships so they'd have to wait to have them repaired," Sacha muttered.

"Yes, that too." Caldwell pulled on his collar again, as though it had grown suddenly tight around his neck. "I changed the charts in shallow water, where a ship was likely to hit a boulder but not sink. I didn't want any wrecks that might put lives at risk."

"So you have half a conscience?" Sacha growled. "Excuse me if I'm not all that impressed."

"Look, I paid an employee at the RCS to give those maps to certain ships, like I said. And only after I wrote Washington several times explaining that the captains were flagrantly breaking the law and asking to have the ships seized. As I'm sure you're aware, nothing happened. How the wrong maps ended up being widely circulated, I don't know. You'd have to talk to the clerk at the RCS. It was never supposed to be this big."

"I still don't understand," Sacha snapped. "Why not support Dr. Torres's study? Why not throw your weight behind mine? Then we'd have a larger chance of accomplishing things in Washington."

Caldwell's eyes turned sharp again. "Because that study might lead to the quotas being lowered. It's not something I'm willing to risk."

"But it's also the legal way of going about things. And if it means you take fewer seals for a handful of years while the population recovers, it should be worth it."

"Except your method of stopping the poaching isn't going to work. The RCS has only three ships for all of Alaska. Even if they sent three more, that wouldn't be enough to curtail the poaching. Better to let sailors think the waters are cursed or too treacherous to pass through. Better to let rumors spread about ships filled with pelts springing leaks in their hulls so the entire cargo haul is ruined."

Sacha could see the logic behind it, even if it was sneaky and underhanded. Even if it had led to several ships being damaged. Caldwell had enough of a conscience to change the charts in places where the ships weren't in danger of sinking, but where the wreck was likely to ruin a load of pelts. No one had died yet with the false charts, and no one likely would. And he also had to admit that Caldwell's family had paid dearly for their hunting rights on the Pribilof Islands, even if it was far from fair that the sole right to hunt seals should go to one family.

"That's a touching story," he said. "But at this point, you're better off saving your explanation for Marshal Hibbs."

"Marshal Hibbs?" Caldwell blanched. "You turned me into the Marshal?"

"Did you think I was going to look the other way? Let ships keep running aground."

"I will ruin you. You. Your shipping company. Your entire family. Say good-bye to any chance of ever getting the *Aurora* back."

Sacha straightened, drawing himself up to his full height. "On the contrary. I actually expect to get the *Aurora* back—sometime tomorrow. And you're going to facilitate it."

"You expect me to . . ." Caldwell shook his head, then took a menacing step forward. "I don't think you understand. Marshal Hibbs is going to be too scared to investigate me. And even if he does, nothing will happen once he turns the information from his investigation over to the prosecutor."

"You seem awfully sure about that," Alexei drawled. "Makes me wonder if Eric isn't the only person you're paying to lie for you."

"Maybe that will work." Sacha leaned forward, meeting Caldwell's gaze. "Maybe you can slip money into people's pockets and get your legal troubles to disappear, but you can't get rumors to disappear. And mark my words, Caldwell, if the *Aurora* isn't back in our possession by tomorrow night, those rumors will spread.

"And while we're on the topic, you cheated Kuluk's tribe out of money, trading them blankets instead of giving the sum you promised them for their pelts." Sacha pulled a piece of paper out of his pocket. "I estimate you owe them this much. It had better be on my ship when we depart for Barrow in a few days. Otherwise those rumors will come back to haunt you."

"You can't do this," Caldwell rasped, his face mottled with rage.

"I can and I will. The choice is yours." Sacha didn't wait to hear what Caldwell said next. He was done giving the man any more of his time. So he turned and strode out into the night, leaving his brothers to follow.

39

She couldn't sleep. Again. Maggie shoved herself to an upright position on her bed. Even with the conversation she and Evelina had shared yesterday, she'd done nothing more than toss and turn and stare at the ceiling all night.

What if Sacha didn't love her enough to give up the sea? What if, even after his trial was done and he went to Barrow and he had a chance to think things through, he chose to walk away from her?

She'd stay faithful to God. That's what. She'd trust that God had a desire to teach her and grow her through whatever happened next.

Evidently she needed to learn to turn her thoughts over to God too, so she didn't end up plagued with worry for the rest of the summer.

She sighed and shoved the covers away. Maybe she needed to spend more time praying and less time worrying. With dawn cresting over the mountains in the east, she knew the perfect place to go and pray before the rest of the house awoke.

She stood and slid her shawl onto her arms. Perhaps there

was still a bit of cold coffee from last night in the kitchen. There probably wasn't enough time to warm it if she wanted to watch the sunrise, but she could still drink what was left and start a fresh pot for everyone else.

She reached for the doorknob, then paused. Because while it would be nice to pray on the deck as the sun came up, there was nothing wrong with praying now too. She tilted her head up to the ceiling. *Thank you, Father, for all you've done for me. Now help me trust you with whatever comes next.*

She already felt calmer as she stepped into the hall, then headed down the stairs, trying to avoid the spot on the third step from the bottom that always seemed to creak. She wasn't expecting the entryway lamp to be lit at the bottom of the stairs, though, and when she turned to head to the kitchen at the back of the house, voices echoed through the hallway—along with the scent of fresh coffee.

The door was closed, likely to keep the noise from waking others. She turned the knob and pushed the door open to find all four of the Amos brothers sitting around the table. She'd known the *Halcyon* returned last night. Even though she'd been in her room when Alexei and Sacha had stomped into the house around midnight, she hadn't been able to even try sleeping until she knew Sacha was back.

It didn't look like any of the brothers had gotten a wink of sleep. All four men wore wrinkled shirts and trousers. Shadows lingered under their eyes and tired lines wreathed their mouths. But she could tell they didn't plan to go to bed anytime soon. The table in front of them was filled with papers, some maps, some ledgers, and some business projections.

Alexei picked up one of the papers and was about to say something when she stepped forward. "What's going on? Is there something I can help with?"

"Maggie?" Sacha turned his head, then blinked at her,

almost as though he was too tired to believe she was standing there. "What are you doing up? Did we wake you?"

"I came down to watch the sunrise from the porch, but I wanted coffee first." She headed around the table toward the stove. "May I have some?"

"Of course. Help yourself." Alexei waved his hand toward the percolator.

"I'll come with you." Sacha pushed to his feet.

Maggie pulled a mug off the shelf and blinked at him. "To get coffee?"

"To watch the sunrise." He nudged his chair under the table and picked up the coffee in front of him.

"Oh . . . um . . ." She shifted her weight from one foot to the other, her palms turning suddenly damp. Hadn't she just been praying about trusting God with whatever came next? So why was she suddenly nervous about Sacha watching the sunrise with her? They'd certainly watched the sunset plenty of times, and it had never made her stomach feel as though a horde of butterflies had taken flight inside.

"You're certain you want to watch the sunrise with me?"

Sacha scrubbed a hand over his face. "I'm an oaf, Maggie. And a dunderhead and a clodhopper, and I need to apologize. You and Ainsley and Finnan are all more important to me than captaining a ship, and I was wrong to ever ask you to marry me without first agreeing to give that up."

"I . . . ah . . ." She looked around the room, only to find all three of Sacha's brothers watching them. "Perhaps we should talk about this on the porch."

"Oh no, please continue." Mikhail leaned back in his chair, a smirk on his face. "This is the most entertaining thing I've seen all year, and Sacha hasn't even gotten on one knee yet."

"That's because I'm not going to ask her to marry me with

an audience." Sacha scowled at Mikhail, then looked back at her and tilted his head toward the door. "Shall we?"

"I . . ." He intended to ask her to marry him? After telling her that she was more important to him than captaining a ship. Did that mean . . . ?

She was too nervous to think about what it might mean.

She'd spent yesterday praying, yes, but then she'd spent all night worrying. She was supposed to tell Sacha she'd wait until the end of the summer for him to decide how he felt about her, and he was supposed to take that time to think things through.

But here he was, apologizing and saying he intended to propose again in a few minutes? He didn't even know how the jury would rule. Did he intend to marry her even if he was going to spend the next five years in prison?

And should she say yes if he did?

Her palms grew damper, and the still-empty coffee cup in her hands felt suddenly heavy.

"Maggie?" Sacha held out a hand for her. Not an arm where she could rest her hand as was proper, but his large, wide hand. "Come, love. We need to talk. Just the two of us."

Somehow she managed to set her mug back down and walk around the table. The moment she slid her hand into Sacha's, warmth shot up her arm and straight into her heart.

He was silent as he led her out of the kitchen and down the hallway, but he paused in front of the front door and reached for one of the coats hanging on the pegs beside it.

"It's going to be chilly." He draped the coat around her shoulders, and she was instantly surrounded by his scent.

Then he opened the door, placing a hand on the small of her back as he led her outside. The touch made a warm shudder travel up her spine.

He frowned at her. "Are you still cold even with my coat? We can talk in the parlor."

"No." She hadn't even felt the chill of the morning. "It wasn't the cold. It was . . ."

How you touched me. But she wasn't going to say that, so she drew in a breath and looked out at the mountains. Dawn in Sitka truly was beautiful, with the mountains in the east and vibrant rays of pink and orange reflected on the water below.

But it was hard to concentrate on the beauty surrounding her with Sacha studying her, his eyes intent as they scanned her face, then swept down the rest of her body.

"Was this what made you shudder?" He stepped closer, then reached out and touched a hand to her shoulder. Again, warmth spiraled through her, and she trembled.

"I see." The corner of his mouth tipped up into a smile, but his eyes were serious. "I meant what I said inside, Maggie. I'm a clodhopper and a dunce and the biggest oaf to ever walk the planet. I had time to think about things on the water yesterday, and I never should have asked you to marry me without agreeing to stay in Sitka. When we learned Tavish died, I expected you to give up your biggest dream—your family's land and shipyard on Lake Michigan—without being willing to give up any of mine. It was selfish and unfair."

She licked her lips. "But you love the sea. I could never ask you to give it up for me."

"I love the sea, yes. But not as much as I love you. Giving it up isn't a hardship, not when it means I can fall asleep next to you each night, or kiss you whenever I please, or spend ten thousand sunrises standing on this very porch with you, watching the sun come up."

Oh how she wanted to sink into those words, to believe them and treasure them and hold on to them forever. But she'd seen this man aboard the *Aurora* with the wind in his hair and his face tilted toward the sun. Seen him behind the helm and standing at the bow.

"Are you certain? I don't want you to offer me something you'll end up regretting in the future."

He pressed his eyes shut and groaned. "That you even need to ask makes me wish I'd handled things better. Yes, I love you more than a ship, or being on the water. It was only selfishness that made me want both at the same time, and I plowed ahead without stopping to think of what would be best for both of us, or Ainsley and Finnan, or the children I hope to one day have with you."

Sacha sighed, his shoulders rising and falling with the puff of air. "Even without you, it's time for me to stop sailing so much. Bjorn is getting too old to manage the shipyard, and the only siblings I ever see are Alexei and Yuri. And I don't even see them enough. There was a time when my family needed me on the water, but we have men who can fill my place on the *Aurora* now, and I'd rather be here with them—and with you."

Maggie sucked in a breath. The words were almost too much for her to take in. It was supposed to take until the end of August for Sacha to come to this decision. And here he'd made it yesterday, before she'd spent last night lying awake in bed.

"What if the jury convicts you? What if you end up sentenced to five years in prison? Would you want to marry before or—"

He clasped his hands around her ribs and hefted her up until she found herself sitting on the railing. "Didn't I tell you?" He moved closer to her, his hips touching her knees. "The trial is over, and the charges against me are being dropped. That's what we stayed up all night working on."

"They're being dropped?" she squealed. "How? Why? What happened?"

He chuckled. "I'll tell you in a minute, but I want to finish the other conversation we were having first. Do you believe me when I say I'd rather be here with you than on the water?"

She sunk her teeth into her bottom lip. "Yes, but I hope you'll still be able to take trips sometimes. Like maybe you can still go to Barrow? I know you love sailing the Arctic."

The smile that spread across his lips was so soft and warm that it wrapped around her like a blanket. "I intend to go on the water every now and then, but I also intend to have you with me. The *Halcyon* felt awful empty yesterday without you there."

"It did?"

"Turns out my short trip yesterday without you was all it took for me to realize I don't want to be on the water again without a certain woman by my side." He got down on one knee in front of her, then pulled something small from his pocket and reached out, taking her hand. "Maggie McDougal, will you marry me?"

She stared down at the top of his head, at the light-brown hair streaked with blond from endless days beneath the ocean sun. Then she slid off the railing, warmth filling her chest as she said, "Yes, I'd love to marry you."

He slid the ring onto her finger, a simple gold band with an oval-shaped emerald.

"It's beautiful."

"It's not quite the color of your eyes. But it was the closest shade I could find from my mother's collection." He stood, then folded her in his arms. Again, she was surrounded by the scent of him, by the strength of his arms and the heat of his body and the love he had for her.

"You just made me the happiest man alive," he whispered against her hair.

"That's good to know, because I'm pretty sure I'm the happiest woman alive."

"Ten thousand sunrises. Don't forget." He bent his head

and kissed the side of her neck. "I want to watch each and every one of them with you."

Maggie looked up into Sacha's eyes, those deep pools of kindness and strength that had first captivated her heart on the deck of the *Aurora*. In them, she saw not just the man she loved but a future filled with hope and happiness and shared dreams.

"Ten thousand sunrises," she whispered back, then pushed up onto her toes to kiss him.

Epilogue

Sitka, Two Weeks Later

Kate stood at the back of the warehouse watching as Sacha and Maggie danced together and grinned at each other with goofy, lovesick smiles.

Two weeks wasn't nearly enough time to plan a wedding, but Maggie and Sacha had managed to pull it off—with Evelina's help, of course. The old warehouse, which was usually used for town dances, had been strung with flowers and garlands, the seamstress had busied herself making a wedding dress, and the fiddler and bass player in town had agreed to the wedding date.

Now the entire town of Sitka was celebrating with Sacha and Maggie—just like they'd celebrated with Evelina and Jonas when they married at Christmas.

"You're not planning to dance?"

Kate looked over her shoulder to find Mikhail beside her. She thought she'd just seen him on the dance floor with one of Bjorn's daughters, but somehow he was standing beside her.

She shouldn't be surprised. The man moved like a mountain lion, his movements quiet and graceful.

"Well?" Mikhail nudged her shoulder. "You should go out there. There's not nearly enough women for the men to dance with."

There never were at dances in Alaska. Men outnumbered women by a margin of ten to one or better. At the moment, there were several male couples dancing together, not because there was anything romantic between them, but just so they could have partners.

"That's the problem," she muttered. "I go out there once, and I'll be stuck dancing all night."

"Since when is that a problem? You like to dance."

"Since half the men I dance with will propose to me when the music ends."

Mikhail leaned back against the wall and crossed one ankle in front of the other, his posture lazy, even though there was nothing lazy in his intelligent golden eyes as he watched the crowd. "Maybe you should take one of them up on his offer."

As if she could. Or rather, she couldn't take one of them up and still be a doctor.

Not that she cared. She'd rather be a doctor than have a husband. She'd made that decision shortly after graduating from medical school, and she didn't regret it.

But sometimes, when she saw how happy her sister was with Jonas, how happy Sacha looked with Maggie...

She swallowed the lump climbing its way up her throat.

"You know, if you find a man and marry him tonight, you might be able to get out of chaperoning Sacha and Maggie on their honeymoon voyage."

Kate snorted. "That's not what I'm going to be doing."

Mikhail shrugged, his eyes still scanning the crowd. "All I

know is you couldn't pay me enough to be on that ship to Barrow in the morning."

She narrowed her eyes at her brother. "That makes me think you should come along. It's not like you to have anything else to do, seeing how your expedition finally got canceled last week. You never know. One day you might get hired to guide an expedition up by Barrow."

"I'd rather stay here and help. Alexei's of a mind that I should learn how to manage the shipping routes. Besides, like I said, you couldn't pay me enough to be trapped on a ship with a newly married couple. They'll be canoodling each time you turn the corner. Just look at them now."

Mikhail nodded to where Sacha and Maggie stood on the dance floor, not moving to the lively reel the fiddler played, but standing in each other's arms, slowly swaying to the music. Then Sacha leaned down and kissed the side of Maggie's jaw.

It was true, all the touching and canoodling could be a bit much, especially since she, Ilya, and Inessa all shared the top floor of the trading post in Juneau with Jonas and Evelina. It seemed like those two were always hugging or kissing or whispering in each other's ears.

But there was still something sweet about watching Sacha kiss Maggie on their wedding day. Just like it had been sweet to watch as Sacha insisted that Maggie come with him to Barrow, which meant putting a rush on the wedding.

Ainsley and Finnan were heading to Juneau with Evelina and Jonas until they returned. But since Kate administered medical care in the northern villages, she still needed to make the trip. Yet at the end of the day, her big, gruff, burly brother who traveled the world suddenly didn't want to leave home without the woman he loved. And that made Kate want to smile.

"You'll find a man one day. Don't worry."

"What?" Kate snapped her gaze back to Mikhail. "What makes you think I want one?"

He snorted. "The way you're looking at Sacha and Maggie, at Evelina and Jonas."

She stiffened. "Don't be ridiculous. I'm a doctor, and I've yet to meet a man who appreciates that."

"Yes, but one day you will. And when that happens . . ." Mikhail shrugged, then sauntered off, blending in with the rest of the crowd a moment later.

And leaving her to stand there on the edge of the room, watching everyone else enjoy the life that seemed to be passing her by—and to wonder just what it would feel like to have a man love her as thoroughly as Sacha loved Maggie.

A note from Naomi...

Wow, sometimes God gives us blessings in the ways we least expect. I'm so glad both Sacha and Maggie realized that though life isn't always sunshine and roses, God can use trials to bring about good.

I know Sacha and Maggie already have their happy ending, but I couldn't resist writing bonus scene from their wedding day. It'll give you a little glimpse of just how happy the two of them will be as they start their new life together—and I think you'll love it. If you want to read it, follow the link below and type in your email, so I know where to send it. https://geni.us/AK2Bonus

*And if you want a head start on Kate's story, turn the page for a sneek peek.

Above all Dreams

Juneau, Alaska; April, 1887

It was the first day of the rest of his life, and he didn't know what to think of it.

Nathan Reid drew in a breath of cool, damp air as he stood on the wharf, watching as townsfolk assembled and dockworkers pushed carts up and down the gangway of the ship he'd taken from Seattle up to Juneau. It was a thing of beauty, with a sleek hull and a series of three towering masts. It had cut through the water seamlessly on the journey north, but unloading cargo from the massive ship was sure to take several hours.

Which meant he didn't know how long he'd be waiting for his trunks.

Nathan stretched his hand at his side. It felt empty without his medical bag, but space had been rather cramped in the bunkroom, and the voyage had been so short—only two days— that he'd elected to pack his medical bag in one of his trunks and place a small bag with only his most basic medical supplies inside the satchel he'd kept with him on board.

A group of people had gathered near the log warehouse down the wharf where the cargo was being unloaded. Should he go there and wait for his trunks? Or should he try to procure lodging first and send for his belongings later?

He looked down at the scrap of paper in his hand. The first mate had given him directions to one of the boardinghouses in town. Perhaps he'd go there first. After all, there was little point in retrieving his trunks if he didn't have anywhere to put them. And it looked like it would take a couple hours before the cargo was unloaded.

Nathan glanced around the growing town that was to be his home for the next couple years. It wasn't nearly as polished as Boston or Washington, DC or even New Orleans. Instead it seemed Juneau was comprised of ramshackle log buildings, most with the bark still on the logs, as though peeling off the bark would have taken too much time when the buildings were being constructed.

The directions in his hand said he needed to go right, toward the heart of town. He glanced at the map a final time, committing it to memory, and then stepped off the wharf straight into a thick puddle of mud.

He blinked as the mud soiled not just his shoes, but the hem of his trousers. The street hadn't looked that muddy from the wharf. Was all the ground this soft? He'd read that Juneau received an inordinate amount of rain, so much so that some biologists called it a rain forest, but he hadn't expected this much mud in the road itself.

Nathan extricated himself from the puddle, though the ground beside it was still soft, just not so soft it swallowed half his shoes. The boardinghouse. He couldn't let himself get distracted. His first order of business was to procure temporary lodging. His second order of business was to have his trunks delivered. And his third order of business was to rent or buy a building that could be used as a temporary medical clinic while the hospital was being built.

He didn't know how long it would take to find a building. Was there an empty one in town, or was every last structure being put to use given the fast growth of the town? Hopefully he'd be able to find a vacant building somewhere, and he'd have that either purchased or rented by tomorrow night. And then he'd hang out his shingle and...

What?

Hope that townsfolk simply came to him? A new doctor that they'd never heard of before?

At his last position in New Orleans, he'd gone to an already existing hospital and helped enlarge it, then started holding one-day medical clinics in some of the smaller towns on the coast.

But Juneau didn't have an established hospital for him to work at. They didn't have anything.

Perhaps he'd made a mistake. Perhaps he should have taken that position in San Francisco rather than begging the director in Washington DC to allocate funds for a new hospital in Juneau.

Again, he stretched his palm at his side, as though doing so would help relieve the tension coiling inside him.

A shout sounded from farther down the road, followed by the pounding of animal hooves. Nathan glanced up to find a wagon with four people careening his direction. He dashed toward the side of the street, along with most of the other people in the road—never mind the second mud puddle he had to trudge through.

The wagon rushed past, then man on the bench fighting to control the reins while a panicked woman clutched two children beside him. Shout and cries filled the air as more and more townsfolk became aware of the runaway wagon.

Dear Father, please let that man slow the wagon. Nathan tossed the prayer towards the heavens, then started racing after the wagon. A doctor would be needed if it crashed.

The wagon veered hard to the right, heading toward a building that looked to be the general store. Two men sat on the porch playing checkers over a barrel, and a woman and her children were sitting on a bench, likely waiting to be picked up.

"Lookout," Nathan shouted, his chest heaving.

Others called out warnings too. But the people on the porch hadn't noticed the commotion farther down the street, and time seemed to slow as they looked up, seeing the wagon careening toward them with only seconds to spare. The two men leaped from their seats, scattering checkers cross the wooden planks of the porch, while the woman grabbed her children and dived to the ground, attempting to shield them with her body.

The wagon collided into the porch with a deafening crash, its impact sending splinters of wood flying and a wheel spinning off the wagon. One of the pillars cracked beneath the impact, folding forward so that it half rested on corner of the wagon.

The porch roof sagged, then groaned. And there was one sickening moment where Nathan imagined it collapsing, all those boards and shingles crushing the people seeking shelter below. But then the creaking ceased, and though the roof sagged, the remaining pillars seemed to support its weight.

Nathan wasn't sure when he'd started running toward the accident. All he knew was that he was pumping his feet as quickly as he could, wishing for the medical bag that was packed in his trunk. He couldn't do much with only the bandages, carbolic acid, and stitching needle in his satchel, but he had to at least try to help.

"Someone get the doctor!" a shout rang out.

There was no doctor. That was part of why the Marine Hospital Service had chosen Juneau for its next hospital. No doctor in town except a drunkard. It would take forty minutes or better for the doctor at the Treadwell Mine across the channel to get to Juneau once he was sent for.

Nathan leapt onto the porch and skidded to a halt in front of one of the men who'd been playing checkers. He was clutching his leg, a large gash staining the thigh of his trousers red. "Here, let's put some carbolic acid on this and then bandage it. We need to clean the wound and stop the bleeding."

He fished in his bag for the blue bottle of carbolic acid and a cotton swab. In truth, the cut might need stitches, but he needed to treat injuries in order of severity, and he didn't yet know how injured the wagon passengers were.

"It hurts!" a groan came from the other side of the wagon. "Someone help! My shoulder's on fire."

That sounded like a dislocation. Nathan quickly dampened the cotton ball with carbolic acid, then thrust that and a bandage at the man's friend beside him. "Clean his wound with the cotton swab and then wrap it. I'll be back in a minute."

Nathan crossed the porch to find the wagon's passengers. A woman and girl knelt on the ground, muddy but seemingly unharmed, but a man lay beside the wagon's wheel, clutching his shoulder and groaning.

Beyond him, a boy sat propped up against the wagon, tears streaming down his face as he clutched his arm. "It hurts, mommy, it hurts."

"There's Dr. Pritchard." A man stood near the woman and gestured across the street, where an older man with graying hair and a medical bag in his hand stumbled toward the accident with the swagger of a drunken man, never mind it was only three in the afternoon. "Looks like you're in luck. Doc Pritchard even had his medical bag with him in the bar."

The woman glanced at Dr. Pritchard, her jaw tightening. "That man is not touching either my husband or my son. Someone get Dr. Amos."

"I'm here. I'm here." A female voice called. A second later, a woman appeared from around the back of the wagon, followed by a large, lumbering man with red hair.

There was another doctor in town? Nathan frowned. Had he just arrived? There was only supposed to be one doctor, a drunkard, meaning the town didn't have adequate medical care.

He nearly stepped forward and offered to treat the man with the shoulder dislocation, but something held him back. If there was another doctor, did they need him here in Juneau too? He gave his head a small shake. No. Juneau had already been chosen for the public health trial and plans had been set in motion. The Marine Hospital Service wouldn't change location simply because another doctor had moved to the area.

Nathan expected the large man with red hair to head straight toward the driver with the dislocated shoulder. But the woman got to him first, kneeling on the muddy ground without a care for her crisp blue skirt and white shirtwaist. In fact, it was the woman holding the medical bag, not the man.

Nathan's jaw fell open, but he forced himself to clamp it shut, forced himself to stay rooted to the floorboards of the porch as he watched the woman probed the driver's shoulder.

The driver howled in pain. "I thought you were supposed to help me! Crazy woman doctor. Yer just making it hurt worse!"

Woman doctor? Again, Nathan felt his jaw open. Was the woman in front of him really a doctor?

No. The report had said nothing about a female doctor in Juneau. And besides, hadn't someone called for a man named Dr. Amos? Surely the woman's name wasn't Amos.

"I'm not trying to make it hurt more, Mr. Cartwright." The woman's voice was both brisk and authoritative. "I'm trying to ascertain the quickest way to get you out of pain."

"Laudanum," the man howled. "That's the quickest way. Just give me some laudanum. I know you got some in yer bag."

"I'll give you some in about thirty seconds." The woman's hands were swift as they moved over his shoulder, probing muscle and bone just like Nathan would do to determine how badly the humerus had been pulled from its socket.

The woman looked over her shoulder at the tall man whom Nathan only now realized had a tin star pinned to his chest.

Not a doctor then, but a sheriff.

"Jonas, I need you to hold him. This is going to hurt."

"No," the driver whined, trying to clamber up into a sitting position. But that only caused him to howl in pain again. "Give me laudanum first, then fix it."

"It can be fixed in less time than it would take to get laudanum out of my bag, let alone give the laudanum enough time to dull your pain."

"Here, give him some whisky." The drunk doctor ambled closer and uncorked a flask, then knelt on the ground and held it over Mr. Cartwright's mouth. "Open up, Jim."

Mr. Cartwright did as asked, and the drunk poured whisky into his mouth until he started to choke.

But the female doctor didn't let anything about the whisky disrupt her. In fact, she'd been moving the whole time, nodding to the sheriff as he knelt by the man's head and murmuring instructions about how to hold him. Mr. Cartwright was still trying to swallow his mouthful of whisky when she gripped his arm and gave it a sharp tug.

Cartwright spit out his whisky and screamed, dampening the front of the woman's shirtwaist with the amber liquid as a popping sound filled the air.

Then the man slid back to the ground, a hand clutched over his shoulder as his breathing slowed. "Feels better already. Thank you, doc."

The woman didn't so much as flinch at the whiskey now drenching her chest, or even smile at the compliment. Instead she rolled her eyes and turned to the sheriff. "Give him—"

"I'm here." Another woman rounded the far side of the wagon. A woman with auburn hair and green eyes—a spitting image of the female doctor. The new woman took in the situation in front of the wagon with a glance. "Do you need anything?"

"Mr. Cartwright dislocated his shoulder. Give him a small dose of laudanum while I treat Benny." Then the woman moved her gaze to look directly at the sheriff. "I suspect Mr. Cartwright was drunk while driving his wagon. I smelled whiskey on his breath before Dr. Pritchard offered it. "

The sheriff crossed his arms over his broad chest and moved his gaze to the brown-haired woman who'd been in the accident. She was still kneeling on the dirt with an arm wrapped around her son's shoulder. "Is that true, Mrs. Cartwright? Was Jim drinking?"

The woman twisted her hands together, then launched into an explanation of how the mining claim they'd staked was no good, with barely enough gold to pay for a sack of flour despite all the months of work her husband had put into mining it, so they'd packed things up and had decided to head back to Chicago.

Nathan let the words float past him as he watched the

woman doctor work on the boy with what looked to be a broken arm. Of course, he couldn't say it was broken without examining it himself. But she was going through the exact steps he would when determining whether a break existed, and where it might be.

And all he could do was stand there and watch. To be fair, no one else seemed to be injured. The women and children from the porch might have some bruises, but they were already making their way down the street away from the commotion. And the two older men playing checkers...

Nathan forced his gaze away from the lady doctor and turned. He should inspect that gash more closely and see if it needed stitches.

But the man was already limping toward him, holding out the bandage. "Thank you, sir. Appreciate your help. I put the smelly cleaner from the cotton ball on it, but I'm going to have Kate here look at my gash before I wrap it up. Make sure it don't need stitches."

"Kate?" It was the only thing he could think to ask.

"Kate Amos." The man shoved his hand toward the female doctor. "The town doc. Didn't ya' just see her fix Jim's shoulder? She's that good at patchin' everyone up, even if she's a woman."

Right. A woman doctor. In Juneau. And the whole town seemed to know her, which meant she hadn't just arrived.

So why hadn't she been included in the report from last summer?

The man limped down the steps, his friend beside him, leaving Nathan alone on the porch. He looked around again, scanning the area to see if anyone else might need medical care. But it looked like everyone had either gone back to shopping inside the general store, or come outside to watch Mrs. Amos—or was it Dr. Amos?—fix up the...

Crack! Something snapped above him, and the pillar that had been propped up on the wagon gave way. An ominous groan sounded, and Nathan glanced up just in time to see an object falling toward him.

Then it slammed into his head, and his world went black.

KATE STARED at the pages in front of her, trying to make sense of the words in the light filtering in through the window. Of course, she might be able to concentrate a little better if the rocking chair she was sitting in didn't creak each time she pushed it backwards.

How did her sister stand it? Sitting still for so long and knitting—because that's what Evelina did, knitted—or read a novel. Not an article from the New England Journal of Medicine on head injuries or apoplexy or heart failure. No. Her sister read fluff.

And liked it.

Kate shifted in her seat, trying to get comfortable, but there was little hope for it. It was a hard, wooden chair, after all. One that creaked whenever she moved it.

She huffed, shifted again, then tapped her fingers on the arm of the chair and looked up. Her sudden need to fidget fell away in that moment, as her eyes landed on the dark-haired stranger lying in the bed on the opposite side of the small room.

What brought you to Juneau, Mr. Reid?

And what had he been doing on the porch of the general store earlier, when everyone else had the sense to vacate it after the crash?

The door to the room opened, and her twin sister peeked inside. "Oh, he's still sleeping. When I realized you were in here, I assumed he'd woken up."

Kate sighed, tapping her fingers on the arm of the chair once more. "No he hasn't woken yet."

Evelina stepped farther into the room, her rich auburn hair cascading down her back in thick waves. "He's not unconscious again, is he?"

Kate glanced at the small clock hanging on the wall. "I roused him about forty-five minutes ago, just to make sure his head injury wasn't getting worse. He woke, told me his name and where he was from, and then went right back to sleep."

"Oh really?" Evelina's green eyes lit with curiosity. "Where's he from?"

Kate frowned. "New Orleans, most recently, it seems, but he gave me a whole list of places. Charleston, Portland, Norfolk, Washington DC and Boston. And he might have said Chicago too. I really don't remember. Oh, and somewhere called Marquette. Have you ever heard of it?"

Evelina shook her head. "No. But it seems odd for him to have lived in so many places. He doesn't seem old enough to have traveled that much."

"I'd guess he's thirty or so." Did that mean he moved every year or two?

Evelina looked at him for another moment, as though also trying to make sense of the conundrum laying before her, then sighed and turned her direction. There was something graceful and gentle about the movement, about the way her shoulders rose and fell and even how she turned.

Then again, everything about Evelina was graceful and gentle.

Kate should probably hate her twin for it, for the way Evelina had such a calming effect on everyone around her. But her sister was far too kind to hate, and so the two of them were best friends, even if she often felt like a walking ball of destruction next to Evelina.

"Go. I'll sit with him for a spell." Evelina nodded toward the door, as though almost being able to sense what she'd been thinking. "I can tell you're feeling antsy stuck in here."

And that was why she couldn't hate her sister. Evelina was always doing things like this, making sacrifices for others or sensing when someone was upset and comforting them.

Kate might be good at saving people's lives, but Evelina excelled at mending people's hearts.

"Well? Are you going to leave, or just sit there scowling at me?"

Was she scowling? She hadn't meant to. She relaxed the muscles in her face—or at least, she tried to relax them—but nothing inside her wanted to calm down. Not after being pent up inside this room for over an hour. Not with knowing so very little about her new patient. And not with the image of that board hitting his head stuck in her mind, repeating itself over and over again.

"It's not your fault, Kate." Evelina crossed the room and rested a hand on her shoulder. "You understand that you can't blame yourself that he got injured, don't you?"

Kate swallowed. How did her sister do that? It was almost as though Evelina could read her mind. And Evelina had such a way of setting people at ease.

Kate was quite certain the only kinds of emotions she ever evoked in people set them on edge. Unless, of course, she was doctoring them. Then people seemed happy with her, even if she was a woman.

She reached up and rested a hand atop Evelina's on her shoulder, and something about the simple gesture brought a small bit of stillness to her soul.

Then her mind drifted back to that afternoon, to the panic that had overtaken her when she'd realized the porch roof was about to fall "If I would have seen him standing on the porch, I would have told him to move."

"You were a little busy treating a dislocated shoulder and a broken arm."

Yes. And to be fair, the porch roof hadn't looked unstable. One moment it seemed like the damaged pillar just needed to be reinforced, and the next, the entire thing had come crashing down.

Kate rubbed her forehead. "I still haven't thanked Jonas. I can't imagine how much worse Mr. Reid would be had Jonas not realized what was about to happen." After that first board fell and knocked Mr. Reid unconscious, Evelina's husband had realized the roof was about to collapse and pulled Mr. Reid off the porch with only a half second before the rest of it had come crashing down.

"Oh, that's what I was coming to tell you. I learned what your new friend's name."

"He's not my friend. And like I said, he told me his name when I woke him earlier. It's Nathan Ried."

"All right, but do you know what he does for a living and why he's in Juneau?"

Kate quirked an eyebrow at her sister.

"He booked passage north on the *Alliance* as Dr. Nathniel Reid, meaning he's a scientist of some sort.

"Doctor?" Kate frowned. "What's he here to study?"

Evelina shrugged. "What do they all come to study? Either geology or geography or biology. I think Mikhail said something about an expedition of biologist studying the flora and fauna of Southeast Alaska this summer."

"So where's the rest of his team?" Kate rubbed her forehead. "And why isn't he in Sitka? That's where most of the expeditions leave from." Something wasn't making sense.

Again, Evelina's shoulders rose and fell on a gentle shrug.

"Perhaps you should wake him and ask, just to make sure you can still rouse him."

"No." He'd regained consciousness after being struck by the board and had maintained it while they'd moved him to her examination room, after which he'd fallen asleep. She'd already roused him once, his eyes weren't dilated, and there was nothing to indicate a serious head injury. "Let him sleep. The journals are all claiming that while unconsciousness is bad, sleep aids in the recovery of a concussion."

"Is that what you've been reading? A fancy journal article about concussions?" Evelina glanced down at the book Kate hadn't bothered to close. "And here I hoped you'd picked up one of my novels."

Kate rolled her eyes. "I'm sitting still, aren't I? That should count for something."

"Yes, it should. But you don't need to sit here. Dr. Reid should be fine by himself for a bit, and if you're really that concerned, I can sit here."

Kate looked at the stranger again, running her eyes down his lean body. He wasn't overly tall or broad of chest, not like Evelina's husband Jonas or their brother Sacha. But there was something lithe and strong about him, something that made her hate to see him lying there so weak, especially when he'd been on that porch after the accident trying to help others.

If only she would have realized the roof was about to give way a few seconds sooner.

"Did Jonas arrest Mr. Cartwright?" she asked.

"He did, and Mr. Cartwright is none too happy about it, seeing how he planned to leave on the Alliance. Jonas says he'll need to pay to replace the collapsed roof before he can leave town. You can imagine how Mr. Cartwright feels about that."

Kate winced. She could, in fact, imagine the tongue lashing Jonas would have received after telling a man with no money that he needed to come up with money before he could leave Juneau. Of course, it served the man right for drinking himself into a stupor and then climbing onto a wagon with his wife and children. "Just tell me Emma Cartwright has a place she can stay with the children"

"Jonas said he'll probably work for a few months over at the Treadwell Mine to pay back the general store. They have company housing, so at least there'll be a roof over his family's head and food in their bellies. That sounds like more than they had up in the mountains."

It did. Gold fever was a real thing. Men made such a big deal of coming to Juneau and prospecting for gold up in the mountains, but she only knew of a handful of men who'd struck it rich. Most men ended up poorer when they left than they'd been when they'd came, and the weather and isolation on the mountains could be particularly brutal on families.

But Treadwell Mine on the opposite side of the channel was a full-fledged mining and ore refining operation. With tunnels that ran deep into the ground, they had hundreds of jobs available to anyone willing to work them. Of course, workers had to deal with the constant stench from the chlorination plant and ceaseless pounding of the stamps at the mill that crushed the rock from the mine so that gold could be extracted. It wasn't the kind of place most men worked for very long, but they did provide housing for their workers, so it would be a good fit for the Cartwrights until debts could be paid.

"I just hope they're able to get back to Chicago soon," Kate muttered.

"Lina, are you in here?" The door to the sickroom opened, and Jonas peeked his head inside. A smile lit his face when he spotted his wife. "There you are."

"Are you finished at the jail?" Evelina headed straight

toward him, then pushed up onto her tiptoes and pressed a kiss to his cheek.

Jonas hooked an arm around her waist and pulled her against him. "I am. Did you save me some dinner?"

Kate was tempted to roll her eyes. It didn't look like Jonas was half as interested in dinner as he was in his wife. The two of them were utterly besotted. In some ways it was sweet, but there were certainly things she didn't enjoy about living with a newlyweds.

It was an issue she was hoping to rectify by the end of the summer. At that point, she'd have enough saved up to purchase the old storefront downtown. It had an apartment above it, and with a few modifications, the first floor could be converted into three separate examination rooms plus a parlor.

It was getting harder and harder to treat her patients in the tiny room inside her family's trading post. And with the growing number of people calling Juneau home, the town certainly needed a proper medical clinic.

The longer she practiced, the more accepting the town became of her, even if she was a woman doctor. When faced with using her services or Dr. Pritchard's, most people had sense enough to pick her. Like Emma Cartwright earlier that day. She'd been racing toward the wagon when she'd heard the woman's voice ring out over the commotion, proclaiming that she wanted Kate to treat her husband, not a drunk.

The words had made warmth rush through her even before she'd rounded the wagon and realized that Mr. Cartwright had dislocated his shoulder.

"Jonas," Evelina giggled, her voice soft and breathy. "Stop. Kate's here."

Kate glanced at the door, where Jonas had wrapped his arms around Evelina and was nuzzling her neck. "Yes, Kate is here, and Kate can also hear you. Perhaps the two of you should go canoodle somewhere else."

She'd hoped to embarrass them, but Jonas's smile only grew as he stared down at Evelina, his arms cinching tighter about her. "Canoodle? That sounds like an excellent plan. Come on, sweetheart."

He tugged her toward the door, his eyes riveted on his wife. Kate just shook her head as the door closed behind them. Hopefully they made it into another room before they started kissing. The last thing she needed was someone stumbling into the trading post to find her brother-in-law smooching on her sister.

Again.

Kate blew out a breath, then moved her gaze back to the journal article on concussions. She really should finish it. It certainly had useful information. The problem was, she could only read a handful of sentences before her mind drifted to her...

A groan sounded from the bed.

Kate was out of the chair in an instant. "Mr. Reid?"

"My head," he whispered, his hand moving to his forehead. "It hurts."

"You suffered a concussion."

"The lamp." He kept his eyes shut, his hand pressed to the side of his forehead, where the board had struck him. "Can you dim the lamp?"

She hadn't lit a lamp. The sun set so late in the summer that it wasn't necessary, even though it was after eight pm. But Kate moved to the window and pulled the curtain shut, leaving the log room shrouded in near darkness.

"Thank you." The man breathed a sigh of relief, even though he had yet to open his eyes.

"I don't suppose you have any phenacetin."

Phena... what? Kate stepped closer to the bed. The other two times Dr. Reid had woken, he'd been lucid, but now he was mumbling gibberish. Perhaps that board had hit him harder than she'd realized.

"I'd prefer willow bark tea to laudanum," he said, his eyes still shut. "Do you have any of that?"

Well, that comment at least made sense. She touched a hand to his forehead. In fact, willow bark tea had been the first thing she intended to offer. She didn't like giving laudanum to people with head injuries. While it dulled the pain, it also dulled their other senses, making it hard to determine if the symptoms of a person's head injury were getting worse or improving.

"Yes. I've already got some hot water upstairs. Let's get you sitting up, and then I'll fix your tea. Would you like some supper too?"

"Yes, thank you."

"If you can push yourself up, I'll reposition the pillows behind you."

Mr. Reid did as asked, planting his slender yet strong arms on either side of himself on the bed and raising into a sitting position.

Or rather, he tried to raise himself into a sitting position. But the moment he moved his head, he made a heaving sound.

Kate reached for the bucket that she'd set beside the bed for that very reason... but she wasn't quite fast enough.

Order your copy of *Above all Dreams* on Amazon.

Author's Note

In the late 1860s, shortly after the US purchased Alaska from Russia, the government commissioned an official study of the northern fur seal so that hunting limits could be set. As unbelievable as it seems, that study (which I reference in *Whispers on the Tide*) concluded that up to one hundred thousand bachelor bulls could be taken from the Pribilof Islands each summer without impacting the population.

The US government, reeling over how much the purchase of Alaska had cost them, decided to manage the seal hunt in the most lucrative manner possible—by charging one company an exorbitant amount of money to hunt the seals for the next twenty years, and then exacting an additional bounty on each seal that was killed.

At first this seemed like a good plan, and the US government started earning some of its money back. But then the price of seal pelts shot up, making them a valuable commodity. Given how large the Bering Sea is and how far seals can swim, the Revenue Cutter Service found patrolling for poachers nearly impossible. On top of that, Canadian, Russian, and

Japanese ships also started hunting seals in the international waters near the Pribilof Islands, where female seals would hunt food for their young. There was little the United States could do about international hunting, and the seals killed at sea (called pelagic sealing) during the summer months were almost always females with pups on land who would then starve. Often, these female seals were pregnant, meaning three seals were being killed for only one pelt.

The scientist in charge of the original 1869 study was named Henry Wood Elliott. He was from the Smithsonian Institution, and while his first study provided a valuable assessment of how many seals could be harvested on the Pribilof Islands each year, Elliott had no way of knowing how both American poachers and international ships would use pelagic sealing to damage the seal population. After hearing rumors about the declining seal population, he returned to the Pribilof Islands in 1884, fifteen years after completing his original study. He found the seals nearly gone and immediately started advocating for a seven-year ban on all seal hunting so the population could recover.

The US government did not grant his request, and even if they had, enforcing a hunting ban on the other nations engaging in pelagic sealing would have been impossible. This began a twenty-seven-year-long struggle for Elliott, who fought and lobbied for a seal-hunting ban, only to be denied repeatedly as various presidents and their cabinet members came into power. Once it became clear to the new administration how much money the government was making from sealing, the government refused to address the looming extinction of the seals.

In spite of opposition at the uppermost levels of government, Elliott succeeded in drawing enough attention to his cause, and the seal population had declined so rapidly, that in

1911, the United States, Russia, Japan, and Great Britain (which also represented Canada) held an international seal convention. All four countries then signed the Hay-Elliott Fur Seal Treaty, which Elliott authored. It banned all open-water seal hunting and allowed seals to be hunted only on land.

After this treaty was signed, the US banned all seal hunting on land for five years to allow the population to recover, and the US government has closely managed the population of northern fur seals ever since. This culminated in 1972, when the US banned all commercial hunting of marine mammals, which included seals, whales, and otters.

The characters of both Dr. Torres and Sacha Amos from *Whispers on the Tide* are loosely based on the real-life figure of Henry Wood Elliott. Without his conservation efforts, the northern fur seal would likely be extinct today, or if not extinct, then endangered and in need of protection and extensive rehabilitation efforts.

At its lowest point, before the Hay-Elliot Treaty was passed, scientists estimate the global seal population was 100,000 to 300,000 seals, down from a population of over two million only fifty years earlier.

Today the global population of the northern fur seal sits at 1.1 million. The species has been steadily recovering ever since 1911 and is no longer in danger of extinction.

As an author, I'm aware that *Whispers on the Tide* dives a bit deeper into historical details than most of my previous novels, but when I learned about the near extinction of the northern fur seal, I wanted to write a book that highlighted the work of Henry Wood Elliott and the impact that a handful of concerned people can have on our world. I find it inspiring that one man was able to push back against large corporations and government agencies and create a policy that will benefit our world for generations to come. Thank you for letting me share that story with you.

If you're hoping for another story that highlights the good one person can do in a community, you'll also enjoy Kate's story. It's coming next in *Above All Dreams*, and much like *Whispers on the Tide*, it will show the impact a person who's dedicated to doing the right thing can have on others. (Plus, you'll get to meet the man who's finally able to slip past Kate's defenses and convince her that falling in love might not be so terrible.) You can order your copy of

Above all Dreams on Amazon.

Acknowledgments

Thank you first and foremost to my Lord and Savior, Jesus Christ, for giving me both the ability and opportunity to write novels for His glory.

As with any novel, an author might come up with a story idea and sit at his or her computer to type the initial words, but it takes an army of people to bring you the book you have today. I'd especially like to thank my editors. Erin Healy's keen insight and ability to understand my characters and their worlds have made my novels shine in ways that I had never thought possible, and I count it a privilege to work with her. Jennifer Lonas is the newest addition to my editing team. Her eye for detail helps me to deliver a polished, professional book to you every single time. And then there's Roseanna White, one of my longest friends and biggest encouragements in this industry. She answers my random emails, helps me brainstorm when I get stuck, and points out many ways to make my books stronger.

Many thanks to my family for working with my writing schedule and giving me a chance to do two things I love: be a mom and a writer.

Also, thank you to the hospitable people of Juneau and Sitka, Alaska, especially Rich Mattson with the Juneau-Douglas City Museum, and Hal Spackman and Nicole Fiorino with Sitka

History. The three of them answered question after question and provided numerous images and book recommendations to help me bring this small slice of Alaskan history to life. And finally, thank you to Susan Benson, a resident of Alaska for over twenty years, who preread this novel looking for any mistakes or inaccuracies.

About the Author

Naomi Rawlings is a *USA Today* bestselling author of over a dozen historical novels, including the Eagle Harbor Series, which has sold more than 500,000 copies. She lives with her husband and three children in Michigan's rugged Upper Peninsula, along the southern shore of Lake Superior, where they get two hundred inches of snow every year, and where people still grow their own vegetables and cut down their own firewood—just like in the historical novels she writes.

For more information about Naomi, please visit her at www.naomirawlings.com or find her on Facebook at www.facebook.com/author.naomirawlings. If you'd like a free novel, sign up for her author newsletter.

Made in the USA
Middletown, DE
20 July 2024

57755647R00252